THE BRIMSTONE SMELL FOUND ITS WAY INTO THE CONJURING CHAMBER—

The lights in the room flared, then seemed to reverse themselves: the silvery glow became an inky black luminescence.

"It comes," Silvas said to his companions.

Renewed thunder covered his words. Silvas raised his staff in both hands, parallel to the floor, chest high, and extended it toward the window. Flickers of light and dark flowed through the window and filled the room. Sparkling outlines of demonic figures appeared.

Silvas faced the two demons squarely while he chanted continuously in the language of power. He wove nets to capture the elusive figures that dared challenge him in his own lair. Each attempt to snare the demons failed though and sparked new peals of their horrible laughter.

"You feeble mouse. Your nets cannot touch us," one of the demons screamed. "We've come for your soul."

THE SEVEN TOWERS: THE WIZARD AT MECQ

RICK SHELLEY

THE SEVEN TOWERS:
THE
WIZARD
AT
MECQ

A ROC BOOK

ROC
Published by the Penguin Group
Penguin Books USA Inc., 375 Hudson Street,
New York, New York 10014, U.S.A.
Penguin Books Ltd, 27 Wrights Lane,
London W8 5TZ, England
Penguin Books Australia Ltd, Ringwood,
Victoria, Australia
Penguin Books Canada Ltd, 10 Alcorn Avenue,
Toronto, Ontario, Canada M4V 3B2
Penguin Books (N.Z.) Ltd, 182–190 Wairau Road,
Auckland 10, New Zealand

Penguin Books Ltd, Registered Offices:
Harmondsworth, Middlesex, England

First published by Roc, an imprint of Dutton Signet,
a division of Penguin Books USA Inc.

First Printing, June, 1994
10 9 8 7 6 5 4 3 2 1

PROLOGUE

I sit here alone now, with little future and a past that is becoming rapidly irrelevant. I have little need—and less desire—to lie. My tale is the truth, no matter how greatly it differs from the histories that others have offered. Few others have observed the passage of time from my vantage, and of those few, none has chosen to set down his observations for others to read. When the truth of our past is lost, we are all diminished. I would build a levee against the flood of lies and errors that threatens to overwhelm all truth.

I write of time and change, of gods and demons, of good and evil—all inevitably connected. I write of glory and shame—always intimately related. I write of life and death—for neither is complete without the other. I write not to offend but to enlighten. Perhaps I write only to satisfy some need in my own soul—if I have such a creature—but I hope, I *believe,* that my words will satisfy others, on some level. That may be the one vanity remaining to me.

The hot breath of summer blows lightly across me. It is fitting. For I start my narrative on a hot summer day such as this, in England, in the Year of Our Lord 1238. And there was great evil on the wind.

1

A man on a horse.

Without waiting for a tug on his reins or a spoken command, the horse stopped at the crest of a low ridge. The late morning sun was almost overhead. The man leaned on the pommel of his saddle and stared into the valley ahead and at the village it sheltered, off to his right a little.

" 'Yea, though I walk through the valley of the shadow of death,' " the man quoted softly. It was not quite a prayer, but neither was it an expression of derision at the drought-stricken valley in front of him. Though the man shared his true name with no one, he often allowed himself to be called Silvas.

The horse snorted.

"This looks like a scene from some mad priest's fevered nightmare," Silvas said. The voice sounded tired, perhaps depressed. In any case, it didn't seem to fit the speaker. Silvas appeared to be in his middle twenties, brawny and rugged, his skin tanned and weathered where it was exposed. The eyes that slowly scanned the valley were dark gray, almost black, with tiny flecks of indeterminate lighter color. Those eyes were sunk too deeply in his face for someone who otherwise appeared to be in the prime of manhood. Mostly the face was balanced and strong, though marred by a few dark wrinkles that made him appear brooding even in repose. His hair, light brown streaked with sun-bleached blond, reached almost to his shoulders, coarse and roughly cut. Silvas had the heavily muscled arms and shoulders, the callused hands, of a warrior, but he was dressed in simple traveling clothes of gray above knee-length riding boots. He carried no weapons but for a long dagger with an ornate hilt that he wore on his belt.

Silvas dismounted with the exaggerated care of the old or infirm and stood next to his horse, Bay. Although Silvas was over six feet in height and two hundred pounds in weight, he was easily dwarfed by the animal.

"The smell isn't right for a priest's nightmare. Those have a unique odor," the horse said, turning his head to look down at Silvas. Bay was an equine giant, over eight feet tall at the withers. He was built along the bulky lines of a knight's destrier, exuding raw power with every movement. His hair was a reddish brown, as befitted a horse of his name, with white highlights mixed in through the full, flowing mane and tail. Bay's voice was a deep, rumbling bass, but his diction was clear, his accent that of the educated classes.

"One more wart on the butt of the kingdom," Silvas said. "There can't be many that we've missed." He spoke softly, with resignation or pity rather than distaste. "I always feel that by the time we finish riding circuit, I'll look like the decrepit old man these peasants always expect a wizard to be."

Bay snorted again, clearly in derision. "Why must we go through this gnashing of teeth every time we approach a new village?" he demanded. "It sheds no light, offers no comfort, adds no truth to the world."

"We go through it because I choose to go through it," Silvas replied sharply.

"Are you afraid to admit your feelings even to yourself?" Bay asked. "There is nothing wrong with passion."

"Passion? I have some great challenge to face—sometime, somewhere. All this . . ." He didn't finish the thought. Instead he turned away from the horse and stared at the village below.

"You chose your life," Bay said impatiently. "You help all these people along the way because you would not turn your back on them if you could."

Silvas merely stared at the village, not even attempting to frame a reply.

"That is the village of Mecq," Bay said after a moment. "The hill below the village, to the right on this side of the

river, is Mount Mecq. The ridge on the other side is
Mount Balq. The river between is the Eyler."

For a protracted moment Silvas remained silent, absorbing the scene. Finally he said, "It doesn't look like
much."

"This *should* be a fertile valley, like those around it,
and in better times it has been," Bay observed. The valley
was clearly anything but fertile now. The Eyler wound
past the village toward a gap between Mount Mecq and
Mount Balq, winding generally north through the English
countryside toward Wales and the Irish Gulf. The only
water visible in the riverbed was a thin trickle in the bottom of a watercourse that could have carried a hundred
times the volume without threatening to overflow its
banks. The village stood on the near side of the river, on
the higher bank. Most of the valley, and the fields of the
villagers, were across the river.

"The valley beyond the river is a floodplain," Bay reported. "In years of normal springs floods, the fields soak
up enough water to return plentiful harvests. Mecq was
once a prosperous village. But the floods have been poor
for years, scarcely enough to grow a minimum of grain
and vegetables to see the people and their few remaining
animals through to the next harvest. The rains have been
scant even longer, for more than a generation. Hunger
and illness are common here."

"They could easily dam the river to hold water," Silvas
suggested. He never questioned the accuracy of information Bay gave him. Whatever the sources, Bay's facts
were never wrong.

"It has been attempted," Bay replied. "The last time it
occasioned a short and inglorious war with the Duke of
Blethye, whose demesne lies just downstream of the twin
hills of Mecq and Balq."

Silvas let his gaze drift north along the Eyler past the
village to the sharp cleft that carried the meager stream
and a narrow road between the two hills. By focusing his
vision tightly, Silvas could see objects at any distance in
his line of sight as clearly as he could at arm's length. It
was but a minor application of his will, of his magic. On
the crest of Mount Mecq, the nearer height, a small cas-

tle, no more than a simple tower and low curtain wall, stood guard over the pass between the hills.

"The thane of Mecq has not the manpower to defend a dam against Blethye," Bay said, as if he could read his rider's mind, "and perhaps not the will. He sends messages of impotent anger and pleading to the king, but the fief is minor, too far from His Majesty's thoughts for him to send warriors. And the Duke of Blethye holds an important section of the border for him."

"There is evil here," Silvas said.

"There is evil everywhere," Bay countered.

There is indeed, Silvas thought. He took several steps away from the horse and continued to scan the valley: bone-dry earth clung to the roots of grain in the fields; peasants worked, their faces thin and devoid of expression; painfully thin animals tried to graze on scant grasses that were dry and dusty.

Life in these villages is never easy, but here it may be harder than it should be, Silvas thought. He breathed deeply and slowly, trying to make his mind a blank, a blotter to absorb the atmosphere of Mecq and its environs. His efforts were never completely successful. The threads of the past were too strong, too visible. The threads of the future, their ends hidden in inner mist, were too much in his thoughts. *They end somewhere,* Silvas reminded himself. *They could even end here.* For a moment that realization made him lose his concentration. He had no guarantees, not even that he would live to face the special challenge his Unseen Lord had prepared him for.

"It seems there will be work for us in Mecq," Silvas said.

"There is always work for us," Bay replied.

"But I have a feeling about this," Silvas continued, as if the horse had not spoken. The sudden ripple of apprehension he felt turned to something much nearer to anticipation. "There is more here than we see, perhaps even the unknown work I must perform to win my freedom." He had spoken of his pact with the Unseen Lord in that fashion for so long that he now even thought of it in those terms.

"Perhaps," Bay agreed, dragging the word out and twisting it around, tired of this routine. "*Perhaps* I shall take the time someday to remind you of all the places you have said that. And *perhaps* the sooner we reach this village the sooner we will finish whatever we must do there."

Silvas neither responded nor took the hint. He was too lost in his thoughts drifting along familiar byways. It was several minutes before he spoke again.

"I can't help but think that the future would be easier to face if I knew what it is that I must face, and where, and when." He spoke softly, as if merely distracted by a chance thought. The words came slowly, as if from far away. *What is the challenge I must face?*

"If you had to lead a horse through fire to get it safely out of a burning stable, how would you do it?" Bay asked, just as casually.

"Tie a cloth over his eyes so he wouldn't panic at the flames," Silvas replied, not thinking about the question or his answer. It was too basic.

"Perhaps your continued ignorance is that sort of cloth," Bay said.

In one way or another Silvas and Bay had covered this point scores of times in their years together. When they were at rest and comfortable, the discussion could be quite protracted and philosophical—a pastime, a game. At times like this, facing a new village with its mostly common problems (but always with the chance of something rare and dangerous), the talk could be tense, abbreviated.

"Eighty, maybe a hundred cottages," Silvas said after he had stared a little longer at the village that was a little over a mile to the south. "Two larger, substantial buildings in the center of the village, facing each other across the green. Another at the edge of the village, by the river." The cottages were ranked around the village green and the two large central buildings. The road from the crest led down to the village and continued on from the far end, leading to the gap between mounts Mecq and Balq, with a secondary road climbing to the castle on Mount Mecq. Silvas hardly considered it a guess when he identified the larger buildings at the center of Mecq as parish church and village inn, or the one by the river as the mill. The church had a modest spire and cross. The mill's water wheel was visible, its lower end hanging in air, not touching the water of the shrunken Eyler. On the near side of the mill, a pair of oxen walked a circle, harnessed to a geared apparatus that would turn the millstone inside.

"They're long used to water shortages here," Silvas said as he studied the mill and the ruts the oxen had worn in their circular marching.

"In a year of plentiful rain Mecq still does well, but such years have been increasingly rare in the last generation," Bay said. "Mecq does best in years when the surrounding valleys have far too much rain. When the others have just enough, Mecq has drought. This valley alone suffers this particular scourge."

Silvas stood with his hands on his hips and stared directly into the village. There were a few people visible on Mecq's dusty streets, more working in the dry fields across the Eyler, pulling the few weeds that took water from the grain. Silvas felt the misery in Mecq. It tugged at him. After a few minutes, Bay walked over and positioned himself for the wizard to mount.

"All right," Silvas said when he finally noticed the horse. "I don't suppose I'll learn anything more by standing here."

"Not that you can't learn more easily by going into the village," Bay replied, but softly.

Silvas turned to the animal. Bay had two stirrups on his left side, one at riding height, the other lower, making a step so it was easier for Silvas to mount.

Silvas mounted and settled himself comfortably in the saddle. He held the reins loosely. Bay needed no direction and couldn't be counted on to take it if given. Silvas started a soft chant while the horse followed the trail down into the valley toward the village. The chant was more prayer than conjuration.

Oh Lord, let me continue to be a fit vehicle for executing your will. Open my eyes that I may see what I need to see. Give me your direction, your help. Protect me that I may continue to protect your people.

Although Silvas had spoken that prayer many times, it was never an empty formula. He directed it to his Unseen

Lord, the god Silvas *knew* existed but had never seen, the god who sometimes functioned through him.

Never an empty formula. *If I am, then He must be,* was the way Silvas had reasoned it out many years before. The wizard felt his skin begin to tingle. The hair on his arms stood up. The power was there again, flowing into him, through him. Silvas mumbled a prayer of thanksgiving. If he no longer paid full conscious attention to the words of these prayers, it did not mean that he took the arrival of this token of his master for granted. And the influx of power now did not mean that he was devoid of power at other times. There was a power that was always his, constant, reliable, the basis of his wizardry, conferred by the test of initiation—considerable enough on its own . . . and then there was this additional power that came when he approached a new village or town and faded when he left it behind after doing his master's will there.

"I am a wizard of unbroken line, master to apprentice, *fahn olduvia estu megidoay,*" went the ritual affirmation, as much a part of Silvas as his names—both the open and the hidden.

"Breathe in the smell of this place," Bay advised after they had covered half the distance from the ridge to the nearest cottages. "Flare your nostrils and drink it in." The horse spoke softly now, as if afraid that someone might overhear. Bay *never* let outsiders hear him speak.

Silvas took one deep breath and then another.

"My nose is not nearly as sensitive as yours," the wizard said.

"It need not be," Bay replied. "The gates of hell might almost open on this valley."

"I told you there was evil here," Silvas reminded Bay. "I don't need to smell it."

Bay did not reply. He merely continued toward the village. Bay's walk looked incredibly slow, but his stride was so long that the look was deceptive. Occasionally someone in the village or fields looked toward them. A racing horse would have caused worry, fear, perhaps even panic. A horse barely plodding along would cause no more than a moment of curiosity.

Silvas continued to cast his mind ahead, seeking any clues to the work that might await him in Mecq. The problem of water was obvious, but the pervasive sense of evil he felt was unusual enough to concern him. Despite Bay's earlier jibe, evil of this depth was *not* everywhere.

Closer to the village, the more common smells of rural August became apparent—the odors of grain in the fields, people, animals, manure, and rotting garbage. The plan of Mecq was as common as its smells. Cottages with their small garden patches lined both sides of the road. More cottages were arrayed in rough arcs behind the inn and church and facing the ends of the village green. A faded wooden sign over the inn's door—a red boar facing a tawny bear—marked the hostel as the Boar and Bear. The church was no larger than the inn. Both were built of rough-cut stone. The church had a wooden spire above it.

People. A small boy ran into the Boar and Bear. A man in the garb of a friar came out onto the small veranda of the church. A few faces peered out of cottage doors or paused in their labors long enough to glance at the approaching horse and rider. Silvas knew that Bay would be the first focus of attention. He always was. No one had ever seen a horse of Bay's size. People looked at the animal first, then wondered what sort of man would have so majestic a steed. They would see that he was no knight in armor or courtier in fancy dress. And there were no bulging saddle packs to suggest that he might be an itinerant peddler.

People started to gather in the village green, but not many of them. When Silvas reached the edge of the "green"—its grass mostly a sunburned brown—only a score of people wore their curiosity honestly enough to stand in the open and stare . . . but more watched from the shadows of their cottages.

Bay ambled out into the center of the square and stopped a little closer to the inn than the church. People moved forward or back, coming to rest in a loose arc about twenty-five feet from the horse. Silvas let the reins drape loosely on Bay's neck and sat with his wrists crossed over the saddle's pommel. A few people edged closer. Most stayed well back. No one really cared to meet his gaze. Those who did so inadvertently looked away quickly.

The friar crossed briskly from the church, his eyes on

Silvas more than on the horse. He didn't flinch when Silvas met his stare. Another man, larger, burly, came out of the Boar and Bear. This man's arms were heavily muscled, his hands rough with work, the joints of his fingers swollen and knotty. He stopped ten feet from Silvas, several paces in front of the other villagers. The friar stopped at his side.

Silvas nodded to them, then slowly scanned the rest of the small gathering of the curious. There were an even two dozen people watching him with suspicion, open wonder, or both.

"I am known as Silvas. I am a wizard," he announced. That brought a considerable reaction. It always did. A few people took a step or two back, but almost as if they didn't realize that they were moving. Others crossed themselves instinctively.

"I have come to Mecq because you have need of my services," Silvas continued. "I will provide such help as you require, that I may honorably give. I will stay until all of those needs have been met or until I am needed more urgently elsewhere. And then I will leave. I ask no payment of any kind for my services. My reward comes from another place." He glanced up briefly. *Let them make what they will of that,* he thought.

"I do not even require that you provide for my maintenance while I am here. If I stop at the inn for ale or wine, I will pay for what I order. If I require the services of any of your craftsmen, I will likewise pay full value for my needs."

He stopped and looked around at the people again. There was no sudden outpouring of welcome, no rejoicing that he had offered free service. Most of the faces wore their suspicion openly. Silvas was a stranger. That was indictment enough for many people. He *said* he was a wizard. He *said* he would help. He *said* he would take no payment for his services and that he would pay for anything he needed from the villagers.

He said.

Silvas kept any emotion from showing on his face. None of this was a surprise. None of it was new. Villagers along all of the marches were like this, whether they faced Celts, Norsemen, Germans, or Franks. Strangers

were rarely good news. Outsiders brought trouble if they
brought anything. Silvas was accustomed to these silent,
not quite hostile receptions, but they did rankle at times.
Finally he let his gaze rest on the friar and on the man
with the heavily muscled arms. The friar stepped forward,
coming within a few feet of Silvas. His companion stayed
with him, hardly a half step behind.

"Welcome, sir," the monk said. He gave Silvas the
scantest of nods and drew a cross in the air ahead of him.
"I am Brother Paul, vicar of Saint Katrinka's here, vicar
of Mecq." He pointed across the green at the small
church. Brother Paul stood just under five feet tall, so he
had to tilt his head back to meet Silvas's gaze. He was
extremely thin, but the extent of his emaciation was concealed by the robes he wore. "I am a friar of the White
Brotherhood, an initiate of the Lesser Mysteries."

"Friar." Silvas nodded in greeting, then blinked and
reached out with his mind to touch the borders of the
monk's power. Faint but noticeable. *I couldn't expect more
in a parish like this,* Silvas told himself. He easily detected
the monk's clumsy attempts to touch *his* power. "Your being here may be of assistance," Silvas said, brushing aside
the vicar's probing with hardly a thought.

"Forgive my asking," Brother Paul said, "but are you
a loyal son of Mother Church?"

" 'He who is not against us is on our part,' as it is written," Silvas replied. "I have often worked alongside the
White Brotherhood, but a member, no."

The monk's face relaxed, but only a trifle. He was
clearly not ready to surrender his reservations despite Silvas's show of candor. *He is cautious, he does not leap to
judgment,* Silvas thought. That was not always the case,
even among the White Brotherhood. The White Brotherhood, order of nearly all of the popes Silvas could name,
was the largest and most powerful order in the western
church, both pastoral and mystically militant in mission,
known formally as the Congregation of the Guardians of
the Faith.

"Welcome to Mecq, Lord Wizard," Brother Paul said,
nodding a little more deeply with this second greeting.
"This honored burgher beside me is Master Ian, proprie-

tor of the Boar and Bear Inn. You'll not find better provision or service in the finest inn of St. Ives."

Silvas shifted his gaze to Master Ian. Ian was taller and not nearly as thin as most of the villagers around, but he could by no means be described as fat.

"Master Ian." Silvas nodded. "You have the arms of a blacksmith, not of an innkeeper."

"Aye, sir." Ian's voice was gruff, gravelly. "I also do what smithin' we need." He glanced at Brother Paul for an instant before he returned his attention to the wizard. "I'd not make such lofty claims for my inn as the good friar, but I'll warrant there are more places worse than better, in St. Ives or elsewhere. Might I ask what ye'll be needing in the way of victuals and lodging?"

Silvas grinned, then stopped quickly. People sometimes misinterpreted that gesture from him. "I'll likely stop by for a flagon or two of ale before the sun sets, but I have my own provision for the rest," he said. Without looking, Silvas knew that nearly every pair of eyes around him flicked their glance toward the rear of his saddle. There were no packs, no saddlebags, no sign of any provisions.

"What sort of wizard would I be if I could not provide for my own comfort?" Silvas asked loudly. He sat straighter in the saddle and spread his arms out to the sides. As soon as he started to chant, everyone moved back, giving him more room for whatever he was about to do. Even the vicar and innkeeper stepped quickly out of his way.

They'll have no doubt now that I'm a wizard-potent, Silvas thought as he started the incantation. He never prepared people for this demonstration. It was the only "revenge" he ever took for the cool receptions he received.

"Dar fistu sprath. Dar estu demiese. Fichu kevry sprath." The words boomed out and echoed around Silvas, carrying volume of their own that did not depend on Silvas's wind.

Wind. It comes. Silvas closed his eyes and repeated the chant. It was significantly louder the second time, though he put no more force into it. He didn't need to see what his magic, and the power of his Unseen Lord, was producing. He knew. But the people of Mecq could not be certain what was coming. A couple of them scurried for cover, not waiting to witness whatever this wind would bring. But more of the people stood riveted in place, unable to move.

Silvas kept his eyes closed and brought the incantation into his mind. A small breeze started to eddy, stirring up dust in a perfect circle just wide enough to encompass the giant horse. The swirls of dust turned into thin white smoke. Then the circle widened until it was a dozen feet in diameter and the smoke thickened as it sought its way toward heaven. The spectacular visual display was only for times such as this. Alone on the road, Silvas used less ostentatious means to open the way to his home. *This* show was intended to impress the uninitiated.

Others: Brother Paul crossed himself. Most of the other villagers followed his example automatically, even if they were staring at the smoke and didn't see the vicar's reflexive gesture.

As the circle of smoke rose to hide the horse's withers, a few of the people, including Brother Paul, saw the ghostly image of an immense castle with many towers. The castle seemed to be contained within the circle of smoke ... but at a great distance, approaching rapidly. The illusion, the paradox, was so compelling that Brother Paul grabbed his rosary beads and clung to them, seeking comforting strength.

Silvas's chant was clearly audible to those around the circle of smoke, loud and insistent, but no ears could hold on to the words long enough to fix them in their minds. The words, cadent and insistent, seemed to instantly erase themselves from every mind. No villager would be able to repeat these sounds of power that could not be grasped except by those with power of their own. Brother Paul came closest to comprehending the essence of the chant, but even he failed to grasp the words. An initiate of only the Lesser Mysteries, he knew that this was something that only those much more powerful in magic than him could ever hope to hear and hold. But he could see the approaching castle for a few seconds longer than the few others who saw it at all. The castle was huge, perhaps as large as the entire village, but it was also circumscribed by the twelve-foot circle of smoke—smoke that continued to climb straight into the heavens.

"Like the pillar that guided the children of Israel in the desert," the vicar mumbled. He had crossed himself so often since the smoky circle started to form that he consciously stopped himself when he realized that he had started again. He couldn't show fear or his flock would be terrified beyond belief.

The tower of smoke finally rose until its upper end—if it truly had one—was lost in the distance, blurred by the sun. The cylinder seemed perfect. Brother Paul walked around it, hand held to within a couple of inches of the crisp border. He could feel the hot tingle of power there, even if he could not touch it or fully understand the power that maintained it.

Are you really on our part, or against us, a tool of the Devil? the friar asked himself. He had seen wizards before. He had not spent all of his life in the backwater parish of Mecq. But none of the wizards he had seen before had displayed this level of power as their introduction.

We shall have to see, Paul promised himself. There was no fear in him, not of this wizard or any other. If the power of Silvas was too much for the country vicar . . . well, in the White Brotherhood, no brother ever stood alone.

2

As the circle of smoke rose around him, Silvas waited patiently for the translation to complete itself. The view inside the rising cylinder of smoke was different than the view the people of Mecq had on the outside. The smoke faded and disappeared completely soon after it rose above Silvas's head. The shape of his home came into focus around him. The Glade was an old wizard's castle set in an out-of-the-way valley of the Pennines, somewhat to the north and considerably to the east of Mecq, almost at the far eastern end of the Pennines, not all that far from the border with Scotland. The Glade had been built of stone at a time when most fortresses still had wooden palisades. Even today most new castles lacked many of the features of the Glade, or the Seven Towers as it was sometimes called. Kings would be in awe of Silvas's home, if kings were ever invited in. No regal residence had towers that stood so high or walls so sturdy.

Overhead, the quality of the sky changed when the smoke vanished. The blue seemed crisper, purer. The difference was subtle, but Silvas marked it as he always did. The air he drew in with each breath was sweeter, fresher, cooler.

"Home," he muttered softly. The tug he felt in his chest was not unusual. He was bound to the Glade with a depth of emotion he himself did not fully comprehend.

The main gate was just in front of Bay. The towers of the gatehouse rose on either side. A smaller pedestrian gateway passed through the gatehouse to Silvas's left. Auroreus—the wizard who had built the castle before the Goths sacked Rome—had wanted to make a statement. The Glade was invulnerable to common attack. The drawbridge was wide, and next to it a stone causeway crossed the moat from the smaller gateway.

Silvas looked around carefully, as if he had been away for years and not just since early morning. The Glade's keep rose before him, a hundred feet high and 70 by 140 feet long, connected to the curtain wall and to the lower buildings within the bailey—the tables, storage houses, and such that were built against the inside of the curtain wall. The bailey of the Glade was larger than Mecq's village green. Mecq might almost fit within the castle walls if not for the buildings already there.

"The Seven Towers still stand," Bay said drily.

"They stand," Silvas agreed. The last flickering of the translation had ended. They were indeed home, hundreds of miles from Mecq.

A small figure ran out of the keep, his legs churning as if he hoped to make up for diminutive size with effort. There was something peculiar about the way his knees bent, as if those joints were constructed differently, but that was the least of the peculiarities about him.

"Bosc," Silvas said.

The little figure bobbed his head. Up close, no one could ever mistake Bosc for human. The features of his face were heavily porcine. If his head lost its mop of tightly curled, thick brown hair, it might actually be mistaken for the head of a pig. Bosc was little more than three feet tall. His nose was flat, his ears pointed and set too high, flopping a little to the sides. His hands each had a finger less than human hands; his thumbs were stubby, set far too low and at the wrong angle. Boots covered four-toed feet. Clothing hid the curly brown hair that covered most of his body. The skin of his face seemed a ruddy gray—ashen but touched with blood. His movements were jerky, inelegant, like a puppet on strings, controlled by an inexpert puppeteer.

Silvas dismounted and handed Bay's reins to Bosc. He bowed first to Silvas and then to Bay. Equal bows. Bosc always showed them equal respect.

"Everything is ready for you, Lord Bay," Bosc said, straining his neck to look up toward Bay's eyes.

"I could use a couple of apples," Bay said. "My mouth feels the need for something both sweet and tart."

"We have new apples just up from the village," Bosc said quickly. He led Bay off toward the stables. "Would you like them before or after your wash and grooming?"

"Before *and* during," Bay said. "Something to occupy my taste buds. I need to think and I always think better over apples."

Silvas brushed dust from himself, slapping at his clothes and stomping his feet while the two moved off, Bosc running to keep up with Bay's slowest walk. For all his power and insight, Silvas did not fully understand either of them. Bay was not merely his steed. Bosc was not merely Bay's groom. They each had power of their own, and veils that protected their secrets, whatever they were.

When Bay's tail disappeared around the corner of the keep, Silvas shook his head and walked toward the main entrance. He felt a sudden urge to climb to the crenelated battlements atop the keep to look out at the long valley that held the Glade, and at the peaks around it. The ability to return home on a few minutes' work was precious to Silvas, his link to the tradition and power that he represented. The Glade always remained where Auroreus had built it more than eight centuries before. The various villages of the marches remained where *they* were. The tower of smoke was merely a magical device that let Silvas travel between two fixed points without taking the time that would be needed to ride between them. It would take perhaps weeks to ride between Mecq and the Glade. It had taken four days to ride to Mecq from the last village Silvas had visited. *If only I could move the smoke from village to village without riding between them* was a thought that came often. But the passage always had to be opened at the far end from the Glade, whether in a new village or just when the day's ride was done. Silvas had never been able to expand the magic to avoid the days of riding between stops.

"It might let you fall out of touch with the countryside, with the folk," Bay had once suggested. "You might close your eyes to too much. Not to mention the way you would terrify villagers each time your tower of smoke appeared in their midst and we rode out of it."

"It would save you as much time as me," Silvas had replied.

"The exercise is good for both of us."

* * *

Rainbows and birds flew circles over Silvas, singing songs of welcome, complete with harmony and counterpoint, a rich musical mosaic to accompany their bright colors. The unique birds of the Seven Towers were part of its lore ... and the token of a promise. Silvas stopped walking and looked up to whistle his own greeting. The birds came down, bringing their circles closer to his head, arranging themselves like strands of a small tornado rising above the wizard.

"Joy to my heart," Silvas said softly, smiling at the birds. They could hardly help but lighten his mood. "I would be lost without you to greet me."

He looked off at the curtain walls then. Sentries covered every side. Some of them appeared to be kin to Bosc. They made excellent watchmen but poor warriors. Others on the walls looked like a cross between humans and wolves—not werewolves or shapeshifters, but perhaps mistakable for them if they strayed far from the sanctuary of the Glade. Even the birds that cavorted around Silvas might easily be mistaken for supernatural. Their colors—each bird a single solid color—were far too bright and pure for normal birds. Their songs were too melodic. But within the Glade notions of normality had nothing to do with visible distinctions. Whatever their nature or place of origin, all of the Glade's inhabitants were there because they belonged—drawn in by Silvas or his predecessor ... or by the Unseen Lord who provided their power.

One of Silvas's earliest memories was of asking Auroreus about all of the strange beings that inhabited the Glade. Auroreus had been ancient then. He had been old when he built the Seven Towers. By the time he brought Silvas in to teach him the craft, *old* was a ridiculous understatement applied to Auroreus. *He looked like a proper wizard* was how Silvas recalled him—long white hair, skin parchment dry and wrinkled beyond description, a prominent nose with a hook that was almost a right angle, eyes so sunken that their color could not be discerned, voice that rasped like fingernails across roofing slate.

"Where do they come from?" young Silvas had asked.

"They are all creatures of our Unseen Lord," Auroreus

replied. The wizard produced a large white marble. Silvas applauded what he thought was a clever piece of sleight of hand. Auroreus's quick frown immediately silenced the boy, though.

"This is our world," Auroreus said in his stern "teaching" voice. He held the marble between thumb and forefinger, rolling it around, holding Silvas's eyes on it. Auroreus closed his hand over the marble, turned his hand over, and opened it to show six dice sitting on his palm. Each die showed a different number of pips.

Silvas's eyes got wide. "That's wonderful! How did you do it?"

"You're missing the point, boy." Auroreus closed his hand and opened it again: only the marble. Again he closed and opened his hand: six dice. "This is still our world, the one world."

"But you have six dice."

Auroreus rolled the dice onto the table. They landed, each with a different number of pips showing again.

"Watch closely, boy," Auroreus said, pitching his voice to induce just the proper level of fear in his seven-year-old apprentice. He picked up the dice that showed one and two pips, held them at an angle to each other, and pushed them together. Silvas had watched from just inches away. He knew that this was not sleight of hand. The two dice had merged into one object that had . . .

"Sixteen points, forty-eight surfaces," the old wizard supplied.

"Keep watching," Auroreus cautioned. One by one, he added the remaining dice to the construct. At first more points and surfaces appeared, but then the points became less distinct, the surfaces blended into each other, and when the sixth die merged into the others, only the round marble remained.

"Keep this with you, boy," Auroreus told Silvas. "Let it be a reminder."

Silvas still had the marble. He wore it on a long chain over his heart. Thinking of it, he lifted a hand to cover it. Then he continued his interrupted walk to the keep. He stopped again near the door to sing with his birds for a few moments. Their minds touched him as readily as their songs—undemanding affection, simple contentment.

"Ah, how I wish I could be as you," he said. Sometimes the birds repeated his clumsy trills. At other times they sought his echoes for their music.

"How I envy your serenity." Silvas finally raised his head and blew across the palm at them. They replied with a three-note line in unison and climbed away from him, heading for their nests at the tops of the towers.

Silvas swung open the door to the keep and was almost knocked down by the bounding welcome of his cats, Satin and Velvet. He barely had time to take a secure stance before they jumped against him. The cats were identical except for sex. Satin was the tabby, Velvet the tom. In coloring they appeared as Siamese cats, dark points and milky coats. But in size they were tigers, weighing twelve hundred pounds between them. Despite their size they were domestic pets, friendly as any cats could be. Their purrs were deep and throaty, their games rough. Silvas had to play with them for a moment or they wouldn't let him pass. Then Velvet and Satin fell in beside their master, one on each side, and accompanied him through the keep.

Silvas walked the length of the great hall, returning the greetings of the half-dozen retainers who were about. There was a broad formal stairway in the corridor that bordered the side of the great hall, and several other ways up to the wizard's private quarters, but Silvas went to a narrow flight of stairs concealed behind a huge tapestry that covered the wall at the head of the great hall. Stone stairs spiraled up to the wizard's private apartments above the great hall—and beyond to the eastern tower of the keep.

He heard a soft humming before he reached the landing that led to his quarters, a voice as musical and pure as the birds outside. Carillia was waiting, letting him know that she knew he was coming. The song came from the large parlor, near the landing of the stairs he was on. *She even knew which way I would choose today,* Silvas thought. He stopped on the landing. Briefly he glanced up the stairs that led to the top of the east tower, another seventy-five feet up.

"Another time." He would not climb to the battlements with Carillia calling to him.

Carillia. No one who ever saw her could possibly mistake her for anyone else. To Silvas she was the divine model of Woman, perfection in beauty and grace. She stopped humming as Silvas reached out to open the parlor door.

"I felt you coming," Carillia said as Silvas stepped inside. He smiled, as he did whenever he came into her presence. Her hair, brushed out at waist length, was a delicate mahogany auburn, glossy, with a slight wave. Her eyes were an impossibly brilliant green, like paint scooped wet from an artist's palette. Slender and perfectly proportioned (to Silvas's eyes), she was dressed in layers of filmy silk that clung or flowed by turns, almost as if they were possessed of a magic of their own, a sorcery that made them show Carillia to her best advantage at any given moment. Her voice was a tonic whenever she spoke, musical, relaxing, a powerful weapon even without magic—and she did have a powerful magical presence, an aura that flooded Silvas with peace.

"You must have heard my heart pounding with anticipation." Silvas pitched his voice to a seductive register without even thinking. He found it difficult to speak to Carillia in any tones but those of love. He crossed to the couch where she reclined as Romans had once reclined on their *lecti* to dine. Silvas leaned over and they kissed. When their lips touched, both felt the tingle of anticipation and the warmth of gratifying memory.

Velvet and Satin circled the couch, as if looking to make sure that no threats were hidden, then took up positions at either end, snuggling down into position slowly.

"Ah, my dear heart," Carillia said when the kiss ended. She raised a hand and snapped her fingers. The sound was not loud, but a servant, one of Bosc's porcine kin, came scurrying immediately into the room. "We need a tray, Koshka," Carillia said as gently as she spoke to Silvas. "That wine and a selection of fruit and cheese. Quickly, please."

"Yes, my lady, at once." Koshka's voice was high-pitched and had a trace of gurgling about it, almost as if he were drowning. He bobbed his head and hurried out of the room with the same inelegant speed that Bosc had displayed.

"Here, my heart." Carillia pulled her long legs off of the couch and sat up. She patted the cushion next to her. "You look so tired already and it's barely noon." Silvas started to sit, but caught himself halfway.

"No, love. I need to bathe first. If I sit now, it'll be too hard to force myself up again."

"Where are you now?" Carillia asked.

"A place called Mecq, just another marcher village that smells of manure and other rotten things."

"Listen to yourself," Carillia urged in a voice tinged with sadness. "You don't normally speak like that of a new place."

Silvas blinked twice, thinking not just of the few words he had just spoken, but also of his earlier exchanges with Bay, and his private thoughts.

"You're right, as usual, my love." His voice suddenly sounded exhausted. He sucked in a deep breath. "Mecq is no worse than any other village of its kind. Most of its people are undoubtedly good and true." He shook his head. "And I've been . . ." He stopped and shook his head again. "I'm not sure I can explain. Since Bay and I first came in sight of Mecq, it has weighed on me. There is a foreboding too vague for me to make sense of it." He shrugged. "I am tempted to think that this is where I must meet my grand challenge." Saying that to Carillia was much different than saying it to Bay. Silvas did not share idle grousing with his love.

"When it comes, it comes," Carillia said, rising from the couch. She was as tall as Silvas though much more delicately framed. She put her hands on his shoulders. "When it comes, whatever it is, you will meet it properly and with honor, and you will come out of the exchange the better for your efforts."

"You believe that, don't you?" Silvas asked, wonder—or perhaps merely surprise—plain in his voice.

"I know you, my heart," she said. "I know you have power and courage beyond what *you* believe you have."

"You almost make me believe it as well." *What magic you have*, he thought, staring into those impossibly green eyes. *A fountain of faith that you let me drink from whenever I feel a doubt.*

"I don't believe, I know," Carillia said.

Silvas smiled and kissed her with more warmth than before. "And I call myself a wizard." He chuckled. "But now, love, I really must wash this stench off. Good people or not, their village still reeks."

They kissed once more, then Silvas broke away for his bath. Servants had begun hauling hot water as soon as they spotted him entering the keep. His routine was well-known. When he traveled, he required a bath immediately upon his return. Auroreus had been thoroughly Roman. The habit of fastidiousness was only one of many he had left with the young boy he had selected from the mists as his successor.

Another back stairway led from the living quarters to the kitchens. Koshka had gone that way. The stairs wrapped around a narrow shaft. A long rope connected to pulleys at top and bottom held hooks to hoist buckets of hot water up to the master's bath. Servants would work on both ends of the hoist, preparing the tub.

Silvas stripped before he entered the bathroom, hurling his dusty travel clothes toward a corner, keeping only the belt with his long dagger when he went into the room with the marble tub. He laid the dagger on a small table and climbed into the water to bathe. He scoured himself with enough concentration to shut out worries about what Mecq might bring. Thoughts of Carillia stayed with him, her looks, voice, fragrance. *The way she gentles me with a word.* At times like this he could only think of her, not about her. Like Bay and Bosc, Carillia remained something of an enigma to him.

Servants returned to dump buckets of clean hot water over Silvas after he had scrubbed. He dried himself and dressed in silk that had come from the farthest corner of the earth. He never affected the long robes that had been Auroreus's common garb. Silvas preferred the style of the eastern nomads—loose shirt that hung to his knees, equally loose trousers, both in a blue-black that would draw in the eyes of anyone. A person with powers beyond those of the flesh might notice ghosts of arcane symbols floating in the inky darkness of the silk, shimmering,

moving. Silvas buckled the belt with his long dagger over
the shirt. The hilt was ivory, jeweled with stones in all the
colors of the birds of the Seven Towers.

When he returned to Carillia, Silvas found that Koshka
had been and gone again, leaving a large gold tray with
bite-sized chunks of fruit and cheese and a crystal carafe
of pale green wine. Carillia handed Silvas a golden goblet. He drank deeply. This wine was slightly sweet and
spicy, a white wine from the foothills of the Alps. Silvas
recalled the vintage immediately, and the first time he
tasted it. The discovery had been a joy, and the wine remained a delight every time.

"This is fast becoming my favorite," he told Carillia.

She smiled. "I know. That's why I had Koshka bring it.
I felt you would have need of it today."

Silvas sampled the treats on the tray. "Not too much
just now," he said, as much to himself as to Carillia. "I
need to visit the local inn, the Boar and Bear, before the
afternoon ends. These villagers are as leery of strangers
as any. I may have to put in more than one appearance
before any will come to me with their problems." Silvas
could not, by the code his Unseen Lord imposed, do anything for them until they asked for his help.

Carillia didn't respond. She merely selected a small
wedge of Persian melon from the tray for herself. She ate
the bit of melon daintily, then licked her fingers to get rid
of the juice.

"I'll show you Mecq before I go, unless you'd rather
not," Silvas said.

"But of course, my heart." She got up from the couch.
"I always want to see where you are working. Who
knows, I may spot something to help you."

Silvas smiled. "You have often enough, my love."

Carillia linked arms with Silvas, and they went out to
the landing and took the spiral stairs up one long flight,
into the lowest level of the east tower. The tower rooms
were Silvas's work area. The first room they entered was
a library filled with scrolls and books—hundreds of vol-
umes, a pope's ransom of hand-copied annals and trea-
tises. A second spiral staircase, this one of iron, led up to
another room. This chamber was large and almost bare. A
pentagram of colored crystal worked into the stone floor

dominated the room. Silvas held Carillia's hand and led her across the conjuring chamber, carefully skirting the pentagram, to a small doorway in the far wall. The cats followed Silvas and Carillia to the doorway and then curled up, remaining in the conjuring chamber.

There were more stairs beyond the door, small and steep, rising to a small turret that projected from the side of the tower to look out over the curtain wall. A series of narrow windows let the viewer look around two-thirds of a circle.

"The village of Mecq, my love," Silvas said. Only from this one location in the Glade could this scene be viewed. From any other window or any vantage on the battlements, only the normal environs of the Glade were visible.

"It is a very hot summer day in Mecq, is it not?" Carillia asked after looking out through each window—as if the next might truly show her something that none of the others could.

"Very hot and dry. Heat shimmers over the fields and dust dances against it."

"Yet look, my flesh is chilled by it." Carillia held out her arms for Silvas to see the gooseflesh.

"There is evil in Mecq," Silvas said, aware how like a formula that was beginning to sound, "and you are so sensitive."

"I feel that the Devil walks the streets at night in this village." Carillia shivered against the ethereal chill. Silvas laughed softly.

"Now you sound like some backland nun. I might expect that from one of these villagers, love, but you?"

"You do not mock me," Carillia said—an observation, not a rebuke. "You are right, my heart. There *is* uncommon evil here."

"I would never mock you, my love." Silvas sighed. "I almost wish you had told me that my fears are baseless." He moved closer to her. Their shoulders touched as he looked out at Mecq. The view put them high above the village green, with the inn at the left and the church at the right. Even the spire of St. Katrinka's was below them. There was a handful of people standing around, staring at the Glade . . . rather, at the pillar of smoke that concealed it from their sight. Other people came to look and then left quickly, most crossing themselves at least once.

"And I will have to uncover this uncommon evil and fight it before our Unseen Lord lets me leave this place."

"We have bested evil before, my heart," Carillia said. "We shall again, whenever we meet it."

We will best it, Silvas thought, *perhaps every time but once. But that time, if it comes . . .*

"I think you are about to have a caller. There is a rider galloping down from the castle of Mecq." Carillia pointed.

Silvas nodded and focused his gaze. The rider appeared fairly nondescript, dressed too well to be merely a soldier or peasant. He wore no armor, but his tabard bore a crusader's cross on the left shoulder, and there was a broadsword at his side. The horse was gray, dappled.

"I doubt this will be the thane himself," Silvas muttered.

"Shall we go down to meet him?" Carillia asked when the rider stopped to talk to a couple of farmers at the edge of the village.

"There's no hurry, love," Silvas said. "For now I'd rather watch and get some measure of the man."

Silvas had no trouble following the dumb show below. The rider asked questions. The farmers replied and pointed toward the pillar of smoke. The rider said something else and nodded curtly, then spurred his horse and rode to the edge of the column of smoke.

"I am Henry Fitz-Matthew, steward to Sir Eustace Devry, thane of Mecq," he announced loudly. Silvas and Carillia could hear him as clearly as if he were in the room with them.

"I'll admit him," Silvas said. "There's no need for you to come along unless you want to meet this man for yourself."

"I would just complicate your meeting, my heart." Carillia smiled and drew her fingers softly across Silvas's cheek. "If he is important, we may chance to meet later."

Silvas nodded. "And I think I should keep the kittens up here," Carillia added. "Master Fitz-Matthew might not take kindly to their attentions."

"He'll have enough to occupy his mind," Silvas said. He kissed Carillia and descended quickly to the court-yard, angling toward the pedestrian entrance through the gate tower. The permanent stone bridge disappeared into the smoke. Silvas plunged into it without hesitation and emerged at its outer edge, almost directly in front of Henry Fitz-Matthew.

"I am Silvas. Please, follow me in." Silvas took a step to his right and entered the smoke at a slightly different angle, to escort his visitor across the drawbridge.

Fitz-Matthew dismounted and led his horse. The gray animal balked at entering the smoke, but Fitz-Matthew kept a tight grip on the reins. He himself showed some re-luctance, but stayed only a step behind the wizard. As the smoke closed around him, Fitz-Matthew heard his horse's hoofs striking the wood planking of the drawbridge and looked down in surprise. When he looked up again, the massive gate to the Glade stood open before him. He could immediately see that the castle was much too large to fit within the column of smoke. He stopped and looked over his shoulder. He could no longer see Mecq.

"You have nothing to fear, Master Fitz-Matthew," Sil-vas said, waiting for his visitor. "Come on inside."

Fitz-Matthew moved slowly between the gate towers into the courtyard and then stopped to look back at the smoke through the gate. Shock was plain on his face. He tried to speak but couldn't get any of the words that were rising through his throat to come out. Silvas gave him several minutes to struggle against the shock while he broadcast a silent spell of calming at the horse. There was no need to make the animal suffer, and the impossibility of the situation had outraged the horse as much as the master.

Fitz-Matthew was no taller than the village peas-ants, though he did appear better fed. His face was weath-ered. He had clearly done some fighting, but he was no knight. *A peasant raised in station for some service ren-dered,* Silvas thought. He finally relented and broadcast his calming spell at the man as well as the horse. Even with that Fitz-Matthew needed a moment to find his voice.

"You have an impressive home, Lord Wizard," he fi-nally managed, shakily. "I'd not have expected anything so fine in a pillar of smoke." He had the proper words, but the voice had not the cadence or fluidity of his station.

"I believe you have some message for me?" Silvas prompted after another moment of fumbling by the steward.

"Aye, sir. Sir Eustace Devry, lord of Mecq, loyal vassal of His Majesty, sends his regards and requests you come to call as soon as is convenient." Once into the substance of his message, Fitz-Matthew recovered some of his poise. The words were still right, but not the tone. Silvas smiled. Beneath the diplomatic phrasing, the message was blunt. *Get yourself up to the castle of Mecq at once. Sir Eustace waits to pass judgment on you.*

Silvas gave the man a moment to squirm, staring him in the eye, holding his gaze, not letting him look away. Mecq might be the fief of Sir Eustace, but the Glade was Silvas's, and the extent of the Seven Towers ought to give Eustace's steward some idea of the power he had come to call to account.

"If you've nothing else to do in the village at present," Silvas finally said, his voice as smooth as any courtier's, "I'll accompany you to your master now." He put only the slightest stress on *your,* uncertain that Fitz-Matthew had acquired enough polish to catch it.

"That would be my honor, Lord Wizard," the steward said . . . but his voice was shaking again.

3

Almost as Henry Fitz-Matthew spoke, Bosc came trotting around the corner of the keep, leading Bay. Silvas didn't have to look. He heard Bay's shod hoofs on the cobblestones and knew that Bosc would be with him, scurrying to keep pace. Silvas watched the steward's eyes. Fitz-Matthew hadn't completely recovered from the shock of the Glade, and here were two new blows for him to absorb. *He must have been told about Bay,* Silvas allowed, though rumors could scarcely do justice to Bay, and there was no way that Fitz-Matthew could have anticipated Bosc.

"He's no demon, Master Henry," Silvas said steadily. Fitz-Matthew jumped as if he thought the wizard had read his mind. *If so, let him keep his delusion,* Silvas thought. *It may make him easier to deal with later.*

"I have n-n-never seen his k-k-kind before." Fitz-Matthew stepped back, closer to his own horse.

"Not all that is unknown or different is evil." Silvas loaded his words with what authority he could muster without preparation.

"And your horse?"

"Is a horse. Bay is quite a steed. You'll not find his equal anywhere."

"I can believe that!" Fitz-Matthew blurted that without a stutter.

Bosc handed Bay's reins to Silvas, then ducked into the nearest gate tower, keeping Bay between Fitz-Matthew and himself as much as possible, hardly giving the stranger a chance to see just how different he was. Silvas smiled as the tower door slammed. Bosc would not discomfort himself by thinking of an outsider's eyes staring as he ran back toward the stables. He took the circuitous route to spare himself, not the visitor.

"He comes from a distant land, Master Henry," Silvas said. Fitz-Matthew was staring at the door Bosc had gone through. "Far beyond the land of the paynim even, where few crusaders have dared to wander."

"And *you* have traveled to this distant land?"

"I have traveled to many distant lands," Silvas said evasively. He mounted Bay. Fitz-Matthew mounted his own horse, and frowned when he saw just how far above him the wizard now towered.

"Shall we be going, Master Henry?" Silvas asked calmly. "I'd not like to keep your master waiting." Once more he added just a hint of stress to *your*. "It would hardly be polite."

"As you say, Lord Wizard."

"Stay close as we cross the drawbridge," Silvas advised.

Fitz-Matthew was plainly relieved to return to familiar surroundings. Silvas watched Fitz-Matthew as they rode, though without seeming to. His higher vantage allowed him considerable freedom, even though the steward kept looking up. It was an uncomfortable position for Fitz-Matthew. It reinforced the feelings of inferiority that everything about the wizard seemed to encourage.

I but do the will of my lord, Fitz-Matthew told himself. He was Sir Eustace's voice in the village, throughout the fief, passing on his liege's orders, often sitting in judgment in Sir Eustace's court, with his lord's full authority to settle disputes among his vassals. In one fashion or another Henry had served Sir Eustace all his life, and served his father before him. Sir Eustace's father had died following the old king off to the crusades when Eustace was but fourteen years of age and Henry but five years older. Henry had been in service to the Devrys as long as he could recall, first scrubbing pots and running errands in the kitchen when he was so small that he couldn't *move* some of the pots without help. Henry had later been page, squire, and man-at-arms to Sir Eustace's father and then to Sir Eustace, though because of his birth Henry could scarcely hope to win the spurs of knighthood, certainly not in a place like Mecq.

Henry watched the wizard as closely as he dared. He hoped he would have a chance to warn his lord to be careful of this one. Sir Eustace could be abrupt in his words and judgments.

"Ye've traveled far?" Fitz-Matthew asked after they left the last of the village's cottages behind.

"Far and long," Silvas replied. "My life is one of wandering. My duty carries me to many places."

"*Duty* I understand," Fitz-Matthew said, as much to himself as to the wizard.

Silvas nodded. Fitz-Matthew had more questions, but every time he started to ask one, something made him put it off. The road up Mount Mecq to the castle switched back and forth. Even someone who traveled the road frequently did well to pay attention to the course. Henry accepted that as sufficient excuse for not continuing to question the wizard.

In places Silvas could see the scars where brute force had chipped away the native rock to put in the narrow road. At the switchbacks the rock had been used to build retaining walls to support the upper portions of the turns. In places the way was steep, but mostly the grade was gentle. The builders had taken what advantage they could of natural ledges. The curtain wall of the castle was right above the top leg of the road. Soldiers inside could rain rocks, arrows, or spears down on any attacker over a considerable distance.

"It's a good location for a fortress" was the only positive thing Silvas could think to say about it. "Is this the only access?"

"Aye, unless ye kin walk straight up like a fly," Fitz-Matthew said with a pride that betrayed how few castles he had seen.

Even before they reached the gate, Silvas decided that site was the only advantage the castle could boast. One wall overlooked the only route up the hill, if Fitz-Matthew was right. Another wall looked down on the gap that carried the Eyler and the road that paralleled it. *An ambitious thane might defend that pass without many men, if he truly had the will to,* Silvas thought. But without its hilltop location, the castle would be unable to withstand determined assault. The curtain wall was only

eighteen feet tall, and not thick enough to withstand the
battering that a first-class catapult could inflict. But no
catapult could be brought to bear against the hilltop.

Inside the walls, there was only a small bailey with
wooden outbuildings leaning against the curtain wall. The
keep was of the same mountain stone as the outer wall,
but it was no grand tower, only forty feet in diameter and
not much taller. Castle Mecq had never been intended as
anything more than it was—the sole seat of a minor
knight with a minimal establishment. Silvas spotted only
three men on the walls, and two of them were above the
gate.

"The pass below is the only connection to the demesne
of the Duke of Blethye?" Silvas asked casually as they
entered the bailey.

"Not the only connection, but the only near one," the
steward replied. "There's another route eight leagues to
the east, beyond Mount Balq. That pass is good enough
for riders, though slow, but very difficult for wagons."

Fitz-Matthew rode right to the entrance of the keep and
Silvas followed. Ten stone steps clung to the keep's
wall—one last defensive gesture. The steward whistled
loudly, and a young boy ran out of the stables at the far
side of the bailey. The boy stopped short when he saw
Bay, and hesitated long enough for Fitz-Matthew to yell
at him.

"Come on, boy. No time for gawking. Take care of
Marivel and our visitor's steed." Fitz-Matthew and Silvas
dismounted. The stable boy came toward them, but not as
quickly as before. He took the reins of the steward's
horse, keeping that animal between him and Bay. The lad
looked up at Fitz-Matthew again, as if hoping for a re-
prieve.

"Bay is a gentle beast, lad," Silvas said, smiling reas-
suringly. "He'll be no trouble at all."

"Aye, lord," the boy said unsteadily, staring at Bay
over Marivel. He glanced quickly at Fitz-Matthew again,
then walked around the head of Marivel, closer to Bay.
Silvas handed him the reins.

"His own groom is no larger than you, lad," Silvas
said. Bay let his head down, low enough for the stable

boy to pat his muzzle. The boy did that cautiously, and seemed relieved that Bay didn't bite the hand off.

"Now off with you, boy," Fitz-Matthew said roughly. "He's just a horse, even if he is large."

Silvas followed Fitz-Matthew up the stairs into the keep. The inside was everything the wizard expected— dark, smelly, and cramped. The great hall occupied the entire entrance level. Stairs led up and down along the wall to other levels. A long trestle table reached almost to the single door. At the other end, a short cross table was elevated only a few inches above the longer board. The few arrow slits in the walls didn't allow much light to enter. Most of the illumination, poor as it was, came from torches along the walls, flames that added more soot and smoke than light. Chickens and dogs seemed to have free run of the great hall, and the straw that covered the floor was none too fresh.

Silvas halted just inside the door and looked around. Soot stains climbed the walls above the torches. The ceiling was almost a uniform black. Silvas finally let his eyes rest on the one man sitting in the room, at the center of the head table. That had to be Sir Eustace.

"The Wizard Silvas," Fitz-Matthew announced loudly.

"Bring him," the figure at the table said. Fitz-Matthew gave Silvas a nervous look.

"This is my lord, Sir Eustace Devry." The steward tried to cover his nervousness with volume. He gestured and Silvas walked slowly across the room toward the head table. The wood of the tables and of the benches that flanked the lower table were dark and shiny, polished by grease, dirt, and ages of use. Only the small head table had individual chairs, three across the side that looked down at the lower table and one on each end. The chairs were as greasy and old as the tables and benches. Sir Eustace sat in the center. That chair was somewhat larger than the others, but still of simple construction.

Your peasants could hardly live more squalidly than this, Silvas thought as he stared at Sir Eustace.

The knight did look as though he might once have been an adequate warrior. His arms still looked powerful, but the body had gone to flab from too many years of riding a table rather than a horse. The face was developing jowls that were imperfectly hidden by a scruffy beard. Eustace's nose was bulbous and laced with thin lines of red and blue. He could be only in his early forties, but might easily have claimed another decade from his appearance. His hair was gray and thinning. His face was wrinkled, the skin drawn around his eyes, loose on his cheeks.

"You are the stranger who raised all this smoke in my village?" Eustace demanded as Silvas crossed to the table. The knight's voice was unpolished and hoarse. He leaned back in his chair and stared openly at Silvas.

"My lord," Fitz-Matthew said before Silvas could speak. He hurried around to his master's side. "I was inside that pillar of smoke. There is a castle within, the likes of which you wouldn't credit, it's so grand." Fitz-Matthew tried to whisper, but it was a poor effort. Eustace frowned at him and turned to Silvas again. Fitz-Matthew retreated to the wall several paces behind Sir Eustace.

"You claim to be a wizard?" Eustace demanded.

"I am what I am," Silvas replied, nodding slightly.

"Where do you come from?" Eustace made no effort at politeness. His questions were all pitched as demands.

"I come from beyond your valley, Sir Eustace, perhaps from beyond your ken." Silvas let a touch of amusement show in his voice, expecting it to rile the abrupt knight.

"If you fear to say where you've come from, perhaps you're fleeing the justice of someone else you've angered." Eustace gripped the arms of his chair.

"I fear no man," Silvas said sternly. "I ride my circuit, doing the bidding of our Unseen Lord." He controlled his voice like a musical instrument, pulling precisely the tones he wanted from it.

"We have our vicar to handle our souls," Eustace said.

"Souls are not my province."

"Then why have you come to my land?" Eustace shouted, almost rising from his chair. He stopped himself and settled back, releasing his tight grip on the arms of the chair.

"I was drawn here to provide what help Mecq needs." Silvas made the statement neutral. He watched Eustace without permitting himself to feel either like or dislike for

him yet. Silvas did not judge lightly. Sir Eustace clearly
had the training of a warrior, not of a courtier, and his
lack of manners was of less import on the marches than
in one of the court cities. And even in London his de-
meanor would not be unique—or even uncommon.

"Just what makes you think that Mecq *needs* your
help? And what sort of help do you think you can provide?"

Silvas opened his face in a cold smile. He knew the
effect that smile had on some people. Eustace's eyes narrowed, but that was his only visible reaction.

"I have spent my adult life traveling from town to village, providing the help of my calling." Silvas spoke very
softly, focusing Eustace's attention on the words. "I have
come to Mecq because Mecq has need of my talents. It
isn't important what I think Mecq needs. I don't come to
impose my opinions. I come to ask what Mecq needs.
What would Mecq have me do for it? Once I know what
you and your people need of me, I'll know what I can do
for you."

"And what will this bounty cost us?" Eustace demanded, though he too lowered his voice.

"I accept neither fee nor maintenance from those I
help," Silvas replied.

"What do you take me for?" Eustace shouted. "I'm not
an idiot babbling in a pigsty!" This time he did stand and
lean toward Silvas. "You want me to believe that you'll
solve all our problems and take no pay for it?"

"Regardless of your belief, I do what I do because it is
my sworn duty to our Unseen Lord." Silvas remained
calm. "I need no gold or silver from those I help. The
power that lets me help you supplies all of my wants."
Silvas glanced toward Fitz-Matthew, who was doing his
best to edge farther away. The steward seemed to have no
thought of repeating what he had seen of the wizard's
home.

Eustace leaned farther forward, resting his fists on the
table and putting his weight on them. But before he could
say anything more, there was an interruption.

"Excuse me, but I just heard that we have a visitor."

Sir Eustace and Silvas both looked to the side. The
woman who had spoken had stopped midway down the

stairs from above. She hesitated, then continued to descend, coming over to the head table. Eustace straightened up and softened the scowl on his face as the lady approached.

"This stranger calls himself Silvas. He claims to be a wizard." Eustace faced Silvas again. "My wife, Eleanora."

"My lady." Silvas bowed to her as to an equal. She curtsied and smiled at him.

"If we had known of your coming, we could have prepared a proper welcome," Eleanora said. She could be no more than half her husband's age, if that. No great beauty, she was modestly attractive and moved with a certain grace. She had not yet been frazzled by life in such meager circumstances. Silvas responded to her easy warmth with a warmth of his own.

"You're very gracious, my lady. But, alas, my comings are never announced in advance. I scarcely know myself where I'll be drawn next."

"It's all so exciting," Eleanora said, ignoring the irked looks of her husband. "I'm sure I've never met a wizard of power before. I saw your pillar of smoke over the village. It must reach clear to heaven. That is an impressive demonstration."

Silvas's smile grew. "It is but the link my master allows me to my home." That statement seemed to transfix both Eustace and Eleanora for a moment. The lady glanced upward, unable to restrain herself.

"I have scores of questions to ask," she said when she brought her gaze back to Silvas, "but I couldn't, not while you're standing here without so much as a drink to ease your throat. You *will* stay to dine with us this evening, won't you?"

"It would give me great pleasure, my lady, but unfortunately, this evening is impossible. Another time I would be more than happy."

"Then tomorrow for certain." Eleanora's back was to her husband. He was fidgeting, showing his impatience, but seemed reluctant to interrupt her.

"I will be delighted, my lady." Silvas bowed, getting his acceptance in before Sir Eustace could veto the invitation.

"I am so happy," Eleanora said. "I hope you will forgive my untimely curiosity, but I simply *must* ask one question now. What has brought you to Mecq? We are so far from everything here."

"The marches are where I spend my time, my lady," Silvas said. "I have come to offer what help I may to ease whatever problems your people have."

"Oh, that is *wonderful* news. Obviously our most pressing problem is the sorry state of the river. We need water, good wizard. If you can find us a reliable source of water so our people can grow proper crops, you will have done us a very great service."

"I suspected that water might be a concern." Silvas delicately understated the obvious and showed no hint of the relief he felt that someone had specifically asked him to deal with the problem. "I could see that the Eyler is far below its proper level." His oath was to proffer only the help people asked for. He could not interfere if his help was not requested.

"It seems that it has been like that forever, though of course it hasn't," Eleanora said. "I've only seen the Eyler fill its banks once, during a spring flood. The troubles started long before I came to Mecq as wife to Sir Eustace." She looked at her husband. He had seated himself again and let his face go blank.

"My husband has often told me that the river hasn't been what it should be since he was a small boy. His father led the attempts to dam the river so our people could have the water they need. It was difficult building the dam, and dangerous, and when it was finally finished, the Duke of Blethye came in with his army and forced the villagers to dismantle the dam stone by stone. Lives were lost when the water broke through. The king is too involved with foreign intrigues to pay proper attention to a dispute like this."

"His Majesty has an empire to see to," Eustace said gruffly. "He is my liege lord. I am his loyal vassal."

"And the Duke of Blethye continues to wait for us to act again," Eleanora said, with just the briefest glance at her husband. "He says he won't abide any interference with the water supply of his vassals. Not that they need the Eyler. Blethye is plentifully watered by three other rivers, each carrying more water than the Eyler does at the flood, and smaller streams beyond counting."

Silvas glanced toward Eustace, waiting to see if he would inject another comment, but the knight remained silent.

"So," Silvas said finally, "the ideal solution would be one that provided Mecq its water without drawing Blethye back through the gap."

"Or even better," Eustace said suddenly, "a solution that destroyed Blethye, body and soul, damn his eyes."

Eleanora and Silvas both looked at Eustace. He was staring at the table in front of him, one fist softly thumping the surface. After a moment Silvas turned back to Eleanora.

"I look forward to dinner tomorrow, my lady," Silvas said. "But for now I must take my leave. I have work to begin."

"Do you have any idea how long your work will take?" she asked. "How long it will be before our people have the water they need?"

"I will act as quickly as I may on that, and on whatever else is asked of me, but such a powerful effect requires study first to find the proper way."

"I am sure you will do what you can," Eleanora said. "It is so wonderful to have hope at last."

"Hope?" her husband asked sharply. He finally looked up. "How do you find hope in empty air?"

"Now, my lord," Eleanora said. "We have a guest."

Noisy footsteps clattered on the stairway from above. A girl, perhaps sixteen years old, came into the great hall. She didn't stop until she reached the landing and turned. Then she looked at the group of people as if seeing them for the first time.

"Oh, I didn't know we had company, Father." But she didn't look at Eustace. Rather, she locked her eyes on Silvas. And the tone of her voice put the lie to her words.

"This is the wizard Silvas," Eleanora said. "He raised the pillar of smoke in the village. Lord Silvas, this is Maria, my husband's daughter by his first wife." There could be no more than five or six years between Eleanora and Maria in age, and they looked nothing at all like each other. Eleanora had coarse flaxen hair and light brown eyes. Maria had dark brown hair that was glossy and fine, and her eyes were a very dark bluish-gray.

Silvas bowed his greeting as Maria walked toward him. The girl was attractive in a wholesome country sort of way, though Silvas thought that she might well look plain in a more regal setting. He closed his eyes for a second, as if to banish such thoughts. Maria's skin had lost none of its youthful glow and softness yet. There seemed to be light in her eyes. There was really no physical comparison, but something about Maria's eyes called Carillia to mind, just for an instant.

"I was on my way through to the scullery," Maria glanced toward her father and Eleanora but quickly returned her gaze to Silvas. She took another step closer to him.

"I didn't know we had company," she repeated. Her features were delicate and pleasant, her smile warm. But Silvas thought that she might yet have trouble finding a husband. If she wasn't betrothed by this time ... Sir Eustace could hardly provide the kind of dowry that might win her a fitting mate, not from a fief like Mecq, and without dowry Maria might easily end up in a nunnery. Unless Mecq itself became her dowry at the death of her father. *A question worth considering,* Silvas thought, but not one he could politely ask.

"Well, we *do* have company." Her father apparently could not avoid brusque speech, but he did try to smile over the words to his daughter. "If you're going to the scullery, then on with you, go."

"Yes, Father." But Maria made no move toward the stairs leading down to the windowless level below the great hall.

"The wizard was just ready to leave," Eustace said, staring at Maria.

Her "Oh?" had too much feeling. Eleanora and Eustace both stared at the girl. She hardly noticed them. She was still staring at Silvas.

"He's coming to dinner tomorrow," Eleanora said. Maria's face reddened as she realized what the others must be thinking of her.

"Till then, ladies, it has been my pleasure." Silvas di-

vided one bow between them, then directed another to Sir
Eustace. "Your leave, sir?"

Sir Eustace nodded and gestured vaguely toward the
door without looking at the wizard. Silvas bowed again
and strode across the room. He didn't need to look back.
He could feel the eyes of the others following him: Henry
Fitz-Matthew, still by the far wall; Sir Eustace, who undoubtedly still wore a scowl; Eleanora, who had asked
him to tend to Mecq's water supply; and most definitely
Maria. The girl's stare was almost like a pair of hot pok-
ers pressed against the back of Silvas's head.

4

Silvas reined Bay to a stop on a switchback halfway down from Castle Mecq. He looked down at the village, then gazed along the valley toward the ridge where they had stood earlier that day to take their first look at the area.

"Sir Eustace enjoys being awkward," Silvas said softly. "You might think he just sits there waiting for someone to badger." He hesitated a moment. "But he doesn't seem particularly evil, just bad-tempered. It's his style." He laughed. "It might be nothing more than poor digestion."

Bay didn't reply, even with a snort. Although no one was close enough to overhear, he didn't care to take chances—a matter of discipline, he liked to tell Silvas.

"But we have our charge at least," Silvas continued. "I thought it might take longer for someone to openly ask me to take care of the water. I didn't count on the good lady Eleanora being so talkative, so cooperative." He chuckled, then flicked the reins. "Let's go to the inn, Bay. See if anyone else is ready to open up."

There were cooking fires burning in most of the cottages now. Thin plumes of smoke found their way out doors and through holes in the roofing thatch. The women were preparing what would be the only real meal of the day for most of the villagers. The fields across Eyler had been deserted. Only a few people still worked in the small garden patches behind their homes. Brother Paul was pulling weeds in the garden behind his church. Everyone would be at supper by sunset, and most of the villagers would be in bed before full dark.

As they neared the Boar and Bear, Silvas spoke softly to Bay. "I'm going in for an ale or two. You can go home or wander the village if you want. I shouldn't be over-long." Bay stopped in front of the inn's open door, and Silvas dismounted, leaving the reins draped over Bay's neck. The horse remained still until Silvas entered the inn, then he walked slowly across the green, not quite toward the column of smoke.

Although the open door admitted some light, the Boar and Bear appeared even darker than the great hall of Eustace's castle. The ceiling was lower. There were no lights burning within. Silvas stopped just inside the door to let his eyes adjust to the gloom. Along the wall to his left, two kegs rested on trestles. Master Ian stood in a doorway leading to a back room, looking toward the front. Two villagers sat on a bench at one of the two trestle tables in the public room. Each farmer had one hand wrapped firmly around an earthenware mug. They stared at Silvas but showed no other reaction to his entrance.

"Ale all around," Silvas announced. He sat at the table with the villagers, across the trestle and closer to the end. The clink of money drew the eyes of the farmers. They looked at the coppers as they spun and settled. Then their gaze moved back up to the wizard. Silvas nodded a greeting. They nodded back. One farmer raised his mug and took a long drink. His companion followed suit, just an instant behind.

Master Ian hurried to fill the order. He brought Silvas a mug, then took the mugs of the farmers after they drained the ale already in them to refill them.

"And yourself, Master Ian," Silvas said when he brought the refilled mugs back to the farmers. The innkeeper nodded and touched a finger to his brow. He brought his own mug back to the table and stood there to raise it to the wizard before he drank.

"I thank ye, sir," Ian said, wiping foam from his mouth. He took his due from the collection of coppers on the table and slid them into the leather purse hanging from his belt.

Silvas took a long pull at his ale. It was everything he expected it to be—thin, bitter, and barely drinkable—but he didn't let his reaction show. When he set the mug down, he nodded as if in approval. Master Ian was undoubtedly his own brewmaster, and Silvas didn't want to offend the man over something he probably could not help.

"It's been a dry year here, I see," Silvas said after a moment.

Ian nodded forcefully. "Aye, it has, one dry year after another." He took another long drink of ale.

"Yer can't grow food without water," one of the farmers grumbled, half under his breath. The bitterness in his words was obvious.

His companion nodded and said, "One o' these years we'll jist dry up complait like and blow away i' we don' get better rains."

"Sometimes now, when the wind blows, ye can see the dirt jest blowin' off the fields," Master Ian said, his voice soft and sad. "If we don't start getting rains the way they should come, year after year, if the Eyler don't come back into its banks the way it did when I was a lad ..."

"The vicar says it's jist God's way o' testin' us," the second farmer said. He shook his head. "E'en Job wasn't tested so to tears."

"Mikes a man wounder," his companion said. Both raised their mugs to take long drinks of their ale. Silvas followed suit.

"Before I leave," the wizard said, "I'll solve your water problem. That is my promise to you, to all the village."

Master Ian and the farmers stared at him for a moment before anyone spoke.

"God bless yer if yer can, Lord Wizard," the first farmer said. Then all three drank their mugs dry. Silvas finished his own and ordered another round.

"I'll do whatever must be done for the water," Silvas said while Ian was fetching the second round, "but I doubt that's the only need you'll have of my services. There's not a village in the kingdom that can't use the help of my sort now and again."

There was no quick responses. Ian brought the mugs back and collected his coppers. Everyone sampled. The farmers and the innkeeper looked at each other, out the door, and back at each other before any of them looked at Silvas.

"There's Giller's mam," one of the farmers said with a

grin. "Her hens won' lay a rooster egg for naught. She says she's been witched."

"Aye, there's little blights enow, I'd say," Master Ian said, nodding slowly. "But good water an' plenty'll solve 'most all of 'em, Lord Wizard. We have water an' most folks'll figure all else is fine."

"Whatever the problems, I'm here to help," Silvas said, quickly downing his second mug of ale. "Anyone can come to me, any time. I'll hear a call at my gate." He didn't explain and none of the others asked what he meant.

"Thankee fer yer help, sir," the first farmer said. "And thankee much for the ale. It shore goes down proper, it do."

Silvas nodded and got up. He wished the others a good day and stepped out into the village green. He saw no sign of Bay, but that didn't worry him. Whether Bay was roaming the village or back in his stable, he could take care of himself—and if there was trouble, Bay could broadcast the news to Silvas, well enough to draw his help. The wizard stood on the green for a moment, taking deep breaths. Master Ian's ale had enough punch behind it for all that it lacked.

Daylight was almost gone. The sun was below the ridge to the west, throwing long shadows into the village and beyond. Above, the sky was still bright. There were red swirls in the sky west of Mecq's valley, too far away.

A peaceful little place, by the looks, Silvas thought, somewhat mellowed by the ale and by the wine he had drunk earlier. But he could still feel the evil that surrounded Mecq. Silvas turned slowly, looking in every direction, casting his mind out, gingerly feeling the aura of the place.

There's evil enough here, for certain, he told himself, not for the first time. There was neither fear nor triumph in his eyes as he walked to the smoke and the Glade within.

I will do my best was a promise to himself as well as to his Unseen Lord and the people of Mecq.

The great hall of the Glade was arranged differently than the halls of most castles. Instead of one long lower

table butting against a shorter head table, there were a
half-dozen tables spread around the great hall, with the
head table set off a little on its dais. The different races
of retainers had different requirements. The tables for
Bosc and his kin were lower, the benches adapted to their
different legs. The lupine warriors also had unique needs.
Their tables were wider, and almost as low as those for
Bosc's people. The lupine kin preferred to eat squatting
next to their tables. Chairs and benches remained alien to
them. Only the humans sat on normal seats at normal tables.

There were people of all three sorts in the great hall
now, many more than there had been at noon. And
Carillia was standing on the dais at the head of the room
when Silvas entered. She stepped down when she saw
him and met him halfway.

"I was wondering if you would be delayed," she said
after they shared a light kiss of greeting.

"Whenever I'm away, I can't wait to get back to you,"
Silvas said. They smiled at each other and Carillia linked
her arm with his as they walked to their table on the dais.
Silvas stopped when he spotted Bosc coming into the
hall, just long enough to confirm that Bay had returned.

"There has been activity today," Carillia said when
they were seated and servants started bringing the first
courses of food. "A horse and rider left Mecq while you
were at the castle. They crossed the river and headed upstream, across the valley at an angle."

Silvas considered that news for a moment, then nodded
lightly. "St. Ives lies in that direction." It was the only
likely destination for a rider from Mecq, particularly now.
"Brother Paul must have sent for instructions from his
bishop about me." He chuckled. "The vicar of Mecq is a
cautious fellow, my love, that's for sure."

"Do you know his bishop?" Carillia asked.

Silvas shook his head. "There's a new man at St. Ives
since last I was there." It had been many years. Bishop
Hugh had been an ancient then, long past his time.
"Bishop Egbert Barlowe has the see now, as far as I
know. He must know me by repute at least. If nothing
else, he'll know that I have His Majesty's countenance."

"And what do *you* know of Bishop Egbert?" Carillia asked.

Silvas shrugged. "That he is an adept of the Greater Mysteries within the White Brotherhood and not a mere nepotistic appointee." That meant that Bishop Egbert would have considerable magical substance—much more power than Brother Paul, if not nearly as much as Silvas. The gradations were relatively clear. An initiate of the Lesser Mysteries would possess only minimal powers. He might have a dozen spells for commonplace magics at his command. An adept of the Greater Mysteries would have a lager number of magics, some of them of considerably more power. But a wizard . . . years of study, followed by a grueling process of initiation, made him almost a demigod, with quite extensive resources at his command.

The wizard turned his attention to the meal for a few minutes.

"In any case," he said after washing down food with a long drink of wine, "it will take better than two days, almost three full days, for a rider to reach St. Ives from Mecq. Add whatever time it takes Bishop Egbert to reach a decision and get it back to Mecq. We may have close to a week before we have to consider Egbert Barlowe in our calculations."

The evening meal was the main repast of the day in the Glade. It was not a meal to be hurried. Silvas's great hall was a cheery place most evenings, light and airy. Tall windows showed a disregard for physical assault. Mirrors on the walls reflected and multiplied the available light, whether from the windows or from fireplaces, torches, and candles within the room. In winter, thick glass panes were carefully fitted to the windows—carefully because everyone who worked with them knew the tremendous expense they represented. Many years had passed since the last time a pane had been accidentally broken. The retainer responsible for that accident, one of Bosc's people, had anguished more over it than Silvas had.

Musicians played through the meal, changing places so one group could eat while the others provided the light airs that Carillia always praised so highly. Guards finished their meals and hurried out to relieve the sentries on the walls so they too could get a hot meal and a little warm companionship. Servants brought more food in from the kitchen and carried off empty platters. The scullery staff took most of their meals in the kitchen, and preferred it that way. Their food was hotter and there were fewer hands reaching for a share.

Before the new shift of guards left, Silvas stood and banged on the table for attention. The hall quieted quickly. Everyone turned to look.

"We are in a new village tonight," Silvas said. He didn't raise his voice, but his words carried to every corner of the hall. "Normally that doesn't much affect any of you. This one *might* not either." He paused and looked around before he added, "Or it might." That he spoke of it at all would have given most of his people that idea. "There is a strange feeling to this place called Mecq, and until I know what it represents, be on your guard. I'll want to know at once of anything out of the ordinary, no matter how minor you think it is."

It wasn't the first time that Silvas had delivered that sort of warning, but the instances were rare enough that it struck home. His people sat or stood and looked at him, searching his face for clues, taking his words seriously, as he knew they would.

"Tell those you relieve on the walls," Silvas said, his eyes flicking from one sentry to another. When he sat down again, the new shift of guards hurried out. Slowly the atmosphere in the great hall returned to something approaching normal, though no one was quite as animated as before.

"You *are* worried," Carillia said softly, leaning close to Silvas so that no one else would hear.

"I am," Silvas agreed. "Until I can chase this feeling to its source to find out why there is such a sense of evil about Mecq, I'll feel much safer knowing that everyone is as alert as possible. Trouble in Mecq could flow over to the Seven Towers."

The evening meal continued after Silvas and Carillia left the great hall. One of the first changes Silvas had made when he inherited the Glade from Auroreus was to stop the tradition of meals ending when the lord of the castle got up from the table. "I've had too many of my own meals cut short," he had explained at the time. Everyone knew what he meant. Auroreus had been prone to eat quickly and sparingly, and to leave the great hall before most had a chance to fill their bellies.

Carillia went straight upstairs. Silvas went out to the mews, to the large enclosure at one end that was Bay's.

"People do not sleep well in Mecq," Bay said when Silvas entered.

"Tonight, or in general?" Silvas asked.

"Both, obviously," Bay replied. "There is much fear in the village. Many lie awake listening for the Devil's footsteps at their door."

Silvas sat on a bale of hay. Unlike the ordinary horses in the rest of the stable, Bay could be trusted not to gorge himself on fodder left within reach.

"I wonder if it is not more resignation than fear," Silvas said. "Fear is the common lot of peasants, especially on the marches where warring armies might come through burning and killing at any time."

"That kind of resignation is but fear carried on too long for the edge to remain," Bay said. "It is still fear. They bar their doors at night, sleep clutching crucifixes and rosaries, and wake with a quick *Hail Mary* at any sound. Judgment Day would surprise no one in Mecq."

"It's more than the water," Silvas said.

"Much more," Bay agreed.

"Even the vicar may not realize it."

"You heard about the rider?" Bay asked.

"Carillia told me."

"The vicar must have some sense of the danger, even if he can't name it, or he'd not be so quick to send for news of us," Bay said.

"Perhaps. But he probably won't discuss this feeling with me until he decides that I'm not the threat. Or until his bishop replies."

The two were silent for a moment. Bay paced back and forth a couple of times, then stopped near the door. The top half was open to give him fresh air. Silvas remained seated.

"Have you decided how to give Mecq its water?" Bay asked finally.

"I haven't thought hard on it yet," Silvas replied. "Water should be easy, if not for the threat from Blethye. It would be a hollow victory for Mecq if the duke came in as soon as we left and overturned our work."

"Blethye has grown uncommon strong of late," Bay observed. "One might wonder at that."

"How has he grown strong?"

"A question that may need answering before long," Bay said. The conversation lapsed into silence. Silvas sat with Bay until Bosc came in. Then he got up, stretched, and wished both horse and groom a good night.

Silvas stopped in the center of the courtyard, senses reaching out to the sentries above the gate and on the walls, feeling for any hint of alarm—and finding none. Then the wizard looked straight up, bending his head back. The sky was ablaze with the points of stars, a rash of lights across the heavens.

"A few drops of rain from each of you," Silvas whispered. "But I doubt you have even the scant water Mecq husbands." He had tried to look closely at a star once, when he was still an apprentice new to the gift of telesight. He had focused and reached out toward the brightest star in the night . . . and had nearly had the eyes burned out of his head for his rashness. The ball of raging fire had nearly consumed him. Only the quick intervention of Auroreus had saved him. "Some visions even the gods are denied, lad," Auroreus said after tending the young Silvas's injuries. "I should have warned you about this." There had been none of the shouting that Silvas had expected.

"Someday," Silvas whispered, scanning the sky. "Someday." Memory of his burns returned. He would not challenge the fires of heaven yet.

Carillia was pacing the length of the small sitting room that adjoined their bedchamber, hesitating each time she passed one of the room's two windows to look out into the night. She wore only a light robe of silk now, so fine that it was nearly transparent. Her brows were knitted in an uncommon expression of deep concentration or worry. She hardly seemed to notice Silvas's arrival, and that in itself was evidence of great agitation.

"What bothers you so, my love?" Silvas asked, not attempting to disguise his astonishment. Carillia stopped pacing and faced him.

"I don't know," she said, and the music of her voice was oddly discordant, with almost a tangible anguish. She took a deep breath. Silvas watched as she carefully banished all signs of her concern. When she spoke again, her voice was calm, her face showed no hint of bother.

"Ah, my heart." She moved to Silvas and took his hands in hers. "It's just a fancy that came over me. Likely it's no more than a reaction to what you told our people at supper."

Silvas didn't believe that any more than Carillia did, but he didn't question her explanation. It would serve for the moment. Velvet and Satin came out of the bedroom, and Silvas could see that even the cats looked less serene than usual.

"Morning will come as always, my love," Silvas said. He drew Carillia into his arms and kissed her lightly. She relaxed, softening in his grip. Then Velvet and Satin were with them, and the cats were looking for attention as well. They needed a lot of stroking before they would settle down in front of the bedroom door so Silvas and Carillia could enter.

The soft lights of the night came in through the bedroom window. The darkness was only partial, even after Silvas extinguished the last of the candles. The wizard and his lady required little more light than the cats in order to see.

Silvas undressed, setting the belt with his dagger on a stand at the head of the bed. Carillia dropped the robe from her shoulders. For a moment she stood silhouetted against the window. Silvas and Carillia moved toward each other and met in the center of the bed. They moved smoothly from soft kisses and light caresses through to the harder passions of their love. Mecq disappeared from their thoughts in the regular renewal of their pillow vows. The light of climax, when it came, was nearly as bright as the star Silvas had once tried to look into ... but this light was without pain.

Afterward, as Silvas and Carillia snuggled together to slide into sleep, Velvet and Satin pawed their way quietly into the bedroom to take up their usual positions at either side of the bed. Sleep was another soft caress in the dark, a peace that moved outside time into eternity ... and ended with the frantic screams of the cats.

5

The sudden shrieks from Velvet and Satin brought Silvas and Carillia out of sleep immediately. The first cry of the cats had hardly begun before Silvas sprang up out of sleep, instantly alert, already rolling toward the side of the bed and starting his response.

"Eyru, reygu mavith. Eyru, sprath tourn." The first spell of defense was out of his mouth as he started to move. The walls of the bedchamber developed a soft luminescence, a pale silvery glow that would silhouette any foe of flesh or spirit that might intrude while it shielded the beings who belonged in the Glade from the eyes of outsiders.

Silvas quickly pulled on a robe and buckled his knife belt around him, automatic reactions. He ran toward the door and reached out with his mind to gauge the nature of the assault. He had no doubt that the alarm meant an attack. Satin and Velvet ran ahead of Silvas, and Carillia was at his heels. At the door Silvas grabbed a seven-foot quarterstaff. The staff, with a ferrule of silver at one end and one of iron at the other, was useful in certain magics, and it was also handy for dealing with physical enemies.

On the run, Velvet and Satin quit caterwauling. The humans behind them were much slower, but the cats paused at every corner to look ahead and to wait. They knew where to go. They led the way up to Silvas's conjuring room without instruction. The silvery luminescence was brighter there. The cold white glow of the walls was bright enough to read by. The crystal pentagram in the floor gleamed like icy fire.

Silvas plunged straight to the center of the pentagram, and his arrival there increased the light in the room. His incantations increased as he cast his mind out, his searching thoughts chasing away like ripples in a pond as he sought the source of the alarm and broadened the protective shield around him, and around the Glade. Silvas could sense his soldiers hurrying to their posts. They might have little strength against magic, but sorcerers and demons often came in the company of physical warriors.

Carillia and the cats had steered their way around the pentagram. Even the cats knew that they did not belong within its lines at a time like this. Like Carillia, Satin and Velvet went to protected neutral zones near the walls, into crystal circles laid into the floor like the lines of the pentagram. Unlike the white glow of the pentagram, the circles glowed a light pink. There was a series of these rings around the room. Carillia went to one. The cats moved to circles at either side of her. The animals sat back on their haunches, claws extended, eyes fixed in intense feline concentration, staring past the edges of the pentagram in the center of the room.

When the screams of the cats wakened her, Carillia hadn't stopped even to put on a robe. She stood naked in her circle, body tensed, leaning slightly forward as if ready to leap at an attacker or meet his charge. Her lips moved quickly as she uttered silent chants of her own. The look on her face was one of single-minded intensity. She stood as ready to defend herself as Silvas and the cats did, and nothing about her suggested any doubt about her ability.

Outside, the thunder started with a soft rumble and grew louder as it pulsed for many seconds before the first bolt of lightning streaked past the window, so close that it seemed certain that it must have actually struck the Glade. More lightning came. The thunder continued to echo off itself. Heavy rain pelted the wall and came in through the glassless window. The lightning and thunder were no mere spectacle. The storm surrounded the Seven Towers, but even so, it served more as a frame to what happened inside. The glow within the conjuring room faded and pulsed with each shock. Another lightning bolt struck close to the keep. Its report was so loud that it momentarily drowned out the sounds of Silvas's chanting and the renewed screams of the cats.

The brimstone smell of the lightning found its way into

the conjuring chamber with a strength that was almost overpowering—too strong, too intense to be only physical. The lights in the room flared and then seemed to reverse themselves: the silvery glow became an inky black luminescence, providing pale silhouettes against the dark glow. But there was no loss of vision for Silvas and his companions.

"It comes," Silvas said.

Renewed thunder covered his words, but Carillia and the cats either heard him anyway or got the message in more direct fashion. The cats bared their teeth. They no longer bothered to scream their alerts. Now they hissed a warning for whatever was coming.

The storm outside ended—or at least it was blocked from the awareness of those inside the conjuring chamber. The danger was closer now, and much greater than that of lightning.

Silvas raised his staff in both hands, parallel to the floor, chest high, and extended it toward the window. Flickers of light and dark flowed through the window and filled the room, the light bleaker but more intense than lightning. Unaided eyes could never hope to adapt to the strobing of blinding light and eternal blackness that came and went in cycles much faster than the eye could blink. Motion seemed stopped by the rapid alternation of light and dark. Thunder rolled continuously, no longer connected to individual flashes of lightning. It grumbled from the depths, then crescendoed into a deafening roar, with the next wave building over the dying echoes of the last.

Sparkling outlines of demonic figures appeared within the room as burning lines that seemed to mute the storm in the chamber without really lessening its fury. The bodies and faces of the demons became more visible during the dark. The flashes of light could not obliterate their forms, though. A smell of rotten eggs and burning rock built within the chamber. Terror flowed from the figures, a visible effluence, and a new sound of ethereal laughter, intimidating enough to make the soul quaver.

Silvas faced the two demons squarely while he chanted continuously in the language of power. He wove his shields and attempted to weave nets to capture the illusive figures that dared to challenge him in his own lair. Each attempt to snare the demons failed, though, and sparked new peals of their horrible laughter.

"You feeble mouse. Your nets cannot touch us," one of the demons screamed. Each word was ringed with scorn and echoed with laughter. The faces of the two demons broadened and grew, becoming larger than the bodies. The mouths gaped open to show razor-sharp fangs and gullets full of the fires of hell. Heat flowed out and over Silvas, singeing the hair on his arms.

Despite the heat pouring over his face and arms, Silvas felt ice grip at his feet, locking them in place. A chill breeze blew up under his robe at his command, a shrinking, tightening wind. He touched the iron end of his staff to one intersection of the pentagram, and cold fire flared up, momentarily overriding the strobing of light and dark that had ushered in the demons, chilling the fires they breathed, freezing the flames like the steam of breath on a cold morning. The demons' laughter faded with the blaze and returned as that cold glare died away and the flickering regained its dominance.

The demons either came closer to the pentagram or grew larger again. Their outlined figures made it impossible for Silvas to judge which. He increased the pace and volume of his chants. The walls of the chamber seemed to fade and disappear, no longer competing with the flashing that supported the manifestations of the demons. Silvas found himself standing on what appeared to be a mountain peak that towered so far above the rest of the world that nothing else was visible. He stood on a small flat area that protruded into infinity. He was barely aware of the presence of Carillia and the cats.

The duel consumed him.

Silvas focused the lines of force that rose from his pentagram. The only constant now was the pattern of glowing crystal around his feet. The lines were clear, bold. The planes of force that rose from them shaded into ultraviolet, beyond the vision of anyone without the magic to see them. In the center of the pattern, Silvas remained conscious of himself and of the long staff in his hands. The quarterstaff was almost part of him now, a bar joining his hands.

Pain reached fiery fingers into his brain, pulling and
twisting, stretching his mind out of shape. His body
seemed ready to evaporate beneath his tortured head. He
heard Bay neigh loudly, a battle challenge, not a cry of
fright. For an instant Silvas could see the giant horse rear-
ing in the stable, front hoofs pawing at the dark, caught
up in some duel of his own. Bosc was at Bay's side. The
little groom had knives in both hands, and the thin blades
had an icy glow of their own.

That image disappeared but not permanently. It kept
flickering back, part of the general strobing that continued to surround Silvas. But he could not see the enemy
that Bay and Bosc faced.

More visions flashed in to seize Silvas, forcing themselves on him. He saw himself staked out on the ground,
tiny insects by the million marching in columns onto his
body. Each bug took a single bite of his flesh and
marched off the other side. Mote by mote he was being
consumed, a meal that would last for an eternity.

Off to the side, Silvas saw a new image of himself
appear as the first faded into the dark. Knives raked
his body, digging deeper with each pass, turning thin
scratches into deep channels of purple blood that flowed
and ebbed in tides of their own, growing into sea waves
of impossible dimension, drowning him in his own blood,
pulling him under.

Silvas felt himself being drawn forward, pulled from
the center of his pentagram toward the lacerated vision of
his body. The ice around his feet started to crack, stab-
bing his ankles. He fought the pull, reaching within to focus his chants and energy more tightly. He forced the
images of the two demons to reappear, and with them in
sight he could hold his position.

The demons came back larger or closer once more.
There was detail to them now, dimension. Their horns
curved forward, black and sparkling. The teeth in their
gaping mouths were long wedge-shaped daggers. In place
of the earlier fire, black and purple blood welled up in
their throats and overflowed, dripping from their swollen
lips. Their laughter was even more grotesque than before,
gurgling through the blood. It folded itself around Silvas,
pressed in on him.

Once more Silvas dropped the iron ferrule of his staff to an intersection of the pentagram. This time he didn't just hold it to bring light back to the confrontation. He went down on one knee, his hands sliding along the shaft as he lunged, dipping the silver ferrule toward the demon that seemed to be closer. When the silver of the staff touched the ghostly outline of the demon, bright yellow fire flamed and the demon's laughter turned, for an instant, into a scream of agony. The demon withdrew and Silvas stood again, bringing his staff back up.

"Eyri, reyqi mavith," Silvas shouted, turning the tense of his spell. *"Eyri, sprith cyclane."* He turned the nightmares that showed him being eaten or sliced to bits and threw them back at the demons, reversing the time flow to show him being reassembled. For a moment more the demons seemed to retreat before his counterattack, but not for long.

Silvas saw himself again, a larger than life figure hurtling toward him. Black claws ripped at his face, reached into his mouth, down his throat. Demon claws pulled him inside out. Bloody innards dripped and flopped as they were hauled out of his mouth. Fires licked at the inverted mess that was supposed to be him.

The wizard felt his body tremble. The clash of power around him was peaking. He had to focus so tightly on his chants that he had little attention to spare for the well-being of his body. *This has to end soon,* he thought.

A warm breeze started to circle the pentagram, almost too soft to detect at first, hovering at the edge of sensation. More images came and went around Silvas, distracting him long enough that he stumbled and had to scramble to keep from falling.

He saw Carillia and the cats still within their protective circles, but isolated—their circles now cylindrical prison cells. The cats were tense, poised, still ready to spring at any physical enemies who dared to approach. Carillia looked just as intense, as feral as the cats, almost as if she too were ready to leap at any enemy who came within reach. The look on her face was of fury and bloodlust. No trace of her native beauty showed through the battle face.

Silvas saw Bay's front hoofs strike out again. This time they hit some target that remained invisible to the wizard.

Bright sparks flowed from the contact. Then Bosc pounced on another invisible foe. His knives flashed up and down. The blood that spurted out was all too visible.

Silvas took a deep breath, concentrating as fully on that as he did on his spells. He felt the ice form around his feet again, protecting him, reaching up his naked legs to knees and thighs. The warm wind around the pentagram grew in strength and speed. It started to whisper its presence.

The demons moved closer. This time Silvas was sure that they were approaching, not merely expanding ... thought they also seemed to be getting larger. The demons slavered blood and continued to laugh, a triumphal sound now. They seemed oblivious to the wind swirling behind them.

"We've come for your soul, you pathetic insect," they screamed in unison. Blood sprayed from their mouths. Their teeth clashed, grinding against each other as they sharpened themselves with every motion.

The laughter of the demons became a physical force that Silvas could feel trying to dislodge him, trying to push him from the protection of his pentagram. The laughter pulsed and swayed, forcing Silvas to lean against it as he might lean into a gale. The laughter hid the sounds of the warm wind contracting around the pentagram, curling in toward Silvas in ever tightening coils, urging the demons forward, edging them closer without their awareness.

At the instant that the demons were pushed within the outer precincts of the pentagram, Silvas erupted into action, chanting words of power that burst the ice from around his feet and legs. He scraped the silver ferrule of his staff across the crystal lines of the pentagram, then picked it up and swung it so rapidly that the line of the staff blurred into a plane. It appeared to catch fire as it passed through both demons, severing their exaggerated heads from their bodies. The outlined figures fell and flamed as they touched the crystal lines of the pentagram. The lines that had formed their figures danced a final agony like fat in a skillet, and shriveled into lines of ash. But their final screams persisted for many seconds after they vanished.

Then there was peace in the conjuring chamber.
Silence.
The strobing of light and dark ended.
The pearly glow returned.

Silvas took a deep breath and let his eyes drop shut for
an instant. *Only for an instant.* But a force too powerful
to resist grabbed him. Silvas felt himself being tossed
head over heels, spinning into nothingness. He opened his
eyes and saw crowds of flaming rainbows spinning in
contrary orbits around him. Silvas extended his arms,
hoping to slow his spinning and bring some order to . . .
to whatever was happening to him. He noticed that he no
longer held his staff. He chanted, but his spells sounded
hollow, without the power they should possess. The
words were empty, meaningless sounds without their
magic.

Is this defeat? Have I fallen to destruction? Silvas
turned the questions over in his mind, surprised that he
could accept the possibility so easily. *That* brought a
smile to his mind, if not to his face. *There doesn't seem
to be much I can do about it.*

Slowly, though, fear did rise in him. The spinning journey through a kaleidoscopic sky seemed to continue for
an eternity. Silvas fought his way through the fear when
it started to press against him.

*This doesn't feel like death. It doesn't feel like the tor-
tures of hell.* The muscles of his face tightened up. *Whatever those might feel like.* The only vague ideas he had of
what those might feel like were those of the Church . . .
and his magic had carried him too close to the center of
all power for him to take the public teachings of the ma-
terial church literally.

Every effort Silvas made to free himself from the trap
failed. Worse, his failures were so complete that they offered not the slightest hope that he might be able to extri-
cate himself. He tumbled and twisted, carried by a power
he couldn't even touch to gauge. Time lost all meaning.
Silvas watched, and delved within himself to search for
any piece of knowledge that might give him a little leverage. Time had to pass, but soon Silvas had no idea how

much time might be involved. There was nothing to mark it against.

What of Carillia and the others? he wondered. If *he* had earned this—punishment?—then what of the others?

He shouted and his words echoed, hollow, mocking. His voice was distorted beyond recognition. His spells and charms were stripped of force and hurled back in his face, as unsettling as the mocking laughter of the demons he had vanquished in his conjuring chamber.

Or did I really vanquish them? Silvas wondered. It had certainly looked as if they were destroyed. *Or did they merely disappear because their work was finished, because they had trapped me?* He worried at those questions for another time and a half without finding any answer he could have confidence in. *It felt like victory when my staff severed their heads.* His power had worked then, and that power was reliable.

. . . At least, it had always been reliable before.

The rainbows started to pulse, growing and shrinking in size and intensity, giving Silvas some measure of elapsing time. He couldn't be certain of the scale he needed to compare it to, but the pulses did seem closely timed to his heartbeat . . . or his heartbeat was being tuned to the rainbows.

"It doesn't *feel* like demonic force," he said, but his words still sounded hollow, alien.

Silvas's tight cartwheels muted into long, rolling tumbles. The rainbows that flashed past his eyes blurred into huge swatches of blues and greens that slowly developed textures and came into focus, if only momentarily. Silvas felt dizzy for the first time. His eyes could hold no target. As his spinning slowed, his stomach felt more ready to rebel than it had when the motion was at its most frantic. He closed his eyes again for a moment, fighting to control the nausea, and he fell.

Up and down had returned, and Silvas knew that he was falling. Before he could open his eyes, he struck the ground—feet first, sending an agonizing shock up his legs and spine, and then he tumbled. His knees went limp and he rolled, ending up on his back, the wind knocked out of him.

Silvas had no choice but to lie still while he caught his breath. There was a brilliant blue sky above him, a clear, sunlit sky. He gradually became aware of a gentle, spring-like breeze, full of the scents of blooming flowers and growing plants. Still his first thought was to conjure his way home ... but his chants remained empty, devoid of power. He reached for his belt, for his dagger, but even the knife was gone.

The dizziness was slow to recede. Silvas pushed himself to a kneeling position and had to rest before he could get to his feet. He was at the edge of a forest clearing, looking along the arc where the pine trees ended. He turned, half a step at a time, fighting to keep his balance.

He jumped when he saw an old man sitting in the center of the clearing.

Silvas faced him. The man was fifty yards away, sitting motionless on a rock that seemed to mark the exact center of the clearing. *An old man* was Silvas's first impression, but he could find no way to justify it. He stared, trying to focus on the man so he could see him more clearly, but even the gift of telesight was gone. There appeared to be something fuzzy about the stranger's appearance. Silvas could make out no real details about him—not hair color or how lined and wrinkled his skin might be.

But Silvas retained the impression that the man was old.

The stranger raised a hand and beckoned. The gesture was slow but not tentative. Silvas looked around quickly. There was no one else in sight. The wizard walked out into the clearing, slowly, hesitating often.

The old man, if he was indeed old, let his arm drop to his lap. He wore an undyed robe, too loose to show whether he was stout or thin. Silvas saw no weapon, but the stranger didn't come into better focus as Silvas approached. His face, his outline remained blurred, as if there were layers of fine gauze between him and Silvas.

"Who are you?" Silvas asked, stopping ten feet from the old man.

"I am me." The voice was as featureless as the face, leaving no hint of accent or mood. "As you are *you,* Henry, son of William."

Silvas felt a chill strangling his spine. He had shared

his true name with no one since childhood, had not even spoken it aloud in all the years that had passed since he first entered the Glade. The last mortal to know his true name was Auroreus, and *he* was long dead.

"Where am I?" Silvas asked.

"Why, here with me, of course," the stranger said. "Come closer. I mean you no harm."

"*Why* am I hear?" Silvas asked, taking only one step closer.

"You are here because I have a story you need to hear," the stranger said. "Come sit by me."

"If you mean me no harm, why have you tried to strip me of my power?" Silvas took one more step, debating what he should do. The stranger could not be powerless, not the way his form remained so indistinct. But could Silvas overpower him physically?

The stranger laughed.

"Tried?" He laughed again. "I have done nothing to your power. But power such as yours simply does not work in this place." He gestured to the grass next to him. Silvas took a deep breath, then sat where the stranger had indicated.

"What kind of story?" Silvas asked. He felt the urge to do *something*, but there seemed to be no alternative. He didn't know where he was or who the stranger might be. His power didn't work. He could do nothing but listen and hope that the stranger would send him home when the tale was ended.

"Would it sound too incredible if I started this with 'Once upon a time?'—No? Good, because that is how this story should start." The stranger gave Silvas no chance to offer his opinion.

"Once upon a time there was a loving couple. First love, lasting love. They were so wrapped up in making each other happy that little else ever intruded on their thoughts. Now, you might think that this would make for an ideal life. And it did seem ideal to them too, for the longest time. They were happy and aware of their bliss. Joy radiated in all directions, making life so much more pleasant for everyone who was touched by that happiness. But."

There had to be a "but," Silvas thought.

The stranger spoke slowly, softly. Silvas, with nothing better to do, tried to focus on the voice, but the words and intonation were as hazy as the man's appearance. *What manner of power do you control?* Silvas wondered. The answer had to lie in the story. Silvas blinked. Staring at the stranger was hard on the eyes.

"This couple had many children over time," the stranger continued. "Their love was exceptionally fertile. Unfortunately—and here is the tragedy of this love story—they were so consumed by their passion for each other that they had little time for the children their love created. Those children grew up neglected and feeling that their parents did not care for them at all." He paused. "That was not far from the mark, but it was not a hostile disregard. The parents simply did not make room in their love for the score of children they conceived.

"An even score. Twenty. This parental neglect colored the outlook of the children. In some cases it warped them totally. They were forced upon their own resources much too young. Some of them grew up bitter, filled with a hatred that started with their parents and expanded to take in most of creation.

"Not all were *that* bitter, but none escaped completely. They were all jealous of each other, interested mostly—or only—in sating their own appetites for pleasure. The children were rivals in everything, trying to prove themselves—to themselves and to the parents who spared them so little thought through the years.

"No matter what the children did, no matter how outrageous or epic their actions, their parents seemed to pay too little attention. The appearance was not deceiving."

The stranger paused and moved a hand to his face. Silvas couldn't be certain, there was still the haze obscuring the man's face, but he thought that the stranger might be wiping a tear from his eye.

What is this all about? Silvas asked himself. He could find no point to the story.

"When the parents finally did begin to notice the competitions among their children, they were so disgusted with what they saw that they withdrew even further, relying only on each other, doing everything but openly disown the children. They were too ashamed to take that step, blaming themselves—with appropriate but belated vision—for the way their sons and daughters had turned out. And the children competed all the more fiercely, until competition became the paramount fact of their existence."

The stranger paused again and stared at Silvas. The wizard had a fleeting impression of blazing eyes and deep sadness before the veils fell into place again and the stranger resumed his narrative.

"Until death was less to be feared than defeat. By that time the parents could do nothing but stand by while their children fought one another. And once the dying started . . ." The stranger shook his head slowly.

Silvas squinted. *Somehow he's talking about the gods. But what is the point? What am I supposed to learn from it?* Silvas understood that the lesson had to be vital, something that would bear directly on what he was going to face in Mecq.

It did give him some confidence that the old man would return him to Mecq, though.

I have to puzzle this out quickly, Silvas thought. But when he raised his head to ask a question, the old man was gone. There was no trace of him.

Then the green of the forest and the blue of the sky started to spin around Silvas, faster and faster. He felt himself caught up in the whirlwind of nature and there was an instant—or an eternity—of nothingness, and when he opened his eyes again, he was lying in the center of the pentagram in his conjuring chamber.

6

The first sound Silvas uttered was a rumbling groan of pain. Consciousness meant feeling streaks of burning agony and the bruises from his falls. The fleeting thought of escaping pain by retreating into the dark was too weak to match the pain. Pain was reality, as hard as the marble floor Silvas's face pressed against. Movement sent needles of fire deeper into his body. His head throbbed so badly that decapitation might not seem too great a price to pay for relief. Even breathing brought pain. He started to draw his arms up under him so he could rise.

"Don't move, my heart," Carillia said, her voice so close that Silvas knew she had come into the pentagram. As always, her voice was a balm. And the cool touch of her hands on Silvas's shoulders was like a dose of healing lotion. Silvas was content to follow her instructions.

"I know you hurt, my heart," Carillia said. "I'm going to turn you over on your back. Let me do the work. Just don't resist." She waited for a moment. Silvas made no reply.

"Okay, here we go, my heart." Carillia moved her hands. Silvas remained as limp as he could. Movement didn't hurt as much as he had anticipated. There was pain, but it was bearable.

Silvas let his eyes slide open when he went over on his back. Carillia's face was close. That was almost enough to distract him from the new agony in his back and buttocks where the floor pressed against them. Breathing came a little easier. Silvas tried to speak, but nothing came out, and the room started to spin and fade above him.

It's too much, Silvas thought. *I can't make it.* Slipping into the void would be so much simpler. An escape.

Carillia leaned closer. Silvas was on the edge of unconsciousness again, scarcely breathing, when her lips touched his. It was only a kiss, but Silvas felt that she was breathing new life into him. He drew warmth from her lips. His breathing eased. He closed his eyes for a moment but didn't pass out. And the room didn't spin when he opened his eyes again. For a moment neither Silvas nor Carillia moved. Then Silvas tilted his head a little to look to either side. Satin and Velvet sat at the edge of the pentagram, staring at him. There was still darkness beyond the room's window. The interior of the conjuring chamber was lit by candles and torches, not by the glow of the stone.

Silvas ran his tongue over his lips. "Tell me," he whispered.

"When you destroyed the demons, you collapsed." Carillia held his hand firmly. "Your body is covered with hundreds of shallow cuts. It looks as if you were raked by cat claws over and over. I've stopped the bleeding with that salve you keep."

"How long?" Silvas asked, his voice a little stronger. He could feel his body responding to the challenge now.

"Since you collapsed? Not thirty minutes. Not an hour since the cats woke us."

"Seems ... longer." Those words were separated by a deep breath, an involuntary inhalation. Silvas's mind focused slowly, bringing him back from the twin confrontations, first with demons, then with the hazy man who was, in many ways, even more frightening.

It's up to me now, Silvas thought. *I have to go on. If I can.* But he needed to be in much better shape than he was at the moment.

Ogru, belviu dekas Silvari, he chanted within his mind. *Lord, heal the hurts of Silvas.* Even that simple line took almost every ounce of energy he had, but his power— weak though it now was—had returned. He could feel it working within him. That was in itself enough to make him feel somewhat better, but it took long minutes before he had enough strength to actually voice the chants of healing aloud. Then he let the incantations reel themselves off his lips. His voice gained strength as the spells started to work. The crisis was past. There was much that he did not understand about the night's adventures, but it was too soon to worry about them. First he had to make himself whole again.

As soon as Silvas started chanting, Carillia retreated out of the pentagram. The cats moved back at the same time, farther from their master, but they kept their eyes on him. Silvas's chanting brought the pentagram back to life. The crystal lines started to glow. The pentagram was but a tool, but it was a tool of considerable power. When Auroreus created this diagram, he had invested it with a portion of his own magical substance, and his link to the Unseen Lord had forced even more magical energy into the lattices of the crystal.

Silvas's recovery was not immediate. The pain was slow to subside, and while it remained it blunted his concentration. Some of the spells had to be repeated.

This was too close for a first encounter, Silvas thought as he weaved his spells. *Two demons who didn't reach me until I was within my pentagram. They shouldn't have been able to touch me, shouldn't have been able to wound me so, not without a lot more force than I saw. Either my talent is fading or they had help I didn't suspect.* And if the latter was true, then the former was also true. The stranger in the forest came immediately to mind.

I had no injuries there, no pain. But Carillia had told Silvas that less than thirty minutes had passed between the destruction of the demons and his painful waking. He had already had the injuries that pained him so. The body he had worn in his oddly compressed excursion was only a body of mind, a memory of reality. *That must be why my power did not work there.*

That relieved one of his worries . . . in part.

Silvas let his chants die away and took stock of his body. He had no idea how much time had passed, but there had been improvement. He rolled over and then pushed himself up slowly, resting on his elbows before getting up to his knees and finally, most carefully, to his feet. There was still pain. It would take time and sleep to erase that and to finish the work of repair. He looked down at his body. He was naked. His robe was gone, tattered even more badly than his body. The belt with his dagger was on the floor, within the center space of the pentagram with him. Silvas leaned over with difficulty, picked up the belt, and strapped it around his waist. The lines of his many cuts were no longer bright red, but rather a rapidly fading pink, except where dried blood had crusted over the skin.

A single word of command in the old language extinguished the magical glow in the room. Silvas walked out of the pentagram to Carillia. She hugged him gingerly, as if she feared that he might still be damaged. Velvet and Satin came to rub against him. They purred loudly until Silvas reached down to stroke their necks. That seemed to reassure them. They went over by the wall and sat down.

Koshka came to the door and hesitated there. "A new robe for you, my lord," he said in his gurgling voice. He held up the garment and carried it in to Silvas.

"Thank you, Koshka," Silvas said. "How has the rest of the Glade fared this night?"

"A few slates were dislodged from the roof of this tower, my lord," the servant said. "Three men on the walls were bruised by hail before they could take shelter. No one has died. No one is likely to."

Silvas nodded. "There is much to be thankful for, then."

"Yes, lord." Koshka waited until Silvas put on the robe before he scurried from the room.

Silvas slipped the robe on over his knife belt. He took Carillia's arm and led her toward the door. "Thank you for your help, my love," he said. "There was too much here tonight for simply an opening gambit."

"Do you know who is behind it?" Carillia asked.

Silvas shook his head slowly. He ached badly enough to avoid sudden motions. "What I do know is that Mecq is shaping up to be a major challenge."

"A major challenge or *the* major challenge?" Carillia asked. There wasn't room enough for them to walk side by side down the first circular stairway. She let go of Silvas's arm and followed him to the next level.

"By the time I know that, we'll be far deeper in the web than we are now." Silvas waited in the library for her.

"You were badly hurt, my heart," Carillia said, her

worry plain in her voice. "I've never seen you have such trouble with demons."

Silvas couldn't deny that, yet he didn't want to voice a confirmation. "Tonight was unique, my love." He certainly *hoped* that it wouldn't be repeated.

When they reached their living quarters, Silvas saw servants carrying hot water from the hoist to the bath.

"I knew you would want it, my heart," Carillia said. "It will help you recover."

"It will," he agreed. He looked at her. He had not mentioned his strange interlude to her. At first there had been simply too many other things on his mind, like the pain. But now his reticence continued, and he needed a moment to think about that.

My love, I've trusted you with my life so many times I can't begin to count them, but I think I must keep my own counsel on this a while longer. Until I learn whatever lesson it was meant to teach me.

"I need to check on Bay and Bosc before my bath" was what he said. The thought of making the long walk down to the stable and back was daunting. His entire body ached, even if the pain was less than before. But he could not put off this trip.

"A glass of wine first?" Carillia suggested, and even before Silvas could agree, Koshka was coming in with a decanter and goblets.

"You think of everything, my love," Silvas said, managing a smile. He was glad to have the wine to fortify him for the trek.

"I saw part of your struggle while I fought my own," Silvas told Bay. The horse showed no aftereffects, but Bosc had a rag wrapped around his left hand to stanch the flow of blood. Silvas went right to the groom and spoke the spells that would speed healing.

"Vile gnomes," Bay said tightly.

"Perhaps, but with considerable power behind them," Silvas said. "They did not act alone. They couldn't have." Bay nodded emphatically. Silvas watched Bosc's hand as it started to heal, peeling the rag away gently. There was only a single cut, but it was deep and ragged. The spells

Silvas spoke started the mending with almost visible speed.

"It's been a long while since the mere fact of our arrival sparked such activity," Bay said. He was also watching Bosc's hand. "A rider gallops away as hard as his horse will run, and then we suffer this attack the first night."

"Are you suggesting that the two events are connected?" Silvas asked, turning his attention to the horse.

"I make no suggestions one way or the other," Bay replied. "I merely flesh out an observation."

"My own thought is that the rider was sent by Brother Paul to get instructions from his bishop in St. Ives." Silvas said.

"As likely as the other," Bay admitted easily. "You may have to ask the vicar directly. Whatever he says, you should be able to discern the truth of the matter."

"Perhaps," Silvas said.

Bay snorted. "But you won't. It's not devious enough for you."

"Get some sleep, Bosc," Silvas said. "That'll finish the mending for you. A day or two and even the stiffness will leave." When Bosc nodded, Silvas looked to Bay again. "Good advice for us all."

Silvas woke as the first light of dawn entered the bedroom. He had slept soundly once he got back to bed, though there was little enough of the night remaining. And he woke easily, without any real pain. Carillia was still asleep, breathing softly next to him. Likely she would continue to sleep for several hours unless there was more trouble. Silvas rolled over onto his back, away from Carillia. As soon as he moved, he heard the cats stir at the sides of the bed.

Like to be a busy day, Silvas thought. He wondered if Mecq had been subject to the raid in the night. *If so, I'll have villagers at the gate any minute.*

The Glade was mostly quiet. Silvas reached out with his mind. The wizard and his castle were linked closely at all times. Silvas listened to the sounds of the Seven Towers in its normal morning routines, sounds that would have been inaudible even to the cats. There were no harsh notes, nothing to indicate that there was anything unusual happening.

The image of the stranger in the forest clearing forced itself to the front of Silvas's mind. The figure was still blurred. Silvas had the impression that the old man was somehow mocking him, that this image was current, not just a memory of the nocturnal encounter.

I have to find out about him and his story, Silvas told himself. *Quickly. The key to Mecq must be in that garbled tale.*

He got out of bed carefully, more to avoid waking Carillia than from fear of reawakening his pains. He dressed quickly. Motion brought only the faintest reminders of the night's agony—a slight ache, a little stiffness. Those would soon work themselves out. And the marks of the many cuts were nearly gone. Only by focusing closely could he make out the lines.

I need to find that key quickly, Silvas thought as he left the bedroom. *It may mark the difference between success and destruction.* In all his years as a wizard, he had never experienced the kind of . . . interruption that he had been pulled into after his fight with the demons. He had never experienced a place where his power had no reality.

Velvet and Satin started to follow Silvas from the room. He stopped and pointed back at the bed, and they retreated to their spots at either side of it, content to lie down again and relax.

Silvas went up to his library.

There were thousands of scrolls and bound books in the room, one of the largest collections in the Christian world, so many manuscripts that Silvas had no real idea how many there were. Auroreus had assembled the initial collection, and Silvas had often added to it. There were works from everywhere that men wrote their languages down, some in the original tongue, some in translation. Some were even in the ancient language of magic, the tongue of the wizard's most powerful spells. There was no particular order to the collection. "As long as I can find what I want when I want it, what does it matter how they're sorted?" That had been Auroreus's line, and Silvas had never found it necessary to abandon. He stood in the center of the library now and surveyed the collection of books and scrolls piled and pigeon-holed on shelves and in racks of small slots. Silvas knew where he wanted to start, with a scroll that Auroreus had written out for him when he had first come to the Seven Towers, ignorant of virtually everything.

"Your mind's a blank slate," Auroreus had told him the day he brought Silvas into the Glade. Silvas had understood even then that the old wizard didn't mean that as an insult. "We have to be careful to fill it with the right information." During the early years Silvas had often wondered at the information that Auroreus thought right for him to study—stories of famous people, reports of travelers to every part of the world, and (more than anything else) language studies. "The power of language is the power of command," Auroreus had often said.

After a moment's thought Silvas went directly to the scroll he wanted. Auroreus had written this one, a primer on the gods, himself. It had posed a lot of problems for the almost seven-year-old Silvas. Auroreus had written in a polyglot mixture of seven languages, including the ancient tongue of magic. The languages were mixed from sentence to sentence, sometimes even within the same sentence. Silvas had struggled with the manuscript for months before it even started to make sense to him.

But now it was just what he wanted.

Silvas scarcely noticed any longer when his reading jumped from one language to another. The tortures of learning had made him quite adaptable. The same facility carried over to spoken languages. When he talked with people, he replied in whatever language he heard, quickly sliding even into new dialects. To date, he had never encountered anyone who spoke a language he could not follow, though some local variations could be difficult at first.

He pulled the scroll from its niche and went to the window seat to read. Auroreus had taken some pains in lettering the title *DEI ET DEAE,* but beyond that the script was in the scratchy, barely legible handwriting that Silvas remembered so well—difficult to make out in any language.

Below the title *GODS AND GODDESSES,* the manuscript started, *"The gods are real."* Reading on, Silvas could almost hear Auroreus's voice reading it to him.

"You forget that to your deadly peril. Our gods and goddesses do not overlook omission kindly, and those of us who follow the ancient path of the trimagister come often under their gaze."

Silvas read on into the scroll, sometimes scanning quickly, sometimes considering each word carefully, finding the familiar lines that had called him to this scroll.

"There are twenty gods and goddesses who look after our worlds in these times. They are all true brothers and sisters, children of the creators. . . ."

"Do not make the error of confusing the gods with the religions of our world. Religions are made by men exclusively. From time to time, one of the gods may choose to favor a particular religion with his patronage. . . ."

"Adepts of the Greater Mysteries of the trimagister must look beyond the dogma and rituals of any church. . . ."

"The gods have fought, from time to time, over the right to be worshiped in certain ways. The Church of Rome has known at least two different gods. The Unseen Lord who is our patron and benefactor became the god of the Roman Church at the time of Constantine the Great. He was so moved by the ardor and faith of Constantine that he went to war against his brother for the worship of Constantine and all of the new faithful that the Imperator brought to the church."

A lot of the manuscript came back to Silvas as he read. Lines jogged his memory about other lines and about the lectures that had accompanied them. This scroll was only a primer, an outline. Auroreus had often talked to Silvas about the gods, sometimes taking hours to explain a single sentence from *DEI ET DEAE*.

"When the gods do war among themselves," Auroreus had told Silvas late one evening, "it can be a dire time for any mortals who chance to get in their way. I have lived through two major wars of this kind, the one over the Christian Church in the time of Constantine, and then over the new church that Mahomet started. Men make churches as they will, designing new ways to worship the power that they sense but can never really know. A dreamer has a vision. A king feels the need to demonstrate divine support for his claims. Presto, a new religion is born. Perhaps most come and go without any of the gods taking notice, but *sometimes,* a new religion, or a reform in an old one, will look so pleasing to one of the gods that he will adopt it as his own. His power will then flow through the rituals of that religion, making it a real manifestation, giving it true power. Eventually his influence will modify the religion, bringing it closer to his own nature. If only one god is interested in a church, there is no conflict, but if more than one god desires to be the object of a particular religion's worship, or if a god covets a church that a brother or sister already claims, then their feuding can spill over from the land of the gods to our own world."

"When the gods do war among themselves." While Silvas read on through the scroll, his mind kept returning to that one line from one of the hundreds of lectures Auroreus had given him. Silvas kept turning the phrase over in his mind. He finished *DEI ET DEAE* and tied the leather thong back around the scroll. But he didn't get up. He stared out the window, focused completely on that one line.

"That is part of the key," he mumbled finally. *But what more is there to it?* Which *gods are going to war? And Why?* If it was going to touch Silvas, it had to involve his Unseen Lord, the god of the White Brotherhood and of orthodox Christians everywhere.

"Does someone want to unseat him?" That was the most logical guess, but guesses would not be good enough. Silvas got up from the window seat and started to return the scroll to its place across the room. Halfway there, another question stopped the wizard in his tracks.

"Why should I be a target at all?" *How can I make any difference to the outcome? How can I be that important?* It didn't make sense. Wizard though he was, he was still merely a mortal man. His power did not extend to the gods. He could not affect the outcome of their battles.

"Or can I?" He felt a sudden chill, as if the summer morning had turned to a winter night. He looked back over his shoulder, toward the window. The sun was still shining brightly on the Seven Towers.

Silvas shook his head and resumed his walk to the rack where his scroll belonged. Then he heard a thin, reedy voice calling him.

"Lord Wizard!"

The voice came from a distance. Silvas knew at once that it did not belong to any of the residents of the Glade. That meant it was coming from Mecq. He tossed the scroll to a table and hurried up to the turret that let him look out over the village. An old woman was standing near the pillar of smoke that would be all she could see of the Glade.

"I'll be there in a moment," Silvas shouted out one of the narrow windows.

7

There were no magical shortcuts from one part of the Glade to another. Silvas needed several minutes to get down to the gate. His lengthy strides across the great hall and courtyard helped banish the last of his stiffness and take the ache from the repairs to his flesh. He didn't slow down until he stepped onto the drawbridge. Then he took a deep breath and walked slowly through the curtain of smoke onto Mecq's village green.

"You wanted me?" he asked gently. He came out of the smoke barely two paces from the old woman. She put both hands to her chest and turned quickly to face him.

"I'm sorry," Silvas said. "I didn't mean to frighten you."

"I be called Old Maga, and there not be much fer me ter be frighted of," the woman said. She was short and thin, with the wiry look of someone who had spent a lifetime at hard physical labor. Her hair was gathered behind her head, almost solidly gray. Her face was darkly tanned and deeply wrinkled. She wore a colorless dress that showed many repairs.

"What can I do for you, Maga?" Silvas asked.

"It's my sister's man. He needs curin'."

"Come inside and tell me about it," Silvas said. That was a whim. He normally wouldn't have asked a villager into the Glade so readily—not from snobbery but to spare them the shock. Silvas wasn't certain why he thought he should make an exception now, but he gestured toward the smoke. Old Maga looked from him to the barrier.

"In there?" Her voice climbed a little in pitch.

"The smoke can't harm you. My home is through there." When Maga continued to hold back, Silvas added, "Sir Eustace's steward was there and came back out yesterday." Silvas assumed that Maga would know about Fitz-Matthew's coming and going, even if she hadn't seen him herself. Others had seen, and they had undoubtedly talked. But Silvas doubted that any word about what Henry Fitz-Matthew had seen within the smoke would have reached the village yet . . . though it would in time.

"Take my arm and I'll guide you through." Silvas offered Maga his arm. She was still hesitant. Finally she shrugged and gripped his arm just above the crook of his elbow.

"I be too old to have aught to fear." But her grip on Silvas tightened considerably when they entered the smoke, and when they emerged inside the Glade, Maga stopped abruptly and pulled her hand free.

"Holy Mother of God." She crossed herself quickly and stepped to the side, away from Silvas.

"I'm not the Devil, Maga, or one of his workers," Silvas said. He extended his hand. Old Maga looked at it and backed away another step. Silvas sighed. Perhaps his whim had been a mistake.

"I told everyone yesterday that I would take no payment for my help," he reminded her, keeping his voice patient and friendly. "I'm not after anyone's money, honor, or soul." He waited a moment, but Maga didn't speak or come back toward him. At least she didn't move any farther away.

"You said that your sister's husband needs curing," Silvas said. Old Maga blinked at the reminder. "Why don't you have a seat in the shade and tell me about it?" Silvas pointed past Maga along the curtain wall. There were a pair of short benches under the wooden roof that protected one of the Glade's four wells.

"We've got plenty of good, cool water," Silvas added, gesturing more directly at the well. He detoured around Maga, careful not to get any closer. He went to the well and the benches. Halfway there, he stopped and looked back. Old Maga hesitated an instant more, then walked slowly toward Silvas. He went on to the well and lowered the bucket. He was cranking the handle to retrieve the bucket when Maga finally reached the shade.

"Sit and rest," Silvas urged. "Here, have a drink." There were several copper ladles hanging from pegs. He took one, filled it with water, and handed it to the old woman. She accepted the water without hesitation and drank it down, easily a half pint.

"More?" Silvas asked when she returned the empty ladle. Maga met his gaze for an instant before she nodded. Silvas refilled the ladle and gave it to her. Then he took another from a peg and had a sip of water himself.

Old Maga sat on the closest bench and nursed the second helping of water. Silvas sat on the other bench, facing her.

"Now, tell me about your sister's husband."

"My sister Enid be a lot younger'n me," Maga said. She lowered the ladle carefully and kept both hands on it, not wanting to waste a drop. "Her'n her man got a bunch of babes. They bin luckier'n most, six born an' all but one still alive. The eldest, he ain't but"—Maga had to stop and think—"ten year old. The lit'lest was born winter afore last. Now, Enid an' her man ha' always worked hard, like mos' folks here. But now . . ." Maga shook her head. Then she seemed to notice the ladle in her hands again, so she raised it to take another drink.

"But now?" Silvas prompted when she lowered the ladle. Her eyes had followed the water down to her lap.

"Now poor Berl ha' got some wastin' sickness. Brother Paul, he said 'tain't no leprosy, but it's eatin' poor Berl up from the insides like, an' Brother Paul, he ain't been able to help none. Berl be so sick now he cain't hardly do no work a-tall. E'en if he don' die, if he cain't work, him and Enid and all their babes'll starve, soon or late."

"Tell me more about the sickness," Silvas said. "When did it start? How does it go? What's it done to Berl?"

Maga looked up at Silvas for a moment, but lowered her head again before she replied.

"It come on winter afore last," Maga said, and then she nodded, confirming that to herself. "At the first he jist said he done felt weak all the time, and sometimes his head were hot to the touch. It warn't so bad then, jist an ailin' sort of thing that come an' go. Yer know, the way a body'll feel out of sorts now an' again." She looked up to see Silvas's nod. "A fever, we thought, and Brother Paul, he did make Berl's head cool now an' again, but the fever kep' comin' back, it did, an' after a spell it got worse each time. An' then Berl jist started to melt away like. His cheeks begun to sink in, an' his eyes. Now 'tain't much meat a-tall on his bones, he's wasted so far. Sometimes, like now, he's too weak to do much o' anythin', and we wonder is he gonna die. He cain't e'en git out o' bed some days, an' when he can, he needs a stick to walk on, jist to git to the fields and do what little he can. But he cain't go on much longer. 'Less he gets a real curin', he won' see the winter out, if he e'en sees the harvest."

"How is he today?" Silvas leaned forward a little.

"Enid tol' me he had a real bad patch in the night, so bad she 'mos' come to get me to fetch Brother Paul to shrive him. This mornin' Berl's proper weak he is. Couldn't hardly get up for his gruel."

"He's too sick to bring him to me here?" It was hardly a question.

"Be hard," Maga said. "An' he might not come e'en if he were stronger. Berl's got some strong fear 'bout sorcery and sech. E'en Brother Paul's godly fixin' makes him awful skittish."

"No matter," Silvas said. "I'll go to him."

"Yer'll cure him?" Maga asked.

"I'll try. I won't know if I can cure him until I look him over. But if I can, I will. That's why I travel from village to village, Maga. That is how I serve our Unseen Lord."

Old Maga glanced up at the sky and crossed herself, almost dropping the empty ladle in her haste. She stood and hung the ladle back on its peg.

"Enid and Berl, they lives right next to me." Maga wiped her hands on her dress. "We be off up that ..." She stopped and looked around, confusion on her face. The arm she had started to raise dropped to her side. "I don' know which way from here." She shook her head. "It's up off from the castle side of the church. Anybody'll know. We be glad whene'er yer kin come and do fer poor Berl."

"If you don't object, I'll come with you now," Silvas said, also rising. "The sooner I see to Berl, the sooner he'll get better. If you'll just give me a few minutes to take care of an errand here, I'll go straight on with you.

Okay?" Maga nodded once as her hands started a nervous picking at the waist of her dress.

"Have more water if you like. We've no shortage here. I'll be back as quickly as I can." When Maga nodded again, Silvas went off toward the stable.

Bosc was just finishing with Bay, tightening the saddle girth, when Silvas walked in.

"We have a request," Silvas said.

Bay nodded. "An old woman. Someone witching her onions?"

"Her sister's husband has been suffering from a wasting disease for a year and a half." Silvas ignored Bay's sarcasm. "He took a serious turn for the worse during the night. The wife nearly sent to have the vicar administer last rites."

Bay could not miss the implication. "While *we* were dealing with intruders?"

"It wouldn't surprise me, but there's no way to be certain."

"You think perhaps the demons we faced were in Mecq long before we came?" Bay asked.

"For a year and a half?"

"Perhaps since the Eyler fell and the rains stopped falling," Bay said. "Water is life. The troubles of the Eyler must be a focus for all that goes on here."

"I hadn't thought of it quite that way," Silvas admitted. "Still, we need to know the who and the why. Perhaps we should have taken time yesterday to gaze upon the lands of the Duke of Blethye while we were up at Sir Eustace's seat."

"If so, then today will be better than tomorrow."

"And I have the dinner invitation from the Lady Eleanora for this evening," Silvas said. "But first there is the matter of this ailing farmer. I'll walk Old Maga home and tend to him. Then you and I can ride along part of the Eyler, get a closer feel for this river, and perhaps take a look at Blethye before supper."

Bay nodded and Silvas turned to Bosc.

"Go tell the lady Carillia that I'm going out and probably won't be back until evening, that she shouldn't wait supper for me. I'm to dine with Sir Eustace and his family."

"Aye, lord." Bosc bobbed his head quickly. "There's provision here for lunch." He pointed at the saddlebags on Bay.

"A good thought, Bosc. Thank you."

"It was the lady Carillia's orders," Bosc said. When Silvas nodded and smiled, the groom said, "Will there be anything else?"

"I don't think so. But how is your hand?"

Bosc displayed the hand that had been cut the night before. The hair was already starting to grow on the back of the hand, and only a thin scar showed where the gash had been.

"It doesn't hurt at all, my lord." Bosc turned the hand from side to side before he ran to carry Silvas's message to Carillia.

"I need a better feel for this river anyway," Silvas said. "It's time to start planning for the magic to give Mecq its water."

"Wouldn't it be more logical to put your attention to the greater threat first?" Bay asked.

"I promised Mecq water," Silvas replied. "The other, whatever it is, will happen in its own good time. We'll take precautions. But the water needs serious work as well."

"You can't allow yourself to become so carried away with curing warts and finding water that you lose sight of the rest," Bay warned. "If this *is* the challenge our Lord has prepared you for—"

"I'm not losing sight of anything," Silvas said, interrupting sharply. "And if these things are connected as we suspect they are, then I am acting on the one when I act on the other."

"If you're not careful, the Foe will sneak up from behind while you're tending to some minor ill." Bay snorted. "If you're going to walk this old woman home, I'll follow along so you can ride on from wherever she takes you."

Bay stayed well behind Silvas and Old Maga as they walked through Mecq, but the old woman kept looking back. When she first spotted the horse, Maga looked ready to bolt and run. Bay seemed to make her particularly nervous. Silvas paid little attention to that, though he did work a quick spell to ease her mind. Bay made her nervous. So did Silvas and the Glade. Silvas wondered if there was anything that didn't.

Once they got away from the smoke, Maga talked almost constantly.

"Poor Berl ha' had a rough life of it, that's God's own truth. When he was a lad, he was one of the boys what helped dam th' Eyler, an' what had to tear it down again when the cursed duke came in wi' his army. Seems all the good lads as was there ha' had rough lifes. More'n a proper share has already gone to their Maker, an' those as ain't, why they all seems to have trouble aplenty." Maga shook her head. She didn't look at Silvas, hardly looked around at all, except when she glanced back to see that Bay was still following. Maga paid no attention to the few villagers they passed either. Her gaze seemed directed mainly at the path just in front of her feet.

"Mayhap we ain't s'posed to be here no more. The river runs 'most dry ever' year. T'ain't rain enow to grow a weed proper. The dirt up an' blows away whene'er they's a good wind. Don' know how we e'er 'fended anyone so bad as to git all this back." She stopped walking then, so abruptly that Silvas went on two steps before he could stop.

"They say yer promised to fix the water fer us afore yer leave. Is that fer true?"

"It is," Silvas said. "Before I leave Mecq, you'll see the Eyler run as it should." He had assumed, without devoting much thought to it, that the solution would be to increase the flow of the river. He hadn't even considered alternatives like wells. But he took a moment to muse over what he had just said and then nodded. It would have to be the river, one way or another.

Old Maga started walking again. "Bin so long without, we'll need time to recollect what-all to do with water aplenty," she said. "It be a blessing fer true."

A couple of minutes later, Maga stopped again and pointed at a cottage. "This be my sister's cot." It was virtually identical to the rest of the cottages in Mecq, built of rough timbers chinked with a mud-like cement, roofed with old thatch. Maga went to the doorway, looked in, then gestured for Silvas to follow her inside.

"My sister and her babes be in the fields," Maga said.

Silvas had to duck to get through the doorway. It was scarcely high enough for Maga. The smells inside were overpowering—the common odors of a peasant cottage, of people crowded too closely for too long with too little in the way of cleaning or washing. It had taken years of practice for Silvas to disguise the way those conditions affected him, and even many of the lords of the land lived with as little attention to cleanliness. Auroreus had maintained an Old Roman attitude toward hygiene, and Silvas had lived under his rule for too many years to lose the habit himself.

And Silvas could detect the smell of fever over the rest in this cottage. He glanced around the single room. Berl was on a pallet at the back. He was so thin that he scarcely disturbed the outline of the rough-woven blanket that covered him. The man was motionless and silent.

"Berl?" Maga said, so tentatively that she must have worried that he was already dead. Silvas moved past her. He could feel the spark of life, but Berl was clearly at the last extremity.

"I'll take care of him now," Silvas said softly. He moved Maga aside gently. She moved farther away on her own, backing hesitantly closer to the door. Silvas knelt next to the pallet and pulled the blanket off Berl, which loosed an extra dose of noxious odors. Berl didn't move, didn't react at all. His chest scarcely lifted with each shallow, widely separated breath. His face was drawn and thin, marked by dark splotches.

The sickness isn't natural, Silvas noted at once. *It was brought on by magic.* He started chanting a series of spells to sustain the man, to simply keep him alive through the longer work it would take to cure him. The effort brought sweat to Silvas's forehead.

I recognize the stink of this work, Silvas realized soon after he started prying into the magical web that was draining life from the farmer. Recognition might have come even sooner if he hadn't been so busy making sure that Berl wouldn't die. Silvas stood and took a single step back from Berl's pallet after a quarter hour of intense conjuring. Berl was out of immediate danger, but Silvas hadn't yet begun the real work of curing him.

"This is the work of a minor adept of the Blue Rose." Silvas spoke aloud but to himself.

"The Blue Rose?" Maga asked. Silvas turned. He had forgotten that she was in the cottage with him.

"You know about the Blue Rose?" Silvas asked.

"They's heretics?" she ventured.

"That's what Brother Paul would call them," Silvas agreed. "Myself, I'd just call them evil."

"Aye." Old Maga nodded solemnly. "Anyone who'd do *that* to a man be evil as Satan himself." She crossed herself. "Can yer still help poor Berl?"

Silvas nodded absently. "I'll help him." His mind really wasn't in the conversation any longer. There were too many thoughts screaming for his attention.

The Blue Rose Cult. It had been a long time since Silvas had last needed to undo any of their handiwork, and there had never been anything this thorough. But their hand was obvious in Berl's illness. Another connection came to Silvas quickly. *They're likely behind the problems with the river as well.* The chain of thought continued to forge new links. Members of the Blue Rose called themselves Christians, but theirs was a religion of violence and terror, centered on the image of God as the Punisher, not the Redeemer. The White Brotherhood and the orthodox Roman Church called them heretics and worse.

If the Blue Rose is behind the water problems, then one of the gods must have put himself behind their cult. Maybe more than one, Silvas reminded himself. For a moment the implications of that pushed aside his concern for the sick man. It was a vital piece of the puzzle he had been working at since coming to Mecq, since he had sensed the evil at the edge of the valley.

And where does it go from here? Silvas wondered. He looked down at Berl again. He remained unconscious, but perhaps his breathing was a little stronger than before. It was time to get on with the work of healing.

If I cure him of the Blue Rose curse, they may discover my presence here too soon. There was a slight chance that they didn't know who he was yet, what power he carried,

what Power he represented. But his interference with
Blue Rose magic might draw retribution quickly, possibly
an attack more perilous than demons in the night. But
there was no real question in Silvas's mind, no hesitation.

When *I cure him.* The wizard kneeled next to the pallet
again and put his hands on Berl's chest and forehead. He
went straight into the series of spells that would both cure
the man and protect him from any return of the "curse"
that had followed him for much of his life.

"Here I am," Silvas said very softly. He knew that his
work would speak much louder to those who could hear
it.

The work of curing Berl took more than a quick incantation. That was why Silvas had woven a sustaining spell
first. But Silvas moved quickly into the flow of the longer
work. He felt a change coming over him, an acceptance—
even an eagerness. At the moment he had no doubt at all
that the great challenge that had loomed over him all of
his life was about to appear.

The sun was directly overhead when Berl dragged in a
sudden deep breath and opened his eyes.

8

"He'll need two or three days, and plenty of feeding, to get him back on his feet," Silvas told Old Maga out in front of the cottage. "He's bound to feel weak for a bit." Maga just bobbed her head, eyes wide, too astounded at the sudden improvement in Berl's condition to speak.

"I know things are rough, so maybe this will help." Silvas reached into the purse on his belt and pulled out a silver coin. "You ought to be able to get several good meals for Berl and his family from Master Ian for this."

Maga looked at the coin for a moment before she extended her hand. The hand shook. Maga seemed torn between staring at the coin and at Silvas. "I ain't ne'er seen one o' them," she added.

"It's got the king's head on it." Once more Silvas found himself questioning the wisdom of one of his whims. There was a chance no one in the village, except perhaps Master Ian, had ever seen silver money. Copper pennies would be rare enough, and silver coinage was new in England. "Remember, Berl needs plenty of food, as much as he can eat, for the next few days. That's the only way he'll be fit enough to work the harvest."

"I'll see to't," Maga said. "Lor' bless yer."

When Silvas turned to leave, Bay was staring at him. The horse didn't speak, but he didn't have to. The wizard could imagine the comments Bay had in mind. *You can't resist getting involved, can you?* If they were alone, Bay might go on for quite a while about Silvas's gesture.

It wouldn't do to have my first magic here go wrong, Silvas thought, rationalizing his gift. *If he died because he didn't eat enough, they'd never know it wasn't my fault.*

Silvas mounted Bay and turned him toward the river.

As they started away, Old Maga called out, "Lor' bless yer," again, and Silvas felt his face redden.

Mostly to take his thoughts away from Old Maga, Silvas mulled over the question of Blue Rose involvement in Mecq's troubles. The Blue Rose had been around for generations, but surfaced only rarely. The White Brotherhood was harsh in its punishment of Blue Rose heretics. There had been an invasion of one district in Burgundy when several villages went over to the Blue Rose thirty years before. The Church had declared a crusade.

"Old Maga's brother-in-law suffered from a most uncommon ailment," Silvas said after they were clear of the cottages. "His illness was the work of a minor adept of the Blue Rose. I could never mistake that work."

Bay stopped walking and turned his head to look back at Silvas. They were too close to the village for Bay to risk speaking, but the look spoke well enough for the moment. Then Bay started toward the river again, moving a little faster.

"Master Fitz-Matthew wore the cross of a crusader," Silvas said softly. "I wonder where he earned it." Bay didn't speak until they had worked their way down the slope into the riverbed.

"You don't think it was just some wandering sorcerer who took a dislike to the man," Bay said then. It wasn't a question.

"The web woven around that man took maintenance over time," Silvas replied. "If the Blue Rose has become strong in Blethye . . ."

"Yet you mention this crusader," Bay noted. "Do you think the Blue Rose's connection to Mecq may lie elsewhere?"

"Something had to draw their attention to Mecq," Silvas said. "If Sir Eustace's father served in the crusade against the Blue Rose in Burgundy, or perhaps Blethye himself caught the heresy."

"But there is no need to look so far afield yet," Bay said.

"I know. It really doesn't matter where the contagion came from. It must be close now. I need time to think, Bay. One way or another, there is a lot going on here for such a small village. Let's work our way upstream for a bit, then we'll turn back toward Blethye."

That was all the direction Bay needed. The horse picked his way along the riverbed. The Eyler was just a meager stream meandering along the deepest part of its bed, rarely more than a yard wide or two feet deep. Bay stopped to take a drink.

"There's nothing evil about the water," he said. "It's just muddy from being so low."

Silvas looked down at the water. The Eyler could hold a flow more than one hundred times as great and not come close to spilling over its banks. If the Eyler had been running normally, the water would have been over the heads of both Bay and Silvas. But now . . . the bottom of the mill's water wheel was six feet above the current water level, and the remnant of the Eyler didn't even run under the wheel. The layers of dirt caked on the blades of the wheel showed how long it had been since it was usable.

"This is far enough," Silvas said when they passed under the bridge that crossed the Eyler just upstream from the village. "Let's take a look at the other end and take a climb up Mount Balq."

Bay picked up his pace as they retraced their steps and went on beyond the point where they had come down. The only change in the nature of the riverbed was an increase in the size of the rocks. Closer to the flanking hills, some of the mud had caked up behind rocks, leaving others clear. Silvas gained no inspiration from the ride.

"The smell of evil is here," Bay said when they were halfway between the village and the twin hills. "But it's no stronger here than it was on the ridge when we first saw this place. The smell is vague, not centered on the Eyler."

"I suppose it is possible that the fall of the Eyler was unconnected to the other troubles," Silvas admitted, though he didn't believe that. "It could be that the Blue Rose merely took advantage of a natural event. Perhaps something upstream happened to divert the flow of water."

"Whether or not they were originally connected, they

must be interwoven now," Bay said. "The Duke of Blethye blocked Mecq's attempt to solve their water problems." Bay picked his way up the Balqside bank, cautiously but without great hesitation.

"The water that remains moves swiftly enough," he added.

"A dam should hold enough water for Mecq," Silvas said. "If only they could defend a dam against Blethye."

"Not against Blethye, against the Blue Rose," Bay said.

"I guess I am assuming that Blethye is under their influence," Silvas said. "But if Blethye is a typical marcher lord, he might make the same stand even without heresy. 'This river is mine, every drop of it.' I've seen that attitude all too often. Even His Majesty is not totally immune."

"If you're going to eat that food I'm carrying, now would be a good time," Bay said. They had reached the base of Mount Balq. There was a little shade, and a little grass.

"Meaning that you're ready to eat." Silvas managed a soft chuckle.

"I don't have a feast at Castle Mecq to look forward to," Bay said. "The stable boys up there aren't all that free with their fodder."

"They've had drought here, remember?" Silvas said, enjoying the moment's respite.

He dismounted and pulled the saddlebag off from behind the saddle. He sat in the shade with his back against a large boulder. He had little appetite, but he pulled out the bread, meat, cheese, and wine that had been packed for him. He arranged everything next to him and ate sparingly, mostly just looking up into the sky.

The Eyler River, pitifully short on water. Berl, hurt almost to the death by a bitter magic. The Blue Rose Cult. Silvas's own unusual abduction and return in the night, stolen away without his body.

I don't have enough pieces to the puzzle yet, Silvas thought. It didn't matter how he sorted the bits he already had. The picture remained incomplete.

"It's not just the river," Silvas said after he had done all of the eating and thinking he could take without interruption. "I don't think it's even *mainly* the river. The Blue

Rose is encroaching more and more deeply into the lives
and souls of the people here. They have power behind
them now."

"Power they didn't have when Pope Innocent had them
driven from Burgundy?" Bay asked.

"It would seem so." Silvas stood and stretched. "Have
you had enough of this dry grass?"

Bay snorted.

"Then it's time we looked at the demesne of the Duke
of Blethye." Silvas looked up the slope of Mount Balq.
"It shouldn't be a difficult climb." There was a scattering
of steep rock outcroppings, but the slope was mostly gentle. Silvas could see the narrow tracks where cows and
sheep had grazed along the side, though not recently.

"Mount up," Bay said. "We've wasted enough time today. You still have a dinner engagement to make."

Bay took the slope as directly as he could, picking his
way toward the shoulder of Mount Balq that overlooked
the river. Some three hundred feet up, there was a ledge
that extended around the end of the ridge.

Silvas dismounted when they reached that ledge, thirty
feet below the level of Castle Mecq on the other hill, and
walked around to look down on the land of the Duke of
Blethye. Bay followed him.

"We should have made this trek in the morning," Bay
said. "Now we'll have the sun in our eyes."

"Not completely," Silvas replied. Most of the valley
beyond lay to the northwest. The sun came in from the
side.

"Who would believe that Mecq lies next to that," Bay
said. The valley beyond was lush with green and gold,
even so late in summer. The grain fields were full of tall
wheat and rye. The pastures had plenty of green grass and
fat flocks and herds.

"It is a rich land," Silvas said. "Yet the duke begrudges
Mecq its water. To look at it, they would never miss a
drop if the Eyler stopped flowing through the gap completely."

"*That* is evil," Bay said.

Silvas went to the edge of the ledge and looked down.
The sides of the twin hills that face Blethye were much
steeper than the sides facing Mecq. No human army could

come over that barrier. They would have to come through gaps, like that which carried the Eyler.

"Give me a few moments to study this place," Silvas said. He focused his telesight and scanned the greener valley as closely as he could, gazing farther away with each pass. There were villages, churches, a broad strip of forest almost due north of Silvas's vantage, and two impressive castles, both set behind broad moats that lacked nothing in the way of water. Occasionally Silvas narrowed his vision enough to let him study the faces of people his eyes happened across in the distance. Simple faces. There was no great evil written on any of them that Silvas saw.

He kept up his searching until his eyes ached from long staring. He had to blink repeatedly to ease them.

"I can feel the aura of power over the land," he said when he finally turned back to Bay. "Nothing identifies it as the Blue Rose, though. There is simply nothing definite to the feeling."

"They do not think themselves strong enough to wear their evil openly yet," Bay said. "You wouldn't expect notices posted on every tree."

"But there is too much power, Bay, even for a congregation gone over to the Blue Rose. That would mean, at most, a few minor adepts of any power. I might expect this level of power over the Seven Towers." Silvas mounted Bay and turned him toward the slope leading back into the valley of Mecq.

"This might really be it, the place where we face our climactic battle." And that did not express Silvas's true feeling, the absolute conviction that this was indeed the place for that fight.

"It might," Bay said neutrally. "But I repeat my advice. We shouldn't run to such conclusions too soon. There might be great evil here indeed, but perhaps not *the* great evil you were trained to meet."

Silvas sighed. "There is always that darkness. It plagues me no end." His voice betrayed his frustration. "How can I prepare for the unknown?"

Silvas lapsed into a silence that lasted until they were on the last switchback leading up to the castle of Sir

Eustace Devry. Silvas needed that time to force his mind
away from the recurrent frustration that came from his
pledge to his Unseen Lord. Despite that Silvas knew that
he would not wish himself free of the vow. It let him do
what he wanted to do in life—even if the price was a constant uncertainty.

I've had many a year to use the gifts, he reminded himself. Auroreus had trained him well. The old wizard had
made his own arrangements with the Unseen Lord, different from the vow extracted from Silvas. *Conditions were
different then. There was no grand Empire of the English,
no Holy Roman Empire.* At times, especially of late, Silvas had difficulty remembering just how different the
world had been when he became Auroreus's apprentice,
and how much different yet it must have been when
Auroreus took his initiation and made his promises to the
Unseen Lord. *Tiberius ruled in Rome. Christ still walked
among mortal men.* And when Auroreus brought Silvas to
the Seven Towers, the Roman Empire had fallen in the
west. The Glade was far beyond the pale of civilization.
The Norsemen had yet to begin their ravaging. Silvas had
won his initiation long before the first Viking raiders followed the coastline around from Daneland to the Celtic
kingdoms on the north and northwest shores of Europe, to
the area that was then called Angleterre, the country of
the Angles. Mostly the Celtic warlords had been a match
for the Norsemen, but there had been a couple of powerful sea kings who had managed to forge their way inland
almost as far as the Glade. And other adventurers had
come by land, crossing through the low country of the
Frisians into Scotland and Northumbria.

"We've seen a lot, you and I," Silvas said softly. Bay
merely bobbed his head up and down. Silvas wondered,
as he had so often, if the horse could read his mind.

We have *seen a lot,* Silvas thought. From a half-dozen
kingdoms hard put to survive the onslaught of the Celtic
tribes of Wales, Ireland, and Scotland on one side, and the
relentless press of Franks and Teutons on the other,
Angleterre had become England, unified by Egbert and
his successors, until the French marriage of Ethelred II
and the Norman dynasty that followed him extended the

English sway beyond the estuary of the Thames and the Rhine, down the French coast to the Loire and beyond.

"Here comes the wizard."

The loud voice above his head gave Silvas a start. He looked up and around. They were almost at the gate of Castle Mecq. A sentry on the wall had called out.

"Well, I *was* invited," Silvas mumbled. Then he chuckled. "Almost a nap," he said in the same undertone. Let Bay make of that what he might.

Henry Fitz-Matthew came out to greet Silvas, not that he offered much of a greeting. "Good day, sir. My lady asked me to see to you."

"Thank you, Master Fitz-Matthew," Silvas said. "Lady Eleanora was most gracious yesterday."

The stable boy who had been so hesitant to deal with Bay the day before showed no reluctance to take the horse's reins today.

Inside, Fitz-Matthew announced Silvas, and Eleanora came toward the door. She had been supervising servants working in the great hall.

"I am delighted that you could come, Lord Silvas," she said. "I was afraid you might have second thoughts."

"How could I stay away?" Silvas bowed, mostly to cover the trace of a smile he couldn't keep from his face. The great hall showed the marks of a lot of work in the past twenty-four hours. Several layers of soot had been removed from the walls. The tables, chairs, and benches had all been scoured. Fresh torches were in the sconces. Two metal candle stands had been brought in to flank the head table. Fresh straw had been strewn on the floor. *I'd wager that Sir Eustace has done a fair amount of grumbling over the bother,* Silvas thought. Then he chastised himself for taking pleasure at the thought of the thane's discomfort.

"Master Fitz-Matthew has told us about the palace you conceal within your smoke," Eleanora said. "If I did not know him so well and trust him completely, I might think he was spinning gossamer tales."

The steward had started to edge away from Silvas, trying to be inconspicuous. When Eleanora started talking about him, though, he had to stop.

"Our Unseen Lord has been generous with me," Silvas

said. "Once I have fulfilled my promise to you and to the people of Mecq, you and Sir Eustace must be my guests for dinner."

"I look forward to that with considerable eagerness." Eleanora smiled widely, but then her face colored a trifle. She fluttered her arms, whether to cool herself or to distract Silvas, he couldn't say. "But come away from the door. Have a seat and a cup of wine. We have a keg of the best vintage from my father's Wessex vineyards."

Silvas bowed again and accompanied Eleanora to a pair of benches near one of the two fireplaces in the great hall. A servant had apparently been watching for his cue. He brought a tray with two goblets of wine.

"Sir Eustace will join us shortly," Eleanora said. "He is finishing a bit of business just now."

Silvas lifted his wine in toast before he sampled the drink. Wessex wines ranged from undrinkable to acceptable. This was one of the better Silvas had tasted. He said so.

"My deepest thanks. My father is quite proud of it. Our family has been making wine since anyone can remember."

Sir Eustace entered the great hall, clomping down the stairs. He cleared his throat noisily to announce himself. Silvas stood and turned toward the stairs. He nodded to Sir Eustace and walked across to greet him.

"Good afternoon, Sir Eustace," Silvas said. "I was just complimenting your wife on this excellent wine."

"Lord Silvas," Eustace said carefully. "My steward informs me that you are a person of some substance."

"I have only what our Unseen Lord honors me with. I do what I may to repay that honor." Silvas was surprised that Sir Eustace was attempting to be tactful, but he was prepared to go far to meet that attempt in kind.

Eustace nodded and called for beer. The servant was much quicker to serve his master.

"We might as well sit at table," Sir Eustace said. "Supper will be along soon, I trust?" He turned that into a question for his wife.

She nodded. "Very soon." Eleanora turned to Fitz-Matthew—the steward had maneuvered his way near the stairs by now—and said, "Henry, would you see to the necessaries?"

"At once, my lady." Henry bowed and quickly scuttled down the stairs, obviously welcoming the excuse to leave.

"I believe that I have found the source for at least some of the difficulties your people have experienced," Silvas said when they were seated at the table. Sir Eustace had the center chair at the head table, facing the lower trestle. Eleanora was at her husband's right. Silvas was at his left. The wizard assumed that the two other places set at the head table were for Maria and Fitz-Matthew.

"That is something for one day," Sir Eustace acknowledged, trying not to make the admission sound grudging.

"A woman came to me to cure her sister's sick husband this morning," Silvas said. "When I tended to him, I discovered that his sickness had been laid on him by an adept of the Blue Rose."

"The Blue Rose!" Eleanora reacted more quickly to the name than her husband did. She crossed herself and leaned forward to look past Sir Eustace to the wizard. "The Blue Rose *here*?"

"Nearby, at least," Silvas said. He turned his attention to the knight then. "You know of the Blue Rose, Sir Eustace."

"Of them?" Eustace nodded slowly. "Heretics. My father fought to stamp them out in Burgundy."

"I suspected as much," Silvas said. "Your steward, he accompanied your father on that crusade?"

"He did, saved my father's life twice." Sir Eustace frowned and looked down at the table. "The third time, both had run out of luck."

"Did the Duke of Blethye take the cross for that campaign?" Silvas asked next.

"Took the cross but did not go," Eustace said. "I know not what excuse he used." He looked up. "Are ye thinking that Blethye is one of these heretics?"

"I don't know yet, Sir Eustace. I would hate to accuse a man unjustly of such a sin."

People started coming into the great hall then, soldiers and servants first. The lower table was nearly half full before Sir Eustace's daughter, Maria, came down from above. Finally Fitz-Matthew returned from below. Maria took the vacant seat next to Silvas. Fitz-Matthew sat at the opposite end, as far from the wizard as he could get.

With more people the great hall became noisy. Special guest or no, Sir Eustace's retainers came for supper in their usual state. Servants quickly brought in food and ale. From several comments that Silvas overheard, this meal was a feast compared to their usual fare. That didn't surprise him.

Eleanora took the lead at steering conversation at the head table. She had to draw her husband out. Left to his own devices, it was evident that Sir Eustace would have gone through supper without saying a word but to call for more beef or beer.

"The last news we had of His Majesty, he was in Rouen," Eleanora said at one point. "That was at Eastertide."

"I'm not sure I've heard anything more recent," Silvas admitted. "Perhaps something about the court planning to return after the spring rains." He shrugged. "Unless there was fighting to be done."

"Have you ever been to court, Lord Silvas?" Eleanora asked.

"His Majesty has been kind enough to received me twice," he replied. That brought stares from all of the others at the head table. "The first time he had heard of me from the deacon at Canterbury. The second time we chanced to be in the same town at the same time. He saw the smoke and came to look." *But not to enter,* Silvas thought. The king had been unready to pass through the smoke.

"Did you see the queen?" Maria asked, reaching out and almost touching Silvas's arm.

He shook his head. "No. The first time I saw His Majesty, it was before the marriage. The second time she did not accompany him."

"Have you traveled all over the kingdom?" Maria asked.

"I have seen most of it, and some lands beyond."

"Have you been to Rome?" Eleanora asked, hurrying to get the question in before Maria could ask another.

"No, my lady," Silvas admitted. "These days, that pilgrimage is difficult even for a wizard."

"Can't you just conjure yourself there in that tower of smoke?" Maria asked.

"You overestimate my abilities," Silvas said. "I couldn't conjure my way here in the smoke. I had to ride in and bring the smoke to me. It always works that way."

"Oh." Maria looked down at her trencher, embarrassed at missing such an obvious connection.

Sir Eustace cleared his throat. When Maria looked at him, he gave her a fierce frown, enough to make her look back down at her food.

"What you said before," Eustace said, "about the Blue Rose. That would explain a lot, would it not?"

"It would," Silvas agreed slowly, waiting for Eleanora to say something about heresy being unfit table talk during the meal. But she didn't interrupt. "But I don't know yet how much of it that it explains. Until I can learn the truth about that. . ." He let his voice trail off, and Eleanora finally did come to his rescue.

"There's time enough for that kind of talk later. Think what it will do to your digestion." She put her hand on her husband's arm. He tried to smile and almost succeeded.

"Whatever," Silvas said. He waved his right hand in a small gesture. "I promised that I would solve Mecq's water troubles. I promised the lady, your wife, and the people of Mecq as well. Before I ride away from your valley, Sir Eustace, you will have the water you need, the water your father struggled to provide."

Sir Eustace turned fully toward Silvas. "That is a considerable promise, Lord Wizard," he said. "From what Master Henry saw, it seems you might have the power to fulfill it. I will be properly thankful if you can." Then Eustace turned quickly away, reaching for his beer and taking a long drink. He wasn't entirely happy with the situation. To have an outsider come in and do more for his people than he could rankled. Eustace emptied his mug and called for more beer.

"A promise of that sort is sacred to me, Sir Eustace," Silvas said. "I would not have made it if I was not confident that I could fulfill it."

"Could I watch you do that magic?" Maria asked. "Or any magic. It doesn't have to be that one."

That brought another glare from Sir Eustace. Silvas looked down for an instant before he looked at Maria. Her attentiveness was becoming an embarrassment.

"This is really nothing to see," he said softly. "And when I do important work, I need to concentrate entirely on that. In any case, the place to look will be at the river. The proof of the magic is more impressive than the magic itself."

"*I* don't think so," Maria said, then she looked away when her father cleared his throat noisily.

Night had settled in firmly before Silvas finally took his leave. Eleanora and Fitz-Matthew accompanied him to the door. Sir Eustace had excused himself by saying that he needed to see to the guards. Maria had been sent to care for her young brother—halfbrother—the boy who would inherit Mecq.

Eleanora went no farther than the door. "Good night, Lord Wizard," she said. "Thank you for coming, and for your promise to help our people. I look forward to visiting *your* home."

Silvas gave her a deep bow. "Soon, my lady, I hope. I thank you for your hospitality."

Fitz-Matthew called for Silvas's horse and waited on the top step until the wizard rode through the front gate. *Just making sure that I'm really going,* Silvas told himself with a smile.

The gate closed quickly behind him. As soon as Bay was started down the path to the valley, Silvas said, "I hope you can see well enough for this road in the dark."

Bay snorted softly.

"It was a full evening," Silvas continued. "Sir Eustace tried to be civil. The ladies were both attentive. Sir Eustace's father was on the Burgundy crusade, but Blethye was not, though he had taken the cross."

Bay did not reply. In the night's stillness, his voice would carry a long way, and there were sentries on the wall above them.

Silvas looked across the valley. The pillar of smoke that concealed the Glade was faintly luminous in the dark—not a pillar of fire, just giving off a soft glow for those who had the power to see it. *Home.*

No lights showed in the village. A farming community would retire and rise with the sun. Most would be up before the sun, ready to work until darkness approached again. And even if they had energy to spare, most villagers would hesitate to venture outside after dark. They would *know* that the Devil might be lurking in the darkness, ready to carry their souls off. To simple folk like those of Mecq, the night held nothing but evil.

Silvas enjoyed the peace of the night. There were no noises to compete with the sound of Bay's hoofbeats along the road. Even the crickets went quiet as the horse approached. No night birds called out.

"If only we get through tonight without a repeat of last night's troubles," Silvas said softly. "I feel the need for a full night of sleep. Sleep may get rare before we finish here."

The hint of motion in the darkness was a surprise. Silvas was looking toward the smoke that hid the Seven Towers and barely caught the movement from the side of his eye. He pulled on Bay's reins and the horse stopped. A figure was standing at the edge of the village green, off to the left.

"Brother Paul," Silvas whispered. Bay turned and headed toward the friar.

"I'm surprised to see you about so late," Silvas said when Bay stopped.

Brother Paul looked up and shrugged. "The needs of my flock come before comfort," he said. "I think you and I need to talk, Lord Wizard."

9

Silvas dismounted, leaving the reins draped loosely on Bay's neck. He walked closer to Brother Paul.

"It's a cool night," Silvas said.

"A blessing in a hot summer like this," Brother Paul said. "It doesn't even feel so dry at night."

"I wondered that you were standing outside without even a light while everyone else is shut up indoors against the terrors that they 'know' haunt the dark," Silvas said. "Do you have a single parishioner who won't swear that the Devil walks the night to claim souls?"

"I have my faith to shield me," Brother Paul said, avoiding the wizard's half-bantering question. "I need no more."

"I hope you never find a time when that is not enough, but you are quite right, we do need to talk. Though I thought you might prefer to wait until you get your instructions back from Bishop Egbert of St. Ives."

Brother Paul smiled. "That might take too long," he said, showing no discomfiture at learning that Silvas knew about his rider. "St. Ives is a long way off, and the good bishop has many flocks to tend."

"Then let us talk, by all means," Silvas said. "The night has no more terrors for me than for you."

Brother Paul gestured toward the front of St. Katrinka's. Silvas nodded and followed the vicar through the open door. There was a single candle burning in a small alcove next to the door. Brother Paul used that to light several more candles on a head-high stand.

"My word may not yet suffice," Silvas said while the vicar was lighting his candles, "but I think I can give you some idea of what Bishop Egbert is likely to say about me."

Brother Paul interrupted his lighting ritual to look at the wizard. "You have the gift of reading minds?"

"Not at all," Silvas said. "But in this instance no such gift is necessary. I am not unknown to the White Brotherhood. We serve the same master even if our paths and charges are different."

"Then what instructions am I likely to receive?" Brother Paul had finally lighted enough candles to suit him.

"A line of scripture, perhaps." Silvas paused *almost* long enough to let the friar say that it wasn't much of a prediction to make in regard to a churchman before he added, "Perhaps something like, 'He who is not against us is on our part.' " Silvas smiled at his repetition of that line. He had used it often over the years.

"Sir Eustace has already asked for the Church's opinion of you, Lord Wizard," Brother Paul said, not bothering to comment on Silvas's quote even though another passage came to mind—about the Devil being able to quote scripture. "Henry Fitz-Matthew has been down here twice today asking."

"Asking for himself or for his master?" Silvas asked.

"The question was put as being from Sir Eustace," the friar said. "The chamberlain did show considerable interest of his own."

"I make him uneasy," Silvas said. He shrugged. "And I don't think that Sir Eustace took any great liking to me at our first meetings."

"Sir Eustace does not take easily to anyone," the vicar said. "He has a lot to occupy his mind in this holding. And strangers make everyone uneasy here, at least until folks know what they bring." Brother Paul went along the side of the nave and stopped in front of the shrine to the Virgin Mary. Silvas moved along with the friar.

"Master Fitz-Matthew has not been the only one to mention you to me," Brother Paul said after a hurried *Ave Maria.* "Old Maga brought her sister's husband in to show me that he had been cured. She carried on at great length and not all that she said was understandable." Brother Paul smiled. "I have never seen her so . . . excited. The cure of her sister's husband was miracle enough, but Old Maga babbled about a great castle hidden within your pillar of smoke."

"She was inside the smoke this morning," Silvas said. "She saw part of my home. Did she have anything else to say?"

"Not too plainly. She said that Blue Rose heretics were out to get Berl. That's her sister's husband," the vicar said. "She got particularly excited then, and I had trouble following what she was saying. Berl finally had to escort her out, she got so agitated."

"I can at least give it to you plainly, what I have learned so far," Silvas said. "Berl's illness was caused by spells cast by an adept of the Blue Rose. Their magics of punishment cannot be mistaken."

"It is beyond my ken," Brother Paul replied. "I know that I failed to bring healing to Berl, and I tried with my prayers and with such minor magics as our good Lord has entrusted me. But what could have brought the man so afoul of those cursed heretics?" The vicar didn't even think to question Silvas's identification of the Blue Rose as the cause of Berl's illness, and *that* startled the priest when he realized that he accepted the stranger's word so readily on such a grave question. *My heart believes the man too easily,* he warned himself. *That is not wise.*

"That I do not know. It may have been simply that Berl was a man of Mecq and somehow convenient for such a punishment. It may be that others here have suffered as well. Sir Eustace's father and Henry Fitz-Matthew were on the crusade against the Blue Rose."

"When I was a novice learning my letters at the monastery, I was taught that Pope Innocent's crusade wiped out the foul heretics," the vicar said.

"You say that as if you didn't believe it."

Brother Paul crossed himself. "May God forgive me, but I have always found it easier to believe in the survival of evil than in its destruction."

"Unfortunately, that attitude is too often right."

Brother Paul walked a few steps toward the center of the church, looking toward the altar. It was a simple wooden affair, not nearly as grand as others he had seen. Even the church at Sarum, where he had spent his childhood, had been much finer. *We serve where we are needed,* he reminded himself. Then he faced the wizard again. "You say that the illness was the direct work of the Blue Rose. Does that mean that we have the scourge here in Mecq?"

"Perhaps not within Mecq, but nearby at least. Berl was not laid low by a simple curse laid on him by a passing stranger. From what Old Maga told me, her sister's husband and a lot of other villagers have suffered uncommonly since they dammed the Eyler and were forced to take it back down. If that is true, then this evil has been working on Mecq for a considerable time."

"I've not been here that long," Brother Paul said. "I can't answer as to the truth of that. But I have heard the tale."

"I have pledged to provide Mecq with a steady supply of sufficient water," Silvas said.

"I have heard that tale as well," Brother Paul said, but softly, not in a scoffing way.

"I don't take vows lightly, Vicar. And I don't leave them unfulfilled. But it won't happen overnight—at least not over *this* night. With the Blue Rose near and hostile, I need time to find a solution that will stand up to their efforts to undo my work. But before I leave, Mecq will have its water—unless I die first."

Silvas closed his eyes for a moment. He still had only the same weak chain of events—Berl's illness caused by the Blue Rose, the tale of the workers on the dam and their alleged "uncommon bad luck," the unnatural shortage of water in the valley, the crusade against the Blue Rose. There was nothing new, but every time he went over the links—tenuous though they were—he became more convinced that there was more at stake than water or the life of one peasant.

"Before I act on the water, I need to discover how strong the evil is," Silvas said. "There may be more at risk than either you or I ever dreamed we would face."

Brother Paul was watching Silvas closely. At those last words the friar crossed himself again, very rapidly.

"You do right, Vicar," Silvas said, nodding.

Brother Paul felt his face grow pale from a chill that was more than night air. *The Millennium is at hand* came to mind. Once more he had to caution himself against accepting anything this stranger said unconditionally.

"Could it be?" he asked, though.

"Could it be what?" Silvas asked. "Armageddon? Götterdämerung? Either is possible." He shrugged. "But perhaps it is too soon to think in those terms." *I am letting my fears run away from me,* he told himself. "It may be nothing more than a small group of heretics banded together to cause what trouble they may. Pray that it is no more, Brother Paul," Silvas urged, and the vicar nodded without even willing it.

Silvas shook his head and looked around. "The night carries me to excess," he apologized. "Even I am imagining demons where there may be none. Unless there is more you think we need to discuss tonight, I'll take my leave."

"You have given me sufficient to disturb my sleep, Lord Wizard," Brother Paul said, "more than I expected."

As he watched Silvas lead his horse toward the column of smoke, Brother Paul pulled his cassock tighter around him. Then he turned and crossed to the altar to kneel and pray.

Silvas could hear the mumbling of Brother Paul's prayers as he led Bay home. The sound was lost as they entered the smoke, cut off by the hundreds of miles that separated the Seven Towers from Mecq.

"You disturbed the friar," Bay observed.

"I disturbed myself as much," Silvas said.

"You have a gift for that."

Silvas did not deny it.

Bosc was running across the courtyard toward the gate when Bay and Silvas entered. The groom always seemed to know exactly when to appear to accept the horse from Silvas.

"Before you two go off, I need a Council this night," Silvas said. Bay and Bosc both looked at him. "I will come for you both when the time is right."

Neither of them said anything. The only response was a slow blinking of both eyes from Bosc. Silvas nodded and the others started toward the stable.

Lord, am I tired, Silvas thought. *This day has already*

been too long, and it is not near finished. The thought made his exhaustion feel greater. He walked slowly to the keep while he looked within himself for the energy to complete the night's work. *I hope we can get through the Council, and the night, without another attack.* The Blue Rose would likely respond to his curing of the peasant Berl. The only question was *How soon?*

"Ah, there you are, my heart," Carillia said when Silvas entered the great hall. She held her left hand out to the side, and Koshka hurried to fill a goblet with wine and take it to Silvas. Carillia moved to intercept the wizard in the center of the hall. "I was beginning to wonder how late they would keep you on the hill."

Silvas smiled, then took a long drink of the spicy wine before he answered. "It wasn't just the Devry family. As I was returning, the vicar of Mecq stopped me and said that we needed to talk. We talked."

"Then you have made an impression on him also," Carillia said.

"Also?"

"Come upstairs and we can talk." Carillia linked her arm in Silvas's. "I have the most interesting things to tell you."

"You intrigue me, my love, but then, you always do." Silvas took another long drink of his wine. Then he handed the goblet to Koshka and went with Carillia.

"Now, what interesting things do you have?" Silvas asked when they reached the small sitting room next to their bedchamber.

Carillia smiled broadly. "Sit down. I'll get you more wine. You have had a most trying evening, my heart."

Silvas sat on the couch and settled himself into the cushions, prepared to let Carillia go through her game, whatever it was. She brought him the wine, a sweet red this time, and settled herself at his side.

"Sir Eustace's ladies have taken a considerable interest in you, my heart," she finally said. "Their thoughts have been most strongly on the air this evening."

"What kind of interest?" It was a minor puzzle, one Silvas was certain Carillia would unravel for him soon. That she could sometimes see into the hearts and minds of people she had never met was no surprise to Silvas. The gift wasn't constant, but when Carillia received, there never seemed to be any errors in her impressions.

"Ah, yes." Carillia smiled more broadly. For a moment she purred almost exactly like one of the cats. Satin and Velvet were snuggled up on the floor, heads down, more interested in sleep than talk until Carillia purred. Then the cats looked up. But when she didn't repeat her "comment," the cats both laid their heads down again.

"The wife first." Carillia closed her eyes and snuggled against Silvas's side. "She sees you as a possible lover, someone to bring a little temporary romance and excitement to her drab life. She has found it hard to adjust to being the wife of such a minor knight at the edge of nowhere. Her life before was not so much different, but even that seems exciting in comparison. She would welcome a dalliance, even if she spent years repenting it." Carillia paused, waiting for Silvas to comment. He took his time. Her tale did not surprise him.

"Others have dreamed that dream," he said at last. "What of the girl? You spoke of both ladies before."

Carillia laughed and tightened her grip on Silvas's arm. "Oh, yes! I don't want to forget the daughter." She paused to get her laughter under control.

"The girl has a very fertile mind, my heart. There is a deep strength to her that even she does not yet realize. She imagines in great detail and in great heat."

"Heat?"

"The young lady sees you carrying her off as your lady." Carillia said it as she would a joke. There was no hint of jealousy or uncertainty. She was simply reporting. "She doesn't even care what her status would be. Make her your wife or your plaything. Either would satisfy her. I find it difficult to believe how detailed, how *precise,* her fantasies are. Her father would be shocked to learn how his young maiden's thoughts drift."

"She was quite determined to take part in the conversation at supper," Silvas said. "It was an embarrassment. And her father wasn't at all happy either. About that, or about me."

"I can't say what he might have thought, my heart. You

know that my gifts do not run in that direction. But do not slough off the girl. She is a rare one."

"You never have any trouble seeing what I think, love," Silvas said.

"Ah, but that is so different. You are my heart."

"And you take my mind from the troubles of the moment so easily." He sighed. "Too easily. I've already told Bay and Bosc, love. I need a Council tonight."

"So soon?" Carillia said, but she quickly covered that with "Of course, my heart. Whenever you're ready."

10

Carillia started preparing for bed. Silvas got a heavy robe and left the bedroom. Satin and Velvet followed him up the stairs into the east tower. The wizard was in no particular hurry, and the cats sensed that. He stopped in the library, but not to do any reading. Silvas went directly to the window seat and made himself comfortable, back to one side, feet up on the seat. He leaned back and rested his head against the stone.

"A little rest before we start," Silvas mumbled. He took several deep breaths. Within a minute he appeared to be asleep.

But some small part of his mind remained alert, active, sorting through what he had learned since coming to Mecq. The cats lay next to the window seat, content to follow their master's example. Silvas didn't discover any new connections in his meditation, but he hadn't expected to. And after a half hour he opened his eyes, turned to drop his feet to the floor, and stretched. The cats were quick enough to get out of his way.

"Okay, kittens, I guess we can go upstairs now." Silvas stood and waited while Satin and Velvet went through their own routine of stretching and yawning, then led the way up to his workshop.

There were fresh candles burning there, seven candles in each of three stands. Satin and Velvet took up positions by the room's two doors, curling up across the doorways to wait for Silvas to get ready. When the time came, they would move to their protective circles. Until then they had these positions.

Silvas was still in no hurry. The others needed time to get to sleep before he could summon them to Council. The wizard walked the lines of his pentagram, looking for cracks or other flaws in the crystal. He had never found one in all his years in the Seven Towers, but he checked whenever he had time. After ten minutes, Silvas was confident that there had been no damage during his battle with the demons the night before. The ashes left from the destruction of the intruders had been cleaned up during the day. Silvas's metal-tipped quarterstaff had also been moved back down to his bedroom. He had seen it there earlier.

When Silvas left the pentagram to look out the window, both cats lifted their heads to watch him. He turned to Satin first and then to Velvet.

"Soon, kittens. You know this takes time," Satin yawned. Velvet stretched. *Time* was of no concern to them.

Silvas leaned out the window to look at the sky. The heavens were clear, the stars bright and sharply etched against the black canopy. On his way to the pentagram, Silvas moved his knife belt, fastening it over his heavy robe. The knife rested comfortably at his right hip, where he could reach it quickly at need.

"Okay, it's time," Silvas said as he stepped inside the pentagram again. The cats moved quickly to the same circles they had occupied the night before. They curled up, making sure that no part of their bodies, not even the tip of a tail, touched the pink crystal of a circle. And they kept their heads up now, on alert.

Silvas went to the exact center of the pentagram. He faced north, with his feet spread comfortably apart. He chanted softly. After a few moments he turned to his right, facing the next point of the pentagram and repeated the chant. He repeated the same preliminary spell facing each point of the pentagram and each point of the compass. A council took some preparation.

The candles in the room seemed to dim by half. The crystal lines of the pentagram and the circles started to glow. When Silvas faced north again, he spoke a different chant, invoking his Unseen Lord. A Wizard's Council was a formal magic, and Auroreus had cautioned the greatest precision in preparation. *"You'll rarely be more exposed than during a Council,"* the old wizard had said time after time. *"You touch others, you include them within your nearest shields. A mistake, even if it does not touch you, can touch those you bring in."*

As he did every time he summoned a Council, Silvas stopped when he had completed the last of his preparatory spells and reviewed them in his mind to be certain that he had omitted nothing. The spells were tools, effective only when used by the proper sort of artisan. Only the combination of spell and wizard could invoke *this* magic. The making of a wizard required both talent and training. Either alone was insufficient.

Silvas closed his eyes briefly to let his wizard's senses reach out around him. There had been plenty of time for the others to get to that deep stage of sleep that made the summoning easiest.

It is time, Silvas told himself. He sat cross-legged in the center of the pentagram, facing north, and moved into the spell of Summoning. The candles went out. The glow of the pentagram and circles increased. The walls and ceiling picked up in luminescence. Light without shadow softened the room.

At the end of the first stanza of this spell, Silvas closed his eyes, but he could still see the room in front of him clearly. The lines of the pentagram, the surfaces of wall and floor, the two cats—all were plainly visible. The spell was working properly.

The conclusion of the second stanza brought a soft hum to the air around Silvas, low-pitched, relaxing rather than annoying.

After the third stanza, Silvas stood—rose up out of himself—and walked to the north point of the pentagram. He turned around and looked at his sitting body in the center, motionless but for a slight movement of the lips as the chanting continued. Then Silvas looked down at the ghostly Doppelgänger that his incantation had expelled. The spirit body was a perfect duplicate of the physical body sitting in front of him, only less substantial. It wore the same robe, had the knife belt strapped on exactly so. But Silvas could see through the facsimile that currently held his consciousness.

He waited until the original seated on the floor reached the end of the fourth stanza of the incantation, then stepped out of the pentagram. Satin and Velvet looked

up at him, then down at him in the center of the pentagram. Silvas's Doppelgänger smiled at the cats but didn't
speak. He knew that Satin and Velvet could see this other
body, just as they could hear sounds that no human could.
The cats weren't bothered by the duplication. They had
seen this magic before.

Silvas walked from the room. *Mentally* he walked, but
the Doppelgänger seemed to float. The legs and feet
moved, but the motion was more glide than step. It was
faster and more direct than he could manage with his
physical body. He *almost* followed the corridors but not
quite. The spirit body took shortcuts that weren't readily
detectable, except that certain parts of the journey were
elided.

The wizard went first to the bedroom he shared with
Carillia. He spoke her name and extended his right hand.
Carillia sat up and then stood, while her body remained
sleeping on the bed. Carillia didn't bother to look down
at the sleeping form. She took Silvas's hand for an instant. Then he gestured toward the door, and she walked
out ahead of him.

When Silvas got through the doorway, there was no
sign of Carillia. The wizard turned and headed toward the
second-floor room in the tower next to the stables. There
he summoned Bosc and gestured the groom through to
the Council as he had Carillia.

Bay was the last to be summoned. The giant horse was
waiting and stepped out of his physical body even before
Silvas called his name. Again Silvas gestured. Bay preceded him, and vanished from the wizard's sight beyond
the stable door, but only for a moment.

Silvas turned, stepped through a wall, and into council.

The room in which Silvas's Council met did not exist
within the Seven Towers. The wizard wasn't certain that
it actually existed, *physically,* anywhere. The room was
poorly defined visually, even more ethereal than the
forms of the advisers Silvas had summoned. There were
walls, ceiling, and floor, but it would be difficult to point
to their exact positions or intersections. The only furnish-
ings in the room were three chairs and a small round table, wood to the eye but insubstantial. They would hold

the Doppelgänger forms they were designed for, but the furniture was as transparent as the rest.

Silvas sat in the middle chair. Carillia sat to his right, Bosc to his left. Bay stood at the table across from Silvas, in the spot that had no chair.

Transparency wasn't the only noticeable difference about the bodiless bodies at the Council. Bay didn't seem so overwhelming in size. Bosc didn't appear so diminutive. They looked the same as usual, but their sizes seemed more in harmony with each other.

Silvas looked slowly around the table. There was a feeling of timelessness about a Council, as if it possessed an instant out of eternity. Bosc's movements showed none of the jerkiness that they did in the flesh. He sat quietly, eyes fixed on Silvas, not even blinking. His hands were on the table, fingers laced together. Bay didn't fidget either. His eyes were directly on a level with Silvas's. Carillia was as serene as ever, a slight smile on her face as she watched her wizard watching her. All three of Silvas's advisers wore auras of calm waiting.

"There is evil in Mecq," Silvas said finally. He spoke slowly and systematically listed what he knew or suspected about the situation in Mecq, labeling *knowledge* and *speculation* accordingly. He spoke of the things that he and Bay had seen and heard since topping the ridge to enter the valley. The only item that Silvas did not mention was his forced audience with the old man in the forest clearing.

"I have made no secret of my feeling that this may be the place for the grand confrontation we have wasted so much time in baseless speculation about over the years," Silvas said after he finished his report. "Everything I see and hear—the attack on us last night, the illness I cured this morning, the connection of Mecq to the crusade against the Blue Rose, and on—strengthens my opinion that we have reached the site of that battle. But it is still only an opinion. I cannot see any details, any certain flow of events from one to two. But the Blue Rose seems to be so deeply involved that there must be more to this than a dispute over water rights."

Silvas paused, but none of the others spoke. They

sensed that he had not finished yet. After a moment the wizard resumed.

"Particularly right now while we meet in Council, I feel that great powers are walking the land, approaching, arming to do battle here. It is a strong feeling, but I can find no clear definition, no focus. I need your counsel."

Carillia was the first to reply.

"I too sense the powers that approach." Her voice seemed subtly different in the spirit, less musical, more forceful. But her eyes were still the deep emerald green of her physical body's eyes, the most vibrant color in the chamber. At the same time the soft blues and greens of her aura changed into richer tones of power.

"I would not dispute anything you said." She looked straight at Silvas. There was no "my heart" in Council. "Mecq is not as simple a country village as it seems on the surface. There are levels of complication and contradiction that make no sense alone. There are mists and storms that divert and disturb any investigation. I have never felt this level of power in connection with the Blue Rose. It is disquieting."

"The ground itself is troubled," Bosc said, knowing precisely when Carillia was finished. There was no servility in the groom now. He was no servant here but an adviser, equal to the others who had been summoned. "The drought has been laid on this land as a punishment, and the land cries out that it has done nothing to deserve such treatment. It can stand little more. If the dryness continues for many more years, the ground will turn bitter and nothing will ever grow on it again."

Bay picked up as soon as Bosc finished.

"There are still too many uncertainties here for—" Bay stopped as abruptly as he had started.

There was a trembling, a shaking, as if the land itself were being upheaved. Bright splatters of light flickered through and around the room, crackling and hissing, leaving a distressed smell behind. The room itself seemed to pulse, moving in and out. Even the table rocked. But no earthquake could affect a Council.

"We appear to be under attack again," Silvas said, extending his mind to gauge the strength of this assault, and to ensure that his safeguards were holding. There seemed to be no immediate danger.

"Bay, you were saying?" Silvas worked hard to keep his voice level, but it was difficult. In Council the others could all detect the slightest hint of uncertainty.

"Too much uncertainty remains for us to plot any active steps in Mecq," Bay said. "We cannot strike accurately until we can see the target."

Silvas looked away from the table again, and Bay quit speaking. The light and sound effects were stronger, interfering. The wizard chanted softly, putting his mind in touch with the outer defenses of the Seven Towers and with the threads of the special defenses he had erected to protect this Council.

"Everything seems to be holding," he told the others when he finished. "I don't seem to be needed to take direct charge." He shrugged. "But the distraction. We might as well bring this Council to an end. As always, I count on your advice."

Silvas closed his eyes and chanted. The others vanished even as his eyelids drooped shut. They would return directly to their physical bodies. Silvas expected to wake and find himself back in the center of his pentagram, where he could take whatever steps might be necessary to turn back this new attack on his home.

He *expected* to find himself back in his pentagram.

He did *not* expect to wake in the midst of an insanity beyond his wildest imagining. He did not expect to find chaos swirling around him, but he could find no better word to describe what he found when he opened his eyes.

He was in a kaleidoscope, in the middle of an earth-rending explosion of sound and color that threatened to deafen and blind him before he could even guess where he might have gone. Everything was too loud, too bright, too fast for him to grasp any of the sounds or images. It was as if he were witnessing a magic that he didn't have the power to grasp, the way the villagers who had heard his first chants in Mecq couldn't hold on to his words as the smoke rose to receive the Glade.

Silvas prayed for help, for guidance. His chants to the Unseen Lord tripped over each other. He felt himself being tossed and tumbled like a leaf in a cyclone, hurled about with no chance to affect his destination or his destiny.

He spoke a spell of calming for himself, and he had not been forced to do that since the death of Auroreus, when he had found himself suddenly master of the Seven Towers and responsible for all its inhabitants. Generations had been born and died in the world since then.

"What is happening?" was not a thought but a cry unheard in the maelstrom. "Where am I?"

He fought panic. He could not identify the visions he saw or the sounds he heard. There was an alienness about it that defied even *his* imagination. The Council had felt as timeless as always. Now time seemed to be rushing to consume itself, to burn itself to extinction.

Silvas took an age and an age to fight his panic, calling on the strongest spells of self-control Auroreus had taught him. As they finally took hold, Silvas was even able to wonder that they had worked at all.

His first guess at the cause of his distress was unavoidable. *I've been taken by the god who has put his power behind the Blue Rose.* He could picture himself being taken to some place of eternal torture. The Blue Rose was the faith of punishment. Their notions of Hell were detailed and pervasive. And if a god had decided that he liked those notions of torturous retribution . . .

But the first guess had weaknesses, and long before Silvas quit spinning and tossing, he had discarded it. *My magic would not work if I had been taken by a god of the Blue Rose. I could not have calmed myself.* That brought a measure of peace to his soul, despite the fact that his circumstances had not improved.

If my magic still works, there must be a way to win free of whatever this is. That turned his thoughts to more productive courses. If there was a solution within his power, there would be a way to find it. He had the training and experience. And now he had the calmness to apply them.

For the first time his brain started to register some of the things he was seeing—an alien landscape that would not fit in any "present" or "past" that Silvas knew. There were people here, wherever "here" was. They were dressed strangely, but they were people and didn't seem to be undergoing the tortures of the damned. There was a lot of stone and metal and glass. Enclosed wagons of shiny metal and glass hurled past as if they had been slung from catapults; no animals pulled them. Noises echoed and screeched, threatening hearing with their constant insanity. The smells were different from any Silvas was familiar with, but the air itself seemed sufficiently noxious for any priest's visions of Hell. There were people walking, others riding in the peculiar vehicles, but no one in this vision showed any awareness of Silvas.

Silvas continued to chant spells of knowledge and power, looking for a key to escape from this place of nightmares. His incantations muted the screaming noises and slowed the mad pace of the people and their peculiar vehicles.

He started to hear faint traces of someone speaking to him. Filtering the static that separated the voice from his mind took longer. Silvas focused himself as tightly as he could on the voice, but still had to guess at some of the words.

"This is the world to which you were born. This is the time and place where Auroreus found you and drew you back to his castle. He scoured all of time for his successor. This is far, far in your future ... if that future ever comes. If you fail, people will not say, 'It would have been better if he had never been born.' If you fail, you will never have been born ... and then you could not fail, and the world that comes, if it comes, will be the world as it would have been had you never lived."

Silvas did not begin to understand, but the voice kept speaking, so he didn't have time to figure it out.

"This world, this time, is so different from the world you know that it would remain completely unintelligible even if I took the time to explain all of the differences in minute detail and answered your questions fully for a year."

The alien scene paled into hazy transparency while Silvas tried to fix the words in his mind and listened for any continuation. But the message seemed to be over. The wizard found himself floating in a bright void, as if he were drifting in a noontime sky—though no sun was visible.

Then, suddenly, Silvas was no longer alone.

The wizard stopped spinning. He seemed to be walking now, though there was nothing but air to support him. A figure approached from a distance. There was light behind the figure, and he remained indistinct, more a silhouette, a shadow, than anything else.

Silvas went down on one knee and bowed his head. He had a sudden awareness that he was meeting his Unseen Lord face to face, or as close to that as he had ever come. The wizard recognized the feeling of power that flowed from the blurred figure against the light.

After a moment Silvas looked up, knowing it was expected. The figure of his Unseen Lord remained indistinct. He couldn't see the figure clearly enough to give any description, but it had always been like that. Their few meetings had always had a dreamlike quality, though none had been quite this dramatic.

Silvas stared up at the face he could not really see. He let his Unseen Lord flow over him, through him, around him, content for the moment to absorb whatever he was about to be given.

"I give you knowledge."

Images flickered through Silvas's mind, too rapidly for him to keep everything before him at once. But the knowledge was being firmly planted. It would be there for him to retrieve later. For the present, all he could hold was an overview, an outline.

He learned how much was at stake in Mecq, or wherever the final confrontation might occur. It was most definitely coming. And the stakes were even higher than Silvas had dared to fear. The gods of the world and time were arming for war among themselves. The outcome of their battle would affect the entire history of the world, past and future.

As that other voice seemed to be saying, Silvas thought. And before the figure of the Unseen Lord vanished and Silvas dissolved back into himself, the wizard was left with one more very clear message:

Gods will DIE before this battle is over!

11

Silvas woke with the feel of cold marble against his cheek. He was flat on his face in the center of his pentagram. Without looking, he knew that his body had to be crossing at least two of the crystal lines. His first thought was to draw in his arms and legs, to get free of the lines of power, but he didn't have the strength. He could scarcely move a finger.

Slowly now, he told himself. *Take your time. Feel out your body. Let your mind search.* Despite his lack of physical strength, there was no clouding of his mind. Silvas breathed as deeply as he could in his uncomfortable position and thought through a simple spell. Feeling started to return to his body. Encouraged, Silvas moved on to the more complicated chants that would bring back his strength.

There were no wounds, no pain. Silvas had not been injured. There was only the exhaustion. A Council was a draining magic to start with. The additional excursion at its conclusion must have been similarly draining, Silvas decided. He pulled his arms and legs in toward his body, and moved his head enough to see that he was now within the five center lines of his diagram. The lines were channels of power when the pentagram was activated. It was quiet now, but this wasn't something to take chances with.

Silvas lay motionless for several more minutes, continuing to attract more power—not magical power, simply the physical energy he needed. There was still work to be done.

As his strength returned, Silvas set his mind drifting around the Seven Towers. There were no alerts, no signs that the defenses had been breached. Whatever the cause of the disruption to his Council, it had not touched the Glade.

Velvet and Satin came out of their circles and over to the edge of the pentagram. Their tails made nervous little twitches, their eyes narrowed as they watched Silvas. They relaxed a little when he started to get up. The wizard paused to rest on one knee, then got slowly to his feet and moved back to the center of his diagram.

"We're not through yet, kittens," Silvas said, and the cats went back to their circles. The wizard took several deep breathes, holding each for a count of twenty before he released it. He turned through a complete circle and ended up facing the north point of his pentagram again. After another series of three slow deep breaths, Silvas started the incantations that would close down the special defenses he had erected for his Council. The spells could have been left to decay on their own, but that was not the way Auroreus had taught him. *Always clean up your spells when you finish, even those that will fade away on their own. That way there is less chance of having them interfere with later work. Surprises are rarely welcome in our craft.*

As he disassembled the individual spells, Silvas examined them closely. Some showed strain, but none had come close to failure. *There had been less power directed against the Glade this night than last,* he decided. *This was no attempt to do real harm.* He wasn't sure what to make of that. It was simply one more fact to keep in mind. Perhaps the rationale would become clear later.

When the last of his housekeeping was finished, Silvas stepped out of the pentagram and the cats came to meet him. There were still nervous, looking for reassurance. Silvas reached down to stroke their necks and to scratch under their chins. "Let's go to bed," he said.

Silvas discovered that his body was still weak and uncoordinated as he walked. He needed to almost consciously direct each step to keep from stumbling. The cats stayed at his side, but a little farther apart than normal, keeping out of his way. Silvas reeled down the corridors and stairs like a drunk.

There was a single candle burning in the bedroom, and it was low. Silvas stripped off his clothes, blew out the candle, and collapsed on the bed next to Carillia. She didn't wake, and Silvas was asleep even before the cats settled into their customary positions.

Silvas knew immediately when he woke that it was far later than his usual waking time. The morning was half gone. It was not a pleasant waking. A sense of foreboding hung over him. The new information his Unseen Lord had given him had settled firmly on the wizard. *"Gods will die before this battle is over."* Silvas didn't speak the words aloud, simply rolled them through his mind. They led quickly to another thought. *If gods will die in this battle, what chance do I have? What chance does any mortal have in that kind of battle?*

Silvas rolled over on his side. Carillia was still sleeping soundly, the muscles of her face totally relaxed. *I am not yet tired of living,* Silvas decided. *How could I ever tire of a life that has Carillia in it?* He stared at her for several minutes, but the rhythm of her breathing did not change. She didn't wake. Finally Silvas rolled in the other direction and sat up on the edge of the bed, moving carefully so he wouldn't waken her.

The cats were gone at the moment. In the daylight they weren't always underfoot. It was as if they knew that they were off duty during the day unless something special came up. They might be in the kitchen eating, or merely curled up in front of a window somewhere, basking in the sun. If Silvas called for them, they would come. But there was no need now. The Seven Towers were peaceful.

There was hot food waiting when Silvas entered the great hall, bathed, dressed, and freshly shaven. He even had a strong appetite. Food would replenish him more readily than magic, and it would hold him longer. Silvas ate quickly and heartily, as much as he might eat in an entire day when no special demands had been placed on his wizardry.

When he had finally sated his appetite, he went to the stable. Bay was munching at his hay. Bosc wasn't around.

"Did you experience anything unusual after the Council?" Silvas asked.

"Nothing out of the ordinary," Bay replied. "Your question implies that you did."

"A strange passage." Silvas told Bay about the first part of it, the journey through insanity and the message he had received. Then he said, "I believe that I saw our Unseen Lord, as much as he can be seen, after that, before I was returned to my body." He withheld the details of his one-sided conversation with the Unseen Lord. The basic substance was enough for now.

"Are you certain you can trust this vision?" Bay asked. "Could it be a deception by the Blue Rose?"

"I believe I can trust it," Silvas said. He shrugged. "I don't rule out the possibility that I trust it because it fits so well with what I have felt from the time we first saw Mecq."

"I am relieved to see that you are finally regaining your sense of caution," Bay said. "How do we proceed?"

"We can only proceed as we would in any such place. I'll do whatever magic the people of Mecq ask of me and start assembling what I will need to solve their water problems. Beyond that we can only wait and be alert."

And for two days, Silvas did little but routine magics. The people of Mecq came to him. Old Maga had spread her tale. Berl was up and about, and by the second day he was back working in the fields—if only lightly. His wife joined her sister in lauding Silvas and his power. The wizard treated all who came to him alike. He listened to their problems and if there was anything he could do, he did it. Each time he looked carefully for the signature of the Blue Rose. Only a couple of times did he find it. Of the other problems, most were minor, and a few were imagined, but Silvas dealt with each person. He talked with them, helped them. Sometimes all that was needed was advice or a show to help people "get rid" of problems that were completely within their imagination.

It was a casual time on the surface. Silvas fell into the languid routines of the village. He spent time in the fields, talking, asking questions about the drought and about the dam that had been built and dismantled. All of the people whose troubles bore the mark of the Blue Rose had helped with the dam. But not everyone who had been party to that work had suffered.

Silvas also spent time walking the course of the Eyler and walking through the dusty fields. Occasionally he would pick up a handful of dust in the fields and let it dribble between his fingers. At one point he borrowed a hoe and dug a foot and a half down into the ground at the edge of a grain patch. Then he got down on his knees and grabbed handfuls of dirt from the bottom of the hole. There was very little moisture even at that depth.

On the third morning after the Council, Silvas didn't emerge from the pillar of smoke in the morning. He spent those hours in his library and conjuring room.

"I think it's time for an experiment," he told Carillia at lunch.

"What kind of experiment?" she asked.

"Partly I want to show good faith to the villagers over their water. A few are already asking under their breath when I'm going to quit talking and produce the water I promised." He smiled and shook his head. "They wait patiently on the seasons, watch their grain grow mote by mote, but they expect me to increase the Eyler a hundredfold at the snap of my fingers."

"The matter of water is vital to them," Carillia reminded him.

"I wasn't indicting them for their hope. But besides the show of good faith, I want to do something very visible to see what response it draws from the Blue Rose."

"That might be dangerous."

"It has to come sooner or later. Drawing action when we're ready for it instead of waiting until the Blue Rose chooses to attack again may work to our advantage." Silvas shrugged. "I have less than inexhaustible patience, I fear."

"When will you put on your show?" Carillia smiled and laid her hand over his.

"This afternoon. The middle of the afternoon should be the best time. I've spent the morning at my preparations. When I go out, you might want to watch from the turret, my love."

"If you think I should," she said.

"You might help me considerably. You may spot any response quicker than I do. Your senses are keen for that sort of thing."

"You think the Blue Rose might respond instantly?"

"I can't guess," he admitted. "But even if they don't, you might find some gauge of the people of Mecq in *their* reactions. Perhaps a hint of something other than relief will show itself."

"You think that the Blue Rose may lie hidden within this valley and not with the Duke of Blethye?"

"It is too soon to rule it out, my love," Silvas said. "If Auroreus taught me anything, it was to be both careful and thorough. And the stakes this time . . ."

"I'll be there, my heart." Carillia gave Silvas's hand an affectionate squeeze.

Silvas emerged from the smoke an hour past noon. Most of the villagers were in their fields. A few tended the garden plots behind their cottages. Silvas walked to the center of the village green, carrying his metal-tipped quarterstaff. In a place where the grass had been eaten down to the roots by the livestock, Silvas used his staff to draw a pentagram in the dirt. He used the silver ferrule for this drawing, putting strength into his strokes, leaving a diagram that was quite visible. He concentrated wholly on his work, speaking the spells that would make this pentagram more than just a design in the dust. The pentagram in Silvas's conjuring chamber might possess power of its own, but the wizard would have to infuse this diagram with power himself. No one appeared to take any special notice of him at first. No one had time to watch the stranger at his games.

At first. Perhaps someone noticed how much time and care he was taking at his task, the look of intense concentration he wore—and then recalled that this was not just any stranger but a wizard who had demonstrated power from the moment of his arrival. The pillar of smoke was a most visible reminder that the stranger was indeed a wizard-potent. Neighbor called to neighbor. Fingers were pointed. People started to take some interest in what the wizard was doing.

When Silvas finished scribing his pentagram, he took up his usual position in the exact center. He leaned his staff against his shoulder, then put his hands on his hips and stretched, working out an ache that his drawing had brought to his lower back. Then he took the staff in hand again and turned in a slow circle, examining every line of his pentagram. It was precise. It was perfect. It would do.

Silvas looked up at the sky and made another complete, slow circle. There were only a few high, wispy clouds. The sun beat down on the dust of Mecq, making it drier with every moment.

Oh Lord, let me continue to be a fit vehicle for executing your will. Open my eyes that I may see what I need to see. Give me your direction, your help. Protect me that I may continue to protect your people.

The prayer was silent. As Silvas went through the words, he recalled the blurry vision he had been given of—he believed—his Unseen Lord. He recalled the dire predictions that had been placed in his mind, the visions of gods arming for war, the warning that gods would die before the battle was finished.

"And I am about to issue a challenge here," he whispered. It had to make him pause. A wizard's power did not make him immune to fear. It didn't rob him of second thoughts, of worry.

Carefully Silvas erected his safeguards. Uncertain how much power he was about to challenge, he took precautions that he would rarely have considered. But he was not planning to remove a wart from a peasant's nose now.

"I am ready," Silvas whispered when he was certain that he had left out no measure of protection that he could take. It didn't stop the fluttering in his chest and stomach, but neither did those sensations deter him.

Once more Silvas started to chant. At first the words were too soft for anyone to hear. Only as Silvas became more involved in casting the web of his magic did his voice become louder. He faced the north point of his newly drawn pentagram, holding his quarterstaff in both hands, low, parallel to the ground, the silver tip to his right, the iron tip to his left. This was a complicated incantation, with stanzas to be addressed to each point and then to each base of the pentagram. At the end Silvas was facing south. His chant had become almost a shout. He could see the beginnings, the materialization of his conjuration.

The sky started to take on new substance. The effect was too major to take place in an instant, but Silvas had speeded up movements high above. The thin, wispy clouds of August expanded and thickened, building into thunderheads. Their bases lowered toward earth, their peaks rose closer to heaven. Near the ground, a mild breeze appeared, moving across the valley from northwest to southeast.

Though Silvas paid no attention to the villagers now, many of them noticed the breeze and took a moment to enjoy the cooling sensation—before they looked toward Silvas. This was not a normal August breeze. The villagers looked up at the sky and saw the new clouds that seemed to grow outward. Some dared to make the leap of imagination. Rain would come. Thunderstorms were not unknown of an August afternoon, though they had been rare for this generation.

A brief summer thunderstorm, no matter how welcome for the moment, could have no lasting effect on the valley's drought, and many of the villagers moved on to that thought in a hurry, while the clouds were still forming, still spreading.

When the sun was hidden and the first drops of rain fell, the temperature dropped suddenly. The breeze got stronger, cooler. Villagers stood facing the wind, arms spread to catch as much of the refreshing air as possible. Some closed their eyes and sighed their relief at even a momentary respite from the heat and drought.

A bolt of lightning flashed, far to the south, beyond Mecq's valley. The thunder arrived behind it. A moment later, there was another flash of lightning, this one off in the other direction, over the lands of the Duke of Blethye.

Silvas remained mostly oblivious to anything close to him. He continued to chant, sometimes moving his staff—raising it above his head, still parallel to the ground, or shifting his grip to point the silver ferrule to the sky. His concentration was too deep for him to notice the cooling of the air flowing by him.

I must be careful, he reminded himself. *The proper amounts in the proper places.*

The drizzle grew to a light rain over Mecq's valley, a soft rain that would have time to soak into the parched ground. It never fell hard enough for it to simply run off into the Eyler and disappear between the twin hills into the demesne of Blethye. Farther off, both upstream and down, the rain was heavier, the wind more furious. Lightning tickled the peaks between Mecq and Blethye, but no lightning struck within the valley. Upstream, the lightning came fast and often, painting jagged lines across the sky.

Villagers started to gather on the green, keeping a respectable distance from the pentagram. Mostly they watched in silence. A few shouted thanks or encouragement. After a time Silvas brought himself out of his deep concentration. It might help to remain within the magic until it was done, but a new thought had come to him.

"Do you see that rain south of here?" he shouted, pointing toward the grayness upstream. "In an hour or two, that water will run through this valley. The least you could do is throw a course or two of rocks across the Eyler. There." He pointed downstream, toward the gap between the hills.

The villagers looked where he pointed, then looked back at Silvas. Fear was plain in many eyes.

"For God's sake, you're not going to build a full dam!" Silvas shouted. "In this storm, Blethye will never notice. And anyway, *I am here now to protect you.*" He loaded the last with power. Still no one rushed off to do the work.

Silvas pointed his staff directly overhead and uttered a quick chant. Lightning flashed by directly over him. The thunder that came with it was immediate and almost deafening.

"I am here!" Silvas thundered in its wake, borrowing such of the thunder's noise as he could. "I will be here until I am no longer needed. Help yourselves while you may."

"To the river," a voice shouted from Silvas's right. He needed a moment to recognize the voice as Master Ian's. "We can't let an outsider do everything for us."

"Our Unseen Lord has sent this man to help us,"

Brother Paul's voice added. "Can we insult our Lord by refusing to help ourselves?"

Brother Paul and Master Ian herded and led the villagers to the river. No one paid any heed to the slow, steady rain falling on them. It was too rare a treat for anyone to run to get out of it. Silvas watched people moving to the river, some six dozen of them, nearly half the adults who lived in the village. Children ran after, or ran on ahead. There was happiness in the voices of the children. Rain was a special treat for them, and they didn't bear the burden of memories of Blethye's anger.

Silvas slid back into the web of his incantations for a moment, checking that every thread remained strong and true. He longed to stay within the web, to see his conjuration through to a perfect finish, but there was other work to do. He spoke a spell of passage and stepped through, out of the pentagram, and hurried after the villagers who were heading toward the river. They might yet need more encouragement from him.

There were plenty of rocks for the villagers to grab down in the almost empty watercourse. Many were small enough for a single person to move. Others required the combined efforts of two or three strong farmers. Master Ian pointed out where the rocks should be laid, against a natural rocky seam crossing the Eyler well below the village. *Perhaps where the previous dam was,* Silvas thought as he shouted his own words of encouragement. *It seems a good place for it.*

Not much could be done in the hour that the villagers would have before the rush of water came downstream. Silvas went down into the riverbed to help. His strength was more than the equal of any of the farmers. For a time Silvas and Master Ian worked together, moving rocks that would have taken three or four of the others.

"I have to watch for the water now," Silvas told the innkeeper after they had lugged a round dozen rocks into position. "Everyone will have to get clear before the flash arrives. We don't want to have anyone drown or get their heads bashed into these stones."

Master Ian merely nodded. Keeping up with the wizard had left him too short of breath for words.

The level of the Eyler had already increased a little behind the stones, and the current was moving faster. Silvas climbed to the top of the bank on the village side of the river and focused his attention upstream, looking with his mind as well as with his telesight. An accident now would undo much of the good his magic was providing. It would be a mark against him in the minds of the villagers, perhaps enough to totally offset the benefits of the extra water.

"Everyone up, out of the way," Silvas shouted when he sensed that the floor was near. "The water comes!"

Few needed a second warning. Silvas watched the people scrambling up, helping one another, urging each other. And then the people of Mecq lined the riverbank, waiting for the water.

It came. It was not a real flood. There hadn't been enough rain for that, but in minutes the Eyler grew to six times its previous size. The makeshift dam held back the water for only a moment. Then it overflowed the rocks and continued toward the demesne of the Duke of Blethye.

"I have to get my lads busy filling the cistern," Master Ian shouted as he ran toward the Boar and Bear.

While the villagers continued to watch the river, Brother Paul came over to Silvas.

"I have received a message from Bishop Egbert concerning you," the vicar said softly.

Silvas nodded. Since there hadn't been time for the rider to return from St. Ives, he knew that the message must have come through magic. Bishop Egbert would have the power to transmit such a message, Silvas realized. Egbert was a man of magical substance, an adept of the Greater Mysteries of the White Brotherhood. Brother Paul's talents would be stretched to the maximum to receive such a message. He could never initiate such communication. He *might* be able to reply in kind if a greater power contacted him.

"Perhaps we should talk where we can be comfortable and won't be disturbed," Silvas said. "May I offer you the hospitality of my home?" He smiled and kept his eyes on the vicar's face. Brother Paul hesitated for only an instant, reminding himself that Silvas had shown no fear of

entering St. Katrinka's during their previous conference.
And besides, there was the bishop's message.

"I would be honored," Brother Paul said with a slight
nod.

12

Brother Paul whispered a prayer under his breath as he accompanied the wizard into the smoke. The vicar had heard the tales of what the inside looked like. Both Old Maga and Henry Fitz-Matthew had described it, so he *was* prepared. Even so, he stopped when they cleared the gate towers and looked around. The castle of Mecq was not the only castle that Brother Paul had ever seen. He had spent the first two years after he took his final vows as a mendicant, traveling the countryside much as Silvas claimed to. Brother Paul had walked, though, and there had been no such refuge as this for him to retreat to every night. Brother Paul had seen castles, including some of the finest in the kingdom, and none could begin to compare with this one.

"It is known as the Glade, sometimes as the Seven Towers," Silvas said.

"It isn't raining," Brother Paul noted. "Has the shower stopped and the sky cleared so quickly?"

"Not at all. It's still raining in Mecq. But we are no longer there. If you were to leave through the postern instead of the main gate, you would find yourself many scores of leagues from Mecq."

"This represents a most powerful magic," Brother Paul said, carefully understating his impression. The pillar of smoke had been enough to convince the friar that Silvas was truly a wizard-potent. Seeing what that smoke concealed made him completely revise his opinion of what *wizard-potent* meant. He could scarcely conceive the level of power that would be required to establish and maintain this magic. Until this moment he would never have credited that any mortal could have done it. He would have termed this a god-like power.

"Our Unseen Lord allows me this refuge," Silvas said, as if he could follow the friar's thoughts. "It is not something I could accomplish on my own."

That brought Brother Paul's eyes back from their sight-seeing. He turned and met the wizard's gaze.

"We are not so much different, you and I," Silvas said. "I believe that we serve the same Lord. Our missions are different. You are of the church-pastoral. My role is somewhat more . . . militant, shall we say. The comforts of the flock are not for all of our Unseen Lord's servants."

"A wolf in the sheepfold?" Brother Paul could not repress the question, but Silvas merely smiled.

"Even the wolf has a purpose to fulfill," the wizard said. "You said that you have received word about me from Bishop Egbert."

"Yes. Quite a long message under the circumstances."

"Come, I'll give you a tour of the Glade and we can talk," Silvas said.

"That might be . . . educational," the friar said after another short hesitation.

Silvas laughed. "An excellent choice of words, Vicar."

Silvas led the way around the courtyard, identifying the various outbuildings. They stopped briefly at the stable, so Bay would see that the vicar had come to call. "You will note that Bay is the only horse of his size here. The rest are quite ordinary in that respect. Bay is unique," Silvas told Brother Paul, thinking, *In more ways than you suspect.* Then they went on to the keep, stopping in the great hall for wine and to sit in comfort for a few minutes.

"In part, the bishop's message was as you suggested," the vicar said. "In truth, he quoted the exact passage you did." Brother Paul managed a look of trifling embarrassment over that. "Even so, I am certain that it was Bishop Egbert who contacted me." He took another sip of wine and complimented Silvas on it before he continued.

"The bishop said that your work is not unknown to the White Brotherhood and that even His Majesty has looked with favor on your efforts. He also instructed me to pose you a question."

"What question is that?" Silvas asked.

The friar closed his eyes as he quoted, " 'Who dies on the altar of Canterbury?' " Then he opened his eyes to watch Silvas's face.

The wizard smiled. The question was from the initiation rites into the Greater Mysteries of the White Brotherhood, something that would be beyond Brother Paul's knowledge.

" 'No one dies there but the ghost of a ghost from another time in another world,' " Silvas said, quoting the ritual response.

"That is the answer I was to look for," Brother Paul said.

"It is not the surest test of one such as I, but it covers many of the possibilities." Silvas smiled. "Unless you would like more wine first, we still have a lot to see. Let me show you the view."

Brother Paul drained his goblet and stood. "I am most curious to learn as much as I can of this place," he said. *I am most curious to learn as much as I can of* you, he thought. Silvas smiled again, understanding the unspoken as well as the spoken message.

"Are you so nearly alone in this castle?" Brother Paul asked as they climbed the main stairs to the levels above the great hall. They had seen only a handful of human retainers since the friar entered the smoke. There had been no sight of any of the non-human servants.

"I have staff enough for my needs," Silvas said. Bosc and his kindred, and the lupine warriors, were very efficient at staying out of sight. It was a "magic" they were long used to performing. They always seemed to know when not to startle a visitor with their presence. "They are busy at their work, I would say," Silvas told the vicar. "I have good people. They do not need constant oversight."

"A most fortunate advantage," the vicar said.

"It is," Silvas agreed, ignoring the hint of sarcasm he thought he detected in the words. "Have a look at this view." They stopped at a window that looked out over the walls of the Glade. Silvas stepped aside to let Brother Paul get close.

"That is certainly not the valley of Mecq," the friar said after a moment of looking at the long, narrow valley with its lush forest and healthy fields, "though there was once a time when Mecq might have looked this inviting." Brother Paul looked for anything that he might recognize, but by the time he took his gaze from the view he had decided that it was no place he had ever been to.

"It is a good place," Silvas said. "I have another view for you." It took several minutes to reach the turret off the east tower so Brother Paul could look out over Mecq.

"It is still raining," the friar noted. Most of the villagers were still out in it. "There will be many with chills and fever by morning, I think."

"They will welcome even that," Silvas said with a chuckle. The vicar nodded in agreement. "How runs the Eyler?"

"Deeper than I have seen it but twice in my years here," the friar said, looking to the side. "I have never seen Mecq from this vantage." He took considerable time looking at his church, the inn and mill, the cottages, even Sir Eustace's castle.

"How can your castle be in two locations at once?" Brother Paul asked when he finally turned away from the view.

"It cannot and is not," Silvas said. "The Glade never moves from the place where it was built. The magic of the smoke merely lets me travel between it and wherever I have erected the pillar. As I said, it is a comfort that our Unseen Lord permits me."

"A most generous comfort."

"It is indeed," Silvas agreed. "But there is a price, as you might imagine."

The vicar's "Yes?" was more question than statement of agreement.

"There is more that we need to speak of now that you have your word of me. Let's go to my library for that."

They had passed through the library on their way up to the turret, as they had passed through Silvas's conjuring room. Going back down, Brother Paul got another surprise. Satin and Velvet joined them in the conjuring room. The sight of the big cats gave the friar a visible start—the first sight in the Glade that had managed to discompose him.

"They are but overlarge pets," Silvas said. "They are friendly to friends."

"They look as though they would . . ." The friar wasn't sure how to finish the statement, so he let it hang.

"They are efficient guards at need as well," Silvas said. Brother Paul nodded.

In the library, a space had been cleared on a small table for a silver tray that held a carafe of wine, two crystal goblets, and a plate of fruit and cheese. Satin and Velvet curled up on the floor, but they kept their eyes on Silvas and Brother Paul.

"Help yourself, Vicar," Silvas invited, gesturing at the food while he poured wine.

"More invisibly efficient servants?" Brother Paul asked as he selected a small cube of cheese. He tried to restrain the impulse to stare at the cats, with only moderate success. They made him nervous enough that his hand started to move to the cross hanging from his neck.

"Efficient, yes; invisible, no," Silvas said. "I would guess that my lady Carillia is responsible for this. She would have directed the servants to prepare for us."

"I would be honored to meet your lady and thank her for her attentiveness," Brother Paul said.

"You shall," Silvas said. "I imagine that she merely waits for us to conclude our discussions."

Brother Paul tasted the wine. It was the same vintage he had drunk in the great hall, aromatic, just slightly sweet, and potent. The contrast worked well with the cheese and with the fruit that the vicar sampled while he waited for the wizard to get to the additional talk he had mentioned.

"There is more at stake in Mecq than water or a few people with illnesses," Silvas said finally. "I have been given—call it a vision. The hows and whys of it escape me, I confess, but somehow Mecq has become a focal point for a major confrontation." There was a limit to what Brother Paul would accept. Silvas wasn't completely certain where he would find that limit, though. The vicar had proclaimed himself an initiate of the Lesser Mysteries, and much of what Silvas had seen and heard was far beyond those.

"The Blue Rose seems poised for an attempt to overthrow the White Brotherhood," Silvas said, speaking slowly now. "For the first time, perhaps, they seem to have real power behind them." He paused and then said, "Considerable power."

"Santanic power?" Brother Paul asked.

"You would call it that," the wizard agreed. "It is even one of the names that Bishop Egbert would have for it." Silvas nodded, mostly to himself. *That should give Brother Paul some clue without calling in question the things he would have been taught.*

"More power than you yourself have?" the friar asked.

"If it is all applied against me, certainly," Silvas said. "If our Unseen Lord did not stand beside me, I would be hopelessly outmatched."

"My flock remains in danger?"

"Grave danger," Silvas said. "They have been in grave danger since the Blue Rose decided that Mecq was important—and I still don't know the reason for that importance. It may simply be the connection of Sir Eustace's father to the crusade against them. There might be more that I haven't discovered yet." Silvas shrugged. "But together you and I may be able to protect the villagers from the worst of the wrath of the Blue Rose."

"You speak so casually, as if you are accustomed to facing this manner of evil routinely," Brother Paul said. He was having difficulty matching the wizard's tone. *Heavenly Father, protect your servant and his flock,* he prayed. *Give me the strength I need to serve.*

"I have never faced it before," Silvas said. "Perhaps no mortal has ever faced so much." *Careful, don't infect him with all of your worries,* he thought. "But I have been trained for this. It is why our Unseen Lord has permitted me the life he has."

"A weapon waiting for the need?" Brother Paul asked.

He has a mind! Silvas thought with some sense of triumph.

"I have thought of it that way," the wizard admitted. *He may be of more help than I expected.*

"Is there anything in particular that I should watch for?" Brother Paul asked. "Anything I can do to guard my people?"

Silvas shrugged. "For a moment I can hardly say. You

will take what measures you normally would, of course. Vigilance is important. The sooner we know of anything happening, the faster we can take whatever specific actions are needed."

Brother Paul took several moments to consider that, sipping lightly at his wine, though he scarcely noticed it. More prayers went through his mind. He felt a trill of fear, but he met that with more prayers for strength and faith. Finally he blinked several times and looked up to see Silvas watching him.

"You have given me a lot to think over—and pray over," the friar said. He looked around. "For now I think I should return to my church. There might be some who would look for me."

Silvas nodded and rose. "With a little rain and water, some may even look for reassurance that Blethye won't come riding through the pass with his soldiers."

"Do you believe His Grace contaminated by the Blue Rose?"

"I have no knowledge of it, Vicar, and I hesitate to accuse a man of such a sin without certain knowledge."

Brother Paul nodded, softly, distracted.

"Come, I'll see you to the gate," Silvas said.

They walked quietly. The friar hardly noticed the walk. He even forgot to worry about the two large cats that trailed behind them. They were in the courtyard before Brother Paul even recalled that Carillia had not appeared.

"I missed my chance to give my thanks to your lady," the vicar apologized.

"I will convey them. Perhaps you will have another chance later."

After Brother Paul left, Silvas stood for a moment just inside the gate. He let out a long breath. Within limits, he could count on the friar as an ally. *Though he is not yet certain of me,* Silvas reminded himself. *He will not commit himself fully, even though I have his bishop's blessing.* The thought of Brother Paul's caution brought a smile to Silvas's face. *So much the better. He will be less likely to fall for any ruse the Blue Rose might try. If only he had a little more power.* Silvas did not discount allies. If he was indeed about to face the challenge he foresaw, he would take any help he could find.

"I have no guarantees," he said softly.

He looked at the clear sky over the Seven Towers and thought of the rain over Mecq. *I should go back out there. If the Blue Rose does respond immediately, I need to see it as soon as possible. In any event, the people of Mecq will worry less if they see me.* Some would undoubtedly see the rain and the increased flow of the Eyler as an invitation to disaster. Some would feel fear as soon as the initial relief started to pale. And if Silvas wasn't there, they would worry that he was leading them to disaster and leaving them to face it alone.

"In a few moments," Silvas said. He went back inside the keep. He wanted to ask Carillia her impressions of the vicar. Even though she had not showed herself, Silvas was certain that she had been close by.

He was just crossing the great hall toward the rear stairs up to his quarters when Koshka came running down from those stairs.

"My lady sent me to tell you that another visitor approaches," the small servant said, puffing just a little. "A young lady riding a horse."

"Thank you, Koshka." Silvas hid his frown until he had turned back toward the entrance. *A young lady riding. I don't need wizardry to guess who it must be.* He walked back toward the main gate, in no hurry. It had to be Maria, and Silvas was far from certain that he wanted to deal with her just then. There was something about her youthful eagerness—even ardor, to credit Carillia's impression—that made Silvas uncomfortable. There seemed to be unsuspected depths to the girl that Silvas was hesitant to explore.

"Lord Wizard!" Silvas heard her call before he reached the gate. "Are you there?"

"I'm here," Silvas mumbled. He took a deep breath while he looked at the smoke. For a moment he considered turning around and letting Sir Eustace's daughter go unanswered.

"But, like as not, she'd just sit there and shout her head off until I did answer." He shook his head and stepped into the smoke. By the time he emerged on Mecq's side of it, there was a smile in his voice.

"Good afternoon, Maria," he said. "To what do I owe the honor of this visit?"

"It's raining," Maria observed, as if Silvas might not have noticed. She held her hand out, palm up, catching a few drops.

"I know it's raining," Silvas replied. "Would you like to come in out of it?"

She actually hesitated for a moment.

"Strange tales have reached my father," she said. "That you live in a fairy-tale palace with soaring towers and all manner of strange servants. I came because I would not like to think that people are making up stories to keep me occupied."

"Your father doesn't think very kindly of me," Silvas said. "I doubt that he would approve of your visit."

"My father does not think kindly of *anyone,*" Maria replied airily, flicking her hand to the side in a gesture of dismissal. "It is raining," she repeated.

"It might be better to dismount and lead your horse," Silvas said, accepting that he would not be able to convince Maria to forgo the visit. "Horses are sometimes averse to smoke."

"*Your* horse isn't," Maria said, as if that were a challenge.

"Bay is quite used to this smoke. He is quite a remarkable steed. Would you like a hand?"

Maria swung herself down from her horse, a young gray mare, instead of answering. *I can dismount without help. I am not a child.* But she smiled at Silvas as she moved to the horse's head to take a tight grip on the reins.

"Tella is well trained," Maria said.

"This way, then." Silvas gestured into the smoke. Despite Maria's assurances, Silvas was careful to position himself close enough to be able to grab for the horse's bridle if Tella reared or tried to bolt to avoid the smoke.

The horse did object, but Maria was able to handle her. When they emerged from the smoke inside the Glade, though, she let go of the reins. Her mouth fell open.

"It hasn't rained at all here!" was her first comment, almost a protest.

"We are no longer in Mecq," Silvas informed her.

Maria did not follow up on that. "This place could not *possibly* fit inside the tower of smoke. You cast dreams before my eyes!"

"You see what you see," Silvas said, sternness struggling with amusement in his voice. "This is my home."

"I've never seen a castle this large." Maria omitted the fact that she had never seen any castle but her father's before. Her sixteen years had been confined to the valley of Mecq. Sir Eustace rarely traveled, and when he did, he didn't take his daughter along.

"May I look through it?" she asked, torn between the forms of politeness and the strength of her desire to see every part of this castle.

"As you will." Silvas gave her another bow and kept his voice polite. He would not be made out to be a poor host, but he was already looking for ways to cut her visit short. Maria didn't get the same tour Brother Paul had, and Silvas didn't linger. They crossed directly to the keep after Maria tied Tella's reins to a ring set in the curtain wall.

Satin and Velvet were at the door of the keep to meet them. But the wizard's first hope for cutting short the visit failed.

"They're beautiful!" Maria said, crouching to get closer to the cats. Satin and Velvet both permitted her to stroke their necks. They nuzzled her sides for a moment before looking to Silvas.

"They are beautiful," he agreed, disappointed that she showed not the slightest fear of the cats—and surprised that Satin and Velvet had permitted her such familiarity on first meeting. The cats were rarely so hospitable.

"What are their names?" Maria asked. Silvas told her, indicating which was which. Then, reluctantly, Maria stood and turned to the wizard again. "I knew this place would be full of wonders. Are there more?"

"No more cats," Silvas said. "Satin and Velvet are the only ones of their sort, and they will not tolerate lesser felines."

"I can hardly wait to see what other wonders you have," Maria said, an unmistakable prompt.

Silvas told Maria a little about the Seven Towers as he guided her into the great hall. There were a number of servants about, but again they were all normal humans.

"What strange benches," Maria said, crossing to one of the tables that served Bosc's people. "How could anyone sit like that?"

"Different people have different ways." Silvas was surprised that she had spotted the benches so quickly. "I have no objection to accommodating other ways." *She has a quick mind,* Silvas thought, giving her grudging credit for that.

"There is someone you should meet," he said as he led Maria up the main stairs to the apartments above the great hall. And Carillia was there, in the larger of their sitting rooms, not the one next to their bedchamber.

"Carillia, my love, this is Maria, the daughter of Sir Eustace." After the two said their greetings to each other, Silvas took Carillia's hand for a moment.

"Maria would like to see all the wonders of the Glade, my love, and I must get back to oversee the rain in Mecq. If you would be so kind?"

"Of course, my heart," Carillia said. Her smile threatened to explode into laughter, but she fought to control it, knowing that Silvas would see her struggle.

"My duty does call," Silvas said with a bow to Maria. "Besides, Carillia can give you a much better tour than I could."

And then he made his exit as quickly as he could. *Maybe now that she knows that I already have a lady, she will turn her fantasies elsewhere,* Silvas thought. Hoped.

13

The rain continued through twilight. In Mecq's valley the shower remained light, giving the water a chance to soak into the fields. Upstream and down, the rain was heavier, accompanied by the sound and light show of thunder and lightning. The Eyler rose slowly as the storm runoff raced through the valley. The simple layer of rocks that the villagers had spanned the river with could hold back only a fraction of that water. Most ran over the top of the makeshift dam and on into Blethye. Even at the height of the spate, the water didn't reach the bottom of the mill's wheel. The oxen continued to tread their circle until they were unhitched for the evening.

Silvas remained in the village until dusk was thick and most of the villagers had retired to their cottages for supper and sleep. The thrill of rain had brought a new kind of exhaustion to them, the exhaustion of celebration. *It is still premature,* Silvas thought, but he wore a smile and said nothing to dampen spirits that had been so quickly raised by a thorough dampening. A number of people came up to Silvas to thank him, or to wish him a good evening, people who had not chosen to take any previous notice of his presence.

The wizard bore no grudges. *It is enough,* he told himself. He never claimed rights on the mere basis of his announcement of his craft. He did not demand that anyone take him on his word alone. In each town or village he had to prove himself again. *That is as it should be* was his long-held belief.

Maria had emerged from the pillar of smoke to ride back to her father's castle well before dusk. She had not come toward Silvas, and he had made sure that he was with a number of villagers as she came through after her tour of the Glade, hoping that company would discourage her.

"This is the best rainfall we've had in some three years," Master Ian said as he prepared to return to his inn.

"It's only the beginning," Silvas told him. "One good rain can't cure years of drought."

"A good beginning," Master Ian allowed, holding out both hands to the rain. "A right good beginning, Lord Wizard."

Silvas nodded politely and Master Ian went off. A few minutes later, Brother Paul emerged from St. Katrinka's and crossed to the river, seeking out the wizard.

"You have won new friends here today," the friar said.

"Which I may lose as quickly," Silvas replied quietly. "This is not all there must be."

"You sound particularly concerned." The friar's eyes narrowed to get a better view of the wizard in the growing dark.

"In part, this rain is a challenge to the power that has held Mecq in its grip so long." Silvas's voice was a mere whisper that no one but the friar could hear. "It may draw a response."

"From the Blue Rose?" Brother Paul asked just as softly.

Silvas nodded almost imperceptibly. "You might be on especial guard this night, Vicar," he said. "I shall."

"I will take your advice," Brother Paul said, his voice showing the trouble he felt in the wizard's words. "Have you any idea what form this response may take?"

"No. I may be better able to judge what remains to be done when it comes, though. It may give me a better gauge of the Foe's strength here."

"It seems a dangerous ploy," the vicar said.

"But necessary. I can't know what I need to offer for the long-term cure of Mecq's ills until I know what power it needs to hold against."

"I will pray for you," Brother Paul said.

"Thank you, Vicar," Silvas said. "We all need our prayers now."

As he walked back to his church, Brother Paul shook his head softly, almost without volition. His command of the craft of power was small, but he could feel the wiz-

ard's troubled soul quite clearly. Silvas might be a
wizard-potent, be he was not without his grave concerns.

Nearly all of the villagers had gone indoors to belated
suppers before Silvas headed back to the Glade. The
ground was soft underfoot. There were small patches of
mud, even a few standing puddles. *A good beginning,* Silvas told himself. *But it is nothing more, and if the price
is too heavy* ... He shook his head, much as the vicar
had, though he hadn't noticed that gesture.

Since sky was still clear over the Seven Towers, dark
hadn't settled as quickly over Silvas's home. Still it was
too late for any greeting from the birds. They would have
settled into their nests before the sun touched the western
horizon, and they would remain there until they sensed
the imminent return of the sun in the morning.

Lights made the great hall bright. There were fires in
both hearths, torches around the walls, candles above the
tables. The people of the Seven Towers were beginning to
gather for supper, and the mood was as warm as the
room. Silvas paused at the entrance just long enough to
see that Carillia hadn't come down for the meal yet, then
hurried upstairs to change into dry clothes.

"I knew you would need these, my heart," Carillia said
when he reached their bedroom. Fresh clothing had been
laid out on the bed. There was even a large, rough towel
for him to dry himself with, and a mug of mulled wine to
warm his insides.

"The people of Mecq are happy tonight, are they not?"
Carillia asked after Silvas showed his appreciation with a
kiss.

"For the moment," he allowed. "They have rain. Some
who have been ill are well. For the moment it is enough."
The shadow that came and went over his thoughts was
not apprehension but, in a way, envy. "It takes so little,"
he whispered.

"They *are* simple folk of the land," Carillia replied.
His whisper hadn't been so soft that she could not hear it.
"A simple life, both in pleasure and in fear." There was
no condescension in her voice. Carillia felt more comfortable around *simple folk of the land* than she did around
courtiers.

Silvas hurried through his change of clothing, and the two of them went down to dinner.

The mood in the great hall was much lighter than it had been the evening before. Before long Silvas felt even his own spirits rising. The folk of the Seven Towers knew that trouble might be near, but that didn't stop them from enjoying the moments that came before.

"Can ye tell us more about the evil that comes?" Braf Goleg, the leader of the lupine warriors, asked Silvas. Braf came to the wizard's table and touched a hand to his brow in salute. The hand was neither human nor truly lupine in appearance, three relatively short digits set at angles that turned the hand into a powerful grasping tool.

"Not yet, Braf," Silvas said, laying his utensils on his plate. "I can't see its form or when it will come." He shrugged. "I don't even guarantee that it *will* come, though I feel certain that it will."

"Or here or there?" Braf asked. His voice, though growling to human norms, was in the polite registers of his kind, and Silvas knew that.

"Or here or there, or both places," Silvas agreed. "Your men are eager?"

"Aye, lord. They have been too long idle."

Silvas smiled at the understatement. The Seven Towers rarely had need of such fierce soldiers. On only three occasions during Silvas's long tenure had they found their talents for fighting actually needed, and never in the lifetimes of any of the current soldiers.

"The time *is* coming, Braf, the time we've all trained against."

There were routines to Silvas's life. Every evening before retiring, there were magical chores that needed doing, and not just when he expected trouble. His mind touched on the normal defenses of the Seven Towers, strengthening or renewing where necessary, inspecting always. The daily routines did not take a lot of time, and they required no special preparations. The Glade had been under these safeguards constantly since Auroreus first raised the walls. They were strong and well tested.

Silvas spent more time than usual at his maintenance this evening.

"We are as prepared as we can be," he told Carillia when he finally joined her in bed.

"You are taking no chances, are you, my heart?" she said as she gathered him into her arms. Without speaking of it, both knew that this would not be a night for passion, merely for sharing strength of their spirits and bodies, holding each other until sleep came.

"I dare take no chances," he told her. "I must offer you all of the protection I can."

She laughed softly. "Not to mention all the others who depend on you, my heart."

Not to mention, he thought—and he did not mention them.

There were a few moments of soft movement between them as they adjusted into more comfortable positions. Silvas went through the disciplined routines of clearing his mind of unnecessary clutter so sleep could come quickly. As the warmth of approaching sleep flowed, Silvas felt familiar sensations of Carillia and him melding together into a greater whole. The feelings were almost those of a dream—but not quite. Where their bodies touched, they seemed to fuse. The warmth became a cocoon that encompassed both, drawing them even closer together, uniting them in a way that their waking bodies could only poorly imitate. Their minds seemed to flow through each other on some primitive level of sensation. They shared no thoughts, but they did seem to share of each other's souls at a time like this. When the union came, it could last through an entire night, holding Silvas's mind, flooding him with a rest that was much better than sleep, strengthening him, rejuvenating him. *I could live on this and never touch food or slide into sleep,* he would tell himself while he floated in the heaven of this spiritual cradle.

It did not come every night.

And they never spoke of it. Silvas believed that Carillia shared the experience, though she had never mentioned it, and he had never asked. *To talk about it openly might ruin it,* Silvas told himself whenever the experience came. He was satisfied to revel in it when the opportunity arose, and to remember it at other times when he needed the reassurance of that deep warmth.

When it came.
While it lasted.

Silvas and Carillia walked together in the shade of flowering trees, enjoying the alternation of warmth and coolness as they went from shade to spring sun and back again. They walked arm in arm, holding hands and leaning against each other. Silvas recognized that they were in some sort of ordered orchard, not in a wild stretch of woods. These trees had been carefully tended by loving hands. The grass had been cleared from around the base of each trunk, leaving a circle of bare soil and chips of bark. That puzzled Silvas, for the short time he bothered to think about it, because he could not recall seeing that kind of detail to any orchard before. But there was too much to absorb his attention for him to pay any great concern to this. There were the fresh scents of spring, a melange of aromas to tickle his senses. And there was Carillia at his side. Wherever they touched, the feeling was that of skin on skin, though they were both dressed. Clothing simply did not affect the sense of touch between them.

Neither spoke. They merely walked. At times Carillia drew Silvas's attention to some sight—a tiny brook meandering past one side of the orchard, small clearings arranged as formal gardens, a doe and her fawn bounding off in the distance. She did all of this without words, and in the same way Silvas occasionally pointed out other sights to her—the patterns in leaves and flowers, a new scent coming in on the zephyr that lightly swirled around them.

And demons rode the night again.

Silvas exploded out of sleep, jumping from bed before his mind had fully returned from its nocturnal walk with Carillia. The frenzy of his movements was almost impossible for any eye to follow. He raced through a spell of protection and delay while he pulled on his robe and knife belt. He grabbed his quarterstaff as he ran out the door. He didn't waste time to see how Carillia or the cats were reacting. They *would* react. They would *know* that attack was coming and respond. This summons was so ur-

gent that the cats didn't growl or scream. Carillia asked
no questions. They all followed Silvas from the room.

The Seven Towers shook at the sudden onslaught of
foes that Silvas could not yet grasp. Going up the first set
of circular stairs, the trembling of the keep became so violent that Silvas missed a step and pitched headfirst. Only
his quick reflexes managed to get hands and arms out to
break his fall. He was back on his feet as quickly as one
of his cats, though, continuing to race for the pentagram
in his workshop.

Silvas spoke words of power. The air around him
crackled with magic, and not just his. Lightning seemed
to flash within the keep. The second set of steps, the iron
stairs, danced with light that prickled against the skin,
drawing sparks—and drawing protests from Satin and
Velvet each time their paws came down on metal treads.
Silvas had no time to spare for calming them. The assault
was already within the Glade.

"Eyru, reygu mavith. Eyru, sprath tourn." Silvas
shouted the spell, loading his voice with urgency. The
walls took on their familiar glow, but it wasn't even this
time. The competing magic cause it to ebb and flow.
"Dar, korbeth mavith. Dar, sprath tourn." He added the
intensifiers and watched the luminescence even out.

Carillia and the cats took their normal places in the circles at the side of the room, but the lines of the pentagram were already fully aglow with power, so Silvas had
to speak a spell of passage to get to the center. Then he
had to waste time testing the space for any lurking enemy. That the pentagram had been activated before he entered was cause enough to require that caution. To be
trapped with an invisible enemy within the pentagram
might prove fatal.

Silvas moved on to chants of power and defense.
Though the Seven Towers trembled at the assault, they
remained standing. The walls provided their protection.
Silvas chanted and he seemed to grow, to expand, over-
flowing the pentagram, even the workshop. Colors reversed. The glow turned dark, and that which was dark
glowed light, casting everything into reverse—the better
to see the demons that must be attacking. Before many
seconds had passed, Silvas seemed to tower over the

Seven Towers, with the castle nestled between his feet, a
child's toy being protected from harm.

The stars were black points against a silvery night sky.
The earth was covered with muted colors, red greenery
against the black of water and the pale yellow of bare
dirt. The walls of the Glade were a muddy red.

Against all that, the forms of the attacking demons
were a brilliant, crackling bright blue. Squadrons of outlined forms circled the Seven Towers and the enlarged
form of Silvas. Darts of crimson shot from black bows.
On the walls of the Glade, Silvas's lupine warriors fought
back as best they could, wielding silver blades that had
been touched by their master's magic. Dark against the
earth, Silvas saw reflections of other warriors moving toward the walls. These warriors themselves were invisible
in this obscure light.

Silvas called on his Unseen Lord. He spoke the words
of defense and brought in the lightning.

The Earth continued to shake.

Silvas spoke more words of power and caused the wind
to turn in circles around the walls of the Seven Towers,
bringing a chop to the water of the moat, bending trees
and grass around it as the wind increased and funneled in
on itself, tighter and tighter, creating a wall as impenetra-
ble as the stone and mortar of the physical walls. The cy-
clonic barrier became a mirror, brilliant in clarity. Silvas
saw his image repeated a thousand times, bent forward
into distortion.

And he saw more.

The storm engulfed Mecq and its valley. The sky was
crisscrossed with lightning. Thunder rumbled continuously. More than one bolt of lightning touched the roof of
a cottage. Only the rain that had continued since the previous afternoon prevented a score of destructive fires.
Some of the soaked thatch smoked for a few minutes, but
none of it was dry enough to sustain fire.

Brother Paul stood before the altar at St. Katrinka's.
The candles lit at either side were scarcely needed in the
repeated toss of lightning. The vicar was deep in his
prayers and in the minor incantations that his station permitted. The friar prayed and chanted. Then he turned and

walked the length of his church to stand in the doorway. There he was not completely protected from the driving rain that had replaced the calmer shower left by the wizard.

It is come to us now, Brother Paul thought. His left hand clutched the crucifix hanging from his neck. His right hand drew the sign of the cross against the storm. Staring into the rain, the friar caught glimpses of the demons riding the night, but his power was not great enough to hold the visions or to see the demons in their full fury. But he knew that they were out there, and his voice found the chants and prayers against them.

Brother Paul could hear the laughter of the demons mocking him. He called on the power of the White Brotherhood, and he felt extra strength flowing into him as he repeated his spells of protection. The laughter of the demons continued, but it was softer, almost sounding more distant.

Old Maga crouched in terror against the cold hearth of her cottage. Unlike some villagers, she didn't keep even a small fire going through the night, except during the coldest nights of winter. Getting wood to fuel a constant fire was more trouble than going next door to get a flaming brand to rekindle her fire every morning.

"This comes from the stranger," Maga mumbled over and over. The terrors of Hell seemed ready to consume her, but she could do nothing but crouch against the stone of her fireplace, waiting for the end to come. The wind rose in strength and volume. The ground shook under her. It seemed certain that the entire village would be consumed by the devil fires lancing the night. The smell of Hell was in the air, the nose-curdling odor of brimstone.

"Saints protect us!" Maga shouted into the storm, but the only answer was a vague sound of laughter on the wind—followed by the growing shriek of banshees screaming for the dead.

There was an even greater terror that Maga could find no words for. After a lifetime of going faithfully to church, of listening to Brother Paul, and to Brother Ezra who had the parish before him, and Brother Alfred before that, Old Maga *knew* that this was a night when souls would be lost. The demons and the banshees who came to oversee their work would carry off both lives and souls.

The mill's wheel began to turn. The river was not yet high enough to flow over the wheel, but it had finally reached the bottom, making it creak noisily as it came back to life after idle ages. Metal fittings screamed in protest as they stripped themselves of surface rust. Wood groaned as if it would split. The millstones inside started to turn, though there was no grain between them.

Next to the mill, the Eyler was a muddy torrent for one of the few times in a generation, frothing and racing past the village, pulling dirt from the banks and carrying it downstream. Some came to rest against the new stones that the villagers had placed across the river. More flowed across that insignificant barrier toward the gap between the twin mountains that bracketed it.

The rain flattened much of the grain in the fields. Most would survive, perhaps, but the storm was a further outrage against crops that had already faced much just to get this far.

Silvas suddenly found himself back within his body, shaking with the force of his magics. He blinked twice, then spoke a spell of passage so he could leave the pentagram safely. "Stay where you are," he said, including Carillia and the cats in the command as he raced from the room.

He climbed to the narrow turret that let him look down on Mecq. The sight he saw now was basically the same as he had seen through the vision of his magic. The village was being assailed by the storm. If anything, it was more violent that Silvas had thought. Demons rode the ridge of Mr. Balq and circled the peak of Mt. Mecq. More rode the surge of the Eyler. Silvas could hear their laughter, and he could also hear the crying of the banshees waiting to collect their due.

"Not yet," Silvas muttered under his breath. He turned and ran back down the stairs, through his conjuring chamber and library, heading for the curtain wall that surrounded the Seven Towers.

"It's come for fair, it has," Braf Goleg shouted when

Silvas climbed to the parapets. The soldier had a gleam in his eye that told the wizard that his lupine commander had already found some targets for his weapons.

"How has it been?" Silvas asked. He too had to shout to be heard over the fury of the storm.

"Some few demon riders have come over the wall," Braf said. "None has survived the passage. They burn and smoke when the silver rips them."

Silvas nodded.

"Have any said anything you could understand?"

"Nay, lord." Braf shook his head violently. "They do naught but scream their fury and pain. I think we are more than they expected."

"That could be, Braf, but don't get overconfident. They may learn that you're not so different as you look."

"Here they come again," one of Braf's warriors shouted. He pointed. Silvas turned to follow the direction.

Ghostly riders showed no substance but only the brilliant blue outlines of their form. There was nothing but the night between the lines. The rain was there, and the forest of the Glade's valley. The demons rode demon steeds, charging through the air, caring not where the ground was or what they rode over in their mad assault.

"Give me space," Silvas said. Braf and the other nearby warriors moved aside, clearing an area that would give Silvas room to swing his staff at full reach if he chose to.

"Eyru, delvi, kepthi, dar." Silvas spoke each word separately, encased in its own web of power. He flung them at the five riders who approached in a tight wedge formation. The words forced some separation among the demons. Silvas adjusted his grip on his quarterstaff, dipping first one ferrule and then the other to scrape against the stone of the wall in front of him.

"Kabri, estu delvu restith," Silvas said, and the forms of the demons started to show some semblance of substance. A pale light filled in the empty spaces of their forms.

"There are your targets, lads," the wizard yelled. Silver-tipped arrows leaped from bone bows. When the arrows struck demon form, there were sparks, moments of intense white fire, longer moments of soul-stealing screams. Three demon riders erupted in the blinding flames of their kind. Their steeds—not horses, not animals of any known kind—shared their fate. But the remaining demons came on, aiming with certainty at Silvas and the aura of power that surrounded him.

Silvas swung his quarterstaff. The silver ferrule connected with the steed of the lead rider. The beast exploded in a white flare, but its rider leaped clear . . . and the quarterstaff went sailing back over Silvas's head into the courtyard of the Seven Towers.

The wizard barely had time to draw his dagger before he was knocked to the parapet by the force of the leaping demon. He was scarcely aware of Braf engaging the other. Silvas was aware of little more than the grinning death's head pressing down against his face and the smell of sulferous breath coming from the demon's empty form. Silvas's wrists seemed clamped, as if by vises. The demon, for all his emptiness, had physical power at this juncture. He had the weight of hell behind him, trying to crush the wizard through the stone and into the ground. The demon's empty skull gaped wide and long, pointed teeth sought to bite away the wizard's soul.

Silvas twisted, calling for the help of his master. With his shoulders pressed against the stone, he found some leverage and started to bring the dagger up. The blade showed the same bright luminescence as the demons, but white rather than blue. The demon shifted his grip, concentrating on the hand that held the dagger. That gave Silvas a chance to roll to the side—enough to get the incredible weight of the demon off of him.

They became tangled. Silvas seemed to get a foot through the demon's middle, where its stomach would have been—if it had had a stomach. The wizard got up on one knee, and the knee would have pressed against the demon's heart—if it had had a heart. And suddenly their positions were reversed. Silvas was on top, pressing down against the tremendous power of the sketchy form. The point of his knife aimed for a target just above the center of the gaping mouth.

The blade cut through the blue lines that marked the demon's face. A flood of putrid smells erupted, almost drowning the screams of the wounded demon. The bright white flare of the fire that consumed the demon blinded the wizard for a moment. He staggered to his feet, reeling from the pain of the intense fire. His arms stretched out, seeking the security of the wall. His feet slid cautiously along the deck, worried that he might step off the parapet to plunge to the courtyard so far below.

"Here, lord, I have you," Braf said, and then the wizard felt the steel grip of his warrior. "This way, lord. 'Tis over for the moment."

"I'll be all right, Braf," Silvas said as some hint of vision returned. There were still bright spots sparkling before his eyes, but he could make out Braf's form. The pain of burning disappeared as quickly as the ethereal fire that had produced it. "A moment. The last of them?"

"I had him for supper, lord," Braf said, cackling. "Though 'twas a close thing who would eat who."

"You are wounded," Silvas observed.

"Aye, but it hurts not yet," Braf replied, glancing at his shoulder.

Silvas put his hands on the shoulder and spoke the words of healing. The wound was deep and poisoned. It was not a simple matter to exorcise this one. It needed time, concentration. There was still work to be done elsewhere. Silvas felt the call, the need. But he took the minutes that Braf's wound demanded.

"There, that has it," he said at last. "And now I must hurry."

"Geffer has your staff, lord," Braf said, pointing into the courtyard. Silvas had to focus closely to see the soldier below holding the staff, starting for the stairs with it.

Silvas met him halfway.

Henry Fitz-Matthew was almost paralyzed by terror—and even more frightened of showing his fear. His fighting days were far in his past, and he had never faced anything like this even then. He was on the battlements of his master's keep, and Sir Eustace was there with him. Eustace was screaming his rage at the storm, waving a sword that had seen no action in too many years. The knight cared not for the lightning that was pummeling the mountain. None struck him or the blade he flaunted against it. Sir Eustace looked down at his few men-at-arms on the walls. They were as helpless as he was. There was no enemy they could strike. Sir Eustace couldn't see the demons riding the ridge or circling the peak. His spirit was not tuned finely enough for that.

But he did feel the evil.

"That wizard brought this on us," Sir Eustace shouted. It wasn't the first time he had made that accusation since the storm roused him from sleep, since he felt the thrill of danger close and charged up to face whatever was coming. The knight looked down at the Eyler. The lightning came so frequently that he had no trouble at all seeing how high the river was getting. And he could cross to the side of his tower and look down at the village and fields. Puffs of smoke now and then showed where lightning continued to strike the thatched roofs that still refused to burn. In the fields, water stood around battered stalks of grain.

"That wizard brought this on us."

Brother Paul remained standing in the doorway of St. Katrinka's. He held his crucifix out in his hand. Both arms were raised against the storm. He stood in supplication and defiance, mouthing what spells he could command, trying to bend the storm around the village, trying to interpose himself between his flock and the ravages of demons and nature. His voice was hoarse from shouting his prayers and spells into the storm. He could see no result, though he took heart every time a puff of smoke from a roof died away without blazing into fire.

Then two bolts of lightning hit the same roof simultaneously, and the roof erupted in dirty orange and red flames. The wood of the walls, and whatever was within the cottage, flamed almost instantly. Brother Paul ran toward the cottage, but no one came out and by the time he arrived, the entire house was engulfed by flames. In less time than he needed to utter a prayer and make the sign of the cross, the home was gone and the fire had leaped to its nearest neighbor.

Brother Paul ran to the next house, screaming a warning. The family ran out into the rain, terror on all their faces as the house fell to the blaze.

But when the second house had been consumed, the

fire went out. No other cottage stood near enough to catch in the driving rain.

"Come back to the church with me," Brother Paul told the family that had survived. "Come out of the storm."

Carillia and the cats had obeyed Silvas's instructions to remain in their guarded circles in the conjuring chamber. When Silvas returned, he said merely, "It continues," before he cleared a passage back into his pentagram. There he moved straight into another series of incantations, trying to fight the assaults on Mecq and on the Seven Towers. He felt the power of his Unseen Lord flowing through him, but the flow remained sluggish, opposed by whatever forces the Blue Rose had mustered. The glow of the walls pulsed, dimming, then brightening again in tune to some greater tide that the wizard could not completely grasp. The wind he had cast around the Glade was reflected within his workshop, twisting around the circumference of the pentagram. He couldn't extend the device to cover the village of Mecq, not without dropping his efforts to defend the Seven Towers—and without those defenses he would not long be able to defend outsiders in any case.

The light pulsed in the conjuring chamber, and it began to pulse within the wizard's head.

Then the light disappeared completely.

It was an instantaneous transition. The light blinked out and then returned, brighter and clearer than before. But Silvas was no longer within his workshop. He was no place he had ever been before.

He needed a moment to gather his thoughts and look around. The terrain was etched with incredible sharpness, everything defined and delineated with an uncanny precision. The sky was a perfect blue, unblemished by any cloud. The sun was a point of perfect orange brilliance. The grass, trees, even the rocks and dirt, all seemed to be painted with a perfect touch.

The plane of ideals, Silvas thought, *the land of the gods.* He could see no reason for him to be suddenly transported there. *It can't be defeat,* he reasoned.

The he saw the armies. The battle of light and dark was joined even on this plane. Heroic figures in plate armor of mirror-like brilliance stood against figures draped in armor so black that it seemed to soak up any hint of light. Swords flashed in blinding strokes. The wounds were clean and lethal. Death came quickly, in glory, even though Silvas recognized that *this* death was more than the simple death of the body. It was a destruction of the soul as well.

"Lord, why have you brought me here?" Silvas asked. His telesight forced him to watch the battle whether he wanted to or not. His vision focused first on one duel and then another, and then he would be given an overall view of the ranks of knights and demons fighting.

Behind those ranks, even more impressive figures commanded the action.

Silvas dropped his quarterstaff and fell to his knees. "I am in the presence of the gods!" The wizard felt an awe that was alien to him. One of the figures behind the lines of bright armor looked his way. Silvas could see nothing of the being behind the armor, but he felt that it was his Unseen Lord. Silvas was drawn to his feet, commanded to watch. The godly figure raised a hand to his face and tilted back the visor of his helmet.

"My Lord, why have you brought me here?" Silvas's voice was a small thing that seemed to have no place on this plain—on this plane.

The distant figure raised his hand and pointed it across the field, toward Silvas's right. Silvas turned and looked. *Why didn't I notice that before?* he asked himself. The ideal plane came to an abrupt end. Beyond it was a desolate wasteland, a desert so complete that it made the valley of Mecq look like Eden. *Now* the dark army was lined up within the desolation, facing the army of shining armor out on the ideal plane.

And—somewhat apart, like Silvas—there was another lone figure. He too was staring at the field of battle. His eyes came to light on Silvas. Their eyes met, their heads nodded.

Silvas needed no further clue. This was his enemy, the foe he must beat to win his own battle over Mecq. The gods and their hordes of shining and dark knights charged toward one another. Silvas's lone opponent charged toward him. Silvas picked up his quarterstaff and moved to meet him.

Silvas chanted for the lightning and it came, but it didn't strike the other figure. Silvas's foe lifted his own staff, and the lightning was shunted aside, bounced back toward Silvas, who met the blast and grounded it harmlessly. A wind grew around Silvas, but it was not his doing.

I have met the Blue Rose wizard, Silvas thought as he worked to unwind the corkscrew wind. He ran forward, crossing the border into the desolation to meet his enemy. Silvas's magic picked up stones and hurled them. He raised eddies of dust and cast them toward the other wizard's eyes. At the same time Silvas had to meet the magical challenges thrown back at him.

The two wizards closed on each other. Silvas swung his quarterstaff, aiming the silver ferrule for one of the metal caps on the other's stick. Miniature bolts of lightning sprung from the contact. The Blue Rose wizard pressed Silvas's staff to the side and whirled his own, trying to hit the juncture of neck and shoulder with a disabling blow. Silvas turned sideways and threw his weight against the other wizard, then spun completely around while he slid both hands toward the silver end of his staff for a mighty swing at the other's head.

The contest went on for a time that may have marked ages in the mortal world. Silvas was hard put to hold his own. There seemed to be little chance of decisive victory. Victory would come only if one wizard made a mortal error, and neither seemed likely to do that.

Very rarely Silvas caught a glimpse of the greater battle being fought by the gods and knights in their anonymous armor, but there too it was hard to see any decision being approached. Warriors died on both sides. Silvas couldn't tell who they were—or even *what* they were. After a few minutes of combat Silvas couldn't even have picked out the figure who had commanded his entry.

Silvas tried to sweep the legs out from under his opponent. The other wizard jumped over Silvas's quarterstaff and returned his own blows, first high, then low. Throughout the encounter not one word was spoken. Neither wizard even grunted with the effort.

It has to end sometime, Silvas thought. He had nearly exhausted his store of tactics with the quarterstaff. Even after ages of practice, there were only so many things a man could do with a wrist-thick, seven-foot-long piece of wood. And the other wizard seemed to know how to meet each of them, and which counterstrokes would be hardest to meet.

The two wizards moved in until they were almost toe to toe, swinging their quarterstaves between them in minimal space. Silvas felt the other staff scrape his knuckles. His right hand stung and went numb. Afraid he might lose his grip completely, Silvas butted his head against his foe.

It wasn't that *hard,* Silvas thought, but the darkness took him anyway.

14

I am still alive was an expression of surprise, not a boast. Silvas felt the smooth chill of the marble floor against his cheek. He felt air pumping within him. He felt pain. He felt stunned, dazed. Mostly he felt drained, as if much of the life force had simply been sucked out of him by some unnoticed demon. He lay as he was for long moments, unable even to open his eyes, too spent to think the words of magic that would speed his recovery.

Old memories were the least demanding of thoughts. They floated in and out of his daze of their own volition, cradling Silvas's mind and body in their flattering veils. For a time Silvas saw himself as the child he had been when he first came to the Seven Towers. He came up against that blank wall within his mind. He didn't remember any time *before* the Glade. As far as Silvas could tell from his memories, he might have been *created* within these walls, a brand new, almost seven-year-old boy with no past and a future already determined.

"Where did I come from, Auroreus?"

The old wizard had chuckled. "You came from your parents, as any child does."

"But where? *Where was I before I came here?"*

Auroreus had never answered those questions, even after Silvas grew to manhood and survived his initiation into the Greater Mysteries of the trimagister.

"You must find those answers for yourself, if you truly want them," Auroreus had said. *"What I* will *tell you is that you do not want to know them."*

"I do *want to know, Auroreus. Why will you not tell me?"*

"I cannot answer the one without answering the other, my son."

Newer memories came with a trifle more weight, floating like waterlogged rafts, bumping and turning, grinding their way past Silvas's attention. He recalled his vision of insanity, of a crazy world or time where people sped by enclosed in shiny wagons of metal and glass, vehicles that went faster than horses could travel, vehicles that had no beasts to pull them.

"This is the world to which you were born. This is the time and place where Auroreus found you and drew you back to his castle. He scoured all of time for his successor. This is far, far in your future . . . if that future ever comes. If you fail, people will not say, 'It would have been better if he had never been born.' If you fail, you will never have been born . . . and then you could not fail, and the world that comes, if it comes, will be the world as it would have been had you never lived."

The words came back to Silvas as clearly as if they were being spoken again. He held fleeting images of the place of insanity he had seen.

"In similar circumstances." That came out almost spoken. Silvas recognized the return of the first glimmerings of strength. He forced himself to take a deep breath, aware of the movement of his chest as he did.

Carillia. The Seven Towers. Mecq.

Silvas dragged his eyes open, but he was careful not to attempt to move anything else. He was in the center of his pentagram, and magic still flowed from the crystal. His face was scant inches from one of the interior lines. There was not the burning pain that had followed his battle with the two demons within this room. There was pain, but more the agony of total depletion, of exhaustion. Silvas mumbled the words of a restorative spell and waited for the warmth to spread through his body.

His hands were at his sides. He looked at as much of the crystal line near his face as he could without moving. Once he was certain that he knew his position with sufficient precision, Silvas started to inch carefully away from the nearest line, drawing his arms and legs in.

After a moment he got his head up enough to look around. Carillia and the cats were still within their protective circles. But the light in the room was wrong. Silvas needed long seconds to realize that what was *wrong* was the time. Full daylight streamed in the window.

"Has it been so long?" Silvas didn't realize that he had spoken the question aloud until Carillia answered.

"It is near mid-morning, my heart." Her voice sounded tiny and distant with fear, and likely with her own exhaustion. "I could see that you were alive. The power did not free us this time."

Silvas took a deeper breath and spoke the words of release. The crystal of the pentagram and of the circles faded. The faint buzzing that accompanied them died away. Carillia hurried across the room to Silvas. She knelt at his side and put her arms around him.

"How stand the Seven Towers?" Silvas asked.

"They stand," Carillia said. "Braf and Bosc have both been to report."

"And?" Silvas asked as he let strength flow back into him. As always, the flow seemed faster when Carillia held him.

"There have been deaths and minor damage to the southwest tower and the wall near it."

"How many died?"

"Braf lost three soldiers, and Koshka's uncle died as well, though perhaps not directly from the attack. He was an ancient of his kind."

"Who should have had leave to grow more ancient yet," Silvas grumbled, feeling the pain of the losses. He forced himself to his feet, then swayed with a giddiness that almost forced him back to his knees before Carillia's touch steadied him. "There is work yet to do." He directed that at himself as he sought to draw in all of the replenishment that his magic could summon.

"Anything of Mecq?" he asked. "They suffered this assault as well."

"I could not look myself," Carillia reminded him. "But Braf said that there appeared to be some damage, a couple of cots burned to the ground, a smell of mourning to the air."

"They will blame me," Silvas said. "Have there been no calls yet from the village?"

"I've heard the voices of the friar and the man from the castle who was here before."

"Master Fitz-Matthew," Silvas said sourly. "Do they remain?"

"I've not heard them for a while. I will check if you feel stronger now, my heart."

Silvas managed a smile. "It improves, my love." His voice remained rougher than it usually was when he spoke to her, but the roughest edges were beginning to fade. "I hope there are not so many nights and mornings like this before we make an end in this place. It wears mightily on my bones."

"You *are* feeling better, my heart." Silvas could plainly read the relief in her voice and in the smile that finally came to her lips.

"It seems I have at least one more fight left in me, my love," he said. "Now, if you would, Mecq?"

"Of course." Carillia left the pentagram and hurried up to the turret that looked out on the village.

"Both men remain outside," she reported when she returned. "The friar paces with such patience as he can muster. The other stares up at the smoke and curses under his breath."

Silvas experimented with movement. He started by clenching and unclenching his fists. He flexed his arms, squatted and bent over, straightened up again. Movement that was too rapid brought dizziness, but as long as he was cautious, he could move freely. He was outside the pentagram when Carillia returned. Satin and Velvet sat near him, watching, still uneasy, still nervous.

"I need to see to our people," Silvas said, speaking as much to himself as to Carillia. "But I suppose I need to hear out Fitz-Matthew and Brother Paul first. They have concerns of their village and masters to deal with." The sigh did not quite escape his lips.

"Koshka will be back in a moment with nourishment," Carillia said. "You must take a bite before you attempt too much."

Silvas hesitated for only an instant before he nodded. He did need food, and a little wine, to hold him until he could sit down to something more substantial.

"Will he find us in the library?" Silvas asked, putting a smile on his face.

"Since he must pass through the library to reach this

room?" Carillia asked, her voice lightening at the sign of his improvement.

"Do I have time to dress before?" Silvas asked.

"Of course, my heart." Carillia took his arm and they left the conjuring chamber together.

Braf came to the library with Koshka, and his report included the names of the dead as well as details on how they had died. He also had wounded soldiers to mention. "None so bad as to need serious help," he assured the wizard.

"I'll stop by to treat them anyway," Silvas said, and Braf's face relaxed a little.

Silvas hurried through the selection of cheese and fruit that Koshka had brought, and listened to Koshka's recitation of how the domestic staff had come through the fight. Silvas was amazed at his hunger and thirst. In just a few minutes he cleared the tray of food and downed two large goblets of wine. Carillia only nibbled and sipped. "I'll have more while you listen to our guests outside," she told Silvas.

"And now I guess I must face them," he said, getting up from his chair with only slight difficulty. His joints seemed stiff, the way Auroreus's joints had stiffened up whenever the weather turned cold and damp. He stretched and twisted a couple of times and then headed out.

His healing work in the soldier's barracks took only a couple of minutes, but Silvas's mood didn't lighten.

It is still too much, too soon, he thought as he crossed back through the great hall. *I am pressed nearly to the limit and there's no end in sight to this confrontation. I need time to think through all that has happened, all I have been shown.* There were magics he could invoke to help him recall every detail of his mystic experiences, the visions—or whatever they truly were. *The answer must lie in them somehow. If I could only find the time to search..*

The sun was bright in a clear sky over the Seven Towers. It seemed impossible that a morning so light could follow a night as dark as the one just ended. Silvas stood in the doorway of the keep and blinked several times at the light before he started across the courtyard. Bay came out from around the corner of the tower, saddled and harnessed. Bosc ran at his side.

"How did you fare?" Silvas asked when they met halfway to the gate.

"Better than you, it appears," Bay replied. "No demons reached the mews this time."

"There was only the terror down the row," Bosc added. *Down the row:* he was talking about the other horses in the stable.

"And you, Bosc?" Silvas asked.

"I had no chance to fight this time," the groom said.

Silvas nodded and turned his attention to Bay again. "We have visitors outside."

"I know. And you were just going to walk out and join them."

"Of course."

"I doubt you could walk as far as the Boar and Bear, the shape you're in," Bay said. "That is why I am here."

"I did not foresee any great need to walk far," Silvas said.

"That obnoxious servant from the castle will undoubtedly have other ideas, and even Brother Paul may have work for you," Bay said. "You appear too weak to get through much," He snorted. "Besides, my presence may have a calming influence."

Silvas smiled. "Intimidating, you mean. Very well. We shall ride, then." He went to Bay's side and mounted. Bosc stood by in case his help was needed, but Silvas managed on his own.

"Sitting *is* easier than standing," Silvas conceded.

The wizard didn't bother to take Bay's reins. He was content to sit and relax, surprised at how much the walk down from the library had taxed his strength. Bay walked slowly through the smoke onto the village green of Mecq. The sky over Mecq remained overcast, though the rain was long over. There was actually some hint of green to the village green now, though still not much.

Brother Paul wasn't caught by surprise. He was looking directly at the point where Silvas and Bay emerged from the smoke. Fitz-Matthew spun around, though. He had been pacing away from the smoke at that moment.

"What have you brought upon us?" Fitz-Matthew demanded when he saw the wizard. "Sir Eustace is looking for answers, and he will not be easily satisfied."

"Good morning, Vicar," Silvas said, nodding at Brother Paul. Then he turned his head. "Master Fitz-Matthew." Bay stopped with his tail only a few feet from the smoke. Silvas leaned forward on the pommel of his saddle.

"You know what happened in the night here?" Brother Paul asked.

"In general, yes. In detail, no," Silvas said. "The Seven Towers was also attacked. I have lost good people as, I believe, you have."

"An entire family destroyed!" Fitz-Matthew shouted. "Only the grace of God kept the toll from being much higher."

Silvas stared at the chamberlain, narrowing his eyes until Fitz-Matthew looked away in discomfort. But he could be put off only momentarily. Villagers started to gather when they saw that Silvas had come out of his tower of smoke. At first only a few came, and they stopped some distance away, content to listen. None of them were yet ready to venture their own questions or charges.

"Mecq has never known such a night," Brother Paul said, his quiet tones a marked contrast to the blustery manner of Henry Fitz-Matthew.

"Nor has the Glade," Silvas replied easily.

"As Master Fitz-Matthew said, there were deaths in the village," Brother Paul said. "Lightning hit their cottage and it was destroyed before they could flee. The family in the next cottage barely managed to escape when the flames spread." He shrugged. "The rain put the fire out before it could claim even more homes." He turned to scan the faces that were watching. A few more villagers had come to stand and wait.

"It was more than a thunderstorm," the friar said when he faced Silvas again. "I saw *things,* things I never thought to see in this life. It makes me wonder what might come next."

"That's something Sir Eustace wants to know as well," Fitz-Matthew said, with only slightly less bluster than before.

The question was enough to draw some of the villagers

closer. They wanted to hear any answer the wizard might have.

"Aye, what more must we bear?" one man asked. "Must we fear for our souls every night?"

There were mumbles of agreement, other voices of concern in the growing crowd. No one thought to mention that the Eyler still flowed much higher than it had of an August in the memory of any of them. Silvas listened and looked, trying to gauge how much fear was really behind the questions. It was clear that Henry Fitz-Matthew still felt the terror of the night assault, perhaps more than most of the villagers. Brother Paul showed no fear. That was no great surprise to the wizard, but it was something of a relief. The friar's faith seemed to be holding up well.

I want to hear more of what he experienced during the night, Silvas thought, but it didn't appear that he would be able to get the time alone with Brother Paul so easily.

"Sir Eustace wants answers," Fitz-Matthew said when Silvas didn't respond to any of the questions.

"Aye, and so do we," one of the bolder villagers said, speaking louder and moving closer.

"You deserve answers," Silvas said, facing the man in the crowd rather than Fitz-Matthew or Brother Paul. "You deserve to know why this has come to you and what may yet come." *I need to make sure that you don't get the idea that my coming to Mecq brought your troubles,* he thought. *If you get that notion, you'll also wear the delusion that my leaving would end those troubles.* Some would take that position soon enough. Silvas had no doubts about that. But he had to try to limit the belief to keep it from complicating his mission even more.

The people were silent, waiting for him to continue.

"I will tell you what I know," Silvas said. "It may take time, so we might as well go over to the church." *You'll all feel more comfortable there as well, no doubt,* he thought.

Bay started walking across to the front of St. Katrinka's. The people followed, and more came from their gardens and cottages. Not many were working in the fields across the river. The rain had left the fields too muddy. At the church, Silvas dismounted and sat on the top step. Bay moved to the side, leaving room for the villagers to come closer. Brother Paul and Henry Fitz-Matthew came to the front. The steward stood with his feet spread apart in a fighter's stance, everything about his attitude remaining belligerent. The friar seemed more at ease. He sat on the second step, off to the side, turned so he could watch his flock as well as the wizard.

Silvas remained quiet for several minutes as more people gathered.

"When I arrived, I told you that our Unseen Lord had directed my path here because Mecq had need of me." Silvas looked around, making eye contact with as many villagers as he could. Most looked away, either immediately or after just an instant of his gaze. Fitz-Matthew met his stare with an angry glare of his own for a moment, but the steward too looked away. Brother Paul was too close, and watching the villagers, so Silvas had no chance to see how he would react.

"The evil of the Blue Rose has been here for an age, perhaps since Sir Eustace's father and others like Master Fitz-Matthew here took the cross to fight the Blue Rose for the Church." Silvas looked at Fitz-Matthew, who looked down at the cross on his tunic. "The fight against evil is every man's duty," Silvas said. When Fitz-Matthew looked up again, there was less anger in his eyes.

"It is my duty as well," Silvas added more softly. He stood up to get a better view and paused for a long moment. More people had come. It appeared as if nearly the entire adult population of Mecq, save those who worked up in the castle, had come to hear him speak.

"The evil has found Mecq. You have only to think of the Eyler, of the rains that haven't come, of the illnesses that *have* come to folks like Berl." The husband of Old Maga's sister wasn't present, Silvas noted. He would still be weak. "Worse trouble was already coming. You couldn't have avoided it no matter what. Even I could not stop it from coming. Last night was only the beginning of this battle. I am here to fight that evil, to do what I can to lessen its effects on you."

Some of the people were staring at the ground or their feet now. Others glanced around nervously. Many had made the sign of the cross. Silvas saw lips moving in silent prayer. Even when he stopped talking there was little change. No one made any attempt to question him now.

"You went through a terrible storm last night," Silvas said. "Lives were lost. You all felt the terror. I went through a storm last night as well. Demons attacked the Glade, off in its true location. I lost good people as well, trusted servants of long years. I share your grief.

"The Blue Rose seeks power in this land. This may be the last place where they still have a concentration of adherents, a foothold." *Certainly I can think of no other reason for Mecq to be so afflicted,* Silvas thought. "They have a hatred for all that the White Brotherhood stands for. And for some reason, be it the crusade in Burgundy or something else, they have a long grudge against the people of Mecq."

The villagers, and even Fitz-Matthew, looked decidedly uneasy, frightened.

"I need to know what your good vicar can tell me about the storm here." Silvas glanced at Brother Paul, who nodded. "I need to learn everything I can so I can better prepare for the next attack."

That brought all eyes to Silvas again. The fear was obvious, and increasing.

"Yes, there will be another attack," Silvas said, his voice little more than a whisper. "Perhaps several. Together perhaps Brother Paul and I can find some way to deal with the Blue Rose here."

Brother Paul stood slowly, as if he were ready to deliver a sermon. He cleared his throat and looked around. When he spoke, it was in his pulpit voice. He looked from Silvas to his congregation and back.

"I saw demons in the sky during the storm," the vicar started. He described the forms, told how they had ridden about, carrying on, seemingly directing the lightning. "The Devil is working against us. He has launched open war against Mecq, for whatever reason. Yes, the *Devil*. The heretics of the Blue Rose are but his tools, accepting their own damnation, glorying in it, wanting only to inflict their pain on all good Christians.

"I have no authority to declare a crusade, but I want you to know, in your hearts and souls, that our fight against the Blue Rose here is every bit as important as the

fight that Master Fitz-Matthew and the father of Sir
Eustace waged so long ago. You know of Berl and others
who have suffered. You know what the lack of water has
meant to all of us.

"And now the Devil's cauldron is boiling. There is
more evil than we have faced before. It is beyond our
ability to fight alone. We are lucky to have the wizard
Silvas here to help us in our perilous hour. Remember, he
has the blessing of Bishop Egbert. He is known to the
White Brotherhood. And he has the countenance of His
Majesty."

Brother Paul drew the sign of the cross in the air and
spoke the words of blessing for his flock. Heads bowed.
Most of the villagers crossed themselves. A few voices.
said, "Amen." And then the eyes came back up to look at
the vicar and the wizard again.

"What will come next?" one farmer asked hesitantly.

Brother Paul looked to Silvas. The wizard shrugged.

"I don't know," Silvas admitted. "The friar and I will
do what we can to learn that so we can arm against it, but
there is a chance that we will not know the form of attack
until it comes."

"Will more die?" another villager asked.

"That is for God to say," Brother Paul said quickly.
"We can but pray for His help, and for His mercy."

"Is there no more you can tell us?" the first villager
asked.

"I keep no secrets from you," Silvas said. In the strict-
est accounting that was not true, but the wizard didn't
count it a lie, and he didn't think that the vicar would either. What Silvas held back pertained to the Greater Mysteries, and the villagers would not believe him if he told
them all that he had seen and heard.

"Sir Eustace will want to hear all of this from you,
Lord Wizard," Fitz-Matthew said. He tried to sound com-
manding, but his words didn't come out that way. His
voice trembled too much for the pose.

"I will come as soon as I may," Silvas replied quietly.

"And now we all have work to be about," Brother Paul
said. He repeated his ritual blessing, and the crowd
started to disperse. Even Fitz-Matthew turned and walked

across the green to his horse tied in front of the Boar and Bear.

"If you would care to step inside for a moment?" Brother Paul said softly to the wizard. Silvas nodded. They entered the church. Brother Paul knelt facing the altar, crossed himself, then stood and turned to Silvas again. Bay stood by the porch, as close to the door as he could get.

"There was more that I saw," Brother Paul said. He crossed himself again. "I do not like to hold back, but this was something I feared to share with my flock."

"I understand the feeling completely," Silvas said.

"Perhaps it was only my imagination," the friar said, though he didn't believe that, "but I thought that I saw the Devil himself coming to claim swarms of souls. A deep voice within me said that we are facing the Day of Judgment, that it may well come here and soon."

"It may," Silvas said simply, and when the vicar crossed himself again, the wizard could hardly fight the urge to echo the gesture.

15

"We might make a tour of the village," Silvas suggested after a moment. "There must be work for both of us."

"There is," Brother Paul agreed. "I've already done the Requiem for those who died, but there is more to do." They left the church together.

"I hope it won't discomfort you if I ride," Silvas said. "I find myself quite spent after the battle."

"I can see. I don't mind. As long as you don't mind waiting for me when your steed gets too far ahead."

Silvas smiled. "Bay is too thoughtful to go galloping off."

They made a very slow circuit of the village, stopping wherever there was a call for their services—at nearly half of the cottages they came to. Silvas and Brother Paul provided what help they could. There were injuries. Silvas dealt with the most serious. Brother Paul took care of the rest, and the friar had his spiritual balm to offer as well, something the wizard couldn't provide.

The villagers were already working to repair their homes, and to rebuild the fire-razed cottage whose inhabitants had escaped. More serious were the damages to the gardens and fields. Scant as the year's harvest would have been, it would be even scanter now.

"We shall need to beg the bishop for help to get through this winter," Brother Paul said softly. "It won't be the first time, I admit."

"If we make it through this crisis," Silvas replied.

"The Lord willing," Brother Paul said.

They were no more than halfway through their circuit when one of Master Ian's lads ran toward them from the inn. "There's a rider a-coming 'cross the valley," the boy shouted. He half turned to point without stopping.

Silvas had to walk a dozen paces to get a view of the rider. He focused his telesight. The distant rider was moving at an awkward trot.

"This might be your messenger returning," he suggested.

Brother Paul nodded. "It might, though it would mean that Bishop Egbert did not keep him long."

"He'll need a few minutes yet to reach us," Silvas said. "We may have time for another stop or two."

The rider almost fell from his horse when he pulled up in front of Brother Paul and Silvas. He was panting so raggedly that he might have been doing the trotting instead of the horse.

"Easy, man," Brother Paul said, putting his hands on the man's shoulders to steady him. "Easy now."

"I have word from His Excellency," the messenger said, the words coming out one at a time, each on a gasping exhalation.

"Yes, but take a moment to collect yourself first."

"Perhaps a drink would help," Silvas said. He gestured to the boy from the inn. "Here, boy, take this copper to Master Ian and bring back a flagon of ale for this man." He tossed the coin and the boy caught it easily, turning to run back to the Boar and Bear.

"Thankee," the man said, starting to get his wind back. "I thankee much, Lord Wizard."

"There, you're doing better already," Silvas said. "Come over to this stump and sit while you're waiting for the ale."

The man seemed to collapse onto the stump more than sit.

"I've ridden hard these days," he said. His gaze moved toward the door of the Boar and Bear. The boy was already emerging, holding the earthenware mug in both hands.

"I gave the bishop your message, Vicar," the rider said.

Brother Paul nodded and said, "Bide a moment. Get a drink of Master Ian's ale in you first, Willam." The boy arrived with the mug. Willam took a long drink and then smacked his lips.

"His Excellency says he knows of the wizard Silvas," Willam said, looking from vicar to wizard and back.

"The bishop has communicated that to me already," Paul said. "But there was more?"

"Aye, more an' some. He gathered the cathedral chapter in solemn conclave." Willam said that sentence very slowly and carefully, as if he had rehearsed it repeatedly so he would make no mistakes. "He's comin' here himself, with such of the cathedral monks as he can bring, an' quick like." Willam paused for another drink. Silvas and Brother Paul looked at each other. Even before Willam continued, both could make an excellent guess at what else he would say.

"Bishop Egbert, he says there's great danger at hand, more'n a country vicar—beggin' yer pardon—could handle." Willam gave Brother Paul an apologetic look.

"I understand, Willam," the vicar said. "I know my limits. I am but an initiate of the Lesser Mysteries. Bishop Egbert is an adept of the Greater. That is as God has ordained it."

"Aye, Vicar." Willam shifted his mug to his left hand so he could cross himself. He finished the ale and set the mug on the stump next to him.

"We will have need for Bishop Egbert and the members of his retinue," Silvas said, speaking across Willam at Brother Paul. Silvas didn't know the bishop, but he knew that as an adept, a *master* of the Greater Mysteries, Bishop Egbert would be a magician of considerable ability ... if nowhere near Silvas's level. And the bishop might understand some of what the wizard had experienced since coming to Mecq. Initiation to the Greater Mysteries of the White Brotherhood took a man beyond the limits of public dogma. *He might even have answers for me,* Silvas thought.

Master Ian came across the green. He held a small keg under one arm and three mugs in his free hand. Willam got up from the stump, and the innkeeper set the keg on it.

"It looked like ye might all have need of a drink," Master Ian said. "An' don' reach fer yer purse, Master Wizard, not for this 'un. I got my lads settin' up fer the whole village after last night." He set the mugs on the stump and started filling them. The first went to Silvas, the second to Brother Paul. Then Master Ian refilled Willam's mug before he filled one for himself.

"Your health, Master Ian," Silvas said, raising his mug to the innkeeper before he drank.

"An' yours, sir," Master Ian replied. He took a long drink, then said, "You might want to drink deep. We have us company comin' down from the hill." He pointed with his mug.

Silvas and the others looked toward Mecq's castle. There was traffic on the road coming down. Silvas narrowed his gaze. Sir Eustace and Henry Fitz-Matthew rode in front. The two ladies behind them were Eleanora and Maria. A number of other people walked along behind, lagging more every minute.

"It looks like help is finally coming from another quarter," Silvas said, not bothering to disguise his lack of enthusiasm for that help.

Brother Paul gave the wizard a quick, sharp glance. "Likely they had their own damages to repair after the storm," he said. "The lightning was even more fierce up on the hill."

"Did Fitz-Matthew say how bad it was up there?" Silvas asked—very softly, turning so that he faced only the churchman.

"He said it was terrible," Brother Paul said. "The look of that was in his eyes."

"Like as not," Silvas said, holding back a sigh and letting the discussion die. *I shouldn't be so quick to judge,* he told himself. *I let the man's style sway me.* He quickly finished his ale and turned to set the empty mug on the stump.

"Best have another while you have the peace," Master Ian urged, refilling the tankard before Silvas could answer.

"My thanks, sir," Silvas said, toasting him again. "I find your thane difficult to deal with."

Master Ian did not reply.

"I expected to see you up on the hill before this," Sir Eustace said as he approached Silvas and the others.

"I thought it more important to take care of the most

urgent needs of the people here first," Silvas replied.
"Brother Paul and I have nearly finished our circuit. If
you would care to join us? There is still plenty of work
to be done to repair the ravages of the storm." Silvas
mounted Bay, not so much because he still needed the
horse to carry him about, but for the height advantage.
Silvas felt stronger after his work in the village than he
had before.

"There is work in my castle as well," Sir Eustace said.
He turned to speak to Fitz-Matthew. "When our people
catch up with us, put them to work here. You can see
what remains to be done."

"Aye, lord," Fitz-Matthew said meekly.

"Vicar, what is left to see?" Sir Eustace said then,
rather than addressing the wizard again.

"We were about to check the mill and then the cottages
on this end." The friar gestured at the dozen houses on
the south end of the village, away from the twin hills.

Eleanora and Maria reined in behind Sir Eustace then.
He took no notice of their arrival. Silvas nodded to the ladies and took a moment to study their faces. Sir Eustace's
wife looked very troubled. Eleanora would not meet Silvas's eyes, looking down, away, anything to avoid him.
Silvas had no difficulty deciphering the change in her.

*She might enjoy a little dalliance with a stranger of
mystery and power, but she isn't ready for so much adven-
ture,* Silvas thought. He knew how he looked, haggard
and probably a little angry. The residue of heavily used
power would be with him, an odor as unmistakable as a
horse's sweat. *She has discovered that she has a much
less adventurous spirit than she thought.*

But Maria showed no such change. She met the wizard's stare with one even more intense. There was a flush
of excitement about the girl that seemed almost sexual.
Under Silvas's gaze she blushed deeply, but she resisted
looking away for the longest time.

Silvas finally started Bay toward the mill. Sir Eustace
stayed at his side, not too close. Brother Paul and Master
Ian followed, and the ladies rode at the rear of the proces-
sion. Bay walked at almost a hesitation step to avoid putting a strain on the two men who were walking—and as
a check against Sir Eustace's obvious impatience to hurry

through this routine. Brother Paul provided a summary of the ills the village had suffered, the dead, the hurt, the damages.

"The men can't tell for certain yet, lord," Master Ian added, "but it looks as like we might lose one part in five of the harvest, perhaps more." Sir Eustace growled under his breath at that, but he didn't speak.

The completion of the tour took another half hour. The Eyler was two feet above the line of rocks that the villagers had laid across the riverbed during the early rain, falling toward that level now that most of the rain surge had passed. There were no serious damages to the last group of cottages, nor were there any injuries among the families that lived in them.

"We withstood the storm better than we might have, God be praised," Brother Paul said when they started back toward the church. "I feared it would be much worse."

"Bad enough," Sir Eustace said in his usual grumbling tones. He stared up at the wizard.

"It would have been worse without help," Silvas said, pitching his voice so that only Eustace would hear him. "The evil that struck in the night has been building here since your father took the cross. Perhaps longer."

"So you say," Sir Eustace replied almost as softly.

"It is my business to know such things," Silvas told him. "When you can do so in private, you might ask Brother Paul to explain just what he saw during the storm."

"Sir Eustace," Brother Paul called from behind. "I forgot. Bishop Egbert himself is coming to help, with the monks of his chapter."

That stopped the knight for a moment, but when he urged his horse onward again, all he said was a mumbled "A crowd of fat bellies to feed."

Silvas considered taking his leave of the others as they neared the pillar of smoke. If Sir Eustace had not been with them, he would have—perhaps inviting Brother Paul and Master Ian in. But he didn't care to extend that hospitality to Sir Eustace, not yet. So he rode on to St. Katrinka's with the others. But he wasn't paying particular attention. His thoughts were back among the Seven

Towers. A good meal, a hot bath, a chance to relax before night—and possibly another attack—came, those were the things he was thinking about.

He was startled when Brother Paul ran past him, toward the front of the church. Silvas looked at the vicar and then toward St. Katrinka's. Bay appeared to notice at the same time, and started walking at a more normal pace for him. Silvas nearly jumped from his horse's back, hurrying to Brother Paul's side.

A rose bush, two feet tall, mature, filled with leaves and thorns, sat next to the steps of St. Katrinka's. There had been nothing there just a couple of hours before. Brother Paul was already on his knees, clutching his crucifix and praying. Silvas stood next to him and stared at the single flower open at the top of the bush. Even better than the vicar, Silvas recognized the threat that the bloom represented.

The single open flower was a large blue rose.

16

Even Sir Eustace was shocked into momentary civility by the sight of the blue rose growing in front of the church.

"How did that get there?" he demanded.

"It wasn't here two hours ago, Sir Eustace," Brother Paul said, getting up to face the knight. "There wasn't so much as a sprout here when we talked to the people before Silvas and I started our circuit."

"They are throwing down the gauntlet," Silvas said, also turning toward Eustace. "The Blue Rose Cult is telling us that they are here and that they intend to own Mecq ... or destroy it."

Eleanora crossed herself. Her face paled. Maria showed no reaction. Perhaps she leaned forward a little more in the saddle.

"Then we must expect more attacks?" Sir Eustace asked.

"More and stronger, I fear," Silvas said. "I hope that none comes before Bishop Egbert arrives to add his strength to the fight."

"He knows how serious our plight is," Brother Paul said. "And Bishop Egbert can travel apace when the need is upon him. I think we may look for him very soon, if not today, then perhaps as early as tomorrow. He should not be more than a day behind our William."

"I hope you are right, Vicar," Silvas said. "I will feel somewhat less besieged when the bishop and his monks stand with us."

"What should we do in the meantime?" Sir Eustace asked, looking back and forth between the friar and the wizard. The frown had returned to Eustace's face. He disliked the need to ask the wizard for instructions. He disliked relying on him for help. But he knew the threat of the Blue Rose. It had taken his father's life.

"Prayer and watchfulness," Silvas said. Brother Paul nodded agreement. "The vicar and I will take what measures we have at our disposal, but in general it comes down to prayer and watchfulness. I will erect what guards I can, but don't count on them to do overmuch. The forces of the Blue Rose are directed here by a wizard perhaps my equal in power." *Perhaps even my master,* Silvas thought, *but he would not say that,* certainly not in front of Sir Eustace. *Pride is a common failing among wizards,* Silvas conceded. *I have my full share.*

"On the chance that the Blue Rose does attack out of Blethye, you might take special care to watch the passes from the duchy, Sir Eustace," Silvas said. "The next attack might be physical."

The knight's face grew the fiercest scowl Silvas had yet seen on it. "We *always* keep watch on Blethye," he said.

"Even at the lesser pass beyond Mount Malq?" Silvas asked.

"Since you put the chance of a connection between Blethye and the Blue Rose in my head, yes."

"There remains a chance that such suspicion is unwarranted, but it is good to be prepared," Silvas said.

Silvas felt exhaustion creeping over him again. Silently he went through a spell for more energy, but he knew that there were limits. He had gotten through this much of the day on magical energy, and the price would have to be paid before long. *What I really need is a chance to sleep through a full night without disturbance,* he thought. *I need to renew myself before the next attack.* He blinked a couple of times and continued to watch Sir Eustace.

"Then we will do what we can to make sure we are not taken by surprise," the knight said. "Is there anything else?"

"I can think of nothing at the moment," Silvas said.

"Nor can I," Brother Paul said. "Prayer and watchfulness are always wise paths for the Christian."

"Then I had best find Fitz-Matthew and see what remains to be done," Sir Eustace said, tugging on his horse's reins to turn the animal. His ladies rode off with him.

"There is worse coming?" Master Ian asked. He had remained silent while Sir Eustace was around.

Silvas nodded. "It could get much worse, Master Ian. I wish that I could promise otherwise, but there are limits to my power—certainly against the Blue Rose."

"Should we not uproot this flower?" Brother Paul asked.

Silvas looked at the bush and tried to decide. "We might as well," he said after a moment. "It won't harm the power that put it there, but it might make your flock feel better."

Brother Paul started to bend toward the plant.

"Hold a moment, Vicar," Silvas said. "Have a care. I wouldn't want to be stuck by one of those thorns. There may be an enchantment laid on them."

"I have stout leather gauntlets that we use in the smithy," Master Ian said. "No rose thorn could ever prick you through them. I'll fetch them."

At last Silvas was able to take his leave. Even though the church was only a moment's walk from the entrance to the Seven Towers, Silvas rode. He was afraid that his exhaustion would show too clearly if he walked. It was a struggle just to keep his shoulders from sagging, but he knew that he did not dare do anything that might, even mistakenly, make the people of Mecq think that conditions were more desperate than they were. *The truth is bad enough,* he thought.

Silvas half expected a call before he got to the sanctuary of the Glade, but it didn't come. When the smoke closed around him, he slumped in the saddle, expelling a deep breath. If necessary, he could always claim that he hadn't heard any call that might come now. Fitz-Matthew and Brother Paul had called and waited before. No one would be able to read any more into a delay now.

Bay recognized the wizard's condition. He carried Silvas right to the entrance to the keep. Silvas dismounted slowly. Bosc came running around the corner from the mews, as usual, but the groom took one look at Silvas and stopped running. But he kept his silence.

"If the attack comes now, you are scarcely prepared to meet it," Bay told Silvas.

"I know." Silvas turned only halfway toward Bay. "I need food and sleep, at least a full night without any drain on my resources."

"At least," Bay agreed. "Do you think we will have that night?"

Silvas no longer had the energy to even shrug. "I hope so, Bay. I hope so." He went inside without waiting for any continuation.

Carillia met him in the main corridor in front of the great hall. "Supper is waiting for you, my heart." She moved to his side, pressing against him as if to take some of his weight on herself. Silvas didn't resist as she guided him into the great hall and up to their table. Servants were bringing in the food on steaming platters.

Silvas ate with more abandon than usual. The smell of food drove his already keen hunger beyond any thought of manners or moderation. There was a thick stew filled with several kinds of meat, a roast of beef, boiled cabbage, peas and carrots, onions, cheese and bread. There was also a platter of fruit, but Silvas hungered for more substantial food. He concentrated fully on eating for an uncommon length of time, hardly aware of Carillia nibbling at the meal with her usual gentility. But Carillia watched Silvas closely, marking how drawn and spent he appeared, worrying about him as she always did . . . and dreading the message she knew she must give him.

She waited as long as she could, letting him eat undisturbed until the pace of his eating decreased considerably.

"My heart," she started, and then she waited until he turned to look at her. "I hate to burden you, but after the events of last night I must suggest another Council. The one we attempted *was* interrupted, you recall."

"I recall," Silvas said, and Carillia felt a flutter of fear at the way it seemed to drain him even more. "And you are no doubt right, my love. We do need another Council." He shook his head. "But it is impossible tonight. I lack the strength to begin a Council, let alone carry it through. If there's time after I've slept, then yes, but I must have sleep first."

"I understand, my heart." Carillia reached out to lay

her hand on his arm. "I only hope that the Blue Rose gives us that time."

Silvas nodded more abruptly than he normally did to Carillia and returned to his eating. But the edge of his appetite was gone, and Carillia's words troubled him. He ate slowly for a few minutes more, then made an end of it. He stared at the platter in front of him, then looked up slowly, his gaze going to one of the hearths at the side of the room.

"I am almost of a mind to sleep on the floor here rather than climb to our chamber," he said.

"You would not rest so well down here," Carillia said. "Come, my heart. You can lean on me through the climb. I at least have had some chance to rest." She pushed her chair away from the table and stood.

Silvas leaned on the table to get up from his chair, but then he straightened up. He looked around the great hall again. Most of his people had finished their meals and left. Everyone had work to do, and long hours of it after the attack of the night before. And few wanted to observe their master when he was so obviously spent.

"I don't think I've been this tired since I completed my initiation rites," Silvas said as he shuffled toward the circular stairway behind the tapestry. "And I was much younger then."

"But not so wise, so experienced," Carillia said, her voice too positive for the words to be intended as mere flattery. She spoke as if she had positive knowledge of that younger Silvas, even though she had not come to the Seven Towers until much later, after the death of Auroreus.

Silvas couldn't even enter into the light banter that Carillia's words, if not her tone, invited. When they reached their bedroom, Silvas sat heavily on the side of the bed, prepared to do no more than cast off his boots before collapsing in sleep. But Carillia was there, helping him out of his clothes, moving the comforter so she could cover him as he lay back and closed his eyes.

Sleep.

Bay raced at full gallop across the plain, his mane and tail flowing with the wind of his speed. Silvas stared at the castle on the horizon. Its towers were white like the chalk cliffs that overlooked Dover Bay, but these towers were blindingly reflective, much too bright for Silvas to focus his telesight on them. It would be too much like the time he tried to see what a star was made of. Silvas couldn't judge how far away the castle was, or be certain that it really was Camelot. He wouldn't know until he reached it.

Reaching it was proving more difficult than Silvas had anticipated, though. Bay's stretching gallop covered the miles quickly, but the towers remained as distant as ever. There was no detectable change in the perspective. Bay pushed on with an eagerness that matched the wizard's. The horse didn't waste time speaking, not even to reply to Silvas's occasional questions or exclamations of frustration.

"Auroreus, will you please at least tell me how many languages there are on this page?" Silvas pleaded, looking up from the indecipherable scroll to his mentor.

The question seemed to startle the old wizard. His eyes narrowed, not in anger but in concentration or puzzlement. Finally he blinked and shook his head slowly.

"I never pay attention to such details, and neither should you," he said. "I write as the thoughts travel through my fingertips. That is the only way to read it as well. The language is important only as it permits greater precision. Some languages do not treat particular concepts as well as others. I use the words that seem most appropriate, most correct."

"But are there not groups of letters that exist in different languages with different meanings? There are only so many letters to use. There must be a limit to the combinations. How am I to know which word, which language, is meant?"

"That is part of the instruction, lad." Auroreus hesitated, then reached for the scroll he had written for his apprentice. Silvas handed DEI ET DEAE to him quickly. Auroreus scanned the page that the boy had rolled the scroll open to, near the beginning of the treatise, and made a low humming sound.

"There are no words here that are not clear as to

*which language they belong to, lad. As you develop a feel
for reading like this, you'll be able to tell the language
without much difficulty, if the question ever really
arises."* He handed the scroll back to the boy.

"But how many languages, please?" Silvas asked,
keeping his eyes on Auroreus, not on the scroll.

Auroreus emitted a long sigh and shook his head again.
"There are only five on that page, if you must know."

"The eldest of the gods is ———." Silvas could not
hear the name. That was a magic that he didn't have the
capacity to grasp. *"The second of the gods is the
lady ———."* Silvas nodded, though he wasn't sure that
anyone was watching him. He couldn't see whoever it
was who spoke to him, but the voice held too much authority for him to speak. He couldn't even question this
voice—unless he were invited to.

The roster of the divines continued. It did Silvas no
good since he couldn't take hold of the names, but he had
to pay attention. He didn't spare much thought on his peculiar surroundings. It looked as if someone had taken a
country vista, cut it into tiny patches, and fastened them
back together without any thought to logic or proper position. Bits of sky were mixed in with the grass. Trees protruded from fluffy clouds. A brook crossed grass, tree
crowns, and sky without deviating from its course. Silvas
himself was sitting on a rock that bobbed along on the
summery breeze, sometimes on the ground, more often in
the sky or coasting among the leaves at the top of the
trees.

*"The first conflict among the brothers and sisters came
in the land of the Hindus, when both ——— and ———
decided that they wanted the worship of the same tribe.
Their brothers and sisters forced an end to that feud, but
the peace that followed was bitter, filled with suspicions
and plots. Neither ——— nor ——— ever forgave the
other. Their enmity continues to this day. In any question,
if one supports a particular side, the other will automatically support the other, regardless of merits."*

Silvas didn't wake, but he felt himself tossing in bed.
He was hot, sweating—as heavily as the Eyler had flowed

before the rain, he thought. The wizard felt a heaviness, something more than his unease at the coming struggle, something less than a warning of imminent peril. He tried to extend his sleeping awareness to Carillia, but he couldn't reach her. Either she wasn't in bed with him or his mind was far more distant from his body and bed than he had thought. Memories and hints of memories pounded at his awareness, demanding that Silvas chase them down the alleys of his mind, taunting him with their incompleteness, laughing at him.

He wished that he could wake up long enough to take a drink. His throat felt dry as the Egyptian desert that Auroreus had told him about. Egypt. Alexandria. The library that had been burned. The way Silvas's throat now burned.

"Silvas, are you paying attention?" The voice was harsh, unforgiving. Silvas blinked and nodded.

"Yes, sir," he replied, not certain who he was talking to. "I'm sure I was." No, I'm not sure, he thought. In fact, I'm certain that I have no idea what he was talking about. Was he really talking? He must have been. Silvas looked around. Where am I? It wasn't the same place as before. It didn't rightly look like a place at all. There were no dimensions, no boundaries, no form within, no sense of "without" to measure it against. It's like the place where I hold my Councils, Silvas decided finally, and that gave him some measure of ease—a very small measure.

"We were talking about the adventures of the god ——— at the time of the Macedonian Alexander, and of the episode in the Egyptian desert," the incorporeal voice said. "The episode of Alexander's announced apotheosis."

The shining white castle was no nearer, not a step, but Bay was slowing, finally reaching the end of his energy. The cadence of Bay's gallop became less regular, the ride became less comfortable. Occasionally he even stumbled, and that was unheard of. Then Bay abruptly dropped out of his gallop into a walk, and stopped.

"It is no use," Bay said. "There's no way we can reach

that castle. It is as I said, you can only get to the castle from inside it."

"*There* must *be a way,*" Silvas told him. "*Others have reached it before us.*"

Bay shook his head spasmodically. "*Then they were already inside before they went there.*"

"*That makes no sense at all, my friend,*" Silvas said sadly.

When Silvas opened his eyes, he could tell that morning had fled completely. The shadows from the window showed that the sun was past the zenith. He had slept eighteen hours, or close to it. The bed clothes were drenched with his sweat. For several minutes Silvas could find no energy to do more than lie motionless. Only his eyes showed any life. Without looking, Silvas knew that Carillia wasn't in bed with him.

"I feel as if I spent those hours hard at work, not sleeping," Silvas muttered. But it would have to suffice. There was another day to face. He had to face it.

17

"Ah, my heart, you are awake at last." Carillia *bustled* into the bedroom. That, and the tempo of her words, caused Silvas to look up in some surprise. He had been so lost in his own thoughts that he hadn't heard her approach, and she was moving and speaking so much faster than usual. There was less of her normal grace. She might almost have been some shopkeeper's wife from the way she came into the room.

"I cautioned everyone to stay away until you woke," she continued. "You were so spent last night that I was determined to let you sleep as long as possible."

Silvas nodded, rather dully. He needed another moment to collect his thoughts enough for speech. "Little enough good the sleep did me, my love," he said, recognizing the hint of wonder in his own voice. "But the night seems to have wrought great changes in you."

The smile Carillia gave him was more mysterious than sweet. Silvas perceived a little additional depth to it, something new in the eyes that topped it.

"The time seems to demand it, my heart," she said. "I knew that I had to be as strong as possible while you recovered your strength." She went to the wardrobe and pulled out fresh clothes for Silvas rather than calling for Koshka or one of his fellow servants.

"I don't know how much strength I recovered," Silvas said, sliding his legs out of bed and sitting on the edge. "For all the hours of sleep, I feel little different than I did at the start."

Carillia finally stopped her *bustling* and stared at Silvas. Her eyes narrowed in a look of intense concentration that was as alien to her normal habits as scurrying about and rapid speech.

"Your sleep was troubled?" The question was tinged more with sharpness than solicitude.

"Troubled and full. And yet . . ." He hesitated, then shook his head. "Yet I can grasp so little of it. The memories are confused, incomplete, like fever dreams."

Carillia laid her hand on his forehead. "You are sweaty but not hot." She looked at the bedding. "If you had a fever in the night, it has broken." For an instant her voice modulated into more familiar tones, but then the new briskness was back. "The water for your bath is being heated. That and a good draught of one of your elixirs will put you as right as possible."

Silvas's new smile almost widened into a grin. He was beginning to find an appreciation for this new manner of Carillia's. "You are probably right, my love." He could hear the amusement in his own voice. "You usually are."

This time Carillia gave him a more familiar smile. "We have to make use of the time we have before the Blue Rose comes again," she said, with *almost* her accustomed softness.

There was a quick knock at the door and Bosc came in, hardly waiting for Carillia's call. He bobbed his head at her, then focused on Silvas.

"I'd not bother you so, but Lord Bay is quite restive." Bosc bobbed his head a couple more times in the peculiarly jerky fashion of his kind. "And I feel most on edge myself, Lord Silvas." He shifted his weight back and forth from one foot to the other.

"What is Bay so restive about?" Silvas asked, noting at the same time that the water was being poured for his bath. He stood and stretched.

"He rumbles and moans like, lord, about this village and about the Blue Rose and a dozen other things all jumbled together, and he paces his stall like there's a mare in heat just out of reach."

"Tell him I'll be out there as soon as I can," Silvas said.

"Aye, lord." Bosc bobbed his head one final time before he hurried out the door.

"It appears that everyone is out of sorts this morning," Silvas said quietly, heading for the bathroom. "The evil of the Blue Rose is still working on us, in one fashion or another."

"We are merely preparing to face it, my heart," Carillia said. She didn't bother to follow him to the bath.

Silvas settled himself in the tub and closed his eyes. The water came almost to his chin. It was hot, steaming—too hot at the start, but that meant that it would remain comfortable longer at the end.

I need time to think, Silvas told himself. *If I could but remember all that I experienced in the night.* But the images and sequences had come so rapidly on the heels of each other that each new segment had overlain and erased the one before. Try though he might, Silvas could do no more than capture isolated scenes and phrases, and that bothered him.

The lacunae might be the most important parts. That seemed to be the way of life, even for a wizard-potent. It was like trying to reconstruct a fine Italian mosaic from one tile in ten, not knowing what the complete picture had originally been. Silvas spent the time in his tub trying to recall the general pattern of his nocturnal experiences.

After a few minutes, he took a deep breath and slid down in the tub until he was completely submerged, and he stayed down until his lungs felt ready to burst. When he pushed himself up he took in several deep breaths of the humid air. He leaned back, head against the stone of the tub, eyes closed, while water dripped from his hair and face.

Nothing, he thought. There weren't even enough fragments of the puzzle in his mind to space out the framework for the missing majority. *And it might be vital.* There were certain spells he could try, but they would take considerable time and energy, and Silvas doubted that enough of either remained for him to spend them, particularly since those spells were not certain, not when he applied them to himself.

As the water started to lose its warmth, Silvas hurriedly went through the motions of scrubbing, trying to scour himself into greater alertness. Satin and Velvet came prowling into the bathroom. Each sniffed at the water and at Silvas. Their growls were more throaty than normal, their movements as uncommonly edgy as Carillia's had been.

"This has got to all of us, hasn't it?" Silvas said softly. He didn't reach out to pet the cats. They wouldn't appreciate wet hands. The cats left the room, but they were back in less than a minute, going through the same routine of sniffing the water and Silvas before turning to leave again.

"You want me to hurry too?" Silvas chuckled. Satin growled in a particularly short-tempered fashion. Silvas chuckled again. "If I thought it would help, I would have foregone my bath, kittens. But it wouldn't help, and it won't help for me to hurry now. But I am nearly done."

The cats fled the bathroom when Silvas stood to get out of the tub. Staying meant getting wet as Silvas splattered and splashed and toweled himself dry. Satin and Velvet were no more thrilled with wet fur than any other cats.

Silvas felt much better when he returned to the bedroom to dress. Carillia was gone. Satin and Velvet came and went, as if they were still checking to see how much longer he would be.

"Such impatience," Silvas said as he adjusted his knife belt. "It's not like you." The cats left the room again.

Breakfast—a selection of fruit and cheese, with spiced wine on the side—was waiting for Silvas in the small sitting room. He sat but did little more than sample the food.

"I think I'm ready to face the world now," he said after only a few minutes. "At least for a time." He stood and stretched, then headed for the stairs. His first stop had to be the mews.

Bay was pacing rapidly around the confines of his stall. Though it was much larger than most, even compared to Bay's unusual size, the stall was hardly sufficient for such frantic pacing.

"You want to go out into the bailey so you have more room?" Silvas asked when he looked in the open top of the stall's half door.

"It would not be room enough," Bay said, coming to an awkward halt. "The itch I have makes me want to run as far and as fast as I can, in any direction. Or even in circles, if the circles are large enough."

"That wouldn't help," the wizard said, uncomfortable at the echo of his own dream. "We could ride forever and not reach our destination."

Bay nudged open the bottom half of the door with his nose. Silvas stepped back to let Bay come out of the stable.

"Bide a moment," Bay said. When Silvas nodded, Bay started along the wall, moving from a walk into a slow canter, an easy lope that consumed distance quickly. Bay lapped the courtyard a dozen times before he returned to Silvas.

"It is not enough, but it must suffice for now," Bay said. He looked closely at Silvas. "They told me you were sleeping."

"I was, little good it did me," Silvas replied. "My slumber was long but not easy."

"It shows," Bay said. "Are you fit for what may come?"

"I won't know until whatever may come does come," Silvas said. "I feel better than I did when I first woke. I might have the strength to get through the next hours." He looked at the sky. There were no clouds over the Seven Towers. "I didn't stop to look at Mecq," Silvas said, as much to himself as to Bay.

"Braf says that the sky over Mecq remains overcast," Bay said. "When you had not appeared by mid-morning, I bade him look for me." The turret that looked out over Mecq, or whatever location the pillar of smoke was in, was as far out of Bay's reach as the stars were for Silvas. The narrow circular stairway leading to that turret was much too small for the horse.

"You told Sir Eustace to be especially watchful of the passes from Blethye," Bay said. "You could make the passage much more costly for Blethye, if that is the source of this disease."

"If," Silvas said, seizing the single word. "But focusing too narrowly on Blethye might make us overlook an attack from elsewhere until too late."

"Not focus, simply prepare," Bay said. "Something to make the more distant pass even harder for soldiers.

Something to drop on the near pass if an army tries to come through."

"And the energy it would take?" Silvas asked. "The Blue Rose wizard appears to be my equal. I can't afford to waste myself now, not when every confrontation already drains me so thoroughly."

"As for wasting yourself . . ." Bay started. He didn't need to finish. Silvas glared at him anyway.

"The levels do not compare," Silvas said. "Anyway, it is all part of the dance. The Blue Rose was behind many of the ills I cured here, and mending the injuries was just as important. I couldn't give the enemy the satisfaction of seeing their evil abide, or endanger our support any further."

"We have come too far to worry about support," Bay said. "If the battle is upon us, they have no choice but to support us or perish."

"I can't be that callous," Silvas said. "If we forget the people we help, how are we different from the Blue Rose?"

"I leave you to worry about theology," Bay said. "It is enough for me to worry about survival. If we don't survive, what use are we to anyone, including these people you want to help?"

"I'm going to the village," Silvas said. "More than half the day is gone. They will be wondering if something has happened to me. They'll need reassurance."

"They'll want to know how you will prevent another storm coming over them, or worse. And they'll want to know when you will fulfill your promise to provide them with adequate water."

"An easy prediction, Bay," Silvas said, his voice softening a little. "I know the questions that will come."

Bay remained within the Glade. Silvas emerged from the smoke and headed for the Boar and Bear. Apart from Master Ian, there were only a couple of boys in the public room of the inn, trying to put some order to the place.

"Good afternoon," Silvas said as he entered.

"Lord Wizard," Master Ian said, nodding politely.

"I'll have a mug of ale, if you please, Master Ian," Silvas said, taking a seat at the nearest table. "And if you have any food ready?"

"There's stew a-simmering," Master Ian said as he filled a mug for the wizard.

"Stew and bread would do nicely," Silvas said.

Master Ian brought the ale, then went for the food. When he came back, the innkeeper gave Silvas time to taste his stew before he spoke.

"Some folks has been wonderin' if somethin' was wrong," Master Ian said then. "As the day moved along, as it were."

Silvas looked up and shrugged. "The storm, and the work yesterday, took a lot out of me. I needed time to gather my strength against the next time the Blue Rose strikes. Wizardry is not a simple affair of muttering spells and waving arms. It is work at least as hard as farming ... or smithing."

Master Ian shrugged back at the wizard. "I'd not know about that. But that's another thing folks has been askin' about. The *next* time. It worries 'most all of us. We be simple folks. All these magics and all. It begins to tug at folks' innards."

Silvas dragged his bread through the stew's gravy and leaned close to the bowl to eat off that end while he waited for the innkeeper to continue.

"Simple folk may not know about all the high-flown things that be the bother of wizards, but they can see that the storm that come chasin' your rain was unnatural."

"Aye, it was." Silvas wiped his hand across his mouth, then reached for his ale before he went on. "It was a weapon hurled by the Blue Rose, another punishment for Mecq."

"Or was it merely sent to test *you*?" Master Ian asked.

Everyone has had their tongues loosened, Silvas thought. *Is that natural or more work of the Blue Rose?* That brought a fleeting smile to his mind: *I begin to see their work in everything.*

"At this point one cannot be separated from the other," Silvas said, clearly not the answer Master Ian had expected. "The *form* of the attack was clearly a response to my gentle rain. The *fact* of the attack was not."

"I've heard more than one ask today why you cannot

make good your promise of water and leave," Master Ian
said. "Folks think that if you go, the Blue Rose may follow. Or turn their attention elsewhere for a bit. Some go
so far as to say that we'd be better off if you just left,
even without the water."

"My leaving would not divert them," Silvas said. "The
Blue Rose has condemned Mecq for whatever reasons. I
didn't draw them to Mecq. The presence of the Blue Rose
is what drew me here. To help. Our Unseen Lord sent
me." Silvas drained his mug and handed it to Master Ian
for a refill. When the innkeeper came back, Silvas took a
long drink and set the mug down.

"The water problems are tied directly to the evil of the
Blue Rose," he said. "Unless they are defeated here,
things can only get worse for Mecq, and everyone else.
That is most especially true if I run away from the confrontation."

Master Ian was clearly not satisfied with the explanation.

"Ask your vicar," Silvas suggested. "If needs be, wait
and ask Bishop Egbert himself, since the good bishop re-
alizes that this matter is serious enough to draw him out
of St. Ives. Whether we like it or not, Master Ian, there's
no turning back for anyone now."

The frown didn't leave the innkeeper's face, but the
look of intense concentration did.

"As to the water," Silvas continued, "I will make good
my vow unless I perish in the fight. That too is possible."
That admission was enough to send Master Ian back to
his kegs and mugs. Silvas returned to his stew. It was beginning to cool, but it remained surprisingly good. *Or
else my hunger was greater than I cared to admit,* Silvas
thought. He thought about asking for another bowl, but
Brother Paul came into the inn and Silvas put off
thoughts of eating another helping.

"Good afternoon, Vicar," Silvas said, making a gesture
for the friar to join him at the table.

"God's peace to you, Lord Wizard."

"Master Ian. Ale for the three of us," Silvas called. He
drained his tankard and set it down. He pulled out the
coins for his meal and the extra ale and dropped them on
the table.

"I have had additional word from His Excellency," Brother Paul said while he watched Master Ian drawing the ale. "He will arrive in Mecq today."

"That is welcome news," Silvas said. "I have hoped that he would arrive before the next attack."

Master Ian arrived with the drinks, and the three men shared a long pull at their tankards. Then Master Ian asked Brother Paul some of the same questions he had put to Silvas. The vicar's responses were similar, which did little to improve the look on Master Ian's face. But news of the bishop's impending arrival did help a little. After a few moments the innkeeper went back to his work.

"Has Sir Eustace been told yet how soon the bishop will arrive?" Silvas asked as he got near the bottom of his mug.

Brother Paul shook his head. "I was about to send someone up when I heard that you had come in here."

"Then I might as well carry the news," Silvas said. "That will also give me a chance to hear whatever new complaints he has thought of since yesterday." *I am certain he will have new complaints,* he thought.

Silvas wasn't surprised to find Bay emerging from the smoke, fully harnessed, as he approached it. The surprise, if there was one, was that Bay had not been waiting at the door to the Boar and Bear.

"The bishop will be here this afternoon," Silvas said before he mounted. "We carry the news to Sir Eustace." Since they were in Mecq, Bay didn't reply. Silvas almost wished that he had been able to give Bay the news within the cover of the Seven Towers, just to hear the horse's comment.

Silvas stopped Bay just before they reached the castle on Mount Mecq. The wizard looked across the valley, focusing his telesight in the direction of St. Ives, scanning the possible approaches.

"No sight of him yet," he said softly. Bay went on to the gate of the castle and inside. There were six men-at-arms on the wall now. Their attention was concentrated to the north, on the duchy of Blethye and on the gap leading through to it.

Sir Eustace was waiting for Silvas. The knight had obviously been warned of his approach, and Sir Eustace had progressed far beyond mere unhappiness.

"I marvel that you have the gall to present yourself before me," Sir Eustace shouted as Silvas entered his great hall. The knight stepped close to Silvas, completely unconcerned that the wizard was a foot taller than him.

"I will remind you that Mecq is *my* fief," Sir Eustace said, still shouting. His face was the deep red of anger. "It is *my* responsibility to determine what help *my* people need and deserve. I am as upset about the deaths and destruction as you claim to be. Most likely *my* concern is even greater. Mecq is *my* village. These are *my* people." He loaded each possessive with as much volume and anger as he could.

Silvas kept any show of emotion from appearing on his face. *After what I have already heard today, this should come as no surprise,* he thought. Anything less would have been incongruous.

"I don't like outsiders coming into my demesne uninvited," Sir Eustace continued. "I thought I made that clear at our first meeting. And I will not abide outsiders confusing the loyalties of *my* people and placing them in great danger. *My* people have hard enough lives without you risking their usefulness to themselves, and to their liege lord."

When Sir Eustace finally seemed to run into a void for a moment, Silvas gave him the vicar's message. "Bishop Egbert will reach the village today, perhaps well before sunset."

"*More* trouble!" Eustace said. He turned and stormed out of the great hall, climbing the stairs to the level above.

Silvas looked around the great hall, not moving from where he stood. He was alone in the chamber. "It seems I am dismissed," he said softly, with more than a trace of amusement. Sir Eustace's rage didn't call forth a like response from the wizard. The changes in everyone that day served not only to exaggerate the knight's anger, but also to put it in a different perspective.

Silvas started for the door. The session with Sir Eustace had been shorter, if no less sour, than he had ex-

pected. *The mood Sir Eustace is in, I should rejoice that
he left so quickly,* Silvas told himself. It was almost
enough to make him laugh.

He was halfway to the door when he heard light steps
hurrying down the stairs into the great hall from above.
Almost against his will he stopped and turned. It was, as
he had suspected, Maria. Silvas waited, letting her expend
the energy to cross the hall.

"I was afraid you would leave before I could get
down," she said.

"I was just leaving. Your father is particularly angry
with me today."

"He fears that you will make him look bad before the
people of Mecq," Maria said. Her tone seemed to suggest
that Silvas had already done that . . . and that she enjoyed
her father's discomfiture.

"*I* think it's wonderful what you have done," she said.
"You are so brave to stand up to the heretics who killed
my grandfather, so bold to challenge them. My father
wishes that you would leave. I wonder that you don't. It
would be safer for you, and you wouldn't have to face the
ingratitude of my father and Master Fitz-Matthew. It
would serve them right if you left and made them face the
heretics alone."

"My duty would not permit that, even if I were base
enough to flee in the face of danger," Silvas said. The
words sounded stuffy, and that was intentional. Sir
Eustace's wife might have lost her yen for the wizard, but
Maria obviously had not.

"There is that as well," Maria said, moving so close to
Silvas that they were almost touching. "I have never met
a man like you before."

Silvas slid half a step back, but Maria hardly noticed.
She moved forward into the gap as if they were tied together.

"You will leave someday soon, though, won't you?"
she asked.

"As soon as the threat of the Blue Rose has been met."
*Providing I survive the conflict. If I don't survive, my de-
parture will no doubt come rather sooner.* "There will
doubtless be other villages that need my help."

"You don't spend *all* your time in tiny places like

Mecq, do you? You get to cities like London and York and other grand places, don't you?"

"At times," Silvas admitted.

"I know you have your lady, Carillia," Maria said. "But I want to leave Mecq with you. There's nothing for me here, and you may be my only chance to escape. Soon enough my father may force me into a nunnery. I can't hope to find a man worth marrying here."

Silvas stepped back again, surprised at the echo of his own assessment of her probable future . . . and even more surprised that she would be so candid about it.

"I could make no promises like that." He held his hands up to stop Maria from coming so close again. "Your father has enough excuses to revile me. And I still have a dangerous battle to face with the Blue Rose." *She makes me as nervous as the thought of that battle.*

"My father has never needed excuses to revile anyone," Maria said. "It is his nature to spew bile at all who come around. He could not think worse of you, and he might even offer grudging thanks if you removed the problem of my future from his shoulders."

"It is too soon to talk, or even think, of things like this," Silvas said. "I must put all my mind to the coming battle." He backed up another step. "And now, young lady, I *really* must be leaving."

"If you must." She didn't bother to suppress a sigh. "I will see you to the gate."

"That isn't necessary."

"But it is," Maria insisted. "My father didn't stay to perform that courtesy. I would not have you think the entire family is so crude."

Silvas bowed to the inevitable.

"I beg you to consider my request as you may," Maria said as Silvas opened the door. "I must escape this place, and you are my only hope."

"As I may," Silvas said, knowing how little that vow cost him.

They crossed the courtyard together. Silvas had Bay at his left and Maria so close at his right that she kept brushing his arm. Then one of the sentries on the wall pointed across the valley and shouted, "There are riders approaching the village."

Silvas hurried up the wooden stairs that led to the ramparts and stared off in the direction that the soldier had pointed.

"There are thirteen riders," Silvas said as he focused his telesight on the group—nearly two-thirds of the way across the valley, "and I see the pennant of St. Ives above them. It is Bishop Egbert and his monks."

The sentry who had spotted the riders scurried down the stairs and ran for the keep. Silvas was a little more cautious descending to the courtyard.

"And now I really must hurry," he told Maria.

18

Bay hurried down the narrow road to the valley as if he were in a race. Silvas made no attempt to slow his pace even though it made him edgy. The drop at their side would hardly be forgiving. But Bay never made the slightest misstep. And when he reached the flat below Mount Mecq, Bay really stretched out to cover the last few hundred yards to the village green—even though the bishop and his retinue were at least a quarter hour away.

Brother Paul had begun to marshal the people of Mecq to greet the bishop. The village could offer little in the way of decoration, but the families were gathering in the village green. The vicar had found some white streamers for the front of St. Katrinka's. They fluttered in the light breeze.

"You saw that he is coming?" Brother Paul asked as Silvas dismounted.

"One of the sentries on the hill spotted the riders. I identified the bishop's pennant."

Brother Paul looked across the river. The riders were scarcely visible from this vantage. The vicar couldn't make out the design of the pennant.

"You have exceptional eyes," Brother Paul said, raising an eyebrow. Silvas nodded.

"Will the bishop have time to shake the dust from his robes before the attack comes?" the vicar asked.

Silvas looked around the green, then up at the sky. "Perhaps. So far the Blue Rose has attacked only at night. Whether they will attack tonight or not, only they know." He shook his head. "I am reluctant to hazard a guess."

"At least the bishop should *arrive* before trouble comes," the friar said.

"Or be close enough to come to our assistance," Silvas said grimly.

By the time the bishop's party reached the bridge across the Eyler, the entire population of Mecq, except for those who were working in the castle, had gathered.

The members of the bishop's party were all dressed alike, even the bishop. The white cassocks of their order were covered by traveling cloaks of unbleached gray-brown wool. The bishop himself, according to rumor, never wore the more ornate robes of his office except when he officiated at Mass in his cathedral on special feast days. There was no flurry of dust as the thirteen riders pulled to a halt at the edge of the village green. The ground was soft and moist from the rain of two days before. The dust didn't come until the riders dismounted and started beating at their cloaks.

Silvas scanned the group quickly. Bishop Egbert was easy to identify. For the moment, though, Silvas was more interested in the dozen monks who accompanied him. There was not a fat belly in the group. Although the monks ranged in age from youngsters barely old enough to have taken final orders to men showing the signs of great age, they all moved spryly. Their eyes were clear and deep, and all showed the aura of mystic power.

Bishop Egbert was easily the most impressive of the churchmen. He looked incredibly ancient, immediately reminding Silvas of Auroreus, though except for the air of tremendous age there was no resemblance between them. As the bishop stepped forward, away from the horses, he peeled off his traveling cloak and handed it to one of his monks.

The bishop might dress only in the white robes of his order, but the cassock he wore was not of the simply spun cloth that most monks of the White Brotherhood wore. The fabric was close-woven and polished, and there were innumerable arcane symbols worked into it in a white that was so near the base fabric that only a person with some gift for magic would be able to make out the symbols—not just the traditional Christian devices of crosses and stylized fish, but some of the symbols of the trimagister and the Greater Mysteries as well.

Egbert had long white hair, worn unencumbered by any

cap while riding. His face was deeply lined and rough-
ened by age and weather. He was so thin that he appeared
emaciated, though that look was common in many chap-
ters of the White Brotherhood. Egbert's hands were long
and bony, with fingers that seemed to be half again as
long as they should be, an effect heightened by long fingernails. His eyes were dark and so deep-set that it was
impossible to tell at a glance what color they were.

To those sensitive to such things, he had a clear aura of
magical power, as much stronger than that of Brother
Paul as it was weaker than that of Silvas. Brother Paul
could never hope to be as powerful as the bishop, and
Egbert was clearly not as powerful as the wizard. The auras of the monks who had arrived with Egbert ranged between the bishop and the vicar, perhaps averaging closer
to the bishop. The cathedral chapter of St. Ives could
marshal considerable force in concert, though even together they would never match Silvas in sheer magical
power.

There were several minutes of confusion on the village
green, a babel of voices. Even without the backdrop of
fear, the arrival of a bishop in a small backwater parish
like Mecq would be a major event, one that the parishioners would talk about the rest of their lives.

Brother Paul stepped forward and made his proper
obeisance.

"Get up, brother," Bishop Egbert said. His voice was
high and reedy but strong, showing no edge of age or in-
firmity. The bishop's eyes immediately went to Silvas,
and the wizard stepped forward.

"I am known as Silvas, Your Excellency. We have not
had the pleasure of meeting before."

"Your fame is known," the bishop said. A cautious
smile tugged at the corners of his mouth. "A couple of
the brothers recall the service you did Bishop Alfred
some years back."

Silvas bowed his head respectfully. "He was a good
friend."

"I did not know him, save through correspondence,
more's the pity," Egbert said. "He did give sage counsel,
though."

"He did indeed," Silvas agreed. "His words are missed by many."

Bishop Egbert looked around at the people of Mecq. They had almost encircled the bishop and his retinue—except for an open space on either side of the pillar of smoke. Once the bishop had started speaking, the villagers had fallen silent. Apart from their worries, they would wait for the bishop to give them his blessing. The blessing of a bishop, perhaps available only once in a lifetime for the people of a place such as Mecq, had to count for more than the blessing of a country vicar like Brother Paul.

"I could feel the nearness of the Blue Rose when we entered the valley," Bishop Egbert said, so softly that none of the peasants hanging around the wizard and the churchmen could quite make out his words.

"As did I," Silvas said. "The feeling was not that specific at first, though. I sensed the evil, but it wasn't until I helped an ill villager that I spotted the signature of the Blue Rose." Even more softly he added, "They seem to be directed by a wizard of my own stature, and they have *real* power behind them now."

The bishop raised an eyebrow, but accepted the wizard's estimate. "Perhaps we should defer further talk of this until later?"

"That might be wise," Silvas agreed.

Egbert looked past the wizard at Bay then. The bishop had been doing his best to ignore the horse's uncommon size up to that moment, but he could not ignore Bay for long. Egbert met the horse's gaze. After they had stared at each other for a minute or more, the bishop nodded with at least partial understanding that Bay was more than just an exceptionally large animal.

Then Egbert looked at the pillar of smoke. "That is yours, I believe," he said to Silvas.

"It contains my home," Silvas said. "I would be honored to offer the hospitality of the Glade to you and your colleagues for the length of our common stay in Mecq."

Bishop Egbert didn't hesitate at all. He sensed that Silvas's home would be better equipped that anything Mecq or its thane could offer. "We would be delighted. In turn, let me invite you to attend the Mass I will offer in St. Katrinka's."

To the side, Brother Paul permitted himself a small smile. He was curious about the wizard's reaction to that offer. Stepping inside a church for a few minutes' talk was one thing. But would he be willing to stay through a Mass?

"I would be honored," Silvas said, disappointing the vicar.

"I think tomorrow at sunrise," Egbert said, turning to the vicar.

"As you say, Your Excellency," Brother Paul said. A dawn Mass would not disrupt the daily work of the villagers, and there would be time for the news to get up the hill to Sir Eustace and the people working in the castle. Without much doubt everyone would attend, except for whatever sentries Sir Eustace thought necessary to keep on duty at the castle. He would certainly refuse to abandon his home completely even for the half hour or so of the Mass.

Bishop Egbert turned slowly through a complete circle, looking at the people of Mecq. Then he looked at his monks. All of them had shed their traveling cloaks and stood together in their white cassocks. *Good men and devout,* Egbert thought. Initiation into the Greater Mysteries could be a sore trial for a pious churchman. Many could not suddenly accept a second level of truth above what they had been taught to believe before. Finally Egbert turned back to the vicar and the wizard. But his eyes were drawn toward the castle on Mount Mecq—or rather to the road leading down from it.

"Someone is coming from the castle," he said softly. Both Silvas and Brother Paul turned to look.

"That is Sir Eustace, with his steward trailing behind," Silvas said. *It seems he finally deigns to come down,* he thought. Eustace must have received news of the bishop's sighting within seconds after Silvas identified the approaching riders.

"I was about to offer my blessing," Egbert said, "but I think I should wait for Sir Eustace."

Many of the villagers turned to watch the riders. Bishop Egbert waited patiently. There was no conversation around him. Everything seemed suspended while they waited. Sir Eustace slowed his horse only when he had to, and the villagers made room for him to pass through the crowd. The knight didn't dismount until he was within ten feet of the bishop.

Even before he greeted the bishop, Sir Eustace turned his head to glare at Silvas. The look of anger was suppressed, if not entirely, before Eustace went down on one knee before the bishop. Egbert let him stay down a few seconds longer than necessary.

"Bishop Egbert has accepted my offer of hospitality for his people," Silvas told Sir Eustace as soon as he could. "There will be a welcoming dinner this evening. I would be happy if you, your family, and Master Fitz-Matthew would attend."

Sir Eustace hesitated before he answered. Silvas could almost follow his thoughts from the sequence of looks that passed across the knight's face. Sir Eustace was delighted to be spared the expense and bother of housing the clerics, but angry at being usurped in that function. He didn't care to enter Silvas's tower of smoke, but he also didn't want to slight the bishop or miss the opportunity to be with him.

"Unfortunately, my wife is a trifle ill this afternoon. My daughter is required to care for her, and to look after her young brother. I will be pleased to accept your invitation for myself and my steward."

"And you, Brother Paul?" Silvas asked, turning easily to him. "It would hardly be fitting to exclude the vicar of Mecq."

"Thank you, I would be delighted," Brother Paul said.

Silvas glanced at Bay and nodded very casually. The horse backed away from the group and ambled toward the smoke. Few people paid any attention to his departure.

Finally Bishop Egbert raised his hand for the blessing.

"In the name of the Father, and of the Son, and of the Holy Spirit . . ."

All of the villagers dropped to one knee or both. Many bowed their heads. Some looked at the bishop, watching him draw the sign of the cross in the air before them. All crossed themselves after one fashion or another. Even Sir Eustace went down on one knee again and went through the motions. Silvas remained standing, a little to the side, neither bound by the discipline of the flock—nor concerned about standing so clearly apart. His eyes focused on the bishop. Silvas could feel the power in Egbert's ritual words and gestures. Silvas had never discounted the magic of the White Brotherhood or the Church hierarchy, and this sample gave him a closer gauge on just how much power the bishop possessed.

It was not insignificant.

19

"Quite substantial for a thing of smoke," Bishop Egbert said as Silvas showed him to a large room in the keep of the Seven Towers. The monks of Egbert's cathedral chapter had been shown to a large room on the ground floor, supplanting part of the staff for the duration of their stay. The Glade was rather more accommodating than most castles. The soldiers, servants, and guests weren't forced to make do with whatever space they could find in the great hall or other areas.

"It's not often that I get to share hospitality with outsiders," Silvas said, forgoing the more obvious replies. "It is quite old, especially for England. When Auroreus built this place, Rome was still the seat of empire as well as of the Church."

"I have heard rumors, but remarkably I have found nothing in any of the annals that come to my attention," the bishop said. "It seems that not even the wordiest of brothers has seen fit to mention the rumors for posterity."

"Not a situation of my doing, I assure you," Silvas said. "While I do not seek to spread the fame of the Seven Towers, neither do I conspire to hide its existence." He gestured around the bedroom. "If you have need of anything, a ring of the bell will bring a servant. And through there"—he pointed to a doorway at the rear of the room—"you will find the rest of the accommodations. Someone will be along with a tray, wine and a few odds and ends, to help you refresh yourself after the journey. Dinner will be a half hour or so, I believe."

"Thank you. I have no doubt that I shall find all that I need."

"Will you be able to find your way to the great hall without difficulty?"

"But of course," Egbert said, smiling.

"There is a lot we need to discuss, Your Excellency, but, if possible, perhaps we may postpone that until after dinner."

"God willing," Bishop Egbert said.

"And able," Silvas added. Bishop Egbert nodded. Alone, he found no call to dispute the wizard's qualification. Silvas bowed and left the bishop to return to his own suite of rooms. Carillia was dressing.

"I hope everything is prepared properly," she said. "It is a good thing that Bay was able to warn us that we would have company."

"He left as soon as Bishop Egbert accepted my invitation. I wasn't sure of his acceptance, or I would have mentioned the possibility before I left."

"You were in little shape for that kind of planning when you left, my heart. You feel better now?"

"As you can see," he replied. "The passage of a few hours today has done more good than the eighteen hours of sleep that preceded them."

"How many will there be for dinner?"

"The bishop and his dozen monks. Brother Paul from the village. And two from the castle, Sir Eustace and Fitz-Matthew."

Carillia nodded. "Bay had the count right, then. I wasn't sure but that it might have changed after he left you."

"Bay be wrong on a simple fact?" Silvas laughed. "That would be a first. Are you sure you don't mind playing hostess this evening, my love?"

"Would that I had the chance more often, my heart," she replied. "It is so rare that we do any entertaining."

"It's rare that anyone is willing to chance the horrors of a sorcerer's lair." Silvas laughed again. "I have decided to hide nothing from any of our churchmen. I wouldn't insult the bishop so, or rob him of any information he needs to be effective in the coming fight. None of the secrets of the Seven Towers need be concealed from them."

"I note that you do not include Sir Eustace or his steward in that," Carillia said.

"Prudence seems to indicate otherwise," Silvas said.

"Eustace already holds enough anger for three men. I wouldn't give him any additional load to bear. He might not be able to withstand it." In his own mind Silvas was less charitable to the knight, but he saw no need to share his darker impressions with Carillia. "Once Sir Eustace and Master Henry depart, we can do some serious planning with the men of the Church."

"You think we will have time for civility and careful planning?" Carillia asked.

"That isn't for us to say." His voice showed a trace of sadness. "So far the Blue Rose has chosen to attack in the middle of the night, when evil is at its strongest. If the pattern holds, we should have time for talk at least. I can give the bishop all of the information I have."

"Will you be strong enough for a Council tonight?" Carillia asked.

"I have to be," Silvas said flatly. "And *that* may be the signal the Blue Rose awaits. They may attack during our Council again."

"Then we must be armed as best we can before," Carillia said.

The great hall was bright with lights. Dozens of candles burned smokelessly on high stands. There were torches in sconces and blazing fires in both hearths. Despite the season the room was not overheated, though. Evenings in the mountain valley of the Seven Towers were rarely extreme. And a gentle flow of air found its way through the great hall, clearing away the smoke produced by torches and fireplaces without guttering the candles.

The tables had been rearranged . . . and some had been removed. There was no trace of the special arrangements made for Bosc's porcine kind or Braf's lupine warriors. And only human servants and guards were in evidence. The tables had been set with silver. Loaves of bread, bunches of green onions, radishes, and bowls of fruit had been arranged for the diners. There was plenty of wine and ale. Even on short notice Silvas's staff had prepared a dinner that he would be proud of.

By the time Silvas and Carillia entered the great hall,

most of their guests were already present. Sir Eustace and
Henry Fitz-Matthew had been in the great hall since coming to the castle. They were off by one of the kegs of ale.
To Silvas's eye, they had been partaking rather freely of
the brew. Sir Eustace looked around the great hall, a deep
scowl plain on his face before he spotted Silvas and
Carillia. Fitz-Matthew looked fearful, as if he wished he
were almost anywhere else on Earth.

Brother Paul and one of the cathedral monks were
missing. *They've gone to get the bishop,* Silvas guessed
easily. The rest of the monks had apparently come into
the great hall within the past few minutes. None had
taken a seat yet. A few had wine. Others seemed to be debating whether or not they should indulge before the
bishop arrived.

"There is such a feeling of power about these churchmen," Carillia whispered.

"I would guess that they have all been selected by
Bishop Egbert for their abilities," Silvas whispered back.
He patted the hand that Carillia had on his arm. "The
bishop himself appears quite formidable."

"I would expect that," Carillia replied. Silvas nodded
and they walked across the room, not quite toward their
places at the head table, but not directly toward either
group of guests.

Sir Eustace made a half turn, not completely turning
his back on his host but coming close. Fitz-Matthew kept
his eyes on his master, giving Silvas only one quick, nervous glance. The churchmen were quite attentive, though.
Silvas saw open curiosity in some of them, a more gen-
teel veil of politeness in others.

"The bishop will be with us quite soon," one of the
older monks said, taking a couple of steps toward Silvas
and Carillia before he spoke.

"I hope you find the wine satisfactory," Carillia said,
gesturing at the goblet the monk was holding.

"This is my lady, Carillia," Silvas said.

"Honored, my lady," the monk said. "I am Brother Andrew. And, yes, the wine is excellent." As if to prove the
point, he raised his goblet in toast and took a long drink.
"Quite excellent."

Bishop Egbert came in then, with Brother Paul and the twelfth monk from St. Ives. Silvas went to greet the bishop and to introduce him to Carillia. Then he led the way to the table. Sir Eustace and Fitz-Matthew came away from the ale keg as soon as the bishop entered.

For this occasion the tables remaining in the great hall had been brought together and arranged in a common *T* formation, although the "lower" table wasn't physically lower. Breaking from usual custom, Carillia sat at Silvas's left, giving the place of honor at the right to the bishop. Sir Eustace was at Carillia's other side. Brother Paul and Henry Fitz-Matthew had the first places at the long "lower" table, and the monks from St. Ives filled the rest of the places.

As soon as everyone started to sit, servants came in with the first courses of hot food.

"If you would offer the blessing, Your Excellency?" Silvas asked the bishop as the servants left to get more trays. Silvas wondered if the request would surprise the prelate—as it obviously did Brother Paul and a few of the monks from St. Ives.

"With great pleasure," Egbert said. His grin was warm, knowing. And his blessing was blessedly short. He made the sign of the cross, which was echoed by everyone at the table, save for Silvas and Carillia. Most of the guests took note of that, and Silvas saw a clear cross section of attitudes. Only the bishop and the vicar seemed to show no reaction at all.

The only guests who showed any discomfort at dining in the magical castle of a wizard who disdained the forms of the Church were the two men from the castle of Mecq. The knight wore his customary anger, little modified in front of the bishop. Fitz-Matthew's face was a study in barely suppressed fear. He had reacted to Silvas with fear since first coming inside the Seven Towers.

The meal itself might have taken place at almost any major castle—except that the food tasted better, the table service was that of a king or emperor, and the room was much cleaner, free of the common smells of animals and moldy straw. If Sir Eustace or his steward took any comparisons to their own home, they were not apparent. But even those two men did not slight the food. Though they started slowly, they were soon eating as heartily as any of the monks, whose appetites seemed to belie their gaunt looks.

Bishop Egbert guided the conversation. He and his monks were all talkative enough, given to passing along the gossip that had come their way. News of the outside world was rare in Mecq. Even Sir Eustace managed to occasionally repress his anger long enough to ask a civil question. No mention was made of the Blue Rose or of Mecq's problems—not during the meal.

"A splendid repast," the bishop said when everyone appeared to be sated. His grin had grown wider through the meal. "My brothers and I all offer our deepest thanks." He allowed the grin to dissolve. "May God grant that it see us through the trials that lie ahead of us."

"I don't know which I wish more," Silvas said. "I dread the arrival of this great battle, but at the same time I wish to have it behind me, however it may end."

"An understandable dilemma," the bishop assured him. "You are quite certain that the Blue Rose is behind the troubles here?"

"Positive. Their signature on some of the illnesses I treated was unmistakable. And we have had later confirmation of that." He hesitated, glanced quickly at Sir Eustace and then back to the bishop.

Bishop Egbert nodded. "There is time enough for that later. About immediate measures?"

"There have been two direct assaults," Silvas said. Sir Eustace raised an eyebrow at that. Brother Paul focused his attention more closely on the wizard. "The first was strictly on the Seven Towers. It was the second that included Mecq. And as the second was stronger, more determined, than the first, so I believe that the third will be stronger and more determined than the second. The next battle, when it comes, may well decide the issue." He paused before he added, "For Mecq, perhaps for everyone."

"Have you any idea what form this attack may take?" Sir Eustace asked.

Silvas shrugged. "It's impossible to be certain yet.

There *may* be a more mundane element, a human army, in addition to the weapons that were evidenced before."

"I have too few men to deal with an army," Eustace said quickly. "If I arm everyone in my castle who can handle a weapon, I could hardly turn back the merest outriders of an army."

"You have the advantage of height, and there will be no time for a siege," Silvas said. "The issue will be decided in a day or a night."

"And you do not stand alone," Bishop Egbert said.

"I will defend my land and people to the last," the knight said after a long silence. He stared directly at Silvas.

"There was never any doubt of that," Silvas replied quietly. It was not the time to willfully antagonize the thane further.

Eustace nodded curtly, then pushed back from the table. "It's time I return to my family," he said. "Night is fast upon us and I have work yet to do." Fitz-Matthew quickly got to his feet as well. Silvas and the others rose more slowly.

"Remember, Sir Eustace," Egbert said, "if our Unseen Lord sees us safely through this night, I will celebrate Mass at dawn in the church here."

Eustace nodded, then bowed more formally to the prelate and left, with his steward at his heels. After they were gone, Bishop Egbert sighed as he sat again.

"Sir Eustace is a difficult man," Silvas said. This time Brother Paul didn't feel compelled to offer any defense. Nor did the bishop say anything on the subject.

"If your brothers would care to continue here, the rest of us might retire to a cozier room to continue our talk," Silvas said. "Some things are best said between close walls."

Silvas, Carillia, Bishop Egbert, and Brother Paul left together. Silvas lead the way to a more intimate room just off the great hall. Koshka came in with a tray of goblets and two bottles of the spicy Alpine wine that Silvas had grown so fond of.

"I conceal nothing of pertinence from you," Silvas said when he saw the bishop staring openly at Koshka. Brother Paul also stared, but he was sitting a little off to the side, where his gaping was less obvious. "Seeing one of Koshka's kin is partial explanation for the look of fear that Sir Eustace's steward wears so firmly."

"I have never seen your like before," the bishop said, addressing himself directly to Koshka. "Would you mind coming closer?"

Koshka looked to Silvas, and when the wizard nodded, Koshka bobbed his head and stepped right up to the bishop.

"Extraordinary," Eustace said after a close perusal of Koshka's head. "Excuse my ignorance, please, but do you speak?"

"Yes, Your Excellency," Koshka said in neutral tones.

"I have a couple of dozen of his folk here, and others who would look as strange to you," Silvas said. "They are as human as you or I, no matter how they appear. They come from a place that is so far away that the distance is unfathomable . . . yet they come from a place that is, in some ways, no farther than the great hall is from us here."

The bishop looked from Koshka to Silvas and back.

"You may go now, Koshka," Silvas said. "Thank you."

Koshka bobbed his head and left the room quickly.

"He is a most excellent servant," Silvas said. "His people, and the others, are all good at their jobs and loyal beyond measure."

"Then you are indeed fortunate," Egbert said. His voice displayed no tremors at the encounter.

"I believe so," Silvas agreed. "Now, perhaps I had best tell you all I know of the situation here." He proceeded to do just that, speaking first of the vow he had made to the Unseen Lord so long before, of the purpose behind his lifelong peregrination. When he finally reached the immediate matters, Silvas didn't even hold back the tales of his meetings after the previous Council and after the battles, the murky stranger who appeared to be their Unseen Lord, and the things he had told Silvas. Carillia listened as intently as the two churchmen when Silvas got to those parts, since he had never mentioned them to her.

"If the Blue Rose gives us time tonight," Silvas finally said, "I will summon a Council of my advisers in the spirit. I would be honored to have you and the vicar join us. I would welcome your advice."

Bishop Egbert leaned back. Being an adept of the Greater Mysteries of the White Brotherhood, he had a vague idea of what the wizard was proposing. *It will be something beyond the scope of conclave but similar,* he told himself. He closed his eyes to pray and to meditate on the wisdom and propriety of accepting. *I need to do whatever I may to save this village and thwart the Blue Rose,* he decided. *And I would not willingly miss this opportunity.*

"I accept your offer most eagerly," he said when he opened his eyes. He turned to Brother Paul. "I do not say this in command, brother. I *urge* you to accept, though I must also caution you that what you will experience goes far beyond the Lesser Mysteries. It may test your faith sorely."

Brother Paul bowed his head. "In that case, Excellency, how could I possibly refuse?"

"I will come for you in sleep," Silvas said. "There are certain precautions that I must take before *any* Council, and more so under the present circumstances. We can find a bed for you here as well, Vicar."

Brother Paul hesitated. "If it does not interfere with your magic, Lord Wizard, I belong where my parishioners can find me instantly at need, in the manse of St. Katrinka's."

"It will not hinder the Council, as long as I know where to find you."

"It is your place," Egbert told Brother Paul. "Go in peace, my son."

"A good man," Silvas said after the friar left. "Much better than I would have expected in a place such as Mecq."

"I believe you are right," Egbert said, looking at the door through which the vicar had departed. "When this is over, he will bear examination. He may be fit for more than the Lesser Mysteries."

"That is, of course, your domain," Silvas said. "But I do know that he hasn't flinched at anything he has seen or experienced since I came here."

Egbert sipped at his wine and looked at Carillia. "You have an aura of power around you as well," the bishop told her. "Yet you have been mostly silent this evening."

"It is not my place, Excellency," Carillia said.

The bishop tilted his head to the side. "That is, of course, between the two of you," he said in conscious imitation of Silvas's earlier words. He transferred his attention to the wizard.

"And that horse of yours. There is more to him than his great size."

"You are very discerning," Silvas said. A smile couldn't be helped. *But did you discern just* how *much more there is to him?* he wondered. There was real curiosity behind that. Silvas had never come across anyone who could guess at Bay's true intelligence or his other gifts, like speech.

"We are a community," Silvas said. "I may be a wizard, but I could not function fully without the support of my advisers."

Egbert raised an eyebrow at the word *advisers,* but before he could ask about it, there was a knock at the door.

"Come in, Bosc," Silvas called. Turning back to the bishop, he explained, "I recognized the sound of his knock."

Bosc entered but stopped just inside the door. "The—" He stopped, then started again immediately. "Will there be anything special for us tonight, lord?"

"It's all right, Bosc," Silvas said. "Yes, there will be a Council, if no attack comes first. You will tell Bay?"

Bosc bobbed his head.

"You're not the one who was here before," Egbert said. It was no question. "You have the aura of power as well."

"I but serve my lords." Bosc looked uncomfortable at the bishop's scrutiny.

"I'm sure you do," the bishop said. Bosc bobbed his head again and hurried out of the room.

"What other wonders await me tonight?" Egbert asked.

"I think that any additional wonders will be a surprise to me as well as to you, Excellency. It's about time to begin to think of the night and the Council. If there is anything you need for your own preparations?"

"Nothing special, thank you," Egbert said. "I have my

faith. I have my crucifix and my rosary. I need nothing else."

Silvas inclined his head. "I will come for you when the time is right."

20

A Council was not a casual gathering, no matter how casually Silvas's advisers accepted the notice of a Summoning. Sometimes years elapsed between situations where Silvas felt the need of a formal Council to help with his work in some village or other. The membership of his Council had been fixed since the days when Louis the Stammerer ruled the Holy Roman Empire. Carillia had come to Silvas then. And the last time outsiders had joined in a Council, King Edmund had been looking for a way to break the alliance between the Scots and the Norsemen, to set them fighting each other.

When the talk in the room off of the great hall ended, Silvas and Carillia escorted the bishop to his room before they went on to their own quarters. Carillia started to prepare for bed at once. Silvas picked up his quarterstaff and went to warn Braf Goleg of the coming Council and the possibility of attack while it was in progress.

"We be ready, lord," Braf assured him.

"I trust there was no problem about dinner tonight," Silvas said. "You know why the unusual arrangements were needed."

"Aye, lord. It went well." The teeth that showed when Braf grinned were pointed, the tearing and ripping teeth of a carnivore.

The two made a hurried inspection of the walls and gates. The Seven Towers were sealed off against attack. Sentries and warriors were in place and alert. Finally Silvas left Braf to his duties and returned to the keep.

The central tower of the Glade was quiet. In the great hall, only the fires in the twin hearths were still burning, along with a single torch near the main entrance. Satin and Velvet came to walk this part of the tour with Silvas.

The cats came as hunters now. Their earlier nervousness had been channeled into the exaggerated patience of the stalk. They flanked Silvas as he prowled the halls and larger rooms of the keep, their ears forward, heads moving constantly, looking and listening for any threat. Silvas felt himself slipping more firmly into the same mode. He had to switch his grip on the quarterstaff from time to time, consciously relaxing his hold on it.

The room where the monks were quartered was silent. The last of their chanted prayers had ended, but there was no great noise of snoring yet. On the first level of the keep, the only room that still held talking was the watch room, where sentries could come to spend a moment before or after their turns on the walls.

On the broad staircase leading up to the higher levels of the keep, the cats bounded ahead, going to the next landing and looking along the corridors there.

"You feel it too," Silvas whispered when he caught up. "The feeling that the climax nears." The cats only glanced at him briefly before turning their attention outward again. They would not be distracted from the hunt.

"All right, let's go to work," Silvas told them. The cats led the way back to the other stairs, the ones that led up through Silvas's library to the conjuring chamber.

The cats prowled that room carefully, staying outside the pentagram but otherwise crossing and recrossing almost every inch of the room. Velvet went to the narrow stairway that led to the turret that looked out over Mecq. After a second Satin joined her mate and went farther up the stairs. When the cats remained poised on the stairs, Silvas went past them, all of the way to the turret.

Mecq seemed as quiet as the Glade. There were no lights visible in the village. Smoke came from the Boar and Bear. There were a couple of small lights visible up at the castle. Silvas narrowed his eyes to focus on the walls of Mecq's fortress. He could see two guards walking their posts, and he saw Henry Fitz-Matthew standing above the gate, looking nervously toward the village or—more likely—at the pillar of smoke.

"Such fear is the fuel that feeds the Blue Rose," Silvas mumbled. Fitz-Matthew was clear of the taint of the heretics. The wizard would have felt that presence in the steward, but Fitz-Matthew might not remain free of it if temptation were laid upon him. "No man should have to bear such fear," Silvas said, regretting that he should be the cause of so much of Fitz-Matthew's fear. "It were better turned outward, at the Blue Rose, and tempered into fire." He spoke a quick spell while his eyes remained on the steward, then sighed. "It is the best I can do at the moment." Silvas took one more quick look down at the village, then returned to his workroom.

"I think the time is about on us," he said softly. The cats went to their protected circles.

When Silvas entered his pentagram and started to work the magics that had to precede his Council, he spoke each spell carefully, slowly, taking more pains with precision than he ever had before—and he was always careful and precise in this work. The web of protective spells he wove was intricate and strong. After he finished his normal preparatory work, he added a spell of seeing so he could look at his handiwork to make sure that it was perfect, that there was nothing he could add to make it more complete. Only when he was satisfied with every line and intersection did he lower himself to the floor to begin the spell of Summoning. He took as much extra care with that as he had with the preparatory work, the more so because there were outsiders to bring to *this* Council.

Silvas went for Carillia first, as he always did. She rose from her sleeping body and passed out of the bedroom to wait for him to summon the others.

Bishop Egbert was next. Entering the room he had given to the bishop, Silvas noted the ritual defenses Egbert had deployed. The pattern was familiar, even if Silvas had never seen it executed so meticulously before. He would have recognized the signs of the White Brotherhood in the pattern even if he had known nothing of the individual who had drawn it.

"It is time," Silvas said in the spirit. The bishop responded with a slight show of surprise. Although the eyes of Egbert's body didn't open with his spirit eyes, the eyelids fluttered enough that Silvas felt it necessary to speak an extra spell of safe separation.

"Simply sit up and get out of bed," Silvas instructed when the bishop seemed uncertain how to proceed.

Egbert stood, then looked down at his body. He leaned
over it, as if to insure that it was still alive, then he
straightened up and turned to Silvas. "Walk through
there," the wizard said, pointing to the nearest wall.
Egbert hesitated for only an instant.

It was time to go for the vicar of Mecq. Silvas didn't
consciously plan a course that would take him to St.
Katrinka's. That was unnecessary. He simply passed
through the walls of the keep and the curtain wall of the
Glade straight into the church as if they were adjacent.
Another passage brought him to the small room where the
vicar slept. Brother Paul also looked back down at his
still sleeping body, for longer than the bishop had. But finally Paul turned to Silvas, brought his hands together,
and bowed his head briefly to signify that he was ready
to leave.

"Walk that way," Silvas pointed. When the friar left the
room, Silvas went through another wall and returned to
the Seven Towers to finish his summoning. Bosc and Bay
remained to be gathered.

There was again the sense of a room around them, but
there was no room. The Council gathered on the ridge of
Mount Balq, across the Eyler from the castle of Sir
Eustace, at a point where they could look across at the
castle and down at the river and into the valleys of Mecq
and Blethye without moving more than a few steps. There
were stones at a comfortable height for sitting. Once
more Bay did not appear so large; Bosc did not appear so
small.

Night had been effectively banished. There was the
pale, ghostly glow of a false daylight, a light without sun
or moon, without any apparent source. There were no
shadows or clouds either.

This vantage does not exist, Silvas noted quickly. There
was no small flat area at the near end of Mount Balq.
That did not stop him from taking immediate advantage
of the location. He surveyed all of the terrain, concentrating on the valley downstream, the demesne of the Duke
of Blethye, but he didn't ignore the castle of Mecq or the
village and its valley.

"Do you feel it?" Silvas asked, stretching out his arm

to indicate Blethye. He glanced at Bishop Egbert, who was also surveying his surroundings. Brother Paul stood as close to his bishop as he could get. There remained a trace of apprehension on the friar's face.

"I feel it," Egbert said. "The Devil's armies are at work. The mark of the Blue Rose is close. It was not so strong when we rode to crusade against them in Burgundy."

"You do not wear the cross of a crusader," Silvas observed.

"I wear another cross," Egbert replied. He turned away from Blethye to look at Bay and Bosc. He studied them closely, then turned his attention to Silvas.

"This is a remarkable magic," the bishop said.

"It but provides a setting for our Council," Silvas said. "And this is not the usual setting. Our location was not of my choosing."

Bishop Egbert allowed just the slightest trace of concern to show on his face. "There has been interference already?"

Silvas shook his head once. "I think not. Interference of that sort would have given signs. I think rather that this is the doing of our Unseen Lord, putting us here to overlook the field of our trial."

Egbert moved to the side overlooking Mecq. He pointed and let his hand drift across the cottages and other buildings. "I can almost see the lights of each soul down there. Our charges, the flock we must defend against the wolves of evil."

"But now our Council," Silvas said. Everyone but Bay sat. There were just enough stones. The wizard started out with a quick review, including much of what he had told the bishop earlier. Bay and Bosc hadn't heard some of that, and in any case, knowledge shared in Council ran deeper than the same knowledge shared in the flesh. But time didn't run as rapidly in Council as it did in the world outside. Silvas had no particular worries about wasting too much of the night.

When he finished, Carillia took over. "I do not see the lights of souls seeking our protection," she said, glancing at the bishop, "but I hear their supplications. The fear that runs through Mecq this night is awesome in its pathos.

The final assault of the Blue Rose cannot be long delayed. This fear ripples away from it across this pond, and the point where the stone falls is close." She made a sweeping gesture with her right arm. "The souls of your flock need comforting this night, Brother Paul." She closed her eyes and seemed to withdraw from the gathering in some unfathomable manner.

There was hardly a pause between Carillia's last word and Bay's first. "Armies are gathering, but I can make out nothing of their nature. They are veiled in a mist I cannot penetrate."

Egbert and Paul both stared at the horse. The friar was visibly shaken by the specter of a horse speaking. Bishop Egbert remained composed, but he too felt disturbed.

"Do you speak only in Council, or is this part of your normal power?" the bishop asked.

Bay didn't look to Silvas before he said, "It is part of my normal being. I usually do not speak in front of outsiders, for reasons good and plentiful. But Silvas said that we need hide nothing from you, Bishop Egbert of St. Ives. He said that you have the strength to know whatever may be pertinent."

"And me?" escaped from Brother Paul's lips without his volition. Egbert turned and laid his hands on the friar's shoulders.

"You have more strength than you dream of, brother," Egbert said. "That, and your faith, will sustain you. Our Unseen Lord stands with us."

"That is true, Brother Paul," Carillia said, opening her eyes. She had not moved, but still she seemed to somehow *reappear* when her eyes opened. "His presence is very real to all of us."

The others watched Brother Paul for several minutes. His inner struggle was reflected clearly on his face. Not until resolution was visible there did Bosc make his contribution to the Council.

"I feel the Earth," he said by way of prolog for the outsiders. "I feel her bones and blood the way you might feel the pulsing of life by holding your hand against a man's chest." He held his hand against his own chest.

"Upheavals are coming," Bosc said. "I hear mourning sing through the Earth. I feel passion erupting, shaking everything around it." He shook his head softly. "I do not fully understand these visions. They are new to me." Finished, Bosc looked first to Silvas and then to Egbert.

"I don't know that I can contribute much," the bishop started, his hand moving to his chest, where his crucifix—or its image—hung.

"Look!" Bay shouted. He jerked his head toward the sky over Blethye. Carillia and Bosc had been sitting with their backs to the duchy. Egbert and Paul had been at the side, intent on the members of the group, not on the outer surroundings. And even Silvas, who *had* been looking toward Blethye, had not been watching the sky. They all looked now.

A storm was developing over Blethye, dark purple and black clouds blotting out the artificial light of the Council. The clouds rolled and grew, curling into one another and ballooning, swirling and climbing, coming slowly nearer, presenting a massive front. Yellow-green lightning flashed, showing wine-red highlights to the clouds. The thunder that rolled toward Mount Balq was the sound of whips cracking over a mighty herd of horses' hoofs stampeding through the night. As the clouds grew and thickened, the thunder increased and became independent of the lightning. An evil wind blew up the slope into the faces of Silvas and the others. Faint in the distance, there were ghostly images of demonic horses and riders, the armies of the dead coming to fight for the souls of the living. Even fainter were the banshee cries that Mecq had heard during the previous attack.

"This is not happening now," Silvas said. The words came out slowly and required the full force of his concentration. The impression of overwhelming evil and unavoidable destruction that flowed across the hilltop was so strong that Silvas had difficulty resisting it. When he could force his eyes away from the assault on his spirit, he looked at the others. They all appeared transfixed by the show. Carillia was holding her own, projecting her customary aura of calmness, only vaguely distorted by the upheavals. Bishop Egbert stood with his feet well apart, facing the clouds, his hands raised against the storm. His lips moved as he went through the words of a silent incantation. Beside him, Brother Paul repeatedly drew the sign of the cross in the air before him. Bosc stood with his hands on his hips, face raised to the sky. He showed no reaction to the storm, and neither did Bay.

Suddenly the heavens split open and a blinding light struck the observers, forcing them first to close their eyes against it and then to blink repeatedly to adjust to the brightness. The thunder of phantom hoofs was drowned out by dirges coming through the growing break in the clouds. This was a lethal music that froze the face and threatened to turn souls to ice. It seemed to almost physically swallow the people on the hill.

The music ended. The scene shifted again.

It was day and it was night—at the same time and in the same place. The people atop Mount Balq saw the gods doing battle on a brightly lit plain. But above the battle there was a night sky, with stars shining in their appointed places. There was no way to identify the gods, but none of the people on the hill had any doubt that they were gods. Even Brother Paul, who only knew the Lesser Mysteries that did not include the pantheon, sensed that these were gods and their chosen champions. And some of the gods were falling. The stars above them were snuffed out one by one, the pace of extinctions increasing rapidly.

Total darkness settled over the Council on the hilltop, a blackness so complete that Silvas couldn't see his hand no matter how close he brought it to his eyes. It was as if the universe had ended, leaving only his disembodied consciousness to contemplate the void.

"Carillia?" Silvas waited but there was no reply. One by one he called each of the others and waited for an answer. "Is anyone here?" he asked at last . . . and he heard only silence. He shuffled around in a slow, tight circle, pausing frequently, straining his ears to hear any sound. But there was nothing. Even his feet made no sound when he tried stamping. He clapped his hands. *That* he could hear.

"Where am I now?" brought no answer, not even an echo.

"What do I do?" There was still no response.

He waited, and he listened. Eventually he tried to walk,

sliding one foot forward, just a little, testing his stance before bringing his weight fully forward. He didn't forget that he had been on top of Mount Balq, or a representation of that hill, before the darkness came. Even in the spirit, if he was still in the spirit, he didn't want to tumble from the hill. He couldn't guess what damage it might do to him. He counted his steps. He paused when the count reached ten and called out again, "Is anyone here?" and waited for an answer that did not come. He took another ten careful, sliding steps and tried again. And then ten more.

"If I were still on Mount Balq, I would have fallen off the edge by now, so I must not be there any longer." *Where am I?* was just a thought this time.

"If my body is traveling, I have strayed beyond the pentagram by now," he whispered. That possibility brought a shiver to him. He turned around, trying to be as exact as he could, and he counted out thirty careful steps, hoping that they were the same size as the steps he had taken before, hoping that they would put him back in the protected center of his pentagram—*if* his body had actually strayed.

Silvas sat down, feeling for the ground under him. There was some sort of surface, but he could make out nothing of its composition. He sat cross-legged and rested his hands on his knees.

"Even if there is no solution, there should be an answer." He closed his eyes and started an incantation. But there was no power to the spell. Long before Silvas came to the end of it, he knew that it would not work.

This is not the same as the other time, though. I can feel the power. I simply can't manipulate it. It is just out of reach now, not nonexistent. He couldn't figure out what difference that might make, but it *was* a difference, something to hold on to until he had more.

"Open your eyes. Stand up."

The voice sounded vaguely familiar, stirring memories too deep within Silvas for them to surface instantly. But he obeyed. He opened his eyes and stood. The darkness was gone. There was good light around him now, vague, with no apparent source, but light. The figure of a man— idealized as only poets or artists could ever picture man—

stood some dozen paces away. The only thing missing
was something solid for the two figures to stand on. It
was as if the clear blue sky of a summer afternoon extended in every direction. Silvas and this form of a perfect man seemed to stand on air. The wizard pressed
down with his foot. The air seemed as solid below as
rock ever had.

"Look at me."

Silvas had really not been aware that he had been
avoiding looking at the figure until then, but he looked
now, and the stranger's eyes grabbed his and locked his
gaze.

*"I am your Unseen Lord. I am the god of the White
Brotherhood, the god of all Christians who follow the orthodox Roman Way. I am the Lord you swore your vows
to."*

"I know that, Lord," Silvas replied, shocked at how
thin and childlike his voice sounded next to the voice of
his Lord.

"Come closer."

Silvas could not have disobeyed if he had wanted to.
He stepped forward, striding as if he had a mile to cover
and not just a few yards. Silvas saw pain and fear in the
eyes of his master. That sight brought tremors to Silvas,
tremors that ran completely through him. He didn't stop
walking until he couldn't advance without running into
this god ... and that was unthinkable.

The god put his hands over Silvas's eyes and pressed.
The wizard felt a heat that was intense, incredible, but still
bearable, almost comforting. Silvas was reminded of the
heat against his eyes when he tried to stare into the distant
star with his telesight. That had been pure pain. This was
also pain, but it was an almost enjoyable ache.

Though no further words were spoken for an eternity,
Silvas could feel knowledge and—inescapably—the power
that this knowledge represented pouring into him, much
faster than he could consciously assimilate it. He didn't
worry about missing anything of importance, or forgetting
some vital detail, though. Among the first pieces of knowledge that took possession of Silvas was the assurance that
this would all remain part of him.

And he knew that he was being made privy to many of

the deepest secrets of the gods. That knowledge had to convey a power that was worlds beyond what he had possessed before, something greater than any wizard before him had ever enjoyed . . . or suffered. It didn't make him a god, but it removed him a step or two farther from his fellow men.

The names of the gods were no longer beyond Silvas's ken. He knew their idealized faces, the range and limits of their powers—and even *they* had definite limits, the makeup of their alliances and history, who was on which side, who stood apart or remained undecided. He *knew*, beyond any doubt, that the god holding his eyes was indeed his Unseen Lord, the god of the White Brotherhood and of the Roman Church since Constantine made Christianity the official religion of his empire.

I liked the new pomp and the efficient organization that spread the rites so quickly. It amused me. I took it and made it my own.

I knew that, Silvas thought. *It is part of the Greater Mysteries. Religions are made by men and the gods select from the choices that are available.* More came to him now. While a god remained associated with a church or sect, there was a process of mutual adaptation, one to the other, change on *both* sides.

If the usurpers behind the Blue Rose destroy me—and that is the only way they will unseat me—there will be chaos throughout the world, perhaps the fall of what remains of any civilization. It will be worse than the fall of Rome and it may be more permanent, an eternal age of darkness.

The knowledge became part of Silvas—and more. This fight had become so important to the gods on both sides that the maiming or destruction of the mortal world was preferable to defeat. Knowledge continued to pour into him.

Gods die more easily than churches, the religious power structures that you mortals create.

Silvas took in the last burdens of knowledge. *It is as I feared,* he thought, almost losing awareness of the divine hands pressed against his eyes. *What is coming could be both Armageddon and* Götterdämerung. *Our world could end with no gods surviving to even conduct a proper Judgment Day in its wake.*

He saw armies of the dead fighting alongside armies of the living. Gods and mages would duel, all centered on Mecq—for no reason that Silvas could find within the well of knowledge he had been given. And there was no explanation from his Unseen Lord. He still had only the guesses he had made so far.

The god took his hands away from Silvas's eyes. The wizard blinked several times at the return of the light.

"I have armed and armored you as best I can," the god told Silvas, and then he disappeared, taking the light with him.

Silvas found himself alone in that total darkness again. This time he felt a crushing weight on his soul, a weight without precedent or equal.

21

When Silvas woke back in his workshop, he wasn't surprised at his exhaustion. Since coming to Mecq, that had been the rule. The sense of weight remained, but it was different than it had been in the presence of his Unseen Lord. Silvas was prone, his face pressed against the marble floor. He breathed easily. This time he felt no apprehensions about the drained feeling. For several minutes he was content to keep his eyes closed and breathe as deeply as he could while energy returned to him.

This time the energy returned quickly. A trickle became a flood as power surged through him—a new sensation. *I have changed,* he realized, and then he opened his eyes.

The sensation of weight was immediately explained. Silvas was dressed in a full suit of plate armor. He had never worn armor of any sort before. His craft had always been his armor. *This is like the plate the gods wore in their battle,* he thought. It was as shiny as polished silver. When he got to his knees, he noted that there was even a sword at his waist, and he never wore a sword. It had been many years—decades—since he had even practiced with a long blade.

Standing, Silvas found that the armor no longer weighed so heavily on him. From the feel it might be no more than heavy wool—winter garments, but stiff. Silvas ran his hands over the breastplate. The metal was cold. *"I have armed and armored you as best I can."* Silvas recalled the words of his Unseen Lord and believed that the armor was as strong as a god could make it.

Memories of the Council and its sequel flooded Silvas's mind. There was so much there, knowledge that went far beyond any possible needs of this coming fight.

There's no time to meander casually through the new corridors I see, Silvas thought with a certain amount of regret. In the most direct sense, knowledge was power to a wizard. The more knowledge he possessed, the greater his ability. And Silvas had just acquired a large fund of new knowledge. But there was too much to do. *I need to check on the others. I need to look out to see how much of the demon force is already on the march.* He needed to climb to the turret that looked out over Mecq, and he needed to look over the walls of the Seven Towers as well.

"I think that what we saw in Council was premonition, or the lies of the Blue Rose, but I must be sure," he whispered.

Quickly he spoke the spells to close down the defenses of the finished Council. There was finally time to notice that it was still night outside, though the darkness was waning, and that Satin and Velvet remained in their protective circles.

"Mecq first," Silvas said when he stepped out of the pentagram. "Come, kittens. We have real work to do now."

Even walking was no problem in the armor. The suit was complete, from helmet to cuisses. Only the hands, and the legs from the knees down, were left unprotected. Walking was no problem, but it wasn't silent. The pieces of armor moved against each other. The sword's scabbard rattled against the cuisse on Silvas's left thigh. On the metal stairs leading up to the turret that overlooked Mecq, the unaccustomed noise was quite distracting. Even the cats seemed bothered by it.

Mecq was quiet. Silvas looked toward the sky over the twin peaks. There was nothing that looked like the gathering storm he had seen in Council. Closer, below, the village was already astir for the new day. A few people were up and about. More would be soon. Silvas looked at St. Katrinka's and remembered that the bishop was due to say Mass at sunrise.

"That can't be far off," Silvas whispered. "I should make sure that the bishop has risen."

He stared at the rough cross on top of Mecq's church for several minutes, then turned away from the view of Mecq at last and headed down the stairs. He needed to check on all of the participants of his Council, but Bishop Egbert had to be first. Silvas knocked on the bishop's door, and Egbert called for him to enter. Two candles were burning. The bishop was up, still examining the suit of armor that had been draped over him.

"I woke with this on me," Egbert said.

"As did I," Silvas replied. "Our Unseen Lord told me, *'I have armed and armored you as best I can.'*"

"There was even this." Bishop Egbert picked a mace off of the bed. "I have never wielded the weapons of war, but if I must . . ." He shook his head. "We are forbidden to shed the blood of men. Is it really so important that no blood is shed if we crush a skull or chest?" Though the iron ball of the mace was heavy, the bishop had no trouble waving it on its wooden handle.

"I know you have questions. I have plenty of my own," Silvas said. "But first I have to check on the others who were with us. It's almost dawn. There is no trace of the enemy over Mecq, but how long that will remain true, I cannot say."

Egbert nodded absently. "I will check on Brother Paul myself if you like."

"That will save time. I'll meet you there as soon as I can, and I'll make sure that your brothers here have a guide to St. Katrinka's when they are ready."

Egbert nodded and looked at his armor again. "It will be difficult to get even a surplice over this."

One by one Silvas visited the others, beginning with Carillia and ending with Bay. All were dressed in divine armor. The plate that the giant horse wore seemed almost monumental. It dazzled and shone in the faintest light. All three of Silvas's longtime councilors were unsteady, uncertain, when he first got to them. All spoke of having suffered from this Council as from none before. Carillia seemed especially somber, withdrawn in a moodiness that Silvas had never seen in her before. Bay had lost some of his normal assertiveness. He was quiet, even when he spoke.

"It seems we are indeed ready for the final battle," Bay said almost hesitantly, as if speaking the words might make them true.

"We will all have to go to St. Katrinka's," Silvas decided. "We may need to be together before this day is over, and we certainly need to continue the night's Council in the flesh this morning."

Bay simply nodded. Bosc said nothing, even though he had never left the Seven Towers to visit any of the villages and towns in which Silvas was working. Finally Silvas went back up to tell Carillia.

"I think you are right," she said. On occasion, when the tower of smoke was in a major town, Carillia had gone visiting with Silvas before, but never—obviously—in a situation like this. She moved against Silvas as gently as possible so their armor wouldn't rattle and clash, and put her hands on his shoulders. He put his arms around her, awkwardly with the armor.

"I fear this may be the last time we will ever be together like this, my heart," Carillia said. "A silly, womanly fear perhaps, but I cannot escape it."

Carillia spoke so softly that Silvas almost missed the import of what she had said. He blinked once, slowly, as her words penetrated. But his sense of urgency allowed him time for no more than a brief smile and a transient caress of her cheek.

The four of them walked out of the Glade into Mecq together. Crossing the green toward the church, Silvas and Carillia held hands. Bay was at his other side, and Bosc was beyond the giant horse. The wizard used his quarterstaff as a walking stick. Morning twilight had arrived. There was a chill to the air even though it was summer. The breeze was from the north, from Blethye. They didn't head for the main entrance to the church but to a side door, near the altar end of the nave. There the steps were narrow. Bay could get close enough to stick his head inside so he would be able to participate in the continuation of the night's Council.

Brother Paul hurried toward the door when Silvas and the others arrived. The look of apprehension on the friar's face was almost out of control. Paul was nervous, edgy, and even his voice was a register too high.

"Armor!" was the first word the vicar spoke. "A mace! I have no knowledge of such things. I cannot use this weapon."

"Then pray that you will not have to," Silvas said, looking beyond Brother Paul to the bishop. Egbert was following, not moving nearly as fast as the vicar.

"Pray that none of us will," Bishop Egbert said, putting his hands on the friar's shoulders. "But since they come from our Unseen Lord, we must be prepared to use what He has given us."

"Our Council was interrupted," Silvas said, hoping to hurry past the vicar's nervousness while the group still had time to talk in private. "Obviously the battle we saw, the storm of demons riding, all of that was not actually happening. It may have been prophecy. It may have been warning. I don't know."

"The battle is coming," Bay said. It was the first time he had ever spoken in the presence of outsiders—saving only the Council of the night just ending, and the effect of this was much stronger. It was enough to make the vicar stop trembling.

"That was not a dream," Brother Paul said, moving a step closer to Bay. "You really do speak."

"A talent that I trust will not be bruited about," Bay said. "It would shake the faith of many to hear a cleric talk of a horse that could speak."

Bishop Egbert chuckled. "Have no fear, Bay. Your secret will not escape us."

"The Council," Silvas said. The others turned their attention to him.

"I don't know what happened to the rest of you. Everything went black around me and I found myself alone. Then I saw our Unseen Lord face to face, more clearly than I see any of you at this moment. He laid His hands over my eyes and allowed knowledge to pour into me." There was no time to share one part in a thousand of that knowledge, and Silvas did not try. "If *we* fail in our task, if our Unseen Lord is defeated on this battlefield, Armageddon may indeed be upon us."

"I feel the armies gathering," Bay said. "The legions of the Blue Rose are coming. They will never surrender. They must be destroyed as quickly and as thoroughly as possible. There is no room for mercy, no chance of offering them any chance to recant. And they will offer us no alternative. They have come to destroy, not to convert."

He stared directly at the vicar for a moment. "You, Brother Paul, *must* be prepared to use the weapon that the Unseen Lord has given you. There is no margin for any of us to fall short in our duty."

"Even if our Unseen Lord prevails, I tremble for this village and this valley," Bosc said. "The earth cries out in great agony. It waits to welcome the bones of many people before this day is out. It waits ... for something more, for something of great pain." Bosc shook his head. "I still know not what it means. The earth's blood flows and mixes with the blood of men."

"We have little time," Silvas said. "The people of Mecq will be coming for Mass within minutes. I hear movement at hand. Your Excellency, Brother Paul, this next part is yours. The rest of us will be here with you."

Carillia put her hand on Silvas's arm. When he turned to her, she simply looked into his eyes for a moment. The wizard felt the frightening depths of sorrow in her gaze, but he still wasn't prepared for the words she finally spoke.

"My brother gods and I are come to the final battle of this world, or so we believe."

22

The shock that Silvas felt prevented any open reaction to Carillia's words. He did not doubt what she said, and he certainly could not miss the clear meaning. She was one of the twenty—sister to the Unseen Lord and the others. Silvas bit at his lower lip. He felt pain as well as wonder. *You have concealed so much from me for so long?*

Silvas and Carillia stared at each other for an instant that seemed all out of proportion to its duration. For that moment they might have been alone in the universe, but no words came to either's lips. There was no time for full discussion, and anything less was better left unsaid. For the moment. The others had no chance at all to show any reaction to Carillia's announcement. The first villagers were coming into the church. There was a little light showing outside. The sun had not quite topped the horizon, but it was near. The peasants knelt and crossed themselves, then moved forward into St. Katrinka's. There were no pews. Worshippers stood or knelt as the service required. They did not sit.

Master Ian was one of the first to arrive. Brother Paul hurried to greet him. "May I beg a favor?" he asked.

"Of course, Vicar," Master Ian replied.

"Would you send your lads around the village to make sure that *everyone* comes to Mass? Just have the lads tell any folks who aren't already on their way that it's most urgent. *Most* urgent," Brother Paul repeated.

"Aye, Vicar, I'll do it." The innkeeper turned and left.

At the far end of the church, Bishop Egbert whispered, "It is time for my brothers to join me." He closed his eyes and raised his hands to his temples for a short incantation.

"It might be best if we could get word for the folks up

in the castle to stay where they are," Silvas said when the bishop opened his eyes again. "We may have little enough time later."

"I'll have one of my brothers go up there to tell them to wait, that I will be up as soon as possible to help them and give absolution and blessing before the battle," Egbert said. He started to close his eyes again.

"A moment," Silvas said. "Have him go to the mews for a horse. The grooms will have one waiting. And I will be going to the castle with you, with all my companions. Sir Eustace's castle would seem to be the focal point of the coming fight."

"I'll tell them that we are coming," the bishop said, and both men spoke their silent spells.

Carillia had turned away from them. She took a step toward the altar and stared at the large wooden crucifix that hung there, and at the crudely painted scenes of Golgotha that surrounded it. So softly that no one else could hear, she whispered, "How little of this I have ever really understood." There were tears at the corners of her eyes. After a moment she turned just enough to let her look at Silvas again. He was busy with his chants, facing away from her.

"This moment had to come, my heart," she whispered, so softly that no one could possibly hear. "Whatever happens today, what we had before is lost. My escape is over." She turned back to the altar.

Her tears came again.

"Father, may I have a word?"

Brother Paul had remained near the front entrance to greet his parishioners as they entered. Busying himself with the amenities was less troubling than standing apart and thinking over Carillia's revelation. The vicar was disturbed both by what she had said and by the speed with which he had accepted her words as Truth.

"Certainly, my son," the vicar said. "Come, let's move over to the side." He led the villager off to the corner. "What troubles you?" *As if there weren't enough to trouble any righteous soul,* he added to himself.

"I saw somethin' in the night." The farmer looked down, turning his head first to one side and then the other, hesitant about meeting the vicar's gaze. "I cain't be shore what it were, Father."

"A dream?" Brother Paul prompted.

"No, it warn't no dream. I woke in the night, like— heard somethin', I did. After that storm t'other night, I don' sleep so good."

"What did you see?" Brother Paul asked, anxious to hurry him along.

"Dunno. I *thinks* I saw the Virgin Mary like, standin' in the doorway, hands stretched out like in blessing. It were very plain, Father. I saw her clear as anythin'." He shook his head. "I were frighted, e'en after she told me not to be."

"Go on. What did she look like?" *A miracle, here in my parish?* he wondered. *Or just a troubled soul taking a bit of comfort in a dream?* With all that had happened, and seemed about to happen, Brother Paul knew that he shouldn't be surprised at anything, even this.

"She looked young, she did, and most beauteous, draped all in a flowin' robe. Her hair was long, stretchin' all the way down to here." He touched a point low on his back to illustrate. "There was light all around her. The hair, it were brown with bits of red showin' in the light. Her eyes was a green sech as yer've ne'er seen. I cain't describe it. I don't have the words." He was quiet for a few seconds, his head hanging down. Finally he looked up. "While she were there, she put my soul at ease, she did. I felt blessed. But afore I could say anythin', she disappeared, she did, and then, in the dark, I felt troubled."

"Did she say anything else, do anything?" Brother Paul asked. He forced himself to hold his attention on the man in front of him, though a demanding itch made him want to turn and look toward the altar.

"No, Father, not that I recollect." The man shook his head. "Were it really her?"

Brother Paul had to hesitate before he answered. "I can't know that, my son. Such questions are for more learned souls than mine. I'll tell the bishop after Mass. I think . . ." He stopped and shook his head. "No, I shouldn't say even that. Just hold to that vision in your heart, my son. It may have been real. If her presence shows in your life, you may have been specially blessed."

The man crossed himself, bowed his head several times, then moved away, looking for a spot near the wall, away from the center of the growing crowd.

Brother Paul turned to look toward the altar—and Carillia. Her long auburn hair was hidden, braided and piled up under the helmet she wore now. But the friar had seen it before. And he had seen her brilliant green eyes. He stared at her back for a moment, then let his eyes look to her companions. Silvas, Bay, and Bosc all seemed lost in their magics, whatever they were. Even the bishop had his eyes closed and was standing in a posture of incantation.

"I am being lax in my duties," the vicar mumbled. He spoke a short prayer while he crossed himself, then moved into the few magics of protection he could muster, simple spells for his church and parishioners. He had just finished when he felt a hand touch his arm.

"Vicar, I needs yer a moment."

Brother Paul opened his eyes. The woman was Enid, the miller's wife. She was terrified. It showed on her face, in her eyes. "What is it, my child?" he asked.

"I think I saw Mother Mary comin' fer me in the night, Vicar. She stood by my bed and held her arms out."

"Not coming *for* you, surely," Brother Paul said. "Perhaps you mistook what you saw. The mother of our Lord doesn't come to *take* people."

"Really?"

"Really," Brother Paul said. "Tell me, what did she look like?"

He managed to keep any expression off his face when her description matched the first he had heard. When Enid finished, Brother Paul blessed her and sent her back to her husband.

"I need the counsel of my bishop on this," Brother Paul mumbled. He started to move toward the altar and Bishop Egbert. But yet another villager took him aside before he got there . . . with a similar tale.

St. Katrinka's scarcely had room for all the people of Mecq, and more people were present than usual—Silvas and his companions, and the churchmen from St. Ives. The monks had arrived as Brother Paul was talking to

Enid, the miller's wife. They had come in led by the two gigantic cats Brother Paul had seen in the Glade. The cats went along the side of the church to Silvas.

Carillia remained with her back to the congregation. No one had yet had any opportunity to remark on her . . . resemblance to the vision that had come to some of them in the night. Silvas was obviously deep in his magic. That, especially inside the church, was enough to worry many of the villagers. Bosc and Bay worried them even more. The little fellow was so strange; he looked as if he might call both a human and a hog parents. And the giant horse, *he* appeared to be chanting as rapidly as the wizard or the short pig-like creature, though no one could hear any *words* from the horse. With all the strangeness present, Satin and Velvet were easier to accept, though their size was frightening.

Brother Paul went to the pulpit and started the Invocation. He blessed the congregation and spoke to them.

"Great danger is at hand, my children. You are all to stay inside the church until the coming fight is over. His Excellency the Bishop of St. Ives and the Lord Wizard Silvas have cast what protections they are able to command around St. Katrinka's to shield you from as much of the outside evil as possible." *And to strengthen you against any follower of the Blue Rose who may have come into our midst, may God forgive me for suspicions,* he added to himself.

"As you value your souls, do not leave until one of us tells you it is safe. We go to war, perhaps to Armageddon!" He thumped a fist against the armor that covered his chest. The gesture hurt his hand, but the ringing sound his armor made seemed an effective addition.

None of the greater powers in the church contradicted the vicar. Brother Paul glanced at them, almost wishing that one of them had.

Bishop Egbert hurried through the Mass as he rarely had in his life. Even so, the feeling of power was more intense than usual. The bishop noticed the difference early. At first he was willing to lay that entirely to the nearness of the struggle. He was no stranger to the anticipation that could make the heart pump faster, that could bring such a sharply defined awareness of everything. It wasn't until the elevation of the Host that he knew that this was more. It felt almost as if lightning were surging down into him through his upraised hands. His arms trembled for an instant, but he didn't drop the Host. And he completed the Mass without omission, though he raced through the remaining words even more rapidly. When he reached the closing benediction, he spoke the words of protection with more fervor than he had ever known. Then he reminded the people of Mecq that they were not to leave the sanctuary until they were told that it was safe.

"We go to meet the threat where it will be greatest," the bishop said. "We will be on the mountain overlooking your river and the pass from Blethye. Brother Paul, and the wizard and his companions, will be there with me. I leave you six of my brothers from the cathedral to see to your safety here. You are in good hands. God willing, we shall all emerge from this alive with our faith strengthened." He drew the sign of the cross over them again and then went to the side of the church where Silvas and the others waited.

"We have little time to spare," Silvas told him. "I feel the danger approaching."

"Then let us hurry." With the efficiency of a military commander, the bishop divided his monks into two groups. One of the brothers was already at the castle of Mecq. Five more would accompany the bishop now. The other six would remain. Those six moved to carefully chosen places within the church. One went to the altar. Two went to the far corners. Two more stationed themselves along the side walls, and the sixth found his place in the center, forming the points and focus of a pentagram.

Silvas and the bishop led the way out of the church by the side door to avoid the crowd. At the front of the church, nine saddled horses waited.

"The grooms said to bring this many," one of the monks said.

"I passed those orders to them," Silvas said. "We will ride to Sir Eustace's castle."

Silvas helped Carillia mount. Their eyes met, locked,

for an instant, but neither spoke. Bosc got on his horse without help, though the stirrup was nearly at the level of his chin. Of the churchmen, Brother Paul was the only one who had difficulty mounting. "I can't recall the last time I rode a horse," he explained.

As soon as the vicar was mounted, Bay took off through the village. He didn't gallop, but the other horses, so much smaller than him, were forced into a canter from the start, just to keep from falling behind.

Carillia kept her horse even with Bay. As they left the village, she asked Silvas, "How will you begin?"

Silvas looked at her, surprised—as much by the fact that she had spoken as by what she had said. "Is that a question for you to ask me, or for me to ask you?" The words were difficult, ignoring the deeper questions he longed to ask but could not yet put into words.

"It is for me to ask you, my heart," she said.

"There seems only one way," Silvas said. "I'll tell you when we get to the top."

Bay had already reached the path leading up the side of Mount Mecq, and there was no room for Carillia's horse beside the larger animal. The horses all fell into line behind Bay. On the climb the line stretched out as the more timid riders held back their mounts. Brother Paul had slid to the rear before they reached the hill, and he fell farther behind at every switchback along the climb. Only the two cats seemed unconcerned by the narrow path up the side of Mount Mecq. Satin and Velvet stayed close behind Silvas throughout the climb. At the top of the road, the gate to the castle was open, but the walls held every soldier that Sir Eustace possessed and much of the rest of the adult population of the castle, hurriedly armed against whatever might come. Henry Fitz-Matthew stood on the parapet above the gate. Only Sir Eustace and his family were not in sight.

"Close the gate!" Fitz-Matthew shouted as soon as Brother Paul made it through.

"No!" Silvas shouted back. "We will have to start our fight outside, on the ledge above the Eyler."

"I have my orders," Fitz-Matthew said.

"Damn your orders, man," Silvas shouted. "We begin

our fight on the ledge above the river. Do you value your soul so little?"

That frightened the steward almost beyond reason. His eyes opened wider, and they had been wide enough with fear before. He looked to Brother Paul and then to the bishop.

"Do as he says," Brother Paul said, almost out of breath from the ride. "Sir Eustace will not fault you for it. You have my word."

"And mine!" Bishop Egbert thundered.

Fitz-Matthew nodded an unhappy acceptance.

Silvas and Carillia dismounted and walked back out through the gate together. Bay trailed along behind them. Bosc busied himself gathering the rest of the horses that had come from the mews of the Seven Towers and took them off within the courtyard to tie them to a railing by a water trough.

Silvas went right to the edge that overlooked the Eyler and the narrow pass between the two hills.

"How will you start?" Carillia asked again. She moved to Silvas's side and linked her right arm with his left. He did not withdraw from the contact.

"By damming the Eyler to give Mecq its water," he said. "That is the gage I must throw down. It seems obvious now—Mecq and its water. Those are the keys." He still wasn't sure why they were the keys, or why Mecq and not any other place in Christendom, but they were somehow the inescapable link. The only explanation that made any sense to him was that his wanderings had finally brought him too near the center of the Blue Rose's power for them to ignore the threat he represented.

"Have you chosen your method?" Carillia asked.

"There's no time for finesse. It will have to be brute force, power I could not command before our Unseen Lord laid his hands across my eyes." He turned to face her. "And still I do not know if my power alone will suffice. I may well need whatever help you and the others can give me." He stared into her eyes, looking for anything he might have missed seeing in the generations of men that they had been together.

"You know me heart and soul, my heart," Carillia said softly. "We are not so different as you believe."

"Even a wizard must believe in something outside himself," Silvas said. "My love, sometimes I know not what to believe anymore." Then he had to take his eyes from hers even though so much remained unsaid. He turned toward the gate.

Sir Eustace had come out of his keep. He started shouting as soon as he emerged, demanding to know why the gate was still open. Bishop Egbert replied. The bishop spoke softly, but his words carried as he took the knight to task for his manners.

"At such a time as this, have a care for your soul," Egbert said. "Let not your anger continue to fester, not even against the Foe and his forces that will come against you." The words held such power that Silvas could feel Sir Eustace's people trembling with fear for their master. And Sir Eustace needed quite some time before he found his voice again. When he spoke this time, his tone was more humble.

"I beg forgiveness, Your Excellency. I stand here ready to do what I may to defend my land, my people, and our Mother the Church. Our resources are scanty, but we are at your disposal." Sir Eustace glanced at Silvas and Carillia, who were just coming back through the gate. "We are here to follow your orders, or even those of the wizard if that is your desire." The last came out haltingly, but with no trace of his earlier, habitual anger.

"It is my desire," Bishop Egbert said. "The Lord Wizard Silvas is much stronger in the magic we need to defend the White Brotherhood than I. You will follow his orders as I will myself."

Silvas made no move to take over the talk. There would be time enough for that. He saw no sense in pressing Sir Eustace's resolve so soon. Once the threat was visible, the knight would be less likely to rebel. Silvas was more interested at the moment in looking at the newest spectators. Sir Eustace's wife and daughter were standing at the door of the keep, cloaks wrapped about them against the morning chill. Eleanora's eyes held nothing but terror as she listened to the bishop. There was something else in Maria's eyes, something wild—not fear but determination or something akin to it. Silvas couldn't quite make out what it was, but she held his attention.

Power? Excitement? Silvas shook his head gently. Whatever the difference, Maria seemed somehow more than she had before. She stared at him for a moment, then turned and ran back into the keep. Eleanora was not far behind her.

Bishop Egbert finished with Sir Eustace and came over to Silvas. The knight followed dutifully, his usual scowl replaced by a look of apprehension.

"We are yours to command," the bishop said.

Silvas nodded. "It's time to begin. We'll start out on the flat overlooking the Eyler." After the bishop nodded, Silvas looked to Sir Eustace, who also nodded—if not meekly, then at least without any look of defiance. "Sir Eustace, for you and your men, the task is that which you have already sworn, to defend Mecq and your people. Your place is on the walls of your castle. The work outside will belong to those of us with other talents." Sir Eustace nodded again, this time with more vigor, and when Silvas led the others out through the gate, he climbed to the wall.

"Don't stand too close to the precipice," Silvas warned those who moved out with him—his companions and the churchmen.

"You must intend to begin the fray, since the enemy's storm has not yet appeared," Bishop Egbert said.

Silvas smiled. "One might look at it that way. Or one might say that we merely pick up the gauntlet the Blue Rose cast before the White Brotherhood here a long time since."

Bishop Egbert looked around, then down. "The river?"

"The river," Silvas agreed. He turned a little. "Brother, not so close to the edge," he called to a monk who was within perhaps five feet of it. The monk took another step back.

"Have your brothers stand along the castle wall while I begin," Silvas told the bishop. "Save for Brother Paul. We will include him in our offensive since this is his parish."

The bishop went to speak to his monks while Silvas started to work. The wizard looked around the ledge for a few moments while he started his preliminary chants. The flat area outside the castle was about forty yards long but rarely as much as twenty-five yards wide, from wall to precipice, and on the side of the hill that directly faced Blethye, the castle extended almost to the edge. Silvas switched into a faster chant and used the silver ferrule of his quarterstaff to scribe a large pentagram in the rock. He moved quickly but confidently, drawing lines that were perfectly straight, with angles that were precise. He used all of the room available across the narrow width of the ledge. The segments of this pentagram needed to be as large as possible to serve the purpose he had in mind. Silvas started with the five outer sides, then drew in the inner lines.

When he finished, he stood near one of the points and looked from that to Bay and back. "Bay, is there enough room for you within the point of one of these arrows?"

The horse came closer, staying outside the pentagram while he looked. "Barely," he said after a moment. "I will have to remain perfectly still, and I will have little room to even turn my head from side to side."

"But is it enough, my friend? If I started again, I could hardly squeeze out more than a few extra inches."

Bay looked directly at him and nodded. "It will do."

"Bishop Egbert, I don't know how much use you make of pentagrams, but I find them to be powerful tools. For most applications I would stand alone in the center and erect my shields. This magic will require more. The pentagram will have to be fully populated by individuals of power, one in each point of the star, one more at the center."

Bishop Egbert nodded to show that he followed the wizard's reasoning. "The pentagram is not our most common tool, even within the Greater Mysteries, but it is far from unknown. Place us as you will."

"Bosc and the vicar will have the points nearest the castle wall. I will be in the point overlooking the Eyler. Bay will be to my left, and I would like to have you at my right. Carillia will be in the center."

Silvas turned to look at her. He would certainly have taken his usual place at the center of the pentagram if not for Carillia's admission of divinity. The center was the most important post. It was customary to place the greatest power there. Carillia met Silvas's gaze without outward emotion. After a moment she nodded, accepting his disposition.

"Be careful not to touch any of the lines," Silvas said as the others moved to their assigned positions. "And once in place, don't cross any of the lines or intersections until you are certain that it is safe." He took a step toward Brother Paul. "If you have any doubt, if your power does not yet run so far, any of the rest of us will be able to tell you when it's safe." Brother Paul nodded. His face had paled, but he didn't hesitate to take his position.

Silvas waited until the others were within their assigned segments. He took a moment to survey Bay's position. "You have a little room around you, old friend," he said.

"I am aware," Bay replied without moving even his head. Silvas nodded and moved to his own position.

"It is time," he announced in a loud voice. The six monks from the cathedral chapter were along the outside of the castle wall. Satin and Velvet took up positions flanking the gate, keeping their distance from both the pentagram and the line of monks. Most of Sir Eustace's people were on the ramparts above the ledge.

It is time, Silvas repeated to himself. He turned around within his position to look at the others inside the pentagram.

"Not much is required of you for this part," he said. "Brother Paul, I know you have no experience at this sort of thing. All that is needed now is for you and the others around the points, to clear your minds and project whatever power you command toward Carillia in the center. She will focus that on me, and I will perform the active part."

When each of the others had nodded their understanding, Silvas turned again to face his point and look out over the Eyler. He took a wide, steady stance and started to chant.

It was not a simple magic. Silvas had to draw together many different spells and merge them into a seamless new construction. He started to chant up elementary defenses around the pentagram, waiting to feel the inrush of additional energy from Carillia and the others. Even before that came, Silvas knew that he himself already possessed more power than ever before. *The inescapable result of the knowledge I was given,* he reminded himself. *Even with all this help, I might not have been able to perform this magic yesterday.* He would still have found some way to produce the end result he sought—sufficient, reliable water for Mecq—but the production would have been more protracted, more difficult.

He eyed the near end of Mount Balq, across the river. He focused his telesight and scanned the rock, searching for fissures, making estimates of the power that would have to be applied and just where. Finally the surge of power he was waiting for came. Silvas switched immediately into more intense levels of conjuring, challenging what had always been the upper limit of his power, knowing that he had to go far beyond that old range to manipulate the substances of Earth and Sky.

Silvas raised his arms, his quarterstaff held horizontal in both hands. Then he brought the staff down to eye level so that he was looking over it at the crest of Mount Balq. The sky started to turn a slightly darker shade of blue. A few thin clouds coalesced and began to churn and curl far overhead. Faint white clouds against the blue. Then Silvas spoke the first words of power.

A bolt of brilliant blue-white lightning came out of clear sky and struck the end of Mount Balq, its accompanying thunder deafening. A trace of smoke remained after the lightning faded. Silvas repeated the first words of power, then added more, chanting the sequence over and over.

The lightning came in force now, blue and purple, occasionally a greenish yellow, most rarely white. The bolts came singly at first, separated by perhaps a second. But the intervals quickly decreased until the ridge across the Eyler wore the lightning like a crown of thorns. The thunder became a solid wall of noise, too loud and close, too constant. The people on Mount Mecq no longer truly heard the thunder, they felt it in their heads and hearts, in their souls. Tongues of fire danced on the rock of Mount Balq, only sporadically visible in the greater brilliance of the lightning. Explosions started to make themselves heard over the thunder. Even the ledge on Mount Mecq started to tremble from the force of the assault on the opposite hill.

Dust rose from the top of Mount Balq. Small chunks of rock, then larger boulders, finally immense sections of the hill began to tumble and slide from the top to the riverbed. The trembling on Mount Mecq increased with the rock slide.

Silvas lowered his arms still more, keeping the quarterstaff horizontal. There were new chants now, a new target. The deluge of lightning eased off and finally ended, leaving a halo of smoke and dust on the newly truncated top of Mount Balq. The falling rocks tumbled and continued to break into smaller portions with loud cracking assaults on the numb ears of the people above. The rock spread out in both directions, filling the riverbed.

Water splashed. The rocks stopped the Eyler and gave it a new chop. Dust rose above the splatter and then settled. By the time the last of the avalanche came to rest, the Eyler had been most thoroughly dammed to a point two feet below the farm fields on the Balq side. There was somewhat more room between the dam and the top of the bank on the village's side.

The near end of Mount Balq's crest now looked much as it had during the Council that had met there during the night, a large flat ledge with only a few stones to mar it. The slope of the hill had changed near the Eyler as well. There was almost a sheer drop from crest to foot, giving the end of the hill the look of a stone column braced only by low buttresses.

Silvas relaxed and brought his staff down, resting the iron end on the ground, holding the staff in his right hand, leaning a little against it as he looked at his handiwork. The dam was two hundred feet thick, strong enough to stand against anything that unassisted nature might throw against it, too massive for humans to dismantle. The top of the dam was flat and level, almost as if masons had set the rocks in place. It might be the work of two winters for the villagers to put the final finishing touches to the top of the dam, if they wanted to bother. The dam would not require that attention.

It is a beautiful dam, Silvas thought. Despite the urgency of the moment, he had put his full attention to the details. The dam was strong enough and precisely the proper height for Mecq's needs. It would not end the spring floods, but it would make them more reliable. The village would not be threatened, though. Even at the flood, the Eyler would spill through the gap into Blethye fast enough to avoid damaging the village. And beyond that, there was just too much room for the water to spread across the valley Balqside. Before the village could be threatened, scores of square miles of floodplain would have to be covered, with new water pouring in more rapidly than the "old" water flowed out between the twin hills.

I do not think that is possible, short of another Deluge, Silvas thought. *It is a good job.*

The wizard turned around, staying within his segment of the pentagram. He shouted up toward the castle walls, "I have fulfilled my vow to the people of Mecq." After the din of the thunder, even his loudest shout sounded hollow and distant, even to him.

"You have fulfilled your vow," Sir Eustace shouted back. The amazement he felt kept any trace of resentment or anger out of his voice. He had never dreamed that such a coup might be possible. Whatever might come next, the knight knew in his heart that he had witnessed a miracle.

"You have indeed kept your vow to these people," Bishop Egbert said, as impressed at Eustace at what he had seen—and felt. His ears still rang.

"It may take weeks for the river to overtop the dam," Silvas said in a normal speaking voice, "but I doubt that we will have to wait that long for the Blue Rose to respond. My challenge to them was much too loud."

Almost as he spoke, the sky began to grow night dark in the distance, over Blethye—black and dark purples, shades that immediately called to mind the vision of the Council. The stain over the distant sky expanded and raced toward Mecq. More slowly the people on Mount Mecq caught the sense of thousands of hoofbeats, felt as much as heard, racing ahead of the darkening sky, and a storm wave of fear pressing even ahead of the unseen riders.

Within the pentagram, both Bishop Egbert and Brother Paul fell to their knees to cross themselves and pray. The bishop started to chant the most powerful spells of protection he knew. Over below the castle wall, the monks of his chapter also went to their knees, adding their strength to the bishop's. Even Silvas had to hold his emotions in tight rein to keep from showing his apprehension at the now visible threat of the Blue Rose's anger.

The horror was almost at hand.

23

Silvas watched the approach of the final storm. There was a sour taste in his throat, but he gave no outward sign of how he felt. Inwardly he uttered a prayer. *Lord, lend me your strength for the coming fight. Help me to stand strong for you.* For a moment he seemed to sense Auroreus standing at his side, hand on his shoulder, the way his mentor had often stood by him when Silvas was a boy learning the ways of the trimagister. *I have taught you as best I could,* the old wizard seemed to say. *You have promise. You will serve our Unseen Lord well.* Then the image faded and Silvas felt intensely alone. *I hope I do serve Him well,* Silvas thought, and on a more secret level he added, *And I pray He lets me survive.*

"It's time to stand and fight," Silvas said aloud. The churchmen had fallen to their knees. Silvas could feel their minds struggling with fear. Bishop Egbert overcame his terror quickly and rose, new vigor in his projections of power and resolve. He helped Brother Paul find the strength to get to his feet as well.

Bay was as solid as ever, broadcasting neither fear nor confidence, betraying nothing of his feelings. He stood motionless in his segment of the pentagram, marshaling his own spells, exhibiting more power than Silvas had ever felt from him.

Bosc emitted waves of fierce determination, seeming more like one of Braf Goleg's lupine warriors. Bosc's magic was limited, scarcely more than Brother Paul's, but he was ready to give everything he had in the coming fight.

And Carillia. There was still no time for Silvas to brood on her revelation. He could do no more than think, *How little I have known you, my love, for all our years together.* She wore her power more openly now, but it wasn't the same sort of power that Silvas had felt from the Unseen Lord. Even facing this challenge, Carillia radiated more the power of the nurturer, not the warrior.

Silvas let his mind quest farther, touching the minds of the monks lined up below the castle wall, then the soldiers above them. The monks were deep in their magics, channeling their power to the bishop. When Silvas fully raised the defenses of his pentagram, the monks would be on their own, and in greater danger. On top of the wall, Sir Eustace, Henry Fitz-Matthew, and the garrison watched in terror. There could be no mistaking the supernatural nature of the coming storm, and those men had only physical weapons to defend themselves with. Silvas broadcast a spell of calming and courage to all of them. The spell might not last long, and it couldn't relieve all of their fear, but Silvas knew he owed them what help he could provide. Without help some of the soldiers might lose the last of their courage before the enemy arrived.

The storm expanded over Blethye, spreading to cover the entire horizon even as it continued to advance toward Mecq. The waves of fear that swept out in front of the clouds of night were as real as an Atlantic storm tide washing against the shore, breaking, washing sand back out to sea, to destruction.

"Time runs behind itself," Silvas said softly. "The storm races for us, yet we experience each moment as if it were five." *That is part of the evil,* he thought. "It is simply a way for the Blue Rose to make its terror work harder. If they were as strong as they try to seem, they would not need such artifice." He looked around at his companions. They were watching the approaching storm. Concern, fear, was on every face. *I expect it's on mine as well,* Silvas conceded. *There is certainly cause enough.*

"We are with you, my heart," Carillia said. She managed a smile, but it was tinged with sadness . . . or regret.

Silvas returned her smile. "I know you are, my love." He nearly stuttered over the last two words.

He turned to face the storm again. It covered half of Blethye now, stretching out for miles on either side, curving in at the edges like the horns of the gibbous moon. The leading edge was no more than a mile from the northern slopes of the twin hills now. Silvas started to chant, projecting part of his mind forward to meet the night that flowed across the morning. *I must make my challenge, let them know that I stand ready to do battle.*

The curdling cries of demons, the soul-destroying wails of the banshees who waited like vultures to feast on the souls lost in battle, the laughter of the Blue Rose's gods, all rose to greet Silvas's probe. He chanted, closing his eyes to concentrate on his spells, doing what he could to ignore the leeching of resolve. After a moment he felt the sun burning brightly behind him, heating his back, seemingly enlarging itself to challenge the unnatural night sweeping south toward Mecq. Silvas's armor grew hot, the trembling inside him seemed to ease. He forged ahead with his incantations, feeling stronger, more confident. *Even if I fall, the Blue Rose will know they have faced a battle,* he promised himself. *If a heaven remains when this day is over, the angels will sing of our stand.*

The musics of hell assaulted Silvas. The chanting of Bishop Egbert's monks rose in reply, the traditional plainsong of the White Brotherhood. The music of the Unseen Lord came not just from the monks on the ledge with Silvas, but also from the monks in St. Katrinka's, in perfect unison, though the one group could certainly not *hear* the other.

The people of Mecq huddled together in their church. At first many of them had little real notion what was coming. There was some foreboding, but not all that much more than there had been since the first storm had assailed Mecq after the arrival of the wizard. Some of the bolder villagers stood at the doors of the church for a time, watching the storm gather beyond the twin hills. But as the black night rose to the heavens and stars returned to the sky, terror finally gripped all the villagers so completely that rational thought became impossible. Even Master Ian shrank from the sight and retreated inside the church to lose himself in *Pater Nosters* and *Ave Marias*.

Clear spaces remained around the six monks in the church. The villagers held back from the monks, their chanting, and the almost visible aura of power that grew around them. The monks chanted magical formulas that the peasants couldn't hold on to long enough to really hear. Only when the chants moved from the spells of the Greater Mysteries to the plainsong of the Church Revealed did the people of Mecq find any ease. Familiar hymns loosened the ropes strangling their hearts and souls—for the moment.

It is time, the voice of the Unseen Lord said within Silvas. *You must strike now.*

Silvas lowered his gaze from the Devil's darkness to the plain of Blethye. His telesight came upon him without bidding, and Silvas found himself staring at a single man who stood on the plain, in the center of a pentagram much like the one Silvas had scribed outside the gate of Mecq's castle.

That is Caradoc, the wizard of the Blue Rose in Blethye, the god's voice said inside Silvas. *He is the wick of their attack.*

As I am the wick of yours? Silvas asked, but no reply came.

Silvas focused on Caradoc. He had never heard the name before, had heard no rumor of this wizard. *I did not know that there was another such wizard-potent in all of England,* he thought. That another as powerful as he could operate and gain no fame was amazing. Whether he worked for good or evil, there should have been some rumor of his power. *Unless the Blue Rose has saved him unused for this one moment,* Silvas allowed.

Caradoc was a man of exceeding height, taller than Silvas and thinner, as if fasting had been a way of life for him. *The discipline of the Blue Rose is stern,* the Unseen Lord's voice said. Silvas studied the other wizard. Coal black eyes *(they could be nothing else)* were raised toward the leading edge of the demonic darkness. The face was lined and gaunt, hard-edged with anger and consuming hate. *His passions are those of the Blue Rose, pain and punishment.* The cheeks angled sharply down and inward to a pointed chin of great exaggeration. His robe was an unadorned black, blowing fitfully around him in the winds that his magic had raised against Mecq. His hands were raised, the right one clenched in a fist, the left one. . . . Silvas couldn't make out at first what was wrong with the left hand. It formed no fist. The fingers seemed stiff and bent at unnatural angles so that the hand looked almost like the claw of a hawk. *The punishments of the Blue Rose.*

Silvas transferred his quarterstaff to his left hand, resting the iron tip on the ground just inside his point of the pentagram, and he drew the sword at his side for the first time and held it out over the intersection of the lines, aimed directly at Caradoc. A spell and a word of power came to Silvas's lips without searching. Thunder roared in the heavens and spat out a single bolt of lightning at the Blue Rose's wizard. The lightning coursed directly at the man but shattered against the dome of protection that covered Caradoc's pentagram, sending dozens of ribs of light harmlessly into the ground around the perimeter.

It was too much to hope for, Silvas thought, but he immediately tried again, racing through the spell and adding words that would rain lightning down on the other wizard as heavily as it had rained down on Mount Balq barely a half hour before.

Caradoc, the five assistants in the pentagram with him, and the pentagram itself were covered by a dome of lightning, a solid sheet of white fire that glowed brighter than the sun. But the white fire turned a muddy clay red and then faded into blackness. The last bolts of Silvas's lightning cracked with uncommon loudness and seemed to turn back on the sky.

Within the night of the Blue Rose, the voices of the demons and banshees grew louder and became audible even to ears unaided by magic. Silvas felt his concentration waver as he heard cries of fear from the soldiers on the rampart behind him. Fighting to shut out those cries, Silvas struggled to regain his focus on the Blue Rose wizard, and managed to seal his mind to the task just as Caradoc launched his counterattack.

Caradoc pointed his deformed hand at Silvas, and a blaze of blue lightning seemed to emerge directly from that claw. Silvas imagined, and knew that it was only imagination, that he could smell burning flesh. This blue lightning appeared to move at the pace of a donkey under a heavy burden, leaving Silvas sufficient time to erect an extra shield against it. But before the blue light reached the ledge on Mount Mecq, it divided into five fingers as misshapen as those that had launched it and came at the pentagram from every side.

Though Caradoc's attack was neither as intense nor as powerful as Silvas's opening thrust, Silvas couldn't meet the blue fire as simply as Caradoc had met the white. If he merely shunted the blue lightning aside, it might engulf the monks standing below the castle walls, or even rebound against those on the ramparts. Instead Silvas reached out with his mind, attempting to cup each finger of fire in a palm filled with water. The blue fire faded into red and limped away across the ledge, feeble enough that the monks were able to step clear of the dying tendrils.

But even as Silvas damped the blue fire, black lightning struck from above, a jagged edge of night cleaving the remaining daylight over the twin mountains. This bolt seemed to be directed at Carillia rather than at Silvas, and she was able to respond more quickly than he, raising her hands and shattering the black lightning into bits of black coal and shiny crystals of diamond that scattered and bounced as they hit the ground.

Bay bared his teeth and neighed in anger, faced with some challenge of his own that Silvas couldn't discern. The horse didn't move, though, and after a moment his face relaxed.

"It is truly joined at last," Silvas mumbled, though no one heard him.

Outside Silvas's pentagram, the ground, the hills, even the castle walls and the monks and soldiers were covered by a thin orange haze. An unnatural silence descended with the mist, leaving hollow echoes of emptiness ringing in Silvas's ears. To the north, the infernal night continued to advance, more slowly than before. Its leading edge was within a hundred yards of the foot of Mount Mecq. A new terror advanced more rapidly beneath that mantle of blackness.

"The armies of the night approach," Carillia announced.

"Demons of hell, driven by the Devil," Brother Paul said, astonished that he could actually see something of the enemy even though they were still some distance away and concealed by the necessary night that sheltered them.

"Near enough the mark," Bishop Egbert said. "Lord Silvas, do you have a specific defense in mind for these?" The bishop's voice remained remarkably calm despite a certain quaking within him. He was ready, even eager, to make this stand for his faith.

"How has the White Brotherhood fought the Blue Rose before?" Silvas asked, a mostly rhetorical question.

"We raised a crusade against them in Burgundy," Egbert said, uncertain of the real tenor of Silvas's question.

"You sent a crusade of living soldiers against the living tools of the Blue Rose. Now we are faced by tools of the Blue Rose who do not live, who likely have never lived. Can we not meet them with an army of martyrs who have already died for their faith?" The idea had come to Silvas almost as he spoke, prompted as much by the bishop's response as anything else.

Bishop Egbert stared off toward the coming night and the armies of the never-living while he spoke a quick prayer and contemplated Silvas's suggestion. *While there is time to think, it would be a sin* not *to think,* he told himself.

"It might be the best of all replies," the bishop said. Deliberation did not require excessive delay. Egbert had a quick mind.

"Amen," Silvas said—*so be it.*

He raised his sword and quarterstaff toward the darkness and started to chant. The spells came to mind without searching, although they were ones that he had never used, or even contemplated, before. It was as if they had been especially entrusted to his mind for this battle. After a moment Carillia started to speak in unison with Silvas, and the others in the pentagram fell in automatically, even Brother Paul, who had no idea what he was saying. Words he could hardly have grasped, could scarcely have heard, outside the pentagram flowed easily from his lips. It was as if Silvas or one of the others were driving his throat and mouth as well as his own. *This is of the Greater Mysteries,* the vicar thought. *It takes me beyond where I have ever been.* His feeling was more of wonder than fear. *I always thought that the Greater Mysteries were beyond my talents.*

The cadence of the chant gave the semblance of music. The different registers of the voices gave it harmony, from the clear contralto of Carillia and the reedy tenor of Bosc through the baritones of Silvas and the two churchmen to the basso profundo of Bay rumbling underneath all of the others. The six monks lined up beneath the wall finally picked up the chant, as automatically as Brother Paul had. They seemed to remain half a sound behind the rest, though, giving the chant a tremolo, an echo.

For the soldiers on the walls above, the effect was one of growing noise, sound without form. Neither Sir Eustace nor any of his men had the gift to grasp the words of the ancient spells.

For several minutes there was no visible result. Silvas and his companions within the pentagram could feel the increase of power they were generating, but they could see nothing new. Then . . .

The army of martyrs rose silently from the dirt and rock of the twin hills. It was easiest to see what was happening across the river on Mount Balq, but the same thing happened on Mount Mecq. Soldiers grew out of the earth, already mounted on spectral steeds. The knights and men-at-arms seemed to come from different eras and from all parts of Christendom. Their manner of dress, their weapons and armor varied. All wore a bright white cross on their shoulders, though, whether on ragged tunic or rusted mail. The ghosts of these warriors who had died for their faith were pale images, less substantial than a reflection in a rippling pond, but the blades of their weapons caught the sunlight and glinted. Men rose from both slopes of the two hills. Those who emerged on Mecq's side of the hills advanced over the crests, moving into position behind those who had appeared on Blethye's side. Steep slopes, even sheer drops meant nothing to this army of the dead. Kings and high lords called out their commands, and the martyrs fell into ranks and rode into the sky, moving out under the darkness that had been projected to cover the advance of the demons of the Blue Rose. Under the darkness the army of martyrs became more visible, a pale luminescence that shimmered in subtle ways.

Even the soldiers on the castle walls could see these warriors. Most of the soldiers fell to their knees in uncontrollable fright or desperate prayer. Not even Sir Eustace was immune.

But the terror didn't last. The army of martyrs raised a hymn, and while the words weren't completely audible to those without entrée to the mystic realm, their comfort was. The soldiers on the wall struggled back to their feet as the martyrs charged toward the advancing enemy. When Sir Eustace looked out through one of the crenels, he had regained his customary scowl. This time he focused it toward Blethye rather than toward the people who had raised this latest terror. He even found grudging approval for the fact that the wizard and his allies had dispatched this terrible army into Blethye to fight. *Better there than on my land* was his easy assessment. *Such a fight could leave the land on which it is fought barren.*

The transition was as sharp and jarring as an unexpected slap in the face. Still, allowing for an instant of shock, Silvas recognized the field immediately. *This is the land of the gods,* he thought, and then he spoke the words when he realized that Bay and Carillia were with him, one on either side. Then he recalled Carillia's divinity and felt embarrassment.

"This is not my home," Carillia said. "My home is with you, my heart, always." She leaned against him. Since Silvas held weapons in both hands, they could do little more than touch shoulder to shoulder.

"My love," he whispered. Warmth spread over the edge of fear that remained in his thoughts. *Perhaps we* do *have tomorrows left together.*

At first Silvas was only aware of the three of them. Then he saw the armies of the gods arrayed on the field. Silvas and his companions were in the midst of one army. The second faced them from two hundred yards away. There was little to obviously distinguish between the armies. This was no clash of light and dark, white and blue. This was the land of the gods, and everything was bright and perfect. These warriors were dressed in full metal plate. From toe to top, they were covered in armor that gleamed like the brightest mirrors ever devised. Visors were pulled down on helmets, giving the assemblage an anonymous look. The horses were magnificent, many appearing to be Bay's equal in size. Their coats, where they were visible, were glossy. Their harness was impeccable, and most were draped in armor and in silken finery.

"My brothers and their cohorts," Carillia said. "And my sisters."

"*All* of them?" Silvas asked.

Carillia shook her head. "Some few have forgone any part in this fight. It does not matter. It will debase them as it debases all of us." There was tremendous sadness in her voice when she added, "Yet it cannot be avoided. It must be endured."

If any can endure, Silvas thought—and that startled him, for it did not seem to originate in his own mind.

A trumpet blew.

Hail assaulted the top of Mount Mecq. Ice pellets the size of plums struck with incredible fury. Their impact was blunted by the dome of protection that covered Silvas's pentagram, but only for those within it. The soldiers on the ramparts of Sir Eustace's castle, dressed in chain mail and wearing helmets, still raised their bucklers above their heads to guard their faces. The monks in front of the wall were left with no defense except for the partial protection of the wall itself. They were forced to break off their chanting to turn and face the wall. They hunched over and pulled the cowls up over their heads to try to protect themselves until Silvas and the others in the pentagram could stop the onslaught. Satin and Velvet growled in anger and pain, then retreated under the cover of the gate, hugging the wall on either side to avoid the rest of the storm.

The hail quickly covered the ledge and made the ramparts treacherously slippery. Bishop Egbert took the lead in fighting the hail, calling for holy fire to cleanse it. Silvas lent his power to the bishop's chant, and soon the ice started to burn away with tiny flames that didn't affect people. *The fire of Pentecost.* Egbert's mind projected that thought so clearly that Silvas could hardly miss it. The flames seemed to climb into the sky on ladders of hail, clearing the air.

Silvas looked up to the castle ramparts. The soldiers were slow to expose themselves again, but there seemed to be no serious casualties there. Below the wall, one monk didn't rise. Two of his companions went to check on him. "He is dead," Brother Andrew reported. Brother Andrew had blood streaks on his chest from the hail.

"Look down the road toward Blethye," Bay said. Silvas focused his telesight and scanned quickly.

"The Duke of Blethye and his army," Silvas said. Then he said it again, loud enough for Sir Eustace to hear, and added, "He appears to have a dozen knights, as many archers, and six score men-at-arms. They're over a mile from the foot of Mount Mecq."

Sir Eustace climbed up into a crenel and looked off that way. "Are you sure it's Blethye himself? I can't make out the emblem on the banner."

Silvas described both the pennon and the man he assumed was the duke, and Eustace confirmed it. "Twenty minutes will see them entering the pass," Silvas said.

"We are ready," Sir Eustace said. "Blethye will have far fewer men by the time he reaches my gate."

It is too soon to gloat, Silvas thought. *Blethye is not alone in this battle.* Without the power of the Blue Rose behind him, Blethye certainly couldn't hope to take Sir Eustace's castle with so few men. The approach would be too costly. There were piles of stones just waiting for targets below. The small garrison of Mecq's citadel could bombard Blethye's force with impunity as it came through the pass and climbed the mountain . . . if not for the Blue Rose.

Silvas looked out over Blethye again, but Carillia suddenly cried, "Above!" Silvas turned and she pointed over the castle.

The monsters had no names. There weren't of the traditional demon sorts, but they were clearly raised by demonic forces. And they were clearly visible, even to men with no mystical gifts. At Carillia's cry, everyone looked. The dozen beasts charged through the air, huge mouths agape, wicked long claws on their feet. No two creatures were alike, though all seemed to have been created of parts from many different beasts and then inflated in size. There were bits of scaled hide, sections that appeared as the shells of turtles, the jaws and teeth of lions or bears, lizard tails, bat wings, totally mismatched legs—some had four legs, others had six, seven, or eight, of different lengths, from different origins.

There was no time for fancy work. Silvas saw that these monsters were as willing to attack the soldiers in the castle as the people on the ledge. A quick chant, a single word of power to trigger it. *As your makers enlarged you to attack, I enlarge you in defense,* Silvas thought as his spell lashed out at the creatures. They suddenly doubled or tripled in size. It differed from beast to beast, but the growth stopped only when the pressure within caused them to explode.

It was a messy magic. Bits and pieces flew everywhere. Blood splattered everything.

The earth trembled. The shaking made dust dance. Silvas widened his stance to maintain his balance. But then he felt himself being split, divided.

I have need of you, the Unseen Lord seemed to say.

We *have need of you,* the army of martyrs echoed.

But the physical battle outside the castle of Mecq couldn't be abandoned either. Three separate views fought for the wizard's attention. His mind and senses were stretched from Mount Mecq into the sky where the army of martyrs and the army of demons charged each other, and on to the plane of the gods, where trumpets continued to blare the call to charge. Silvas sensed that—in some fashion—he was physically in all three places at once. Whichever venue he turned his attention to took over the premier place, but only for so long as his thoughts remained there.

Silvas struggled to hold each view, going from one to the next almost instantly, responding wherever the press seemed most critical. But he was only one man, not three, and the concentration required by this juggling act meant that he had to focus very tightly on each task in turn. It left no room for anything else. The battle became an endless series of tableaux blurred into jerky movement, a series of still images giving only an impression of motion. All three fights continued simultaneously regardless of which Silvas was viewing at the moment.

Demons continued to assault the people atop Mount Mecq while Blethye's army advanced toward the pass between the two hills. Overhead, the unnatural night of the Blue Rose finally reached the hills and stretched on into the valley of Mecq. Night came at mid-morning.

In the land of the gods, Silvas found himself mounted on Bay, even though he remained aware of Bay standing in his segment of the pentagram outside the castle of Mecq. Carillia was to Silvas's left, also in both places at once. In the land of the gods Carillia was mounted on a beautiful palomino mare. To Silvas's right in the land of the gods the Unseen Lord sat atop a white charger that was as large as Bay. Off to either side Silvas could see the gods allied with his Unseen Lord, and the army of heroes and demigods they had gathered. Across the plain, not more than eighty yards away now, was the divine army of the Blue Rose, led by the gods and goddesses who were trying to take over the orthodox Roman Church.

The scene that was etched in Silvas's mind was of bright lights, pristine colors, and brilliantly gleaming armor, an idealized rendering of the moment "Before the Battle." The blues were the most perfect blues imaginable. The yellows and reds were the epitome of their hues. It was so with all of the colors and forms. Nothing so ideal could possibly have existed on the mortal plane. Snatches of conversation or thought were tagged to the view. *"It is our moment of glory." "For truth, my brothers, for Truth." "The song we sing today will echo through eternity. It will never be forgotten!"*

At the same time Silvas could *feel* the fear and the pleas of hordes of believers in the mortal world. The people there were somehow aware, at least in their souls, of the tremendous battle that was beginning. They *knew* that it might bring them all to the end of the world. It wasn't just the people huddled in St. Katrinka's in the village of Mecq (though for an instant Silvas could see them inside the church). This voice of terror echoed through Silvas's mind and soul and seemed to be the entire congregation of Christianity trembling against the Day of Judgment.

On the divine plane, the armies of the gods collided. Weapons rang against one another and against armor with the purest bell tones that could be imagined. An intricate ballet of death whirled in almost symmetrical patterns. Blood flowed and spurted—fountains of the most exquisite crimson and scarlet. The cries of triumph or defeat, victory or death, were almost operatic. Death visited the gods, and Death was a visible if ghostly presence, moving untouched among the flashing weapons reaping his most glorious harvest yet.

Laughter echoed over the battle, the laughter of gods at play. Silvas was aware of it, but only on a peripheral level. While they fought their own duels, the gods seemed to be enjoying a split consciousness like Silvas's own. But the gods were watching the fighting on the other levels almost as if they were watching wrestlers compete in the great hall of some mortal lord. It seemed as if none of the horror on the other levels was real to the gods, as if none of it really mattered. That brought an ache to Silvas's gut more distressing that the deaths among the warring gods.

The battle between dead martyrs and never-living demons commenced at the same time as the battle in the land of the gods. This battle ranged over sky and land in a confusion that no eye could completely follow. The colors were not as clean and brilliant as they were in the land of the gods. The dying—if the dead and the never-born could truly be said to die—was not so heroic. If not death, this was a destruction even more complete, a destruction of souls and spirits. The greenery of the earth seemed to wilt and char where the blood of martyrs and demons was spilled. The earth seemed to recoil from the touch. Blood? Perhaps it was something else, but it flowed just as freely in muddy reds and browns, and its loss brought down those who lost too much of it.

The earth seemed to recoil and shake on the mortal level. The quaking started without warning and seemed ready to continue indefinitely. Once more the ground danced under Silvas's feet. Standing became as difficult

as standing in a wagon whose horses were galloping out
of control down a rocky road.

"Mother Earth shows her pain!" Bosc shouted.

It was a difficult moment for Silvas. His eyes were
locked on those of the Blue Rose wizard as they con-
tested the mastery of the pass between mounts Mecq and
Balq. Blethye's army had come to a halt on his side of the
pass, still out of reach of the physical weapons of Sir
Eustace and his soldiers. Silvas had put up a wall of force
in front of Blethye's force, and the other wizard needed to
scribe a new pentagram to penetrate it . . . and as long as
Silvas held him locked in mental duel, the other wizard
could not scribe that pentagram.

Sweat poured off of Silvas's face, soaking the garments
under his armor. Keeping his balance against the earthquake was an additional complication that was almost too
much for his mind to handle. Only slowly did he bring
himself into balance with it all—and the quaking eased
off then. On the plane of the gods, Silvas was also being
pressed hard by the forces of the Blue Rose. The might of
the White Brotherhood was being compressed from both
ends, forced in against itself. Silvas was not the only focus of the Blue Rose's wrath in the land of the gods. All
of the divine forces behind the White Brotherhood were
arranged at the wizard's side. The auras of power over-
lapped, interlaced.

An arrow, perfect in shape but fashioned of the stuff of
stars, struck the line of the White Brotherhood not far to
Silvas's left. One of the armor-clad figures—one of the
gods allied with the Unseen Lord—was consumed by the
flash of starfire. The rest closed ranks and fought on.

"Mother Earth bleeds!" Bosc screamed, his voice
climbing so high that it forced Silvas's attention. The
wizard felt a sharp crack that seemed to penetrate his
head from temple to temple, a blinding pain that made his
eyes water and squeeze shut. He reeled so wildly that he
almost fell. For just an instant Silvas's concentration fal-
tered.

Brother Paul chanced to raise his right hand to draw
the sign of the cross before him. A silver-tipped arrow,

sparkling as if on fire, struck the vicar's hand. Blood spurted.

Silvas focused tightly again. The shaking of the ground stopped—at least for the moment. Silvas looked to Bosc, then followed the groom's outstretched arm. He was pointing south, into the valley of Mecq. As Silvas looked, he heard the echo of faint laughter from the Blue Rose wizard, a laugh of triumph as Silvas's blockade fell and the army of the Duke of Blethye moved into the pass between the two hills.

Mother Earth does *bleed,* Silvas thought as he stared at a sight he had heard of but never seen. *The Norsemen tell of this happening in Iceland.* Molten rock was flowing up out of the ground. It seemed to originate at the spot where he and Bay had rested when they first caught sight of Mecq—*scarcely a week gone by,* Silvas realized with a touch of shock. It seemed so much longer.

The lava appeared to inch along, welling out of a crack in the earth that, at Silvas's first glance, seemed to be thirty feet long and no more than five feet wide. The road out that side of the valley had been broken by the shaking of the earth. Now the molten rock was spilling over into Mecq's valley. Steam rose from the surface, partially obscuring the dull reds and brighter yellows that lurked beneath. *Yellow fades into red that fades to black at the edges,* Silvas observed. *And already I catch a hint of the fires of hell in it.*

"They will not surrender the water of the Eyler to us even now," Brother Paul said, his voice quaking as roughly as the earth had until a moment before. He clutched his bleeding right hand with the left, wrapping some piece of fabric around the wound. His face had paled, but he stood without wavering. "They send a river of fire to block the river of water."

Silvas nodded. His mind, fighting battles on the other levels at the same time, had not moved that far in its thinking yet. He focused his telesight on the lava flow. It was moving much faster than he had originally estimated, and in much greater volume. *It won't take long to reach the Eyler,* he realized. Possibilities chased one another through his mind. The lava might boil away the Eyler, fill its course completely, damming it at the south end of the valley, upstream, undoing his work. It might flow downstream and melt the dam he had already erected. It might flow farther and block the pass between the twin hills, perhaps turning the entire valley into a reservoir that would drive the people out as it put Mecq and its fields under water in the months to come. *If months remain to come,* Silvas qualified. It might even overflow the village, roasting the people inside the church.

Somehow I must stop this river, Silvas thought. *But how?* For once he could imagine no magic that might suffice. This was far beyond anything that Auroreus had taught him, far beyond anything he had taught himself in the years since the death of Auroreus.

He started running through spells of power. He stretched out his arms and drew in energy from wherever his magic could touch it. *I have yet to test my new limits,* he thought, but it didn't buoy his spirits as much as he might have hoped. The power that had enlarged him when the Unseen Lord revealed himself was vast, but the wizard could not know if it would be enough.

Silvas chanted, the volume increasing as his companions within the pentagram once more echoed his words without understanding them. The light faded and surged in time with the wizard's rhythms. The air whined around the pentagram, faster and higher with every phrase.

A silver bubble suddenly formed around the pentagram and just as quickly popped. Silvas looked around quickly and could scarcely credit what he saw. The wizard and his companions were no longer on the ledge outside Sir Eustace's gate. They were down on the floor of the valley, not a hundred yards from the leading ledge of the river of molten rock. Silvas glanced down. Even the pentagram he had traced in the ledge on the hill had been transferred with them. Everyone was still in place.

Is this real or a projection? Silvas asked himself. He focused his telesight toward Mount Mecq. He saw no trace of himself or his companions on the ledge. *Bay's head at least should be visible,* he thought. He moved his gaze to the rampart of the castle. The consternation he saw among the soldiers there was more persuasive. *They don't see us. We vanished.* And finally someone looked into the valley and spotted them. He pointed directly at Silvas.

That was all the time Silvas dared spare on that. The castle's defenders were coming under direct attack again, but for the moment they would have to face it alone, with only the weapons of Sir Eustace's men and the magics of the monks who remained outside the gate. Silvas had a more urgent danger to face. The lava was advancing steadily. The point of the pentagram in which Silvas stood was aimed directly at the molten rock.

"Courage," he said softly. He felt the fear of Brother Paul and, to a lesser extent, Bishop Egbert. "This is where we stand or fall. If we can't stop this river or divert it, the molten rock will entomb us here and the Blue Rose will win."

Except for one brief flutter, Silvas felt remarkably calm. *For once my duty is as plain as the sun in the sky,* he thought. He started to chant, looking around carefully as he worked through preliminary spells, building a foundation of power for the actual work of stopping the flow of molten rock. Carillia looked as serene as ever. She beamed confidence and love at him. Bosc and Bay were calm, ready for whatever came. Brother Paul still fought against an edge of terror and the pain of his wound. His prayers were coming faster and faster. Bishop Egbert seemed to be torn. There was fear, under control. There was preparation, as the bishop worked his own way through to the power of the Greater Mysteries of the White Brotherhood. But he also displayed an unmistakable fascination with the molten rock that was moving toward the pentagram.

Silvas shared, as much as he dared, the bishop's fascination. The lava bubbled and fumed. Steam and tongues of fire rose above it. The wall of fiery rock moved forward, rolling over its own leading edge, like a waterfall in slow motion, advancing a few inches every second. Cinders formed and fell from the periphery. The wall was already near Bay's height, and it seemed to be growing as it approached. *Even tree sap does not run so thickly,* Silvas thought. It was part of the fascination.

And part of the danger.

The other phases of the battle could too easily be forgotten, and they had not ended yet.

The battle between the martyrs of the Church and the never-born demons of the Blue Rose continued. The remains of twice-dead martyrs and never-born-but-once-dead demons faded quickly, but before they vanished, they poisoned the land on which they fell. The battle had progressed beyond the control of either Silvas or the Blue Rose wizard. The martyrs and demons fought with an abandon that mortal warriors rarely could. The demons fought because they had been created to do nothing else, because they understood nothing else. The martyrs fought to save their souls. The terrors of death and the terrors of the night consumed each other in a visible nightmare that spread from horizon to horizon ... but still only on Blethye's side of the twin hills. *We did that much right at least,* Silvas thought with what little satisfaction he could muster.

On this level, Silvas was still locked in a duel of magic with the Blue Rose wizard. Caradoc had found time to scribe another pentagram, almost within the pass between the hills, and to invest it with protective spells. He had a sword in his hand, using it as a pointer. Silvas raised his own sword, spoke a short spell, and watched lightning flash from his blade to the other, a blast that wasn't completely turned aside by Caradoc or his pentagram. *I can reach you,* Silvas projected. The other wizard grinned at him. He raised his sword again and pointed into the sky. Silvas followed the gesture, but he did not see the night that the Blue Rose had brought, or the battle of demons and martyrs.

This transition was like another slap in the face. Silvas found himself back in the land of the gods. That battle had progressed as well, and Silvas found serious gaps in his memory. *I participated, but I don't know what I did.* The battle was no longer that of two colliding armies. The forces of the White Brotherhood had been reduced and compressed. Few of the soldiers who had lined up against the Blue Rose here were still on their feet or horses. Their bodies littered the field.

Silvas was no longer mounted on Bay. He was standing

within one of the points of a divine pentagram. The lines shone like purest gold. The pentagram itself was more than twice the size of the one Silvas had scribed outside the castle of Sir Eustace. Carillia guarded the point to Silvas's left. The Unseen Lord stood in the point to his right. Two other gods—whose faces Silvas couldn't see—held the other points. Bay was in the center, where the greatest power present would normally be stationed. Silvas didn't understand that positioning, but he had no time to question it. The pentagram was surrounded by enemies, and off behind the gods and soldiers of the Blue Rose, Silvas saw a vast cyclone approaching.

It's a trick of the mind, a magic, Silvas told himself. His attention had once more shifted from one arena to another. Now he was facing the Blue Rose wizard at a distance of only a few yards. Silvas's pentagram appeared to have moved again, this time to the pass between Mount Mecq and Mount Balq to physically block the way. But the effect wasn't quite identical to the transportation from the ledge above out into the valley of Mecq. This was not a true transportation.

Only a magic, Silvas reminded himself, *a projection.* He was still at the point of his own pentagram. The Blue Rose wizard was at the center of his. Only magic had brought about this appearance of nearness. Sparkles of light danced on the shields over the two pentagrams and bounced off the hills to either side. The wizards threw every weapon they could bring to bear at each other. Behind Caradoc the archers who had come with the army of Blethye stood waiting, arrows notched to bows, taking shots at Silvas and his companions. The arrows couldn't penetrate the wall of magic around the pentagram, though. *And we are not really here after all,* Silvas thought, uncertain whether that was protection enough. Overhead, the battle between martyrs and demons was nearly finished. Very few of either remained to contest the issue, and they were all locked in what would almost certainly be their final duels.

The Blue Rose wizard launched a ball of fire at Silvas. It grew quickly, blue fire splattering against and then flowing over and around Silvas's pentagram, hiding the

Blue Rose force from his sight. Silvas struggled to quench the fire.

When it was gone, he was once more facing the river of molten rock in the valley. The wall of lava had continued to grow. It was now twelve feet high at the front ... and that front was only a dozen yards away. The heat was overwhelming. Even the dome of magic that protected the pentagram was not enough to completely hold the fire off. And soon the river would bury the pentagram.

There was no time for complicated magics. Silvas took a deep breath and spoke the hidden name of his Unseen Lord aloud. The earth shook underfoot, more violently than it had before, though only for an instant. The air shimmered and crackled. For the barest instant the very fabric of being seemed to vanish and reappear. But the wall of molten rock was still there, still inching closer.

The only changes were within Silvas. He felt tremendous reserves of power being funneled into him on all three levels. His companions in the valley seemed to drain into him. Even the gods around him in the golden pentagram in their land were channeling their power through him, using him as the cutting edge in their desperate last stand against the Blue Rose.

Are they giving *me their energy, or am I* taking *it?* Silvas wondered, but only briefly. Now more than ever, he was too pressed to waste time at idle thought. There was too much confusion. His eyes now saw on all three levels of the battle at once. He stood in three places: in the valley of Mecq facing the lava, in the pass between the twin hills facing the Blue Rose wizard, and in the land of the gods facing the gods of the Blue Rose and the cyclone bearing down on the golden pentagram of the White Brotherhood.

Silvas worked his way quickly through the most powerful spells at his command. The power that was accumulating in him was too much. He felt as if he were expanding, ready to burst from the inner pressure the way the monsters over Mecq's castle had exploded.

He held his sword in both hands and extended it: toward the river of lava, toward the Blue Rose wizard, toward the cyclone that had been raised by the Blue Rose

in the land of the gods. An aura of blinding light ema-
nated from Silvas and his outstretched sword.

*I could not look upon this light from the outside and
keep my eyes,* Silvas thought. *It is brighter than the star
I tried to gaze upon when I was a boy.*

The words of power spoken, Silvas's mind commanded
and his body obeyed, on all three planes at once.

—He stepped out of the golden pentagram in the land
of the gods and cut into the cyclone, cleaving it, destroy-
ing the windstorm, and then he turned and moved into the
gods and heroes of the Blue Rose who had gathered like
vultures waiting for the tornado to finish their work. Silvas moved with blinding speed. It was as if the others
were frozen in time while he moved among them at will,
and his sword destroyed all who wore the Blue Rose.

—He stepped out of the pentagram in the pass between
Mount Mecq and Mount Balq. His now flaming sword
cut through the outer lines of the pentagram controlled by
the Blue Rose wizard. And then Silvas's sword cut
Caradoc in half with a single blow, skull to crotch. He
whirled and, in what seemed to be a single spinning blow,
decapitated the five assistants who had stood in that pentagram with Caradoc.

—He stepped out of the pentagram in the valley of
Mecq with the sword, now gleaming an icy silver, raised
high above his head. He strode forward and swung the
sword into the leading edge of the river of molten rock
. . . and the lava froze, steaming madly for a moment as
it cycled from ember red to coal black in the space of a
breath.

But Silvas did not see the end of that cycle. The sword
came out of his hands, buried in the wall of lava with
only the hilt protruding. Silvas himself pitched forward,
unaware of the burns on his face and hands,
unconscious—or worse—before his head hit the rock
wall. He crumpled to the ground as if dead.

24

I am not dead. The wonder of that realization kept Silvas from noticing the pain for a time. Hands picked him up and carried him—for a distance that seemed incredible. *They can't be taking me all the way up to the castle,* he thought, and that unleashed the confusion in his head. There were thoughts floating around in the maelstrom of his mind, but nothing could record itself over the confusion and the pain. There were obscure images, as of chickens plucking their own feathers; dark sounds that were beyond description; nightmare eternities compressed into instants. Reflections of fears were magnified, exaggerated, repeated. A babel of voices assaulted Silvas's mind, blending into indecipherable gibberish.

The cacophony finally damped away to a low hum in the background. The wheel of kaleidoscopic images ground to a halt. Silvas felt himself being lowered to a stone floor. The pain remained. It was as if the fires of Hell burned in every joint in his body. His fingers throbbed. The rest of him felt even worse.

They've brought me to St. Katrinka's, he realized finally. That brought a measure of comfort . . . and a measure of fear. *Do they know I'm still alive? Or do they think I'm dead? Will they bury me as I am?*

Just opening his eyes took as much concentration as the most difficult magic he had ever attempted. And it increased his pain. Silvas couldn't turn his head or move to see anything more than the patch of ceiling right overhead. And he couldn't hold his eyes open for long.

I am not alone here, he thought.

Cautiously he started a silent chant for strength. Each word caused an increase to the throbbing in his head. The pain was scarcely tolerable, but Silvas forced himself to continue. He needed strength before he could work on healing. He needed strength just to keep breathing.

Strength returned, but slowly. There was a concurrent easing of the intense pain. After several moments Silvas noticed that he had started to whisper his chant aloud. When he opened his eyes again, the task was easier, and he could even move his head a little. Bay stood at the side door, his head poked into the church. Bosc stood next to Bay, inside the church, looking anxious.

Silvas turned his head the other way . . . and saw Carillia.

A hoarse "No!" escaped his lips, twisted and tortured. Silvas squeezed his eyes shut, but reopened them at once.

Carillia. Someone had taken off her helmet and covered her with a blanket. Only her head and arms were visible. Her hair was a tangled mess. Her face was impossibly pale, but her arms, and her left hand, were terribly burned—blackened and blistered. The right hand had somehow escaped the fire. Silvas felt his stomach turn at the horrible look of her burns, but he had to force himself to look away from the burned arms, back to her face. It took a long moment for him to spot the slight evidence that she was still breathing, still alive. The spark seemed faint.

Carillia, my love, don't desert me, Silvas thought, with such little force as he could muster. He closed his eyes and tried to shut out the memory of Carillia's burns. He chanted silently, pulling in strength and projecting healing to Carillia—hoping that he had enough energy to make the spell work. But he wasn't even certain that his spells would have any force on a goddess.

When Silvas opened his eyes the next time, he saw Bishop Egbert standing a little distance away, swaying as if he might not be able to remain standing much longer. The bishop wasn't looking at the wizard, but at someone else on the floor of St. Katrinka's. Silvas raised his head just a little—even that much movement was difficult— and saw Brother Paul sitting in front of the bishop. There was dried blood on the vicar's face and arms, and some slight evidence of burning. Silvas squinted. His telesight wasn't working, but he could see that the thumb and first two fingers of Brother Paul's right hand, the fingers he would normally extend in giving a blessing, were missing. Short stumps were covered by crude blood-soaked bandages.

A soft background of conversation slowly became audible around Silvas. The sounds had been there right along. He had simply been unaware of them. And for a time yet it was just incoherent noise to him. Only slowly did he begin to extract words and meaning. He continued to look around, straining his slowly returning strength. Eleanora, Sir Eustace's wife, was standing near the side of the church. A young boy held her hand. *Sir Eustace's son,* Silvas thought, though he had never seen the boy before. Maria was there too, standing next to her stepmother. They were looking down. Even before Silvas managed to spot the focus of their gaze, he knew it had to be Sir Eustace. And the look he finally managed was enough to tell him that the knight was dead.

The monks from St. Ives moved around the church, tending to the injured, saying prayers over the dead. Counting the monks was too much trouble, but Silvas had the clear impression that there were no longer twelve of them. Whether the missing monks were dead, wounded, or merely occupied elsewhere, he couldn't guess. Many villagers had left the church, but there was a crowd outside the main entrance.

As the words floating around Silvas started to become understandable, he picked up what news he could—while he continued his chants for healing, for himself and for Carillia. The battle had been won. The Eyler continued to fill behind his dam. That lava hadn't destroyed anything vital. It had burned and buried a few cottages at the southern edge of the village before flowing to a halt after it split around Silvas and his companions. But the cottages could be replaced. No one had been inside them at the time. The remains of the river of lava were smoking and steaming as they cooled. The surface was a hard black crust that dwindled down to nothing at the edge of the village. The split ends were ramps leading up to the top, a new road leading out of the valley. The crack that had spewed out the lava was no longer visible. The molten rock had sealed its own womb.

Louder voices flowed over softer ones. Silvas became

aware of a heated discussion between Maria and
Eleanora, though he didn't follow the specifics. He was
concentrating on Carillia, and the pain in his heart left little room for other considerations. Carillia had moved a
little. Tears of pain were escaping from under her closed
eyelids.

Then her eyes opened and the wells of tears overflowed, rushing down her cheeks. Watching Carillia, Silvas was hardly aware that Maria had left her stepmother's
side and was coming toward him.

"My love," Silvas whispered, struggling to turn onto
his side to face Carillia fully. He felt hands on his shoulders, helping him, supporting him so he wouldn't roll
back, and then falling away. He realized that it was Maria, but he had no time for her now. He had no time for
anyone but Carillia.

Carillia's head seemed to fall to the side, toward him.
She blinked twice, slowly, trying to clear her eyes to see
Silvas.

"You have always been my heart," Carillia whispered.
The words came slowly. She was obviously much weaker
than Silvas.

"I am dying, my heart," she said, and though Silvas felt
her words choking him, he couldn't even utter a futile de-
nial.

"Many of my brothers and sisters have already died,"
she continued, pausing after every few words. "The leg-
ends of the immortality of the gods will suffer. Your once
Unseen Lord survives, but all of the remaining gods, including him, will remain diminished by this battle."
There was a long silence before she added, "Even the few
who stood aside and took no part are lessened."

Silvas knew that he alone could hear Carillia. Even
Maria, now kneeling behind Silvas, could not possibly
have heard.

"You have always been my heart," Carillia repeated,
her voice so weak that Silvas could almost believe that he
only imagined that he was hearing her. "Now I have only
one gift left that I can give you."

She rolled more on her side, sliding a little closer. Silvas rolled toward her in reply, meeting her more than
halfway. Carillia kissed Silvas just as Maria put her hands

on his shoulders again, supporting him, holding him as he returned Carillia's final kiss.

But it was more than a kiss. A white light enveloped the three of them, bright enough to make all of the living people in the church look.

Carillia poured what remained of herself into Silvas. In the quick flood of knowledge, Silvas learned that Carillia had taken her injuries because she had broken the lines of the pentagrams ahead of him, absorbing the damage to keep him from falling. And then she had put herself into the sword that he had used to end the battle on all three levels. Her right hand had become the hilt of the sword whose blade remained welded into the cleft of the river of lava.

You gave yourself for me, Silvas thought, uncertain whether enough remained within Carillia for her to hear his thought.

But she was not gone yet. Silvas felt the power—the divinity—flowing from Carillia into him. And he was also aware that some of that divinity was flowing through him, into Maria, because of the way she was holding him.

You are become one of us, was in Carillia's voice, but within Silvas's head. He had no chance to ask questions. Her lips fell away from his, and she was dead . . . and instantly cold. The bright light faded away.

Silvas rolled away from Carillia, and Maria was there to help, to ease him. She knelt over him, and he looked up, his eyes searching her face. Silvas took a deep breath. His pain faded quickly and he felt new power settling into him, restoring him.

There is no going back, he realized. *I can't escape her final gift.* He could sense the basic change within him even if he couldn't understand it yet. *"You are become one of us,"* Carillia had told him.

Am I now a god? he wondered. The idea was incredible but inescapable.

Silvas sat up. He rested only a moment before he got to his feet—shakily, with considerable help from Maria. She was at his side, half behind him. Silvas felt her hands on his arm and back, he felt her *mind* tied to his. He took a deep breath and turned. Her hands fell away as she realized, as quickly as he did, that he was now strong enough to stand on his own—almost completely restored.

The church fell silent. The people seemed to freeze into a silent tableau, aware that *something* momentous had happened but unable to guess what it was. Silvas and Maria stared at each other, their eyes locked together, twin tunnels that let them travel into each other's minds and souls. Silvas could see the frantic play of emotions chasing each other through Maria's mind—knowledge, desire, and even fear—colliding and rebounding insanely, only slowly coming together, finding common ground.

Silvas nodded then. When he spoke, the words traveled no farther than her ears. "You get your wish after all. I think we are linked together beyond all measure and time now."

Maria nodded slowly. There was an entirely new universe within her, demanding her attention, enticing her with unexpected vistas. She could scarcely keep from diving headlong into the novelty, to explore, to *try* to understand what had happened. *I will need forever to come to terms with this,* she thought. And she had doubts that she would ever manage to be comfortable with this *newness* she felt.

"It is our fate," she managed after a long moment of silence.

EPILOGUE

"My work here is over," Silvas said when he noticed that Bishop Egbert and Brother Paul had come to him. He looked around the church at the seriously injured and the dead. "I cannot raise the dead," Silvas said. His eyes returned to Carillia's body. "But I can help those who are still living." He spoke an ancient chant of healing, one that he had never known as merely a wizard, and Maria's voice was right with his through the words.

"Give me your injured hand," Silvas told Brother Paul. Silvas held the hand between both of his and spoke another spell. The vicar's hand grew hot and seemed to pulse, but when Silvas uncovered it, there was no visible change.

"Before the bishop leaves Mecq, you will be able to show him a whole hand," Silvas promised. "Perhaps I should say, 'Before you leave Mecq *with* the bishop' ?" He turned to Egbert, who nodded.

"Brother Paul will return to St. Ives with me," the bishop said. "He is bound for the Greater Mysteries."

"Where will you go now?" Brother Paul asked.

"For the moment I will go home. Beyond that I cannot say." Silvas glanced at Maria. "This world had changed beyond all reckoning. We all need time to find our places again."

Maria walked over to where her stepmother and halfbrother stood over the body of Sir Eustace. She knelt next to the boy, held his shoulders, and kissed him on the forehead, and hugged him tightly. "I will always do what I can to help you, Will," she whispered.

Maria got up and returned to Silvas. They joined hands and walked toward the main door. Silvas stopped, turned, and gestured to the figures at the other door. "Bosc," he said, and the groom trotted across to his master. "Bay, we will meet you outside." The horse nodded and pulled his head back from the side door.

The crowd around the main entrance parted. A light rain was falling on Mecq again, gentle, cleansing, renewing the land.

Silvas and Maria stood at the door of the church for several minutes, until people started coming out of the smoke—Braf Goleg and a half dozen of his soldiers, Koshka and an equal number of his people. Some went into St. Katrinka's and brought Carillia's body out on a stretcher. A few gathered the horses that had carried the monks up to Mecq's castle earlier. The rest flanked them as a guard of honor.

Silvas and Maria descended the steps hand in hand and walked toward the tower of smoke. Carillia's body was borne before them. Bosc and Bay followed. Silvas and Maria stopped for a moment at the edge of the smoke. Bosc and Bay passed on through. Maria waved. Silvas raised a hand as if in benediction. Then they went inside. The pillar of smoke disappeared from the ground up, withdrawing toward heaven. The only evidence that it had ever stood in the center of the village was a circle of lush, beautifully green grass—just the size of the column of smoke.

ROC (0451)

FAR AWAY WORLDS

☐ **RATS AND GARGOYLES by Mary Gentle.** It is a city where the gods themselves dwell and where their lesser minions, the Rat Lords and Gargoyle Acolytes, have reduced humanity to slaves.
(451732—$5.99)
Hardcover: (451066—$18.95)

☐ **ANCIENT LIGHT by Mary Gentle.** Lynne de Lisle Christie is back on Orthe, caught in a battle to obtain high-technology artifacts from a bygone civilization, while struggling to protect the people of Orthe from its destructive powers. (450132—$5.95)

☐ **MAZE OF MOONLIGHT by Gael Baudino.** In this long-awaited sequel to *Strands of Starlight*, can one baron and the last true elven folk save the realm from an invasion of mercenary forces?
(452305—$4.99)

☐ **RED DWARF: *Infinity Welcomes Careful Drivers* by Grant Naylor.** An international best-seller! Not since *Hitchhiker's Guide to the Galaxy* has there been such a delightful excursion into the wackiest regions of the unknown universe! (452011—$4.99)

Prices slightly higher in Canada

Buy them at your local bookstore or use this convenient coupon for ordering.

PENGUIN USA
P.O. Box 999 – Dept. #17109
Bergenfield, New Jersey 07621

Please send me the books I have checked above.
I am enclosing $_____ (please add $2.00 to cover postage and handling).
Send check or money order (no cash or C.O.D.'s) or charge by Mastercard or VISA (with a $15.00 minimum). Prices and numbers are subject to change without notice.

Card # _____ Exp. Date _____
Signature_____
Name_____
Address_____
City _____ State _____ Zip Code _____

For faster service when ordering by credit card call **1-800-253-6476**

Allow a minimum of 4-6 weeks for delivery. This offer is subject to change without notice.